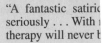
continued . . .

Key to Justice

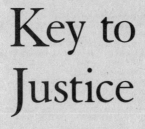

TALIA GRYPHON

ACE BOOKS, NEW YORK

THE BERKLEY PUBLISHING GROUP
Published by the Penguin Group
Penguin Group (USA) Inc.
375 Hudson Street, New York, New York 10014, USA
Penguin Group (Canada), 90 Eglinton Avenue East, Suite 700, Toronto, Ontario M4P 2Y3, Canada
(a division of Pearson Penguin Canada Inc.)
Penguin Books Ltd., 80 Strand, London WC2R 0RL, England
Penguin Group Ireland, 25 St. Stephen's Green, Dublin 2, Ireland (a division of Penguin Books Ltd.)
Penguin Group (Australia), 250 Camberwell Road, Camberwell, Victoria 3124, Australia
(a division of Pearson Australia Group Pty. Ltd.)
Penguin Books India Pvt. Ltd., 11 Community Centre, Panchsheel Park, New Delhi—110 017, India
Penguin Group (NZ), 67 Apollo Drive, Rosedale, North Shore 0632, New Zealand
(a division of Pearson New Zealand Ltd.)
Penguin Books (South Africa) (Pty.) Ltd., 24 Sturdee Avenue, Rosebank, Johannesburg 2196,
South Africa

Penguin Books Ltd., Registered Offices: 80 Strand, London WC2R 0RL, England

This is a work of fiction. Names, characters, places, and incidents either are the product of the author's imagination or are used fictitiously, and any resemblance to actual persons, living or dead, business establishments, events, or locales is entirely coincidental. The publisher does not have any control over and does not assume any responsibility for author or third-party websites or their content.

KEY TO JUSTICE

An Ace Book / published by arrangement with the author

PRINTING HISTORY
Ace mass-market edition / April 2010

Copyright © 2010 by Talia Gryphon.
Cover art by Judy York.
Cover design by Annette Fiore DeFex.

ISBN: 978-0-441-01862-8

ACE
Ace Books are published by The Berkley Publishing Group,
a division of Penguin Group (USA) Inc.,
375 Hudson Street, New York, New York 10014.
ACE and the "A" design are trademarks of Penguin Group (USA) Inc.

PRINTED IN THE UNITED STATES OF AMERICA

10   9   8   7   6   5   4   3   2   1

This is for some of the dazzling women who have influenced my life by word or paradigm: my mother, Eleanor; Jill Marrinson; Charlotte Poetschner; Barbara Finer; Nichole Schumacher; Virgina Sica; Greer Fites; Missy Iske; and, in her own peculiar way, Sophia Wiwczarowski.

And to my wonderful, patient, tolerant sons. I could never have accomplished some of the things I set out to do in my life without your support and encouragement.

To Troy and Reni Wiwczaroski, my nephew and his lovely wife. It's not family without you.

To John Pfeifer, my first writing partner from back in the day and a loyal friend.

As always, to Ginjer Buchanan, my wonderful editor, and Joe Veltre, my fabulous agent. You guys are the best.

Special thanks to my military advisors: Charles Randolph, Sgt. U.S. Army Special Operations Command, Retired; Jon Eppler, Sgt. U.S. Army Reserves Intelligence Analyst; Steven Mills, Sgt. USMC, Retired; Donald Akina, Corpsman Second Class U.S. Navy, Retired.

Talia Gryphon

CHAPTER
1

Virgin. She was a virgin. Again. This was not happening. Thirty years old and a goddamn virgin. Stupid music, stupid Perrin, stupid Vampire foo. Great Ganesh, this was beyond ludicrous. Gillian briefly considered leaping off the back of the black dragon to save herself the trouble of subjecting herself to Daed and Helmut's inevitable question session.

Shit. Damn. Hell. Fuck. No, she couldn't do that. She wasn't that much of a coward, and besides, Aleksei, the morphed dragon–Vampire Lord she was riding, would just catch her in a huge paw on her way down, then yell at her for being an idiot and not relying on him as her partner . . . even though they were still on a relationship break. Sort of.

Sometimes it wasn't worth it, trying to remain in non-bitch mode. Things were much easier when you were able to just shoot whatever was bugging you. Or at the very least, pack up your stuff and depart the area until things calmed down.

That wouldn't work either. She really didn't want to hurt Aleksei or her friends. Nor did she want to jeopardize the newly anointed Rachlav Institute of Paramortal Healing, just when it was beginning to blossom. Some nights it just sucked to be herself. Some nights also sucked more than others. This would be one of those nights.

She felt like a virgin on prom night . . . except it wasn't prom night. It was nighttime in the Carpathian Mountains and she had just been turned down for sex by her ex-boyfriend—if that was what she could call Aleksei—because he had some ridiculous notion of taking her out for a dreamy weekend, romancing her and seducing her gently. In short, he wanted to take her out and treat her like a lady instead of the hardball soldier he'd been sleeping with for the past few months. Inconsiderate bastard.

Gillian realized she was being unreasonable and ridiculous, but couldn't think her way out of their current difference of opinion. On the edge of her consciousness floated the tendril of thought that she didn't want to address: if she let Aleksei do what he wished, make everything perfect for her as only he could do, she might find herself really in love with him. And *that* would suck. She didn't want to be in love with *anybody*, not just Aleksei.

It had nothing whatsoever to do with him being a Vampire Lord; she wasn't prejudiced against mixed relationships like some Humans were. It had to do with someone really needing her in his life, being willing and wanting to commit to her, that scared her to death. Gill wasn't sure she had it in herself to be permanently devoted to anyone. She was horrified of the possibility that she might actually hurt Aleksei if she was unable to commit. As perceptive as she was with her patients and on her missions, she had a major blockage when it came to thinking things through about herself and the "L" word.

The United States Marine Corps had been the only thing that ever held her devotion for very long . . . well, and the people she worked with at the International Paramortal Psychology Association. At least her patients were on a time frame with her. She would give them 110 percent of her attention, concern, knowledge and dedication while they were under her care. After their needs were resolved, she bid them farewell, focused on being proud and happy for their success and moved on. There was no lasting involvement except for the occasional follow-up thank-you card or letters letting her know how they were doing in their lives, which was fine with her. No lasting ties, just satisfaction for having done her job. Right now, with regard to Aleksei, it wasn't a job; it had serious potential for permanency, so she was kidding herself by avoiding the obvious since that was all she had as leverage.

After their near-disastrous moments on the mountain, discovering Gillian's newly "intact" state and subsequent discussion on what to do about it, Aleksei shifted to dragon form to fly them back to the castle. Gillian was uncharacteristically quiet, which had him a little worried.

Damn her, he wanted to give her respect, not take her like an undisciplined young buck on the mountainside. Once again, his idea of chivalry and her idea of antiquated nonsense were at odds. He didn't know how to resolve it any more than she did, but both were willing to keep slogging along and trying like hell to figure it out. At least he hoped they were.

He avoided invading her thoughts. It grated against every protective bone in his body, but was necessary to give her space, let her realize she could trust him with her fears, come to him in her own time. Insisting on further dialogue tonight would be a mistake.

And they say an old Vampire can't learn new tricks, he thought to himself. His smile was an unfortunate grimace coming through the dragon's jaws, but it was there.

It had been a surprise to encounter her regrown barrier. A barrier re-created by the power they had generated in their "group effort," as Gillian would say. Never in his wildest dreams had he imagined such power—power that was his to command. Perrin's magical music had enhanced it, the healers had fueled it and Aleksei had merged it, but she had directed it, channeled it, fired it into all of them. She was truly an amazing female, of any species.

In so many ways she was his perfect match, his ideal mate: strong, disciplined, dedicated, altruistic, kind, loyal and, as an added bonus, beautiful. If only he could get her to stop being stubborn and come to terms with her feelings. He wanted her to accept the idea of them together in a joyous commitment instead of judiciously avoiding a possible emotional entrapment.

Inwardly he groaned. That was going to take time. He had all the time in the world; he would simply have to exercise his iron will in a different way. He would outlast her stubbornness; be there when she came to her senses. Right now she was not ready to buy into what he was trying to sell her.

She loved him; he was sure of it. There were bound to be a few more bumps in the road of their relationship. He was going to have to put big, thick walls around his ego if he was going to keep from snapping. She was worth it; of that he had no doubt. Now, if he could just get her to see what he saw when he looked at her . . . and believe.

Gillian remained torn between being extremely pissed off and grudgingly grateful to Aleksei. That he hadn't fallen on her like a randy stud said a lot about his character. A sense of honor was something Gillian admired above all. She had it, all of the people she loved had it, and Aleksei had it in buckets. That was one point she couldn't argue. Why the hell he wanted her, wanted to go through all the trouble to keep her, was beyond anything she could imagine.

He was remarkable. Powerful, but he refused to use it carelessly and was unwilling to force control or to bring fear. Aleksei was as he always had been even after coming into the full power of a Lord: noble, aristocratic, honorable, honest, stubborn, intractable, chauvinistic, opinionated . . . gorgeous, passionate, tender and bossy.

She was just a scrappy little girl from the foothills of the Ozarks, former Captain, now successful psychologist, sex therapist and poster girl for Paramortal careers everywhere; always a Marine, and apparently a great big chickenshit. And dead, because her friend Kimber was going to fucking kill her if she was now re-virginized as well. Oh joy.

Once they arrived at the castle, Aleksei walked her upstairs and offered to sleep with her if she promised to keep her hands to herself. Gillian kicked off her boots and flopped onto the bed, sprawling over most of the area with an exasperated sigh. Smiling a breathtaking smile, he rolled her onto her side, then lay beside her, curling around her body, sheltering her in his arms. Gill could feel the raw power and sensuality coming from him as she nestled into his warmth. His scent of cardamom and nutmeg was comforting and safe.

There was nothing really to say; they'd said everything on the mountainside. Aleksei had formally asked her for a "date," and she'd grudgingly agreed after he cocked an eyebrow at her and assured her the only way back into his bed anytime in the near future was to allow him this one concession. Gods above, she wanted to work things out with him. Sort of. Mainly she didn't want to fight. At least, not with Aleksei.

He held her tenderly, wanting her to know that she was important to him, that he had never before considered any woman as a long-term partner. Even his former fiancée, Elizabeta, had become his ex-fiancée when he realized she was more interested in what he could do for her in terms of immortality and power than with his love.

He was in entirely new territory himself but wasn't quite as nervous about it as the petite blonde he held in his arms. It was on the tip of his tongue to speak soft words of love and passion to her, but knowing this was Gillian he was dealing with, he refrained. Eventually her breathing evened out and she slept trustingly in his arms.

"Ti amo, mia piccola," he said softly, his voice rumbling in his chest. No, this was not going to be easy. Even in the surface areas of her mind that he had glimpsed, there was a deep-seated fear of being trapped, particularly in a relationship. Suddenly it occurred to him that he'd known her for over two years and had barely heard her mention her family except for their brief conversation after the Ripper incident. He wanted to know more about her, how and where she'd grown up. "Quid pro quo, Doctor."

Gillian didn't talk about herself. She did not whine, wheedle or complain. Well . . . she did bitch a lot, but it was about other things, not the state of her own affairs. Maybe it was a defense mechanism, or maybe it was automatic professional detachment; maybe she was just being a pain in the ass as usual. He chuckled at his thought. Gillian was a lot of things, but she wasn't high maintenance despite her prickliness once in a while.

In fact, Gillian was so low maintenance that her own needs, fears and desires were buried; locked away, where no one could ever reach. She was self-protective, fearless, but with a wall of iron surrounding a vulnerability that broke his heart whenever he'd glimpsed it. She kept her emotional distance from everyone, even him. Other people could disappoint her but she would walk through hell itself to avoid failing a patient or a friend.

That was a sobering thought. Perrin had been right. It was all smoke and mirrors with her. She needed looking after and a safe haven. A person she could talk to, really talk to, whom she trusted, loved and respected. Aleksei hoped to someday be that person. For now, her past was a mystery and the future was looking just as obscured.

Trusting him with her life came naturally to her, as did trusting him with her body. Completely comfortable with her own sexuality, she was as giving with her body as she was with her various professional skills. Trusting him or anyone with her heart was quite another matter. Gillian was her first, best and only sanctuary from the crazy shit she had to deal with on a daily basis and from any accidental emotional entanglements. Her Marine family didn't count. Those relationships were on purpose and Gill loved them like her family. Aleksei wanted very much to be part of that family.

He gently kissed her hair, smoothing it back from her face and covering her up as he rose to leave. All of that was food for thought on another day. Right now, letting Gillian be herself would get him further in her esteem than any magical seduction he could devise. He was learning. Smart Vampire.

The next afternoon Gillian awoke to the lyrical music of Kimber's voice. "Rise and shine, Captain Key. Oh, and thank you very fucking much. Mind explaining to me just what the hell happened to us last night?"

It was a reasonable question, except Kimber rarely ever addressed Gillian by her rank unless she was inordinately pissed. Plus, it was spoken at an extremely high volume and with a grimace.

"What the fuck are you talking about, Whitecloud?"

Kimber recognized the warning in Gillian's voice and countered, "I brought your goddamn coffee, so drink it and then tell me what the hell you, the Romanian stud and your pet masked pianist did to us last night."

She set the cup down on the nightstand by the bed and backed up a pace. Flopping into a chair, she paused in her quest for information to disembowel Gillian with her eyes, then slurped her own cup of Italian roast with sugar and cream.

Blindly, Gillian groped for the cup and found it, shoving her tangled hair out of her eyes and attempting to focus as the powerful beverage hit her stomach and then dispersed its bounty of stimulant into her bloodstream. She fumbled for her cigarettes and lit one, glaring at Kimber through the bluish smoke.

"We healed a lot of people. You were there," she grumbled.

"So were you." Kimber was staring at her accusingly.

"What's your point?" Gillian was trying to think. It was getting easier since her synapses were getting their caffeine fix and excitedly insisting that she focus on the immediate conversation. "Kimber, seriously, what the hell are you talking about?"

"Didn't you go with Aleksei last night?"

"Yeah, so?"

"I went with Pavel."

"*And?*" Gillian was getting supremely tired of this.

"*And* we discovered that I have been 'healed' in the worst possible sense of the word—that's what, dipshit!" Kimber's lovely gold green eyes were positively blazing.

"Shit. You too?"

"*What!* You mean you are . . . ?"

"Yup. Intact and untried."

Kimber kicked the bed and winced when she remembered she wasn't wearing shoes. "Goddammit, I am too old for this shit!"

"That's what I said too. Aleksei wouldn't touch me."

"Neither would Pavel. He said it was about honor or something fucked-up like that."

"Great, so now we're a couple of thirty-year-old virgins in a Country full of sex-on-a-stick males. However, I am supposed to have a 'date' with Aleksei where he wants to do this big romantic seduction thing so I feel special." Gillian sat up and ran her hand over her eyes.

"Aw, that's so sweet!" Kimber squealed, then threw her coffee spoon at Gillian, clipping her on the head. "You dumbass!"

"*Ow!* Why am I a dumbass? I didn't know that was going to happen!"

Kimber slumped back into the overstuffed chair, narrowly avoiding spilling her coffee. "I know. Shit, I'm just pissed."

"No, you're frustrated, sexually frustrated." Gillian's grin was a little too wicked for someone who was yanking the chain of another very lethal Marine. Neither of them had had enough coffee for this conversation.

"I really hate you sometimes." Kimber flipped her off, then sipped her coffee.

"Hey, I'm in the same boat. What did Pavel say?"

"He said the same thing as Aleksei, evidently," Kimber muttered resignedly. "He wants to have a 'special' evening, take me to Brasov or somewhere to a bridal suite in some really nice hotel. Just kill me now."

Gillian nodded. "All the males out there and we get Paramortal Lancelot and Galahad; complete with honor, principles and ethics."

"At least Lancelot was getting laid."

"Let's not go there," Gillian said, swinging her legs over the edge of the bed.

"Now what?"

"I guess we go through with our 'dates,' then everything will be back to normal."

"Normal is a state of mind. We've never been in that state," Kimber observed. Gill didn't bother to argue.

After they finished their coffee and their gripe session, Gillian got organized to go have a brief session with Csangal. She'd promised to drive up to Brasov with Perrin to see him off and return with Helmut and Cassiopeia.

Kimber had decided to go with her so Gillian wouldn't be alone with Perrin. Gillian thought it best to keep a well-defined distance between them here at the end of their professional relationship. Perrin needed to make a clean break from her and his therapy so he could get on with his life. Having Kimber along would make it less difficult for him.

She wasn't afraid of being alone with him; she just didn't want to get into one of Perrin's overly sensitive moments. It was going to be hard enough on both of them when he stepped aboard that plane. His emotions still had a tendency to short-circuit all over the map when he was stressed, especially where Gillian was concerned. He was also the only client who had ever truly gotten under her skin.

Dr. Cassiopeia Delphi, Gillian's mentor, had made it clear that it was all right to care about him the way she did as long as she kept her professional perspective when it was time to say good-bye. Now it was time. Gillian had her emotions hog-tied and stuffed back behind a solid glass wall. It would be hard but she could handle it. Perrin would too; she had faith in him.

Driving down to the Inn to meet Csangal, she thought about Aleksei. *Cronus on a cracker, could he ever do anything spontaneously? No.* She shook her head. *That isn't fair.* Aleksei could be as spontaneous as the next Vampire. He was just more romantically inclined; that was all. As well as being gorgeous, sensitive, charming, really tall, breathtaking, stubborn, opinionated, stunning . . . Oops, her mind was drifting and she nearly missed her turn.

She kept her head down as she got out of the car and

went toward the door. Her thoughts were still so chaotic, she nearly climbed up the outer wall of the Inn when a dark, honeyed voice greeted her from the shadows outside the building.

"Good evening, Gillian."

"Holy shi— Er, hi, Csangal. Sorry. My mind was else-where."

Good gawd almighty, speaking of sex on a stick. The Vampire was so incredibly beautiful that she felt the sting of tears briefly as their eyes met. Sidhe legend said that some of their kind could cause a Human to die of heart-break if they were deprived of the beauty of the Fairy. This wasn't a Sidhe male; this was a Vampire—but damn, damn, damn, he was smoking hot, making her heart wrench in her chest from his sheer loveliness.

"Shall we take a walk tonight?" Csangal wasn't unaware of his effect on the Human female. She had an iron will but, like any other Human, tended to let her guard down around beautiful creatures. So much the better. He needed her co-operation and her expertise.

There was something different about her tonight. He couldn't quite put his finger on it. Her scent was familiar yet not. Something teased the back of his thoughts as she agreed to a walk. They turned from the Inn and went across the road and into the forest.

Gillian noticed that they were on a well-defined trail. "This looks well used," she commented.

"It is. I believe that Radu said they kept nature trails and a garden over here for the guests' enjoyment."

"I've been here for more than two years and I didn't even know about this." Gillian laughed.

"Perhaps you have not had much opportunity for ro-mantic walks in the moonlight, nor had many patients who enjoyed being out of doors more than being inside," he said silkily in that fabulous voice.

The path was wide enough for them to walk abreast of each other, so they talked as they strolled down the moon-dusted lane. Soon, the path opened up into a lovely gar-den; beautiful even at nighttime. It was lit by tiny Fairy lights—not the cheap strands of tiny lightbulbs you could string around your house for the holidays but some variety of teensy, tiny, real Fairies or demi-Fey; real Fairy houses and real Fairy lights.

They looked like will-o'-the-wisps but were stationary. No danger there. Gill knew that if the little suspended ghostly balls of light were seen lazily meandering around a swampy, boggy area, it was best not to follow them. Too often they were affiliated with a malicious Fairy or Sidhe bent on leading the unwary traveler to a nasty moment of personal clarity before they died, drowned in the bog.

Csangal led the way to a comfortable-looking bench by a small fountain. They sat and Gillian listened to where he was going with his story. She stayed well away from him; his sexual draw was as strong as ever and her shields still were not what they should be in order to be near him for long.

He was telling her about when he believed his symptoms first appeared. His beauty was so overwhelming, she had to shift her eyes away momentarily now and then to keep from becoming entranced with him. He wasn't even trying to bespell her. Shit, this wasn't a hazard that she'd ever heard of being mentioned in graduate school, nor one she'd ever encountered before. What the hell was he saying? Origin of his problems? Yeah, that was it.

"I'm not sure I have this correct. You believe your symptoms all started soon after you were Turned? Or was it longer, a while after you were Reborn?" Gillian wasn't quite clear on that point and he seemed to be talking around that issue.

"After, much later," Csangal said quietly, looking away from her, "I became concerned that I really could not remember anything about my maker, my creator. Most Vampires have at least a rudimentary relationship with the one who Turns them, true even back in the age when I was Reborn. It was considered good etiquette to watch over your protégé, as it were. It is the maker's responsibility to make sure his creation rises for the first few nights.

"A number of Vampires never see their first sunset. They

take refuge in the Earth too deeply, or they lock themselves too securely within a tomb. A new Vampire is nearly as weak as a Human until he has fed for the first time. Many die after those first few sunsets, or go mad and become the Revenants, who we all must fear."

"So Vampires don't just automatically know what to do to stay alive? They need a teacher?" Gillian asked, wanting to put her hand on his arm in comfort but cautious of direct physical contact with him. His sensuality was almost overwhelming when sitting this close, and she remembered what had happened the last time.

"Yes, they need another Vampire at least. Preferably their Master or Lord to guide them. They are aware they will need blood to survive, but where to acquire it safely is a lesson to be learned. One of the problems the Master helps the fledgling overcome is where to feed, so the newly risen are not driven to kill their families, friends or loved ones by mistake of proximity." As he said it, something very, very dark crossed his features and then vanished.

Gillian gulped, her hand involuntarily going to her throat, hoping her innate perceptiveness was not clanging the warning she thought it was. She took a shot at it. "You killed your family?"

Shit and double shit. He had murdered his family. She knew it without a doubt before he answered her as her empathy flared in response to his long-remembered guilt. Was this a crime that needed to be reported, considering how long ago it had happened? How unstable was he when it happened? Who the hell would she report it to if she did need to report? How unstable was he right now? Inquiring minds had better fucking find out.

Csangal smiled an empty smile, full of wry regret. "I rose a full Master, Gillian, with no knowledge of the level of my power or the damage I could potentially do. I killed a woman whom I loved in my newly acquired Bloodlust because she was simply there when I rose. I was a fledgling with no one to guide me, but it still burns a hole in my soul that I took her life and possibly the life of our unborn child as well. She told me just days before her death that she might be pregnant."

He subsided, his hands clasped together, looking at the ground. Gill could feel his anguish and horror clearly. Even a mind-blind person would have picked up on his pain.

"That was six hundred years ago and I am still filled with regret, still paranoid that someone might remember and take vengeance upon me."

"I'm sorry," Gillian said softly, grateful that he was making sense and broadcasting appropriate responses to his story. She could do nothing for the woman, now long dead. If no one had acted to avenge her death back when it happened, there was nothing to be done now. Csangal, she could help.

"Why?" he asked, turning those wondrous eyes on her.

"Because it has haunted you for this long. Because you are genuinely sorry and can't repair the damage. I want to help you, but we have to get you to a place where you can forgive yourself too."

"Do you believe that is possible? For me to finally let go of the past and forgive myself for killing someone who trusted me?" There was no animosity in his voice or manner, but she could feel a subtle shift. His hackles were up; she'd better tread carefully.

"I don't know," she answered him truthfully. "I hope you can. I've counseled Vampires in your position before, where out of accident or necessity they had to kill someone they loved. It's difficult but eventually they get past it or they Face The Sun."

"Suicide? I do not think I could bring myself to do that."

"I wasn't suggesting that you could," Gillian explained, her voice completely level.

"At first I didn't know what *Face The Sun* meant," she continued. "It's not something included in textbooks on how to counsel the Reborn. Paramortal Psych was a completely new field when I started. There were a lot of things we didn't know or that were referenced by Human ethics only, since mostly Humans were writing the books and teaching the classes. There are a lot of things we are still learning," she added wryly.

"A couple of years into my practice, I had a patient who asked me to be a witness for them. I didn't know that suicide was acceptable in Vampire culture until then. While it is tolerated in some Human societies, it isn't considered an option in my profession or in my particular society. I had to expand my own thinking and realize that others might consider an action that I found morally wrong."

"And if I did contemplate this as a choice?" The glacial green eyes were wary, questioning.

"I would try like hell to talk you out of it, just as I did for the other Vampire."

"But he went through with it, didn't he?"

"She. She went through with it." Gillian shook her head, still clearly bothered by the incident.

"Could you explain further, please?" His gaze never wavered from her face.

"This woman had lost her husband a year before in an auto accident. She and their son were living with her parents and she was trying to get her life back together. Her most recent lover was a fairly new Vampire himself. Either he didn't know about your Rules or he didn't care, because he convinced her to become Reborn, then abandoned her within the first few nights before she'd gained control of her need for blood."

She shook her head, her own eyes growing sad at the remembered pain of that experience. "Since he wasn't around to watch over her and guide her, she went to ground way too close to her family's home. She wanted the security of her child and parents since he'd left her alone.

"When she rose, her little son was alone outside, catching fireflies in the dark, while his grandparents prepared dinner. It never occurred to her that the need for blood might override her maternal instincts with disastrous results. She said she only meant to hold him, but lost control of herself."

Gillian paused, reflecting on the mother's anguish that

she remembered. "I don't remember how she was sent to me, but she came. It had been several months since the child's death, so I thought it was a good sign that she wanted to talk about it, process all the feelings. In reality all she wanted was to tell her story to someone, on video, so her family would understand what had happened.

"She asked me to be one of her witnesses when she Faced The Sun. I refused at first. I don't believe suicide is ever an acceptable answer for any Being. After talking with my mentors, I realized that I had to accept what was normal in Vampire culture, even if it conflicted with my own moral standards. I wanted to help and support her, so I agreed."

"Whose line was she from?" Csangal asked softly.

"I honestly don't remember. At that point in my career, I probably wouldn't have thought to ask since the importance of individual Vampire Bloodlines wasn't something I was aware of," she said ruefully.

"But now you are?"

"Being here for over two years, learning about it from Aleksei and the other Vampires I've met, helped me understand a great deal."

"Go on with your story, then. I am sorry to interrupt."

"No, it's fine," she responded. "Anyway, she planned it for a winter morning, so the sun would rise late. It was cold, snowing. She picked her child's grave for the location. It was just the two of us and the video camera. Her family wanted nothing to do with her or her plans, so they'd waived their right to attend. Then her former lover showed up. He begged her to reconsider but she blew him off."

"Blew him off?" he asked, puzzled.

"Told him to leave, to forget it; her mind was made up."

"Oh, I see."

"Anyway, she lay down on the grave, in the snow, like she was wrapping her arms around her son. She said a few ritualistic words about this being her entitlement to right the wrong she'd done. She stated very clearly on record that this was her decision, even though I had counseled her against it. Then the sun rose.

"Her lover panicked and left. He was a young Vampire, like I said. I know the older you are, the more daylight you can tolerate, but he ran. I guess he wasn't ready to die or to watch her die. But I stayed. She was so very new it didn't take long. She didn't even scream or cry out, just lay there while the sun turned her into dust."

"Gillian." Csangal's voice penetrated her reflective thoughts. "I am very glad you are so sensitive. It gives me more confidence in you than you can imagine."

His slender, elegant hand reached out and he caught a single tear on her cheek. She hadn't realized that she'd been crying.

"I'm sorry. I just wanted you to know that I do understand your cultural differences, and while I don't agree with all of them, I will support your decisions to the best of my ability," Gillian said firmly, shaking off the sad feeling that remembering that incident always brought.

"No apologies, please," Csangal said adamantly. "I am grateful that you want to take the time to explain why you feel a particular way, or what drives your concepts of our lifestyle."

"Time . . . time! Shit! I have to go, Csangal. I'm sorry but I'm supposed to pick up someone at the airport in Brasov and I have to cut this short for the time being." Gillian leapt to her feet, panicked that she might have really lost track of time and would make Perrin miss his flight.

He laughed, to her surprise, and rose to hug her quickly. "It is all right; please do not be worried. I will be here tomorrow night and we can continue then, if you are available."

"Yes, I will make sure I am here. Thanks for understanding, Csangal. I do appreciate it." She nearly screamed when he impulsively hugged her. His charisma was overwhelming and she felt desire slam into her, hard. Pushing away from him, she backed up a step.

"Sorry, Csangal, but you're lethal." She laughed and shook her finger at him before bolting for the car.

He watched her as she hurried off. Delightful, simply delightful. What was it about her scent that was different? He knew he had affected her sexually just by hugging her, but he really couldn't help it; it was just part of who he was. It was interesting that he could affect her so strongly. She had allowed herself to be very open to him and his feelings.

Yes, Gillian was an interesting woman: Guarded, beautiful, compassionate and a little naïve, despite her professional knowledge. And with no idea of just how lethal he could be.

Gill skidded the car into the gravel parking lot, fishtailing it around to face the other direction. The adrenaline surge cleared most of her empathy circuits of the sensual appeal Csangal had left her with. It would have been hell to be in the car with Perrin and Trocar for several hours like that. Kimber and Aleksei stood with the other two, waiting. Perrin had his mask on, but that was fine. He was handling everything much better since the healing.

"Sorry! I'm sorry—that took longer than I thought it would," she exclaimed as she leapt out of the car, popping the trunk and unlocking the doors in the process. She started to grab Perrin's bags, but he stopped her with an arm around her waist, pulling her back.

"No, Gillian. I am a nineteenth-century man and always will be. A gentleman would never permit a lady to fetch and carry for him, and I will not start now."

"Dammit, Perrin, do you ever get tired of being a sexist?" Gill snapped, then smiled up at him.

He looked good. He was even dressed in a more modern way: collarless black silk shirt, black trousers and black loafers. Only his mask was in stark white contrast. That perfect left eyebrow rose.

"Do you ever get tired of being a pain in the derriere?" But he smiled when he said it.

Everyone laughed at that. Perrin had definitely found his more assertive side and was capable of wielding it freely and confidently. Charming.

"I do not believe she does, actually, since she has rendered it into a fine art form."

Thanks a lot, Trocar.

"I would agree," Aleksei offered. "As she has said, 'it is a gift.'"

Gillian stared at all of them incredulously as they secured Perrin's luggage inside.

"I am in testosterone hell."

Kimber smirked covertly behind her hand at Gillian's reply.

Gillian spun on her heel and yanked open the driver's side door, ordering, "Get in, whoever is going."

Perrin opened the passenger side and leaned in. "Are you certain that your emotions are not going to influence your driving abilities?"

"Get in the goddamn car, Perrin."

Chuckling, he slid in, tossing a leather jacket onto the top of the dashboard in front of his seat. It was a gift from Trocar and he wanted the Elf to see he was appreciative of it. He buckled his seat belt and pried her hand off the gearshift to kiss it.

"Settle down, *amoureux.* You do not have to make yourself angry with me to distract yourself from the fact that you will miss me after I am gone."

Her wide-eyed, openmouthed stare told him he'd hit a nerve. Kimber didn't help since she'd climbed into the back with Trocar during Perrin's remark.

"Hey, Gillian, did you include psychology lessons in his therapy? He's really good!"

Gillian viciously shoved the car into gear and floored it, throwing gravel in an arc behind her. Aleksei blurred out of the way of the multiple projectiles and strode off toward the castle, chuckling to himself. Trocar reached out and snapped his door shut before they reached the end of the drive.

"Yes, indeed, he is. I am impressed with how Perrin's perceptions have expanded during his stay," the Dark Elf observed.

"Shut. Up," Gillian said in a low, dangerous voice.

She flicked on the car's stereo and the soaring music of Howard Shore's *Return of the King* soundtrack squelched the sounds of her friends' and her former patient's laughter. Soon she was smiling too, warmed by their gentle teasing.

Perrin studied the scenery as they drove, a mixture of fear and anticipation growing in his stomach. Every kilometer that would take him farther from Gillian and the Institute was a kilometer that took him closer to his own personal destination of life and living.

Something was different about her tonight. She felt off to him, but that could be attributed to her tenseness over his leaving. Her scent was slightly dissimilar. The sexual receptors he had from his Gargoyle lineage were firing at an alarming rate, and he couldn't figure out why.

What was it about her scent that was wreaking havoc on his system? He'd been in close proximity to her for months and hadn't been this turned on.

Gingerly, he crossed his legs, lifting the leather jacket over his lap, hoping Gillian hadn't noticed the straining erection he was now sporting. Turning his face to the window, he wiped the sweat from his upper lip unobtrusively, jostling his mask a little. What the hell?

He nearly jumped out of his skin as Gillian's warm hand reached under the edge of his jacket and squeezed his thigh briefly, her fingers lightly brushing the inseam of his jeans.

Oh, sweet darling, do not do that now, he thought as his blood surged, filling his cock tighter. Spots swam in front of his eyes.

"Are you cold, Perrin?" she asked, not taking her eyes off the road and returning her hand to the steering wheel, much to his relief.

"No, just a little nostalgic," he managed to say in a level voice.

"Okay, just wondered. You seem a little tense." She reached toward him again but he grabbed her hand frantically before it reached his thigh, recovered, brought it to his lips and kissed her fingers. Dear God, if she touched him like that again, he was going to spill inside his jeans.

"I am a little . . . excited," he said honestly, hoping she wouldn't comprehend the true meaning of his words.

"That's understandable. You're embarking on a wonderful journey into your new life." She glanced at him and winked, taking his meaning as he hoped: that he was excited about his journey home.

Perrin squeezed her hand, then reached over to put it back on the steering wheel. "Hands on the wheel, please. I do not care to die on my way to my fabulous new life adventures," he teased her.

She laughed, then changed the CD to some raucous rock and roll, which she and Kimber began to sing. Strange, she sounded good singing like this; not like before when she sang for him in the cottage. But dear God, her scent was still driving him mad. He had to fight not to allow his hips to thrust. All he seemed to be able to picture was her lying beneath him, writhing in ecstasy as he drove deep and arched into a climax . . . spilling . . .

Merde! He swore viciously in his own mind. He couldn't think about her in that way now or he would embarrass both of them by reaching over to turn the wheel so she would pull over and stop the car. The woods were close and thick. They could run in there, away from the road, where he could brace her against a tree, wrap her legs around his waist, plunge hard and deep . . . Dammit!

Deliberately he tamped down any sexual feelings. He was trembling with need and he had to get it under control before they got to the airport. It wouldn't do to get out of the car with a hard-on of his dimensions. She'd surely notice that. Forcibly he turned his thoughts toward Paris.

He couldn't help but be excited about the idea of experiencing his beloved city of Paris as he had never been able to before. Even the thought of finding a job instead of living off his considerable investments didn't seem quite as daunting today. It was like magic, his change of perception, his newfound confidence; being able to look forward to each day rather than dreading it—it was all so remarkable. Gillian was wrong. He hadn't been the supernatural creature in their professional relationship; she was.

It was a nice, relaxing drive to Brasov for everyone else. When they got to the airport, each of them grabbed a bag or a trunk of Perrin's luggage and they got him checked in. He put the leather jacket on and buttoned it even though they were inside. It was long enough that the hem hit him right above his knee, keeping his still-urgent erection covered.

They couldn't follow him to the gate so they said their good-byes there in the concourse lobby. Kimber shook his hand and hugged him, wishing him well. Trocar handed him an intricately tooled, shimmering leather satchel, which Perrin admired, thanking the Grael Elf for his gift.

Trocar explained that it was made from dragon hide and decorated with Grael protective runes. It was enchanted and would never weigh more than the actual leather it was made from, no matter what was carried inside. He showed Perrin how to untie and retie the intricate knot in the front, knowing the musician was a quick study. Opening the bag, Perrin found a portable CD player and several CDs that Trocar and Aleksei thought he might enjoy.

There was the collection of Howard Shore's full score from the Lord of the Rings movies and Sir Andrew Lloyd Webber's *Phantom of the Opera* on a two-disk, full movie soundtrack. Digging further, the Elf pointed to a portable DVD player and the special edition DVDs to all the movies of the soundtracks in the bag.

Perrin was speechless and embraced the Dark Elf tightly. "Thank you, my friend. I cannot tell you what your and Aleksei's friendship has meant to me."

"You still retain it," Trocar said, serious for once, "For as long as you wish it, if you have need, we will be there."

Gillian watched as Trocar stepped back and gave Perrin the highest accord he was capable of bestowing on anyone. The Grael's left arm crossed over his chest, his fist touching his right shoulder and the quick, almost imperceptible nod of the head symbolizing the trust and respect for a higher-caste Being. Perrin watched closely, remembering the last time he'd seen that gesture one night in Sacele, then deliberately mirrored it back. The Grael smiled and turned away. There would be no more words; he'd said farewell.

It was a moment neither of them had looked forward to. Gillian glanced over at Trocar and Kimber, who had wandered over to a small airport shop to admire some local souvenirs. She smiled at her friends' attempt to give her and Perrin a private minute in the crowded airport.

"Gillian." His voice made her shiver but she turned back to him and, bracing herself, looked into those remarkable eyes a final time. Damn, this sucked. No more Gargoyle crossbreeds for her as patients. Ever.

Perrin looked down into her very green, very bright eyes and wanted nothing more than to crush her against him and kiss her senseless, but this was not the time or the place, nor would it have been appropriate, and he knew it. This was a time for them to move on, remain therapist and patient and congratulate themselves on the success of his therapy.

"Thank you." Two small words, yet they conveyed a wealth of meaning when spoken by a tall, dark and handsome masked man in the middle of a crowded airport concourse.

"It was my pleasure," Gillian said, then instantly regretted her choice of words when he smiled and stepped closer to lightly dance his fingers over her shoulder.

"And mine," he replied, his voice laced with a warmth that had everything and nothing to do with sex. Damn, what the hell was it about her that was so enticing at the moment?

Awkward Moments in Good-bye Situations 101. Gillian stuck out her hand. "Take care of yourself, Perrin. Once again, I am proud of you, and you should be too. I wish you all the best in everything. The Gods know you deserve it. Be happy, Monsieur Garnier. Be happy and have a wonderful life. I have enjoyed having you as a patient."

There. That was so goddamn professional she ought to get an Oscar. She looked him straight in the eye with no tears, no outward reaction at all except a warm smile.

Perrin shifted the satchel Trocar had given him to his other shoulder, then took her proffered hand with a quizzical look on his face. So, she wanted this to be formal, almost impersonal. All right, that was what she would get. He shook her hand with a firm grip, his eyes never leaving hers.

"I wish you the same, Dr. Key. I appreciate everything you have done for me, every effort you have made to ensure my success. Be safe, please. This is a difficult and dangerous profession you are in. I do not want to ever hear of you being harmed or hurt." He let go of her hand and waited for her to turn away.

"*Au revoir, ma chérie,*" he said finally when the silence and the staring at each other became uncomfortable.

"Good-bye, Perrin," Gillian whispered. Tearing her eyes away from his, she turned and started toward the exit, knowing that he would be all right and that she would be all right. She almost made it.

"Gillian."

Shit.

She froze, then slowly turned back. Perrin lifted the bag off his shoulder and set it down, opening his arms. She hesitated only a moment before taking the few steps back to him just as he moved toward her. They met in the middle of the empty space that had separated them. Perrin wrapped her in an embrace generally reserved for a life preserver on the *Titanic* and stroked her hair.

Gillian hugged him back tightly, allowing his offer of comfort. She stiffened a little as she felt the tremendous press of his erection against her hip. Sweet Hathor, he was as hard as a crowbar. Time to go.

"Bye, Perrin."

"Good-bye, angel."

It was Gillian who broke the hug first, putting him away from her gently, then waiting patiently as he kissed her hand. He winked at her, then retrieved his bag. Still smiling, he turned and disappeared quickly into the crowd.

It wasn't until later, when he was seated on his plane, staring out at the wet and sparkling tarmac, that he realized what the hell was wrong with him in the car. The seat next to him squeaked as a young brunette seated herself. She was flushed and excited from nearly being late for her flight; her hands were slender and the left one was decorated with a single diamond ring.

The young lady turned and started chattering with him

as the aircraft rolled toward the runway. Unexpectedly her scent hit him and he was at once hard and aching. What. The. *Hell?* Had he turned into some sort of sex fiend? The plane taxied out and lifted off just as the girl who had been talking incessantly about her upcoming wedding got to the interesting part.

"So you see"—she blushed prettily—"he doesn't know that I really am a virgin. I hope he is happy about it. I'm a little embarrassed. Have you ever known a virgin? Why do you have a mask on, by the way?"

Perrin took a moment to digest what she'd just said and put everything together in his lightning-fast mind. Virgin. Gillian carried the same scent. She was now an intact virgin? It must have been from the healing. The healing that had made such a difference in his face. No wonder his body had been so desperate to mate with her.

Sexually mature females did not remain virgin long among the Gargoyle. He didn't know whether to laugh or cry knowing he'd just left Gillian unopened and untried. Right, he was listening to the girl . . .

"Yes, I have known a virgin. She was the most beautiful creature I have ever known," he answered honestly, thinking of Gillian. "I am sure your fiancé will be most pleased with you, my dear. My mask is due to my appearance being displeasing to some. I had an . . . accident, so it makes me more comfortable to wear it."

"Oh," she said softly, "I hope you will be all right."

"I am quite fine, *chérie*. Now, do go on and tell me about your young man and your wedding."

He let himself be distracted by the young woman's inane babble. It kept his mind off a lot of things and helped pass the time until the plane touched down at Charles de Gaulle Airport in Paris. He also found that it was easier to resist the young girl's scent. There was nothing to tie her to him emotionally. Good. That meant he was more Sidhe, more Human, than Gargoyle where it counted and could resist his baser instincts. Relieved, he hailed a cab to take him back to his home beneath the streets of Paris to begin his new life.

Gillian had sighed in relief as Perrin walked away. He was going to be all right. It stung a little. He really had gotten to her, but she was used to good-byes and could handle it. Really, she could. She drew a deep breath and locked everything in her emotional closet back up again.

"Are you all right, Petal?" Jesus, it was Trocar.

"Yeah."

"Liar," Kimber said matter-of-factly.

"Bite me."

"You're not my type."

"I'm hungry. Let's get something to eat," Gillian suggested, hoping to distract everyone, including herself.

"Replacing an emotional or sexual need with food is not a good practice to start, from what I have read in your psychological journals, Gillian," Trocar said sagely.

"I really hate you, you know."

"No, you do not; you love me." The tall Elf draped an arm over her shoulders and the other over Kimber's, then led them down the promenade to find something to eat and wait for their incoming passengers.

CHAPTER
2

CASSIOPEIA and Helmut arrived right on time. Unfortunately they were on two separate airlines coming in from two separate directions. Gillian went to greet Dr. Delphi while Kimber and Trocar went to fetch Dr. Gerhardt.

It was full dark now, but Cassiopeia would have to be unloaded from the specially designed cargo hold. Since the legalization and recognition of Vampires and other Paramortals, most major airlines had passenger facilities to accommodate their special-needs clients.

Dr. Delphi would have gotten into her shipping coffin at dawn, been picked up by the passenger-cargo recovery van and delivered to her waiting airline. The flight from Greece to Romania wasn't that long, so the coffins of any Vampire passenger and similar compartments containing various Sidhe that could not take the rays of the full sun were kept in a special holding area until their flight was ready to depart.

In Cassiopeia's situation, she would wake in the coffin and then emerge after landing. It was a proficient method and generally easiest on the Vampire. Cassiopeia traveled extensively throughout Greece but generally didn't take long trips that necessitated daytime flight. She enjoyed her status as a Master Vampire and really didn't miss her Day-walking life at all. She was there as a favor to help with Gillian's shielding abilities since her professional relationship with Perrin's special case had strained her control.

Cass had her own agenda as well. She was hoping to lure Gillian back to the Greek location of the Miller & Jackson Center to be her clinical director.

Gillian hurried forward to hug her friend as Cassiopeia came slinking down the corridor. The Master Vampire was jaw-droppingly gorgeous. She looked like a young Greek Elizabeth Taylor: short, curvy, blue violet eyes, stylishly arranged raven hair, double-thick lashes, the whole shebang. The two women embraced and exchanged pleasantries. It had been a few years since they'd seen each other but they were definitely good friends.

They collected Trocar, Kimber and Helmut, with all of his luggage, then piled into the car for the drive back. Discussion was kept light, mostly about the Rachlav Institute and how well it was doing. Cassiopeia was most interested in some of the new information Gillian was coming up with in her dealings with an extraordinary number of varied races and crossbreeds.

Sensing that Gillian tensed when that particular subject was brought up, Cassiopeia refrained from questioning her further until they could be alone for some girl talk. She'd been Reborn in the late 1930s and, like most Vampires, retained some of the social mores of her original time period. Some things were just not discussed unless it involved almost a slumber-party-type atmosphere.

Later, when they had everyone back safely at the castle and unloaded, Gillian and Cassiopeia wound up chatting together in a private study that Gill sometimes utilized for individual therapy. It was cozy and quiet with leather furniture, a fireplace, shelves of books and a small rolltop desk. They were lounging on the overstuffed chairs. Cass was embroidering a lovely picture of the Greek wine festival of Dionysus, and Gillian was drinking tequila.

"So, Perrin's Sidhe blood must have been the catalyst for the Gargoyle magic. That's probably why you had such a hard time shielding with him. I am sorry I missed meeting him." Cassiopeia glanced over at her blonde colleague.

Gillian lit a cigarette and poured another shot. "Yes, but it was more than that. I had to remain somewhat open to him or he would notice. His glamour was more than just glamour. It was like my empathy combined with magic and pure instinct," Gillian responded, swirling the tequila in her glass.

"I do not doubt that, baby girl, which is probably why your own shielding broke down around that new Vampire patient of yours. It was already overtaxed from your original patient; then to deal with that level of Vampiric magic . . . How old did you say he was?"

"About six hundred years."

"Well, darling, there you are. We gain a certain level of power and the skill to wield it through the centuries if we are Masters to begin with. Otherwise we simply top out, if you will; gain quickly and then stabilize. The really old ones like Osiris, Dionysus and their main Courts are astonishing in their abilities. Aleksei will gain more as he ages as well."

"Terrific. Can't wait till he discovers just how far Vamp sex foo can be pushed. Or what other forms he can adopt," Gillian grumbled. She picked up a saltshaker, licked the back of her left hand and sprinkled it lightly with the crystallized condiment.

Cassiopeia's musical laughter earned her a glare from Gillian before her young friend licked the salt off, downed the tequila, then shoved a lime wedge into her mouth and bit down.

She shuddered. "How can you drink that?"

"Want some?" Gillian grinned.

"Not even when I was still mortal would I drink that poisoned cactus juice."

"Of course not. Ouzo is so much better. Just another one of the festive gifts from the Greeks, like that horse," Gillian retorted, grimacing.

"You are a bitchy drunk."

"I am not drunk . . . yet."

"Oh, well, do tell me when you are, dear, so I can be sure to notice the difference in your personality," Cassiopeia quipped smugly.

Gillian flipped her off and poured another shot before continuing. "What was really weird was that Perrin really got to me, you know? I have never met anyone, Human or otherwise, who was so completely vulnerable. You couldn't be in the same room with him and not want to comfort him. I don't know how he lasted as long as he did without having any kind of relationship."

"Probably his defensive magic was strong enough to put off any inquisitive searching. Anyone who accidentally got close enough would likely be horrified by the pull from him and would have run like a rabbit."

"Well, he's gone now. I think he'll make it on the proverbial outside. He's very bright and now is determined to carve out a life for himself." Gillian's voice had a bit of a wistful quality that did not go unnoticed.

"You know, ducky, any sort of Fey is very difficult to detach one's self from," Cassiopeia pointed out. "I am impressed that you did not get completely sucked in by his glamour."

"Really?" Gillian looked skeptically at her friend and mentor. "I was concerned about the therapeutic wisdom of letting him practice being a companion and partner."

"You did exactly what your patient needed," Cass said definitively. "Sex therapy is not just about sex, you know. It is about relationships too. He did not have a clue as to how to have a relationship with anyone. You gave him the tools he needed, my precious girl. Do not forget that."

"Thanks, Cass. I never felt a pull like that from anyone before. It's a bit troubling to send him off into the world by himself, even though I know he's lived and functioned alone for a hundred and fifty years."

"Occupational hazard, love. Some of them get to you. There is no avoiding that. It is the same whether you are Human or not."

"You've had one get to you?"

"More than one, darling Gilly. But I have been doing

this longer than you have," Cassiopeia reassured her. "If you are not too plastered, we can practice your meditation and work on your shielding."

"I am not plastered."

"Yet."

Much later, after they had worked on improving and shoring up Gillian's shields, Cass went off to walk the Institute grounds with Daedelus. Gillian discovered that, despite her best efforts, she wasn't drunk. There wasn't much else to do, so she wandered off to the Great Hall to read by the massive fireplace.

One of Gillian's passions in life was a good book. Rarely did the opportunity arise for her to sit and just read. She tried to make it a point to read through Tolkien's trilogy at least once a year, and she was a huge Harry Potter fan. The newest installment in the Potter series had come in several weeks ago, but with everything that had been occurring, she had no time to sit and read it. Now, engrossed in her book, sipping on a cup of coffee, she didn't hear Aleksei come in, and she jumped when he leaned over the couch to kiss her head.

"Dammit, I thought I told you not to sneak up on me like that!" she growled at him.

Amused, he came around the couch to sit next to her and draped his arm over the back of the sofa, encouraging her to come closer. Gillian ignored him at first, then let him draw her up against his chest.

"*Petite femme têtue,*" he teased her lightly. "Stubborn little woman."

"I am not stubborn," she protested, trying to shift away.

Aleksei held on to her and pulled her closer still. It was a rare moment that he could just enjoy the luxury of holding her. Neither of them had to be anywhere; nothing had to be attended to. He gently rubbed his chin and cheek over her hair. She always smelled nice: snow on clover, even if she'd been smoking, or right after sex—especially after sex. Now with her virgin scent added to the mixture, it was a heady fragrance and he felt himself hardening in anticipation. Firmly, he pushed his feelings down. This was neither the time nor the place. He had a romantic evening planned for her and would see it through.

Gillian sighed and scooted into a more comfortable position against his hard chest. Automatically his arm wrapped around her, securing her against him. She didn't struggle this time, just reached up and patted his hand, then turned another page.

Another scent was on her: alcohol. She'd been drinking. It wouldn't affect her as much since she'd accepted an exchange of his blood. Though it was only once, it was enough to enhance her natural abilities: her strength, her speed, her resistance to alcohol and illness. He refrained from mentioning it, as he wisely ascertained that it would not please her a great deal. He really was getting smarter where she was concerned.

They stayed like that in front of the fire. Neither spoke as Gillian read and Aleksei let his thoughts drift where they would. After a time, he noticed that she hadn't turned a page in a while and her head was heavier on his chest. Gently, he slid the book out from under her hands, careful to keep her place, laying it on the carved coffee table. Shifting carefully, he scooped her up in his arms and carried her from the room. When halfway up the stairs she stirred enough to loop her arm around his shoulder, he whispered softly to her to be still and sleep as he carried her into the room they shared between dusk and early morning.

The tall, raven-haired Vampire Lord laid her on the bed and then, with infinite tenderness, removed her boots and tucked her in. He smiled as he watched her snuggle deeper beneath the down comforter he pulled over her.

It was times like this that Aleksei liked best, when life was simple and uncomplicated for even a few brief hours. Just being with Gillian made him feel content and happy, he realized as he stretched out next to her on the bed and spooned his larger, heavier frame around hers. Whatever their activity, or lack of it, did not matter to him; being with her did. Lying next to her as he was, he could almost feel like a Human man again, holding his lady tenderly in the night.

A brief scowl darkened his breathtaking features momentarily. He wasn't a Human man and never would be again. What kind of life had he innocently gotten her into? He had no idea things would turn out the way they had when he'd initially hired her. With her help, he'd finally crossed the last bridge of his adjustment into the Nightwalker's Realm. Nearly four hundred years as a Vampire, all his wisdom, knowledge and experience, yet this little blonde woman with more heart, courage and compassion than good judgment had, in her quietly supportive way, helped his life make sense; made it complete.

Aleksei knew he shouldn't think that way. There was nothing tying Gillian to him on a permanent basis. With only one blood exchange between them, and a limited one at that, either one could walk away from the other.

He briefly wondered if she would have agreed to see him again after her ethical time period ended if the War hadn't started, forcing her to stay for her own safety. Probably not a good idea to think along that particular path. He might not like the conclusion he came to. Gillian was unpredictable in most circumstances except one: she was an outstanding therapist and never shirked her duty to a patient, no matter what the personal cost to herself.

Perrin's departure had been difficult for her. The masked genius had left an indelible positive impression on all of them. Aleksei knew his initial behavior over Gillian being Perrin's sex therapist was inexcusable. After relenting and seeing the result of her expertise, it had been awe-inspiring to watch Perrin blossom into the man he could have been all along.

Much as she did for me, Aleksei thought to himself. The one difference being that Perrin was far more Human than he was, even being a crossbreed. Perrin could walk in the daylight with her and hold her all night instead of leaving to find shelter within the earth before the sun rose too high. For the second time, Aleksei wondered if he was being selfish trying to win Gillian's love and affection; if she wouldn't be better off with a man like Perrin, who could share a more normal lifestyle with her.

He smiled ruefully as he grazed his hand down her shimmering hair, because he knew what Gillian would say: that her lifestyle wasn't normal by any standards, so that wasn't necessarily a selling point. She would, of course, also punctuate her statement with some sort of profanity and tell him he was off his fucking nut or something to that effect.

Gillian made no excuses for who she was. Maybe it was time for him to do the same. He was a Vampire Lord, head of his own line, not a Human man. There were infinitely more choices and possibilities available to him.

Either she would get over her fear of relationship permanency and let herself love him for who he was, or she would eventually walk away. Aleksei knew that as long as he didn't push her and let her come to her own conclusions, his chances were better for her to stay than if he demanded some form of commitment from her. Besides, he had to grudgingly admit to himself, he really did respect her more than that.

When dawn broke and he reluctantly left her side to find refuge in the rich earth of the Carpathian Mountains, he was more than ready to rest. He'd spent most of the night thinking way too much and was tired. A last kiss on her smooth brow and he took his leave, a strikingly handsome, elegant figure walking confidently from the castle that had been his family home and striding into the depths of the forest to await the excitement of another night.

———◦———

Gillian awoke to the incessant ringing of her cell phone. It was Jenna, calling from Abu Simbel, Egypt. She and Tanis were all toured out and were coming back soon. The two friends chatted and caught up for a little over two hours, with Gillian drinking coffee and getting dressed during the conversation. Gill finally had to leave to meet with Samuel and Esi for some couple's counseling. She wished her friend well and hung up, then got her thoughts together before she went to meet them in the library area that was used for group therapy.

Samuel had approached her with a request for some private therapy with himself and Esi. It seemed that Esi was having some issues letting go of her dead husband's memory and needed to work through her feelings.

Esi wanted to be with Samuel; she loved him, but it still felt a little like she was being unfaithful to her first husband. Gillian was going to see what she could do to iron everything out.

They were already in the library when Gillian got there. Samuel sat on the leather couch, his huge bulk positioned in a sheltering manner next to Esi, who was stiff and prim at his side. A mammoth arm was draped over the back, almost but not quite touching her slender shoulders. Gillian took her seat in one of the large high-backed chairs positioned diagonally from them, tucking one leg under in casual repose.

"What can I do for you two?" she began, wanting to let them set the pace.

"Oh, Gillian, I want this to work so badly. I just don't know if I can get past the memory of Mirko." Esi was uncharacteristically vulnerable and raw. Samuel gently patted her shoulder with a ham-sized fist, concern written plainly over his almost-handsome face.

"Tell me what is good about this relationship, Esi," Gillian said soothingly. "Tell me what it is about Samuel that makes him different from all the other men you've had chances with since Mirko died."

Gill wanted to establish a positive tone to their discussion. Esi had been dating Samuel for weeks. They had accidentally gotten caught in a sexual energy field manifested by Perrin's power-laden metaphysical music the first night he'd had sex with Gillian. Instead of cementing their relationship, Esi had been plagued by guilt over behavior she couldn't have controlled if she'd tried.

Samuel was growing more and more depressed. He'd been miraculously healed by the magic generated by the combination of Vampire, Sidhe and Perrin's powers—or as much as a creature sewn together from spare body parts and brought to life through the astronomical power of a lightning bolt could be healed. As Frankenstein's clinically depressed handiwork, he'd had no hope of ever experiencing love or even life, until he came to the Institute for therapy and inadvertently found Esi as well.

He'd gone from almost repulsively ugly to passably attractive as a result of that fortuitous curative experience. Still a gargantuan man at over seven feet tall, Samuel had retained his dignity and intellect over the years; even expounded on it. The Creator, as Samuel referred to Viktor, had inadvertently given him a brain that was already inquisitive and intelligent.

Samuel's own personality, wherever it had manifested from, had brought a love of poetry, romance and beauty in all its forms. This was the first time in his life that he'd found the courage to explore the possibilities of a relationship.

"At first, Samuel was safe," Esi said quietly, looking down at her hands in her lap.

"Safe? How?" Gillian asked.

"Because I was ugly," Samuel interjected in his bass voice.

Esi nodded. "I'm sorry, Samuel, but yes. I didn't think I could look at you as anything but a friend."

"And I would have been happy to be just that, your friend," he said kindly, squeezing her shoulder.

"Then Perrin's music mojo took us all by surprise," Gillian added.

"Yes," Esi continued. "I wasn't expecting my reaction or Samuel's." She turned toward the Giant, worry plainly written on her face. "Samuel, you have to know that when Perrin's music overtook us, it was so dark, I didn't notice your physical changes until after . . ." She blushed scarlet.

"You didn't notice that he'd gotten more handsome until after you guys had sex?" Gillian prompted her.

"No," Esi whispered. "It didn't matter what he looked like. I was willing."

"Hell, Esi, we all were willing," Gill said with a snort. "Perrin packed a huge punch in that music of his. No one within hearing distance of that music could have remained unaffected." Something occurred to her then. "But that's not what's bothering you, is it?"

Esi shook her head.

"This isn't about the sex at all, is it, Esi? It's guilt over wanting to continue that happy, carefree feeling. You're experiencing guilt because you believe that being happy is betraying Mirko in some way." Gillian knew she'd hit the nail on the head. Esi paled, then slowly nodded her head.

Gillian waited for Esi to make all the connections herself. Samuel wasn't quite so restrained.

"Sweetling, I did not know your first man, Mirko, but I know that if he loved you as you say he did, he would want you to be happy after his death. I know that, Esi, because that is what I would want too. Not for you to mourn for the rest of your life, but to continue living." Samuel's voice was warm and gooey as he gently took her chin in his massive paw and turned her toward him.

"I love you, Esi. As much if not more than Mirko did. I think he would approve of someone like me being around to cherish the woman he loved, now that he cannot."

Wow, thought Gillian, *Samuel's got that romantic, articulate thing going on.* She was silently cheerleading for the two of them. She couldn't let them know how she would like it to play out. This was their life, their relationship; she was just the therapist and had to remain unbiased, at least outwardly.

"And," Samuel went on, "I don't think he would be jealous that you loved me as well. Your feelings for me cannot take away from or even touch the feelings you had for him. You are allowed to love us both. I don't feel threatened by your memories of Mirko. You had a good life and a good marriage with him. It is appropriate that you remember that fondly and with love."

Esi visibly relaxed, leaning into his barrel chest. "You always know the perfect thing to say, Samuel."

A little awkwardly, he draped his mammoth arms around her and hugged her. Esi's torso disappeared amid the corded muscle. "We will work this out, my love," Samuel rumbled. "I want to marry you but I don't want you to have any reservations."

"Marriage?" Esi squeaked from somewhere around Samuel's solar plexus. "You want to marry me?"

Samuel drew back and looked down at her, his face concerned and frowning. "Of course! You did not think I would just leave you after my time here at the Institute was over?" Then he slapped his own forehead. "Well, of course you did. I have not been as clear as I should have been. Forgive me, Esi. I want to marry you and I should have let you know."

She laughed and scooted up onto her knees on the couch so she could hug him better. "Thank you for saying it now, and for understanding everything, Samuel."

His enormous hands picked her up and sat her on his lap, and they started an intense make-out session. Gillian hastily got up and started for the door. "I'll let you two finish working this out. I think you've got everything under control without my help."

"Thank you, Gillian," Samuel and Esi chorused.

"Think nothing of it. I didn't do a damn thing."

Gillian was smiling and lighthearted as she shut the doors behind her. That was the way therapy was supposed to go. One or two well-placed therapeutic phrases and they were on their way to resolving their own problems. Generally it wasn't that easy, but hey, she'd take it.

CHAPTER

3

GILLIAN sat, pen in hand, notepad on her lap, trying desperately to focus on what the hell her newest patient was getting at. His story, much like the *Phantom of the Opera*, was familiar to most people. What most people didn't know was that Dr. Henry Jekyll, aka Edward Hyde, was alive and well and living in Paris. Well, normally he was. Right now he was a surprise addition to her client list, thanks in part to Helmut's Paramortal Psychology public relations campaign, and partly due to the same article that had brought Perrin to the Institute.

Henry had a not-so-classic case of what would have normally been called dissociative identity disorder, if he were fully Human. The Paramortal term for it was fragmentation syndrome, or FS, and in Henry's case, it had been self-inflicted. Technically, any Shifter had FS by default. It referred to the Being literally becoming something or someone else for a space of time. Shifters were notoriously well-adjusted as a whole, except in the case of some with ancestral curses, like Charles Chastel, everyone's favorite Loup-Garou, now deceased.

The dear doctor had been a little too overly ambitious in his experimentations with various Victorian-era pharmaceuticals in an effort to discover whether mankind could divest itself of its beastly nature. Fortunately he used himself as the proverbial guinea pig instead of a patient, or he might have been up on attempted murder charges.

As it were, the tonic he imbibed worked a little too well, literally splitting him in two. The low point in his discovery was finding out that two complete people now resided within his skin and were constantly fighting for supremacy. It made for an exciting life for Henry and an enormous headache for Gillian, who was essentially contending with two people telling the same story in varying degrees of hostility and trying to out-shout each other. It wasn't helping that his face and body contorted with each sentence, finally settling on a horrific mishmash of features that would have done any Gargoyle or Sluagh proud.

Henry was trying to explain how the tonic had somehow unnaturally extended his life beyond normal parameters, while Eddie was viciously interjecting the seventy-five reasons why they shouldn't be at the Rachlav Institute of Paramortal Healing since they weren't really Paramortal, and why being a raging psychopath with an infinite life span was a good idea.

Gillian had to disagree with him on that particular point. Henry had unintentionally stumbled on a formula that, despite everything else, extended a Human life span considerably. According to the fellows at Interpol who had brought him to her, there had been some murmurs of interest in the formula on the black market. The respectable doctor and his counterpart had been sentenced to a newly devised house arrest arrangement that was masquerading as a glorified witness protection program. It kept him alive and kept the formula off the streets, which suited everyone except Eddie for the time being.

Eddie had actually been the one on trial for several murders committed when he had control of their shared body. Henry had nothing to do with the atrocities, but was an accessory before the fact since he'd devised the soul-splitting formula in the first place.

All levels of law enforcement were doing their best to

stay on top of the challenges brought to the table by now having to incarcerate and prosecute various non-Humans instead of just hunting them down with dogs, stakes, pitchforks and torches. Generally the ruling body for the individual Paramortal stepped in and handled the issues on a case-by-case basis and in accordance with their own specific set of rules.

Once in a while, someone did something so outrageously horrid to a non-Paramortal that the Human-run courts were allowed to step in and handle the problem. That was when the FBI, the CIA, Interpol and the International Civil Liberties Union got gray hair, took large amounts of antacids and antianxiety medication and did a lot of praying, knowing they might be teetering on the verge of an interspecies incident by whatever course of action they might take or might try to prevent. Sometimes it just didn't pay to be one of the good guys.

Aleksei, Osiris and Dionysus had put the wheels in motion for their respective countries to join Interpol's informational network. Knowledge was power, Osiris said. So everyone being able to access any possible activities by the Dark Prince and his friends and track them was a good thing. Who said Vampires were stodgy and not progressive?

One particular Interpol agent who was pulling "Weird Shit I Can't Tell My Family About" duty was an Irish Shifter named Galahad Upchurch. He was leaning against the library doors, keeping an eye on his fractured charge and shaking his head as Gillian tried to calm the agitated man. Gill didn't like it one bit that he was in the room, but Eddie had a habit of breaking furniture and people if he gained sole control of the body for any length of time. A Vampire or Shifter was required to manhandle him to the ground if necessary until Henry got control again.

"Dr. Key, may I approach the three of you?"

"Yes, Special Officer Upchurch, you certainly may."

"Please call me Galahad; it's less of a mouthful." He smiled at her and walked toward their seated area.

Galahad was tall, dark and very handsome. His dark auburn shoulder-length hair was pulled back into a masculine ponytail, accentuating his chiseled jawline. His eyes were a dark evergreen color that Gillian had never seen before, but which was striking against his tan complexion.

Reaching them, he put a firm hand on Henry's constantly reshaping shoulder. "That is quite enough from both of you. Let her do her job and try to get you into a functioning capacity or this is not going to work."

"He wants me to be a lemming!" Eddie bellowed, asserting himself for the moment.

"I want us to both survive, you moron!" Henry bellowed right back, clearly not intimidated by his other self.

Gill wanted to bang her notepad against her face, but instead she tried to be helpful. "Look, Galahad explained the situation to me, so let me ask you if I understand your goals for this therapy correctly.

"You have avoided capture, kidnapping and being murdered for your formula for a very long time. However, now, with more sophisticated technology and identification requirements, you discovered you have been under surveillance for at least . . . five years?" She checked her intake forms to make sure she was correct.

"Yes," the two of them growled simultaneously.

"Okay, so you contacted Interpol and asked for asylum. What they offered you was a new identity in exchange for the formula. Have I got everything straight so far?"

"Yes, but I want to take this opportunity to make a new life for myself . . . for us . . . He wants us to remain as we are, where we are most comfortable in Paris, and take on anyone who wants to steal the formula. He says it will be exciting." Henry's voice became higher pitched and more sarcastic.

"I said it is worth being a target if it means we will still know we are alive instead of living in some remote Icelandic fishing village!" Ye Gods, Eddie was loud.

"If you're assaulted by any of these groups that want your longevity formula, you're both in danger of dying," Gillian pointed out. "Plus the fact that if the formula can't be modified to leave out the splitting-people-in-two thing, there are going to be more like you running around and having the same problems."

"Saints preserve us." Galahad sighed.

"No saint, no God and no half-assed therapist can help us. Do you not understand that?" Eddie was definitely in need of some form of horse tranquilizer to lower his volume.

"Henry . . . Eddie . . . " Gillian was having empathy fits over Eddie's homicidal rage versus Henry's righteous anger.

"Perhaps it would be simpler to address the two of them by the name they've chosen for their new identity," Galahad said helpfully.

"Is that all right with both of you?" Gill raised the question.

At their nodded assent, she asked, "What would you like me to call you?"

"Chester."

"Chester?"

"I like chests, and he keeps the formula in one." Eddie howled at his own hilarity. Everyone else groaned.

"Chester Vangarde," Galahad said, rolling his eyes.

"All right, Chester, I am willing to do this but you guys really have to come up with a plan on who's going to talk when during these sessions. I am having a hard time concentrating on what issues are important to each of you and I want to give both of you my attention and show you that I respect both perspectives."

Grudgingly the two halves agreed and, by the end of the next hour, had developed a semblance of a plan with Gillian on how to get their therapy on the right path. To say that Gillian was relieved was a vast understatement. She had a hell of a headache and wanted some aspirin and a very cold soda. After standing as witness while Galahad locked Chester up in the crypt for some quiet time, Gillian thanked them both and then headed upstairs.

"I will accompany you, if you do not mind. Chester has had his outing for the day and is supposed to be studying all aspects of his new identity." Galahad sprinted up the stairs past her and opened the door.

"Thanks." Gill acknowledged the gesture. "How long is he kept locked up every day?"

"Most of the time." Galahad didn't mince words. "He is far too dangerous to allow in a noncontrolled environment, so he is either escorted by an agent or he is under lock and key."

She frowned. "I don't like any situation where a person is isolated most of the time. It really doesn't help anything and causes a lot of resentment."

"Understood, but we honestly have no place to perpetually house him. We periodically move him from one secure area to another, but there is no continuity. He would have been on trial for his crimes except for the ICLU insisting that his formula made him a target, and that to prosecute him rather than protect him would sign his death sentence."

"Where the hell has he been all this time?" Gill wanted to know. "There haven't been rashes of strangled prostitutes or offended aristocrats around Paris recently . . . He's been somewhere, surviving without help, since the nineteenth century."

"He was found unconscious, barely alive, in a forgotten section of the Paris catacombs by a group of Vampires. I do not know which one in particular. He was allegedly under a spell, but most think he had mixed another tonic that put him into a state very much like hibernation. We'll never know for sure. You see what it's like trying to get a straight answer out of them." Galahad chuckled. "I do like him, though."

"Yeah, he's a riot," Gillian said dryly. "How'd you get this assignment, by the way? Were you a bad Werewolf?"

He laughed again. "Not that I am aware of. I was a reader of Stevenson's stories who thought it would be most appropriate to watch over his creation."

"That is very kind of you, Galahad," Gillian said, meaning it. "There are not many who would be as tolerant of him and his situation. Thank you for helping."

"My pleasure."

"I have to run, but I will see you around the Institute."

Gill waved and hurried off to talk with Daed about some possible medication for Chester to level out his moods.

After she explained the situation, Daed rummaged through half a dozen books to determine whether it was better to treat the mood shifts as just a psychological problem or to take into consideration that Chester actually shifted, at least internally. It was one of those situations that made Paramortal psychiatrists wonder what the hell they were thinking when they declared a specialty in medical school.

He stopped abruptly and stared at Gillian, cocking an eyebrow. "How does he feel to you?"

"What?"

"Your empathy. How does he register?"

Gillian frowned and thought about it. "Not like a Shifter; more like a Human with dissociative identity disorder but without the clear individual personality parameters. Emotions scattered . . . all over the place . . . completely chaotic . . . nothing you can hold on to for any length of time."

"Okay." Daed grinned. "That helps a lot. I'll do some research on creating sort of a drug cocktail for him. If I don't have all the meds on-site, I'll drive into town and pick up what we need."

"Great." Gill grinned at her former boss. "I think we have a good chance with his therapy if we can make the meds work."

She strolled down the castle hallway, deep in thought about how she would organize her notes on Chester.

"Buona sera, cara," Aleksei's deep, velvety voice intoned next to her left ear.

"Shit!" Gillian managed to untangle herself from the ceiling. "Dammit, stop doing that!" She punched him in the chest halfheartedly.

He chuckled and swept her up in an embrace, nuzzling her hair with a kiss. "How are you, *piccola*?"

"Busy. Put me down." Gill squirmed and he set her on her feet.

"Honestly, Aleksei, I appreciate your enthusiasm but I don't have time for slap and tickle in the hallway when my mind is on other things." She glared up at him from her vertically challenged vantage point.

He smiled down at her, warming her from her toes to her hair. She shivered under his intimate regard and smiled back, despite herself. "I have to finish working and then we can play."

"I look forward to it." He ran a long, aristocratic finger down her cheek and traced her jawline. "Have a good evening, *dolcezza*. I will attend to my own responsibilities." A quick kiss and a caress on her bottom and he was gone.

"You suck," Gillian said to empty air.

"You should know."

His voice rumbled through her mind, making her blush and feel all gooey. She had to laugh. He had a decent sense of humor for an old fossil. Maybe he was growing on her. Nah. Well . . . maybe. *Argh!*

Walls . . . where were those goddamn walls when she needed them? Actually . . . *did* she need them anymore? More important, did she want them? A sudden epiphany whacked her over the head with the knowledge that there wasn't too much she wanted to keep from Aleksei. That bothered her and comforted her at the same time. She realized that just by being what she needed him to be—her friend, her lover, her comrade at arms—exactly when she needed him to be each of those things, he was fitting himself into her life rather than expecting her to fit into his.

Wow. He really was putting her first, in everything.

He would put any contemporary man to shame with that outlook, Gill thought to herself. Her four-hundred-year-old Vampire Lord had evidently been keeping up with current events and paying attention to one particular Human's laundry list of expectations.

Aleksei smiled to himself after he left Gillian flustered and bemused in the hallway. Tonight he intended to make good on his promise to take her out for a toe-curling quixotic evening. Hopefully by the time they ended their evening with life-affirming sex—accomplished romantically, of course—she would be more open to his suggestion.

Suggestion? No, it was not merely a suggestion. It was a

question. A question he had wanted to ask her for a while, but there was always something else keeping their attention elsewhere. He knew his heart and mind were clear on the issue. Gillian and he belonged together. He wanted her on any terms, but above all, he wanted her to know that he was in her life to stay, and he was willing to bestow a small token as a symbol of that commitment.

Fingering the ring in his pocket, Aleksei hoped she liked jewelry. The only pieces he had seen her wear were her diamond studs and her little claddagh ring. This was a little bit more ornamental but not so gaudy that Gillian would shriek in horror. At least he hoped not.

———————

Gillian finished up her notes on Chester in the smaller study that she had been using as an office. It wasn't as big as the library but it was still enormous. The castle wasn't massive by castle standards but it was pretty damn big. She realized that she hadn't seen all the rooms yet despite having lived there for over two years. She loved history and ancient places, so it was easy for her to feel comfortable in the surroundings. Maybe after her meeting with Csangal she'd ask Aleksei for a tour, or she'd ask the Brownies if Aleksei was tied up being Lord of something. The little Beings knew the castle as well as Aleksei did. They'd practically taken it over since their temporary stay had become more permanent.

Flipping open her phone, she called Kimber to see if anyone wanted to grab dinner before she met with her next client. It was the jolly crew of Kimber, Gill, Helmut, Daed, Trocar and Pavel that headed to another little neighboring village and a restaurant that came highly recommended by Cezar and his brother Ivan. The Werewolf Alpha and his constable brother normally had very different tastes in most spectrums of their lives, but one thing they both agreed on was where the best local cuisine was located.

It was an uneventful, satisfying meal with friends in a relaxed setting. Just what she'd needed, Gillian realized. Life had lately become one adventure after another and it was nice to simply hang out with familiar, comfortable friends, no braid on her shoulder, no one having a meltdown, no one trying to kill them for the moment. She raised her iced tea in salute to her little group.

"I just wanted to say that I really appreciate everyone getting involved with the situation here. It means a lot to me to have you guys with me, and despite bitching about it, I really am glad we're all here together and able to do some good. Helmut . . . the idea for the Institute was brilliant. I am amazed at the amount of patients and the amount of support."

Helmut actually blushed, his ruddy complexion turning even redder. "I am very glad it worked out as well, and that we have such an amazing staff to work with these Beings."

"Speaking of which," Daed interjected, "unless Cassiopeia wants to stay on and Helmut wants to take on his own caseload, we really need to hire more staff. I've got a full load myself between seeing private patients and doing medical director duty."

Kimber piped up. "Pavel says he wants to look into getting a degree. He said that Gillian convinced him through his therapy that being a Paramortal shrink is what he wants to do with himself. When he's not on Wolf guard duty, of course."

Everyone was excited by Kimber's statement, causing the Werewolf in question to blush uncharacteristically. Pavel was well liked by everybody in the pack and at the castle. He was intelligent, reliable and a stalwart friend. Gillian suggested that Helmut and Daed figure out a way to provide the young Alpha with a grant to pay his way through school.

"I . . . I don't know what to say, Gillian." Pavel was truly endearing and humble.

"Just say that if we pay your way through university, you'll stay on here as staff." She grinned at him and patted his shoulder.

"Of course!" Pavel enthusiastically agreed.

"Which brings me to another point," Gillian said, swirling her finger over the rim of her glass. "Apparently a lot of the texts we read in grad school were a teensy bit wrong on a few points. I was thinking we need to revamp a textbook or two, Helmut."

"That's a wonderful idea, Schatzi!" Helmut was excited about the prospect. Gillian was absolutely right. They'd found out more about Paramortals in her two years of involvement in Romania than some field researchers had learned in a decade.

"I think we need to rewrite some of the current curriculum along with more than a few of the texts. I will do some poking around in the stuffy world of academia, which I know you hate, and see what I can find for us to do." Helmut's eyes sparkled with delight at the prospect.

"Great. Okay, I'm almost late, so I need to run," Gill announced, standing up and gathering her things. They all piled out of the restaurant and drove her back to the edge of Sacele. She'd walk into town, just to ensure Csangal's privacy.

On the drive back to the castle after dropping off Gill, Daed proposed another idea. "You know, Helmut, maybe having some scholarships sponsored by the Rachlav Institute would be a good idea, as would some paid internships. It would get us staff in a hurry and we could train them the right way from the beginning."

"Excellent idea. I will find Aleksei and see how agreeable he is to even more people living in his home," Helmut said.

Everyone laughed but they were excited about the prospects as long as Aleksei and Tanis didn't mind their family home being both a retreat of sorts and a classroom. They found the Lord of the Manor in the great room, reading Gillian's latest Harry Potter book.

"Expanding your horizons?" Daedelus asked with a grin.

"I admit, I am a bit confused. I think I should start from the beginning of the series so I understand everything up to this point. Gillian is correct; Ms. Rowling is a wonderful writer and I look forward to reading the entire series."

Realizing they wanted to talk to him about something, Aleksei smiled and laid the book aside. He shifted on the couch and motioned for them all to sit down. "What can I do for all of you?"

CHAPTER

4

"LET me make sure I'm understanding all of this, Csangal," Gillian said carefully, and reiterated what he had told her to the best of her ability. Her eyes never left his face, he noticed, and she was too deep in concentration to respond to his seductive power as she reasoned through what he was telling her.

They were in the midst of a very intense session in a private dining alcove at the Inn. He had just gotten around to sharing with her the crux of his anxiety and depression. Evidently he had put a lot of thought into it and discovered what was really bothering him. Gillian was very pleased with his progress and his new insight. He wanted to find his creator. Find and confront, if truth be told. Csangal was a six-hundred-year-old Master Vampire with no roots.

Some of his issues were directly related to him rising as a full Master with no one to guide him and no one to teach him about the terrible power he now wielded. That oversight had cost him dearly: he'd killed the woman he'd loved due to Bloodlust—the condition all Masters, Lords or standard, everyday Vampires must endure the first few times they rise as a Reborn creature of the night.

Not to mention the enemies he'd made for himself and his family by hunting too close to home in his own village— another sin in the world of Vampire etiquette: never bleed your shelter. Romania had always been a friendly haven to Vampires, since long before the recognition of Paramortals as real and sentient Beings.

Courtesy dictated that a Vampire feed away from its community of origin. Csangal had been ignorant of this fact, hunting and feeding in the area where he'd lived all his life. This did not sit well with the community at large and he was warned to stop. Knowing, by that time, some of the extent of his new abilities, he had ignored the warning and continued as before.

As a result of his disregarding this basic tenet and ignoring the warnings, and because Vampires in general are just hard as hell to find and to actually kill, the townsfolk sent a rather clear but violent message to him via his family. His father was kidnapped and buried alive after refusing to disclose his son's resting place, subject to the superstitious justice of a bygone age, six hundred years prior.

Soon after his father's death, when Csangal retaliated and killed several of the nobles he thought responsible, his mother was taken from her home and burned at the stake. His eldest brother's eyes were burned out and he was buried alive. His younger brother was held captive and used as a pawn by both Hungary and the Ottoman Turks as leverage over Romania's ruler. Romania and Hungary were in the midst of an ongoing war with the Turks. There was a proverbial witch hunt to try to draw Csangal and other nobles out, using the captives as bait. The intent was to banish the ruling class or kill them outright, thereby making peace with the invaders.

Csangal had chosen banishment, but not before turning on the townspeople. In response to the killing of his parents and brother and the imprisonment of his younger brother, Csangal formulated a plan of retribution that Gillian was surprised hadn't been recorded somewhere. She'd have to do some research on it, but doubted she'd really find anything. During the time frame he described, the Turks had been a rampaging presence in Eastern Europe and a lot of atrocities were committed on both sides.

Managing to gain the attention and admiration of a neighboring province's prince, Csangal had been given a small army to command and had defended both areas well. His troops were loyal to the core, so when he asked them for a favor, they were only too eager to comply. They tore through monasteries and estates, murdering nobles and monks, taking the gold and valuables to sell and give back to the villages that had been victimized by the Turks.

Still, there had to be something about this in the history books, Gillian thought. A Romanian Robin Hood and his murderous madcap band could not have gone unnoticed. She felt a faint twisting as her internal alarm system went off, then found she couldn't remember quite why she was concerned.

As his therapist, she had to assume that he was telling her the truth. Patients sometimes lied, sometimes told slanted versions of situations, but generally would revert and confess to the truth—mainly because they realized they weren't accomplishing anything by lying to their therapist or to themselves.

She'd let it go. Csangal had been brutally honest about himself and his mistakes so far. There was no reason for her not to believe that he would fess up when the time was right. She needn't be concerned.

Csangal felt her curiosity, her empathy and her disbelief well up and just as quickly soothed her thinking. Only a Vampire with his extraordinary abilities would be able to do so. He couldn't afford for her to be suspicious of him. He needed her trust. He needed her. Telling her the absolute truth was not an option. He would tell her everything she needed to know and quite a bit more that she didn't, but not now.

He watched her, easily reading her surface thoughts as she scribbled her notes down. Good, good, she was concerned about him, not because of him. There was still something very different about her. Settling back in his seat, he continued his observations.

Her scent . . . there was something about her scent . . . It was . . . intoxicating. Mentally he shook himself. She was Human. There should be nothing particularly intoxicating about her. She might be his therapist at the moment, but she was still food.

What was it about her? He was the predator; he was able to inspire desire, lust . . . acquiescence. The lovely Dr. Key should not be affecting him this way. Prey did not make the Master's senses tingle in this manner. Her scent. What was it about her scent? The aroma of a female, the perfume of . . . purity.

Something clicked in his memory and he knew.

Good God.

Csangal fought not to display his surprise. Of all the things he had expected from Gillian, virginity was not one of them. Yet it could not possibly be true. He had seen her with his own eyes, coupling with that Gargoyle creature.

She lived with Aleksei Rachlav. Aleksei was, to his recollection, a very virile, dominant male. They were definitely enjoying carnal delights together. How the hell was she virgin? If such a thing were possible and she truly was, it was an unexpected advantage for him. A bit more premature than he had planned, but still an incomparable treasure.

He wrenched his thoughts back to the present, noticing finally that Gillian was staring at him. How long had he been silent?

"Forgive me, Gillian. I was lost in my thoughts for a moment."

"Not a problem." She smiled at him. "I didn't want to intrude. You seemed to be so deep in contemplation."

"Quid pro quo, Doctor."

"What?"

"I have given you a great deal of information about myself. Would you care to reciprocate?"

Gillian eyed him skeptically. "Self-disclosure is only appropriate in therapeutic circumstances when it will bring direct benefit to the patient."

"What is your point, may I ask?" Csangal had a rather

eerie look in his eyes that Gill wasn't quite comfortable with.

"My point is, as a Human who is six hundred years younger than you, there is very little reference that I can give you from my life to benefit you as a Vampire. I have to assume you are just being nosy because you've exposed a great deal of your personal issues to me lately. You want it to be fair, for me to be as vulnerable to you as you are to me, but it doesn't work like that, Csangal."

Nosy? She had called him nosy, like some gossipy fish-wife. Csangal could not believe his ears. If she had been any other Human, he would have killed her for insulting him in that manner. That is, unless her newfound state was a true one, then he would indeed have stayed his hand. Still, she did not know whom she was dealing with, evidently. He could hypnotize her easily to find out what he wanted to know, but perversely, now he wanted to raise the stakes on his own.

"Gillian, I am not trying to pry into your personal life, but I notice that you appear to have experienced a sort of"—he paused for effect—"regression."

Their eyes locked. Gillian was hoping that he didn't mean what she thought he did. "What exactly are you saying, Csangal?"

"My dear girl, your scent . . . it is quite different and alluring." He gave her a megawatt smile and she shivered under the full power of his preternatural beauty.

Well, shit. Is it that obvious? Apparently, it was.

To his supreme delight, she blushed prettily, clearing her throat before she answered. "Um . . . yes . . . well . . . that is a little hard to explain."

"I imagine it would be. There would be a great many women who would be clamoring to know your secret."

"It's sort of the . . . by-product of some Sidhe magic." There. That was the truth. Sort of. She prayed he wouldn't pick up on the almost lie.

"That is not quite the entire truth, Gillian." Csangal's surreally beautiful voice tingled over all her senses.

"Dammit, stop probing."

Csangal chuckled. "Freudian slip?"

"I have to go."

Laughing openly, he stopped her with his hand gently on her arm. "I apologize, my dear. I did not mean to make you uncomfortable with my comments,"

Disgruntled, Gillian sat back down, her cheeks flaming, wishing she could disappear or at least shoot herself. She didn't want to say anything to any strange Vampire about what had occurred at Castle Rachlav, or rather the Rachlav Institute of Paramortal Healing. She didn't want to spook and run off either. Bastard. He found a chink in her armor. Vampires did that ever so often. She should be used to it by now.

"No, it's just that, well, it is a little embarrassing that you can tell so much by just my . . . scent." She flushed a deeper red. At least *that* was honest. Fucker.

"I am a predator, sweetling. You are prey. I have to be able to determine certain aspects about you using various senses."

Prey. She definitely didn't like the way he said that. Regrettably, he was being completely honest. Honest, and something else.

Now there really was a warning flickering on her alarm radar. It was lurking under the surface of what he was showing her. Something cloaked, something dark and something he definitely did not want her to see.

This sucked. She couldn't confront him on it right now. Tipping her hand that much, letting him know she knew, would be detrimental to her health at the moment, she was certain.

What the hell was he hiding? Prey. It had to do with prey. Aleksei used the term; so did Tanis; so did every other Vampire she knew. It was the tone he'd used when he'd said it: disdainful, disrespectful, sanctimonious.

He was of Dracula's line. That had to be it. The timing would make sense; he was six hundred years old, Romanian by birth. Yup. He was one of the Fanged Prince's flunkies. No wonder he was making her Spidey senses tingle. Peter Parker would be impressed.

"So, do virgins taste better?" Gill quipped, giving him what she hoped was a conspiratorial smile. She wanted to deflect his intensity while she processed this newfound tidbit of information.

Csangal threw his head back and laughed uproariously. Half the Inn's contingent jumped at the sudden ascent into Vampire hilarity. She was too much. He had made her uncomfortable and she responded with humor.

Perhaps Humans were more interesting and entertaining than he believed. No, no, he could not be that wrong. Amusing, perchance, but still the inferior species; still food. Food might be amusing but one did not become emotionally attached to it.

"Oh, Dr. Key." He was chuckling, wiping his eyes. "You are a delight."

"I'm simply thrilled to have amused you," she said dryly.

"Forgive me"—he was still chortling—"but your new circumstance must present some difficulties in your personal relationship."

She completely missed him saying *relationship* as a single entity. "Yes . . . well, no, my"—Great Ganesh, what the hell was Aleksei to her—"boyfriend has plans for a romantic evening. I'm sure everything will be back to normal soon."

His extraordinary mind was suddenly awhirl. Fate had brought him to her. Fate had dropped exactly what he had needed and prayed for right into his hands. This was a true miracle. A miracle for him. He felt hope leap in his soul for the first time in six hundred years.

Guilt twitched at the edge of his consciousness. He had abandoned his Faith centuries ago, yet God had ascertained in His wisdom to grant him this miracle now. Why? Because *now* was the time. It had to be just that simple.

What had she said? Back to normal? Did she mean sleeping with Rachlav to alleviate this "problem"? This would not do at all. He had to act. This was too great a prize to let slip away in Aleksei Rachlav's bed.

God, fate, karma, the powers that be had delivered this

treasure right into his eager hands. If he ignored it, squandered it, wasted the opportunity, who could say when it would come again? *If* it would come again. He had to act.

"Gillian . . ." His voice was a compelling, sultry purr.

Unable to help herself, Gillian raised her eyes to his and was at once lost in the glacial green regard. Those eyes were so sincere, rife with power, beauty, compassion. She felt her automatic defenses adjust to accommodate her newfound trust for Csangal. He was absolutely honorable; she had nothing to fear from him or his intentions.

No! Her instincts warred among themselves, empathy screaming at her to get the hell out of there fast, away from the treacherous Vampire. This was dangerous. Yet . . . he wasn't dangerous, was he? He wasn't treacherous. He was only a lost soul, hurting . . . A patient, nothing more . . . and so much more. He was beautiful; he was hazardous; he was . . . lying.

The lie was there but she couldn't find the essence of it, nor could she focus her inherent talent toward him. There was no beginning, no end, no specifics in Csangal's psyche that she could pinpoint with certainty. He was more deceitful, more dangerous, than anything she had ever encountered. She couldn't say why or how; she just knew he was supplanting her survival instincts with his own intentions, and she couldn't stop him.

She needed to tell Aleksei. She should call out for Aleksei; she had a link with him, and she needed him. Something was very wrong . . . and yet . . . Csangal needed her. Needed her for some important reason, some great purpose. She would help him. She had to help him. Everything depended on her assistance. It was her job. It was her *duty*.

Csangal studied her as he subverted her own thinking, turning it against her. She couldn't trust her feelings, her thoughts, her instincts . . . but she could trust him. It was difficult, he found. He actually had to exert himself a little to subdue her. She had a much stronger strength of character than he had anticipated. A will and resolve that had nothing to do with Aleksei Rachlav's blood or influence. Interesting. Gillian Key was without a doubt remarkable . . . for a Human.

"What do you need from me?" she whispered, unable to tear her eyes from his.

"Cooperation," Csangal murmured, taking her hand in his own and kissing it.

"Okay."

The gloriously handsome Vampire exited the Inn with his petite therapist tucked under his arm. No one noticed because he had clouded their minds. Nobody on the street saw him shift into a steel gray dragon with mysterious green eyes or scoop the woman up into his powerful forelimbs. There would be no witnesses to tell about the dragon's launch or his flight to the North, toward Brasov; toward his waiting plane. No one could remember exactly whether or not Dr. Key had been in that evening or had met with a client in the private dining area of the Inn. In fact, nothing was there except her scent.

Nothing.

———

Nothing was what Aleksei and Daedelus found once they went to the village to look for Gillian when she didn't return. Aleksei tried to locate her mentally. He hated to invade her privacy, knowing how much she shied away from the depth of intimacy their mental link gave, but it wasn't like her to be late and not contact anyone. When he got the equivalent of a blank void where Gillian's tumultuous presence should have been, icy fear shot through him. Déjà vu. It was just like when Tanis went missing.

"Who was she supposed to be meeting here?" Daedelus wanted to know.

"Dr. Aristophenes, Gillian is a consummate professional. This patient requested complete and total privacy; she would not violate that for any reason. I have no way of knowing her schedule, other than that she did have a patient to see here, this evening." Aleksei uncharacteristically sounded rather put out.

"I didn't mean to cast aspersions on our fair therapist,

Aleksei. I was hoping she had written it down or logged it in the Institute's main schedule on the computer," Daed said quietly.

He looked at the tall, gray-eyed Vampire beside him. Aleksei was more agitated than Daed had ever seen him. Something was very wrong.

"I cannot feel Gillian through our link," Aleksei stated, no emotion whatsoever in his voice.

"You have a blood bond with her?" Daed was impressed.

"Yes, I do." The gray eyes morphed into gleaming silver. Yup, he was disconcerted.

"I have to admit that I am impressed. I never thought Gillian would allow anyone to get that close to her."

Aleksei disregarded his commentary. "Be that as it may, Doctor, she is missing. If you have records on the Institute's main computer, please contact the castle and have Helmut or Cassiopeia look them up." As nicely as it was worded, it wasn't a request.

Daed flipped open his cell phone and quickly dialed the castle. One of the Brownies answered. After a quick rundown about this particular patient's privacy issues, Daed convinced the little Being that he could not be of help and to locate Dr. Helmut or Dr. Cassiopeia as quickly as possible.

"Daed, the Brownie tells me that you need some information regarding Gillian." Helmut's Austrian accent was unmistakable.

"Gillian is missing, Helmut. I need to know who she was meeting tonight for a session at the Inn. It may be important," Daed informed him.

He listened for a few moments, then told Aleksei the news. "She was meeting a Vampire, the new one . . . Helmut says the name she has listed is 'Chahn-gell.' Oh wait—it's spelled C-s-a-n-g-a-l. Csangal."

Aleksei literally went bone white, his eyes wide with obvious alarm as he gripped Daed's shoulders. "*Csangal?* You are absolutely certain that is the name?"

Daed repeated the request to Helmut. Receiving an affirmative, he told Helmut to hold on and reached out to steady Aleksei. "What's wrong?"

"*Csangal* is a Romanian verb, from the Székely dialect. It means literally 'to roam' or 'to wander.' I know it also as a name; a particular name in reference to a specific person. One of many he is known by."

Daedelus wasn't stupid. Aleksei's obvious reaction spoke volumes about a mere name being upsetting to a Vampire Lord.

"What specific person?" Daed felt his own mouth go dry. He was definitely not going to like the answer.

"Dracula. It is one of his secret names known only to his progeny."

"Oh, Jesus."

Ignoring Daed, Aleksei reached out to his mentors: "*Osiris . . . Dionysus . . . Dracula has Gillian.*"

CHAPTER
5

"*I need you, brother,*" Aleksei intoned to Tanis through their link.

"*I will return at once,*" Tanis responded straightaway.

Tanis and Jenna had been in Egypt, trying to sort through their relationship after the Jack the Ripper fiasco. Aleksei's golden-eyed brother had been showing his new girlfriend around the magnificent archaeological finds and museums in the land of the pharaohs.

"*Osiris and a few others will accompany me,*" Tanis told him after a moment.

"*I am grateful and honored,*" Aleksei said to Tanis and to the Egyptian Lord.

"*Of course, my friend,*" Osiris responded. "*Your lady is in dire peril. All efforts must be made to locate her, and quickly. We shall be there within a night.*"

Aleksei managed a brief smile, thinking of Gillian as his "lady," though he knew she would not approve of the moniker. He was grateful beyond words that the Egyptian Vampires would be available to help him.

Dionysus also checked in; he would arrive in Romania sooner than Osiris. Aleksei was immeasurably grateful to the Greek Lord for committing to his cause as well.

"Gillian indirectly brought me my mate," Dionysus said through their link. *"Even without my pledge to assist in Dracula's destruction, I owe my happiness to her."*

"And I thank you," Aleksei confirmed. The Greek Vampire was as powerful and ancient as Osiris. Their assistance, knowledge and skill would be invaluable in locating and rescuing Gillian.

Gillian. Aleksei tried to keep from shaking; whether it was from fear or rage, he could not tell. They had exercised a methodical search of the Inn, of the village of Sacele and of the surrounding area. Still nothing.

This was not her fault. She had taken every precaution: she had told her colleagues where she was going and when to expect her return; she met with her mysterious client in a safe, public place; she was a capable soldier, a brilliant psychologist . . . and very, very Human. If Dracula had taken her, it was because he had cloaked himself exceedingly well. Well enough that even Aleksei had not perceived their deadliest collective enemy being literally on his doorstep.

Dracula had been able to deceive all of them, even with Aleksei's own newfound powers and recent metamorphosis into a Lord. Aleksei recognized he'd been too trusting, too naïve, too altruistic, believing that his province was reasonably safe after the death of Jack. He felt more shame than he had ever known but shoved it aside. Finding Gillian was his only priority. Self-recriminations could wait till she was on his lands and safe in his arms once more. If anything happened to her, he would never forgive himself.

Gillian, or any other Human for that matter, would have been no match for the Dark Prince's spectacular abilities. She had never been completely at the mercy of a hostile Vampire Lord before. Nor would she have any reason to suspect her patient to be anything other than exactly as he presented himself: a Being in emotional pain and need. Nothing in her life's experiences or from her professional training could have prepared her for this.

Helmut and Daed went through her notes from prior sessions with Csangal after Aleksei broke the news about the mystery Vampire's identity. Gillian had written that he was a six-hundred-year-old Master Vampire suffering from paranoia, depression and megalomania; she had indicated that she wanted to research the time line he gave her in accordance with some of the events he quoted. There were also notes in the margins suggesting that she felt uncomfortable with him and his enormous power level.

Aleksei found himself smiling with pride. She hadn't been completely taken in. Something about Csangal had felt wrong to her. Too bad she had not had time to investigate it more thoroughly. Her notepad, keys, phone—everything she normally carried with her was gone. They didn't know if she had discovered something about her patient that had triggered her abduction, or if her kidnapping had been the plan all along.

———

Dionysus arrived with his contingency some hours later. Since he had a prior invitation that had never been revoked, he alerted Aleksei to his presence, sweeping gracefully into the library with a small group of his own Vampires and Werelions. Greeting Aleksei first, he introduced his group.

"Lord Aleksei, my Vampires: Hades, Nyx, Thetis and Persephone."

Hades and Persephone, not surprisingly, were a mated pair. The tall Hades sported collar-length curly auburn hair with a gold circlet around it, and had dark brown eyes and a smattering of freckles over his adorable nose. He looked entirely too cute to be Ruler of the Underworld, as Greek mythos had named him. His mate was nearly as tall as he was. Persephone was a true brunette, her hair meticulously arranged and styled in an ancient Greek fashion. Her eyes were a sparkly dark green in a pixielike face. The couple stood together, arm in arm, and bowed to Aleksei, then to the assembled group.

Thetis was very thin and petite, and had a truly unearthly beauty with her long, wavy, pale blonde hair and shimmering Aegean blue eyes. She looked frail and insubstantial, but Aleksei could feel the immense power radiating from the historical water Goddess and the others Dionysus had brought with him.

Nyx stood a little to the side of the rest, nearer to the Werelion group. Her hair was a sun-kissed dark blonde, her eyes a true robin's-egg blue. She looked nothing like a Goddess of the night, but rather like a tall, willowy Greek girl who spent most of her time gathering wildflowers on the hillsides of Delphi.

"My Barbary Lions." Dionysus indicated the group next to where Nyx stood. "Zelus, Kratos and Bia."

The Lions were all wiry but obviously muscular. They were very tall, sandy blonde and amber eyed. Their family resemblance was obvious from the wide, bright smiles as they greeted everyone. All had thick, dark lashes, which only added to their Shifter beauty.

"How may I be of help, my friend?" Dionysus asked once the introductions were completed.

Aleksei felt warmed by the Greek Lord's show of support. Dionysus was a wild card on a good day. Unpredictable, often unreachable, he chose his involvements and battles carefully. He wasn't squarely in anyone's camp, but one thing Aleksei was positive of: he wasn't in Dracula's.

"Osiris will arrive shortly. I want everyone's input on where Dracula could have taken her. No effort will be spared to find her," Aleksei replied.

Noticing someone missing, he asked, "Where is your lady, Dionysus?"

"Maeti remains home, for now. I have had a few incidents of my own recently. I trust her to look after our interests while I assist you in Gillian's search."

"I apologize. I would have come to you or sent representatives of my own, if you had asked, my friend." Aleksei was discomfited. Twice now, Dionysus had come to his aid. He wanted to be able to return the favor.

The cerulean-eyed Vampire squeezed Aleksei's shoulder lightly. "You have had enough on your plate, coming into your own power and dealing with Gillian. I do not begrudge you your time in your own lands. This situation concerns us all. I am happy to help."

It was little comfort, Aleksei acknowledged to himself. He needed them more than they needed him. He was not yet equal to either Lord's power; his own were still evolving, sliding into place and becoming prominent randomly. They had thousands of years to learn and hone their skills. Nor was he remotely as accomplished as the Dark Lord, who was his senior by mere centuries but a thousand times more ruthless.

Without the help of Osiris and Dionysus, he would be hard-pressed to locate Gillian in time and would have no hope at all of saving her or destroying Dracula. He felt familiar twinges of his depression and fangxiety at the edges of his subconscious and immediately chastised himself for it.

I will not give in to my own frailties. Gillian needs me and I must remain strong and capable for her, he thought to himself.

"Indeed you will, Aleksei. I have complete confidence in you, as does Dionysus." Osiris's familiar touch on his mind brought calm back to his disordered thoughts.

"Call the others; we will arrive shortly." While Osiris's steady faith was inspiring, Aleksei hoped he could live up to his own expectations.

Aleksei soon had everyone situated in the Great Hall. Tanis stood with his brother as the Egyptian Vampires arrived: stately, noble looking and swelling the air with power. Osiris introduced his contingent. Anubis and Sekhmet, most of the Rachlav Institute residents knew. Isis, Osiris's mate, was new to the group. Slender, petite, regal looking, the sapphire-eyed queen of the Egyptian pantheon nonetheless radiated incredible warmth along with her incredible aura of power.

Tall, thin, graceful Tehuti stood next to his Lord and Lady, his dark eyes taking in every detail of the people in the room. Straight, thick black hair cut short like Osiris's graced his head. Dressed in Western-style clothing, like the rest of his contingent, he looked slightly uncomfortable as he tugged at the cuffs of his shirt.

Two Cheetah Shifters completed Osiris's group. Panya and Sidiki were cousins. There was a family resemblance in their hazel, almond-shaped eyes, coffee-colored hair, golden-hued skin and slender, almost delicate build. The female Panya was willowy grace when she walked. Sidiki seemed almost boyishly thin compared to the heavier-built Vampires, Wolves and Lions in the room. He looked a little gangly, despite the clearly defined muscles he sported.

Daedelus, Helmut, Cassiopeia, Trocar, Pavel, Cezar, Luis, Oscar and Kimber ringed the wall behind Aleksei. Luis and Oscar had stayed on for a while at the Institute. A gay Vampire couple was still in the "holy shit" range for a lot of Humans. Vampires had been viewed as exclusively heterosexual, so Luis and Oscar had openly come out to support their alternative-lifestyle brethren. For the time being, the Institute was their safe haven until the public got used to the idea. The Brownies were there as well. Aleksei would have preferred to not have them underfoot; however, except for Gillian's client sessions and the private rooms of the castle, it was almost impossible to keep them out of the discussion. The little folk had a fondness for Gillian and wanted to know where the Human was who had called attention to their species' bravery and usefulness.

Aleksei decided to get a brainstorming session going to determine where Gillian had been taken and why. They all listened as Aleksei spoke of Gillian's last appointment and the unexpected name that had come up.

"Csangal." Osiris's gold eyes glittered with suppressed rage. "That is a name I thought I would never hear again."

"I thought there might be a mistake at first," Aleksei said. "Helmut had spoken it to Daed, who conveyed it to me. Unfortunately it was correct."

"The Wanderer has returned and we did not realize it." Tanis spoke half to himself.

Aleksei's head jerked toward Tanis. His brother hadn't meant the comment as an insult by any means, but he felt very responsible for Gillian's disappearance. None of them realized just how much. The agony in his expression was brief but so potent that it actually made his brother step back.

"I am aware of my failings as a Lord, Tanis. I should have realized what the brushes against my power were. I should have known that only a Vampire of equal or greater power could have caused them, even if they wished for secrecy. I should have acted on it instead of ignoring my unease."

Aleksei raked his hand through his lush black hair, his eyes a steely gray. "I should have protected her, Tanis . . . I should have watched over her better, been more cognizant of the danger she was in and kept her safe. It is my fault that she is now in the hands of that monster. Just say it; we are all thinking it."

Everyone shifted in the uncomfortable silence that followed Aleksei's self-recriminations. Helmut, Gestalt therapist that he was, went to the tall Lord and squeezed his shoulder gently. The muscles were like granite under his hand. He suppressed a gasp as Aleksei turned to pin him with those magical silvery eyes. Maybe he and Gillian ought to write a very detailed journal article on Vampire emotive powers and how to avoid being scared shitless when dealing with a clearly anxious Lord.

"No one, not even Gillian, would blame you for this situation, Aleksei." Helmut's own blue eyes were kind, though his voice noticeably quivered a little. "From what I understand, you are new to your own level of power. You could not have easily identified a number of things you were experiencing."

"I appreciate your candor, Helmut, but it does not excuse my responsibility," Aleksei said quietly.

"No, it does not," Osiris interjected.

All eyes turned to the Egyptian. "However, Dr. Gerhardt is correct. You cannot expect that you would have recognized every shift in the fabric of your environment so soon after your Ascension, nor have anticipated that Csangal . . . Dracula would have come here. What you must do, with our help, is determine the next best course of action. We will get her back."

"If she has been harmed . . ." Aleksei said, beginning to pace.

"I do not believe she is injured or dead," Isis spoke up, her voice clear and pure as silver bells. "He has a specific purpose for taking her; otherwise you would have found her here on your lands, Aleksei, drained or executed."

"What purpose could she possibly serve, other than exercising control over me?" Aleksei frowned at her suggestion, but a small glimmer of hope was forming. If Gillian was indeed a hostage with a purpose, she may live awhile longer.

"I do not know," Isis admitted, "but it is worth taking a little time to research any possibility. At least we would know in which direction to go."

"I might have an idea." Oscar cleared his throat and stepped forward, clearly uneasy.

Aleksei rounded on him like a Rottweiler on a steak. "You were that deeply in your Lord's confidence that you know his future plans?"

"Not precisely," Oscar divulged, paling a little. "But I know that while he was using my estate for a headquarters of sorts, he availed himself of my library quite extensively."

"What the hell was he reading? 'How to Be an Asshole' manuals?" Kimber crossed her arms and squared off with the British Vampire.

"Research, poppet. He was always researching some ancient artifact, epic legend or another. He had a keen interest in ancient religions, their symbolism and various dogma . . . beyond that of your traditional pantheons, my Lords." Oscar nodded in respect toward Osiris and Dionysus.

"Earlier than us or later?" Osiris asked.

"Earlier, much earlier. He was reading the Torah, I believe, when he was last at my humble home."

"I don't suppose your observations include what part of the Torah he was reading, do they?" Helmut was moving along the shelves of the castle's vast library to find a copy of the Holy Book in question.

"No, I am afraid it would not have been healthy for me to be that inquisitive. One does not simply ask the Dark Prince to explain himself in any manner, and it never entered our conversations," Oscar said, shrugging. Luis patted his shoulder in a comforting gesture.

"Surely he was not researching that tired old story about Vampires being descended from Cain," Dionysus exclaimed.

"No . . . no, I think this is something else," Helmut said distractedly, flipping through the pages of the Torah he had located.

"But Dracula did have an interest in who made him. Do you remember, Aleksei?" Tanis asked his brother.

The Romanian Lord's brow furrowed. "Yes, I do remember him mentioning that in one of his rare contemplative moments when he was tormenting me about my Rebirth. He said that while I did not recognize my attackers, at least I had the mentoring I required to survive from my brother. He made it sound as though he had done me a favor, having ordered my execution."

"None of us knows who created us or how we came to be, Aleksei," Osiris spoke up.

At Aleksei's perplexed look, he continued. "Neither Dionysus, myself or Dracula knows how we were Reborn. I have vague memories of walking in Egypt during midday, proudly surveying my lands, my workers and my flocks, but beyond that I have no memory of my life as a Daywalker."

"Nor do I," Dionysus stated. "There are hazy impressions of owning a vineyard . . . and being a wealthy, arrogant man. *That* I remember," he said ruefully. "I know I was more interested in hedonistic pursuits and letting my staff tend my property. Other than that, I cannot remember how or where I lived."

"Every other Vampire that I have personally known has been descended from the three of us. Now that you have joined our cluster, you will have an opportunity to bring others over and strengthen your own line." Osiris watched Aleksei carefully as he said this.

"So there are truly no more than the four of us with a Lord's power?" Aleksei ignored Osiris's comment for the moment. He had no desire to think about that for the time being. Getting inside Dracula's mind to determine his next move was bad enough.

"There may be others, but I have yet to encounter any. I remember hearing tales of a Line of Northmen near the beginning of the first millennium, but I have not heard of them in centuries," Osiris said. "Even though our Lines rarely overlap intentionally. It would not be difficult for a true Ancient to conceal his presence, live in a more secluded area and not announce himself to the world."

"With the Compact, there may be more who step forward." Dionysus's observation quieted the murmurings in the room.

"Aleksei, what belief system or religion did Dracula subscribe to?" Helmut said suddenly.

The tall Lord glanced at his brother for confirmation, then turned to Helmut. "I believe he was born Catholic; however, the Unitarian movement began here in the fifteenth century. He had been Reborn by that time, and as far as I know was more favorable toward the Unitarians than the Orthodox Church, but I cannot say for certain."

"You are correct, my Lord." Oscar nodded. "We had a discussion over religion at one point of time, after he read my book. He laughed at the idea of a man selling his soul to the devil. I found his thoughts rather heretical."

"You are Catholic, then?" Aleksei asked, taking note of Oscar's pretentious predilection. He had never asked to be called anything but Aleksei.

"Not practicing, but I was raised Catholic, yes. Are you?"

"No. Tanis and I were raised in the Unitarian Church. We have a firm belief in the Almighty, but we do not subscribe to traditional Christianity."

Helmut listened with interest, taking mental notes. As liberally minded as he and the IPPA's professionals were, most Humans still thought of Paramortals as completely dissimilar to Humans. They forgot that even "magical" Beings frequently had religious beliefs that mirrored their own. It was one of the circumstances that Paramortal psychology dealt with every day.

"Let me keep looking, then." Helmut sighed, turning back to the extensive shelves of books.

Everyone continued wracking their brains trying to figure out where Dracula had taken Gillian, and why. Daed was poring over Gillian's notes for the fortieth time, trying to zoom in on the pattern in her sessions. He beckoned Helmut over when he could catch the psychologist's eye. The rest of the group in the room barely glanced in their direction as they continued their own discussions.

"There has to be something here, Helmut. We've missed something. *I've* missed something. There's a pattern to therapy, even a loose one. She had to be zeroing in on what his anxiety or paranoia was rooted in."

Helmut slumped into the couch, the Torah balanced on his knee. "I know, Daed, but I've been over it countless times, just as you have. The best I can remember is that she was talking to him about what distressed him. Didn't he say that he did not know his creator and because of it he killed someone? His family?"

"Yes!" Daed said elatedly. "Aleksei! Don't Vampires rely on their progenitor to teach them?"

"Yes. Even if they are not closely bound, it is the responsibility of the Master or Lord to help his progeny gain control in the beginning," Aleksei confirmed.

"Gill writes here that Csangal had a grudge toward his creator for causing him to kill his family." Daed locked eyes with the Vampire when Aleksei laughed harshly at his statement.

"Is that what he told her?"

"Almost, but not quite a lie," Osiris added in an acerbic tone.

"Yes, it says here that he killed his family by mistake because his creator did not remain with him. He wasn't told to rest away from his home and village."

"You have not read much on Romanian history, Helmut," Aleksei said more patiently than he felt. "Vlad Dracula may indeed be angry with his creator, but his wife committed suicide, and killing his mistress was intentional, if that is what he was referring to. At the time, she was all the 'family' he had left, I assure you."

"He murdered her?" Helmut was appalled.

"He did indeed," Tanis responded. "Cold, deliberate murder."

"Why?"

"Because she told him she was pregnant to cheer him up when he was in a particularly black mood." Aleksei's sarcastic response spoke volumes about what he really thought of Dracula and his disposition.

"Vampires can knock someone up?" That was from Kimber.

"Occasionally even a fossil can produce fruit." Aleksei didn't smile this time.

"Do Jenna and Gill know that?"

"Gillian is on the Pill," Aleksei informed her.

"What about Jenna? Come to think of it, where is Jenna?" Kimber stood and walked toward the library door, peering down the hallway. "Tanis? Didn't she come back with you?"

Tanis's face reflected a recent blow to his emotions. "No, she did not. She said she wanted to get away from the 'fanged freak show' for a while. I left her in Cairo, at Osiris's headquarters, as per her request. She will do what she will, go where she will, as I suspect you know from serving with her in the past."

"Dude, I am sorry." Kimber's tone and expression said she really was. "Jen is a bit of a flake on a good day, and with all the excitement . . . like with Jack and everything . . . it doesn't particularly surprise me. I'm sure she'll pop back up at some point."

"If she does, I will wish her well." Tanis looked away. "We decided to go our own way in Egypt, just before Aleksei's call. She mentioned us remaining friends but I am not sure how this is possible if she has no intention of returning."

"*Tanis, I am truly sorry,*" Aleksei said privately to his brother. "*I had no idea. You are hurting, yet here you are to support me in looking for Gillian. I apologize for not noticing your pain.*"

"I am fine, truly. Having experienced two remarkable women after a very long dry spell, I consider myself fortunate indeed," was Tanis's reply.

Aleksei could detect no hidden anger from his brother, no regrets, no masking of any emotional trauma. *"I thought you believed her to be 'the one.'"*

"At first, yes, I did. But as we spent more and more time together, it became apparent that we had different thoughts about our futures. She is young, Aleksei; young and flighty. She is not ready for anything I could offer her. I am not bitter; the experience was good for both of us. It helped me put things into perspective."

His heart clenching in his chest, Aleksei had to ask, *"Perspective? On . . . yourself and Gillian?"*

Tanis looked at him askance. His brother was more sensitive than usual due to the stress of Gillian's abduction. He would be diplomatic now and hit him over the head later.

"Good Lord, Aleksei, of course not. She and I are long past any possibility of a relationship. She loves you, and in time she will see that."

Kimber impulsively hugged him, breaking his concentration with his brother. Smiling down at her, he returned the hug. "Now, let us get back to the half-truths that Dracula told our little sister."

"What else is in the notes, Daedelus?" Anubis inquired, his curiosity piqued.

"Just some things about the atrocities of the Turks . . . some mention of his brother . . . about his concern over his appearance . . ."

That brought a laugh from the Vampires who knew the Dark Prince on a personal level. They explained to the others who hadn't met him that Dracula was easily the most beautiful one of their species that any of them had ever seen.

"His concern was that he was attracting too many followers to him, instead of just the ones he personally chose," Aleksei stated. "He is an egomaniac, a narcissist in the extreme. He blamed his victims for falling so easily under his spell and wished he was less lovely to make acquiring prey and acolytes more of an interesting challenge. Thus his theory that Humans were inferior to Vampires: they were so easily duped."

"That's remarkable." Helmut's voice was skeptical. "We had Perrin, who was terrified of how he looked, and now we have someone who wished for less striking features . . . Humans are not the only ones with fascinating idiosyncrasies."

"Can we please focus?" Daed's annoyed tone brought them all back to the immediate problem.

"He wants to find his creator . . . I wonder if it would be the same as our creator." Osiris looked to Dionysus for his opinion.

"Possibly. Aleksei is really the only true Lord among any of us. We were all created by an unknown Being. He rose a full Lord, knowing his creator, but not knowing his power due to Dracula's interference," the Greek Lord said thoughtfully.

"Tanis is the Master who Turned me from death to Rebirth," Aleksei pointed out for those who didn't know. "I was dying by the road; he forced me to drink from him.

"I was riding alone at night. It was moonless, very dark, very cold. My Human eyes did not see them until they had me. I was bled out by several of Dracula's Vampires and left to die. Tanis is the one who found me, gave me his blood and made certain that I rose with my mind intact. He is the one who taught me our customs; he kept me from losing hope."

Osiris studied his friend for a moment. "That may be, but I suspect your power originated from within you, whereas Dionysus's and mine came from an outside source. I was the first Lord of our breed; he is the second.

"Both Dionysus and I know we did not sire Dracula by blood or seed, nor did any of our lineage. His is a separate Line altogether. Since we were created thousands of years before Dracula, perhaps we should concentrate our search on where our creator possibly came from. In doing so, we may also gain the answer that he seeks and find Gillian in the process."

CHAPTER
6

CONUNDRUM, Gillian thought to herself. That was what this was. She was unrestrained and still armed; she could shoot out one of the sun-shielded windows in the opulently decorated, roomy cabin of the private plane she was currently aboard. It would certainly result in cabin depressurization, forcing a landing in the velvety blackness that surrounded the aircraft. Csangal would be in no real danger, but he would be pissed.

She could shoot herself. That would accomplish getting rid of the immediate hostage situation but would be vastly unproductive with regard to solving the mystery of why she'd been brought along in the first place, and end any hope of getting back to her friends in Romania. Plus, Aleksei would be pissed.

She could shoot Csangal. If she managed a lucky head shot, he would be dead but she would still be trapped in an aircraft with flunkies of various varieties obviously in his employment. They would most definitely be pissed if she killed their boss.

Therefore, going along with whatever the hell her rogue Vampire patient wanted so she could get to the bottom of this and still emerge among the living seemed like the most prudent thing to do. He hadn't hurt her, but he had done a great job with mind control. She couldn't remember leaving the Inn back in Sacele or getting on a plane or where their ultimate destination would be. Great. Now *she* was pissed. Delineating immediate avenues of escape and pondering her current situation wasn't working at all.

Her captor sat across from her, reading some type of scroll that looked like it was written in some very ancient text. It wasn't Hebraic or Egyptian; she was certain of that. There were stacks of books, sheets of notes written in various languages, more scrolls and even a stone tablet or two strewn on the table that separated them, as well as on the seat next to him and on the red carpeted floor.

Since he'd released her mind after takeoff, explaining that he needed her support and company on this venture, she had weighed her option of killing him versus her professional obligation as his therapist. He had been spending their flight time deeply engrossed in his apparent research, while she'd pondered various escape possibilities. Her preoccupation was not going as well as his, and she was beginning to fidget.

Glacial green eyes lifted to her own. "I do apologize again, Gillian, for my unseemly behavior. Controlling your mind was necessary to ensure your complete cooperation without wasting time on explanations at that particular moment."

"Not accepted, Csangal. This is not okay," Gillian growled at him, shifting in her chair to plunk a booted foot down on some of his scrolls on the table. She was just a wee bit scared. Empathy and nerves were firing at an alarming rate. She wasn't currently in any immediate danger, but her options were rather restricted.

"Do be careful, my dear; these are very valuable," Csangal scolded, lifting her foot and removing the scrolls out of harm's way, then replacing her heel on the table.

"Why am I not tied up in the hold or bolted in your coffin? Why am I loose in here when you know damn well that I am armed?" She was also rather confused.

He chuckled. "There is nowhere for you to go, Gillian.

We are thirty-five thousand feet in the air. If you shoot me, you will not have time to kill me before my associates dismember you. If you attempt to shoot yourself, I shall take your pretty gun away. If you attempt to shoot a window out, I shall also take your gun away and quite possibly injure you in the process."

Shit and double shit. Yeah, he could do all that and so much more. She was so screwed.

"What the hell do you need me for? Aleksei isn't stupid; he'll figure out who took me and why."

"Rachlav will indeed eventually determine who took you, but I do not believe you actually know the answer to that yourself."

"What does that mean? I know exactly who you are."

"Do you?" He smiled at her, his sheer beauty making her eyes glaze for a moment. "You know what I have told you. That is all."

She shook her head to clear her mind of his spectacular visage, frowning at him. "But you haven't lied to me. I would have sensed it."

"You are correct. Nothing I told you was a lie, but it was also only what I wanted you to know at the time, Dr. Key." The smile he gave her this time was absolutely chilling.

Stark terror slammed through her in response, putting whatever fear the Ripper had instilled in her to shame. No doubt the reaction he intended. Bastard. Gulping her heart back down into her chest where the damn thing belonged, she asked the obvious question in her most level voice. "Then what do I need to know now?"

"That you are my therapist, my prisoner and perhaps my salvation."

"Therapist I know; prisoner I figured out all by myself. But salvation? How am I going to manage that?" Gill tried to insert a little bravado into her voice. He would not get to her. He simply would not.

"An exchange, Doctor. You for my redemption."

He turned back to his papers and scrolls, leaving her to deliberate what the hell *that* meant.

Gillian unconsciously tapped her front teeth with her

thumbnail, her mind racing at his enigmatic statement. Some nights it just didn't pay to get up in the evening. Maybe she ought to take Aleksei up on his offer and quit doing this for a living. She was getting too old for this cloak-and-dagger shit.

Aleksei. Sweet Hathor, she wished she could tell him where they were going. Shit, she wished *she* knew where they were going.

"Bellissima."

It took all of her discipline not to shriek with joy at the familiar black velvet of his voice in her mind.

"Do not react, Gillian," he quickly warned her. *"I have only just been able to reach you; our bond is very tenuous, as I am still learning my abilities."*

"It's a Vampire named Csangal, Aleksei. He is a Master but more powerful than any I've ever seen. He clouded my thinking . . . I've never experienced anything like it. I couldn't yell for help or I would have. Hell, I don't even know where we are headed."

She sounded anxious but in control of herself as she rapidly fed him only necessary information and didn't elaborate on her own feelings or fears. Confidentiality violations ended when the patient kidnapped the therapist, she thought as she looked around, trying to send him as much information visually as she could.

He sent her a burst of pride and love coupled with his relief that she was alive. Anyone else would have been hysterical with fear, but not Gillian. *"I know,* piccola. *But it is not Csangal who has you."*

Gill paused in her mental pictorial diatribe of the plane, Csangal and the mounds of information he was studying to focus on what Aleksei had just said. *"Who is it, then? Wait . . . Csangal has to be his name. He didn't lie to me, I am sure of it."*

"Gillian, listen carefully. You are Dracula's prisoner. 'Csangal' is merely one of his aliases. You are correct; he did not lie to you. He only misdirected the truth. He is probably taking you to where he believes his creator resides,

possibly for a confrontation. There may be a religious con-notation in his mind, but we are not positive of that.

"Comply with whatever he wants and stay alive, cara. Do not confront him. We are all working together to find you. I will contact you again soon."

His comforting presence was turned off as if he had flipped a mental switch. Gillian lit a cigarette to keep her nervous hands busy. She processed what he'd told her, managing to look reasonably relaxed. It wouldn't do to tip her hand or let Csan— er . . . Dracula know about her subversive commentary with Aleksei. It was all she could do not to freak out about being three feet away from the boogeyman of all Vampires.

Stupid Dracula. Stupid top secret Vampire validation mission. Apparently there were a few things about actual Vampire Lords and their mystical magical foo powers that some nimrod forgot to cover in her Ph.D. program. She was going to have a talk with Helmut, Daed and the board at IPPA about revising the current course material with more accurate information . . . if she survived.

Fuck. This was just getting better and better.

"She is alive!" The relief in Aleksei's voice and bearing swept over everyone in the room.

They were all gathered in a rough circle, debating Dracula's actual intentions in both his mission and with Gillian. Aleksei had been trying periodically to contact her since her disappearance, without success until now. To feel her presence, hear her voice, if only for a moment, filled him with renewed hope.

"Wonderful!" Osiris gave him a sincerely felt smile, squeezing Isis's hand tightly. He genuinely liked Gillian, especially since her very public career was encouraging ever-increasing numbers of Humans to truly view Paramortals as real people.

Isis glanced up at her mate. She knew his interest in Gillian was completely academic. Anyone he held in esteem was well regarded among the general population of non-Humans. Both of them were tremendously fond of Aleksei and Tanis outside the bonds of their sworn loyalty. Gillian Key's importance to the brothers was enough to have brought them here, even without the threat Dracula posed.

———⋄———

"Look, I'm bored out of my tiny little Human mind over here." Gillian leaned toward the document-covered table that separated them. "Why don't you tell me what you're looking for and let me see if I can help you find it."

Dracula's chilly aqua eyes rose and regarded her intently. "I do not believe you can read Sumerian pictoglyphs, hieroglyphics or Phoenician, Gillian."

She sighed. "No, but maybe if you explain it to me, it might become clearer to you. Sometimes the best way to learn about something is to teach it to someone else."

A slight frown creased his perfect brow as he considered her request. "Why the sudden change? A moment ago you were contemplating killing me or bringing the plane down."

"Yes, I was, but as you pointed out, either option would be suicidal." Her eyes locked with his own. Nobody smiled.

"We cannot have you dying too soon, Dr. Key." That was from a completely new female voice directly behind her.

Gillian spun, rising from the chair and standing as far away from the voice as she could. Unfortunately that put her very close to Dracula, but he was a known threat. This new person was a surprise. Gill hated being surprised.

"Who the hell are you?" she demanded, then stared.

It was like looking in a mirror. The woman's hair was more yellow than Gillian's golden blonde, her eyes were a lighter green, but her height, her facial features . . . The word *doppelganger* leapt to mind. She might have been Gillian's sister or close relative.

"I am Elizabeta. Surely Aleksei mentioned during his therapy that he once had a fiancée?" A very smug smile formed on those shell pink lips.

"You're supposed to be dead," Gill blurted out, still wrapping her mind around how much the woman looked like herself. She and Aleksei needed to have a talk about possible clinical transference if she lived through this. Old fears clawed at her psyche. She needed to be sure it was herself he loved and not a facsimile of his former fiancée.

"I was . . . but as you can see, I am quite alive."

"I found her to be most interested in being Reborn, Gillian," Dracula said smoothly. "It seems Aleksei denied her that privilege."

Gillian kept her mouth shut. That wasn't the story Aleksei had told her. According to him, Elizabeta was a gold digger, who was more interested in his ability to make her immortal than in their relationship. Aleksei believed she had died in childbirth, calling his name while married to another man.

What do you say to the suddenly appearing former fiancée of your current . . . boyfriend? "Hi"? No, that wouldn't work. Neither would "Nice to meet you." Trying to sort out appropriately spontaneous. diplomatically phrased responses gave Gillian a headache.

The hell with it.

"Well . . . so here we are. On a plane. Together."

"So it would seem." Elizabeta's eyebrow lifted as she circled Gillian.

Dracula rose, taking Gillian's hand and drawing her back toward him. "Enough, Elizabeta. You have disregarded my order to remain hidden until we reach our destination."

The Vampiress's face reflected her concern. "I am truly sorry, my Lord. I wanted to see her for myself."

" 'My Lord'?" Gillian echoed her.

"Go back with the others and remain there." Dracula ignored Gillian's comment, fixing his gaze on Elizabeta.

Elizabeta nodded and turned away, giving Gillian a deadly glare as she did so. "As you wish, my Prince."

" 'Prince'? Is there something you've forgotten to tell me in our therapy, Csangal?" Gillian asked in her nicest "I'm aware of your trickery, sir" voice.

"I apologize, Gillian." Dracula's voice brought her head around to look at him.

"For springing Aleksei's supposedly dead fiancée on me? Damn nice of you. Thanks."

His face darkened. "Truly, I am sorry for that and for deceiving you the way I have. I suppose it should be clear to you that I have not been entirely honest about who I am." Uncharacteristically, his eyes lowered and he managed to actually look repentant for a brief moment.

This was new. The dreaded Dark Prince showing remorse? Her empathy wasn't flaring at all; in fact, it hadn't since she'd been with him. His power had to be the reason. She clearly hadn't understood just how much power he had until now. Apparently none of her instructors, mentors or any of the Humans she'd studied with perceived the true level of power wielded by a fanged Lord.

As he said, he hadn't actually lied to her at any time, just misrepresented the facts. She should have picked up on it. Hell, Aleksei should have noticed. Thinking back, she realized her senses had only tingled around the Egyptians and Dionysus, despite their impressive age and power. Probably due to them not being secretive shits.

During an earlier conversation with Cassiopeia, her mentor had reiterated what she had already been told: their power took time to develop. If they were destined to be a Master or a Lord, they rose with greater aptitude than their fellows. So, Aleksei's power was technically still in its infancy since the dampening fields had been removed. Dracula, on the other fang, had had centuries to sharpen his considerable skills and, since he wasn't keen on honesty and cooperative living, had honed the skills that would make him what he was: a monster.

Gill settled back into her seat, still watching her host, who again had his face buried in ancient scripts and was writing notes in his own special shorthand. She couldn't read or make sense of it.

Think, Gill, think.

Well, practically speaking, she was a therapist, which she had temporarily forgotten when her Oh-Shit-a-Meter had gone off the scale due to recent events. Technically he was still her patient; she understood a lot about him. And Aleksei had shared some valuable information with her about what he was potentially after. Shit, there had to be a way to find out his true intentions. All right, back to the previous conversation before they were interrupted by what's-her-name.

"As I was saying, why don't you share with me and let's see if I can help."

Aquamarine eyes pinned her for a moment and a slight smile quirked his flawless mouth. "Rest assured, Gillian, you will help me regain what I have lost. I am trying to determine exactly how best to accomplish that."

"What is it you believe you lost?"

"My humanity. I do not know what other word to use, but something died in me long ago."

Gill sat up at that and leaned forward. "You know, Csang— er . . .What exactly would you prefer that I call you now . . . since you pointed out that you're not actually who you claimed to be?"

"My given name is Vlad."

"Vlad . . . as in . . . Vlad Dracula?" There. Now everything was out in the open and clarified. No need for her to fake it and accidentally reveal Aleksei as the source of her knowledge.

He smiled and nodded. "Yes, as Elizabeta so unfortunately revealed, I am the proverbial Dark Prince."

"Fabulous. I won't insult your intelligence by saying it's nice to meet you, because right now this sucks," Gillian said pointedly.

"I understand, my dear."

"You want me to call you Vlad instead of Csangal now, is that right?"

"That is up to you. Either name is correct," Vlad informed her.

Supremely relieved that he wasn't insisting on "my Lord" or any other subservient title, Gillian acknowledged him. "All right, Vlad. I know you are aware that Vampires can never become Human again."

"Not Human, Gillian." He looked at her as if she were a slow pupil. "My humanity. There is a difference."

"My bad. Okay, let's start there. When do you believe you lost your humanity?"

His mouth tightened. "When I killed my mistress. I was too drunk with the power I had received and believed myself to be a God of sorts. It is amazing what a few centuries of wisdom can teach. I know that I lost something precious that I believed could never be regained."

Calling bullshit on that one, she thought to herself. "I see. Pardon me for not understanding, but where does that wisdom fit in with your current beliefs that Humans are an inferior species to Paramortals?"

"You are inferior," he interjected. "Humans are the minority species compared to the thousands of Paramortal varieties in this world, yet your kind presumes to make the rules for all Beings, including those who have sprung from a magical font."

"That doesn't answer the question."

Dracula paused. "I am not certain I understand what you're asking."

"You are labeling a part of yourself as Human—your humanity—and considering it precious to you, yet you perceive Humans as a race or species not valuable in any way to you except as nourishment or prey. How do you reconcile the dichotomy of wanting or admiring characteristics from something you hate? It's like saying you respect a serial killer's organizational skills." She spoke in her calm, quiet therapist voice. Provoking him wasn't on her mind at the moment; buying time was.

Deeply creased frowns on infamous Vampire Lords are never a good sign. Gillian hoped she hadn't pressed a major oopsie button.

"I see what you mean, Gillian. I had not considered this before."

Either he was making an enormous concession to himself and to her, or he was about to be supremely pissed off. All she needed to do was sit back and wait for him to process his own thoughts.

"That does seem a bit ridiculous, when you say it like that." He smiled ruefully at her. There was a glow beginning in the back of his eyes that she wasn't quite sure of.

"Not ridiculous, Vlad, just a different way of looking at it." It would definitely not be a good idea to taunt him about his oversight right now.

He stared at her. He couldn't decide if she was being kind or contentious. "When I was gifted with Rebirth, I knew my power came from the Divine, that I had been given great talents and skills with which to keep my Country safe. I believed that I was an avenging angel . . . until I killed . . . not from hunger, not for food, but because I simply wanted to exercise my abilities.

"My temper grew shorter, my viewpoint less tolerant; I was given these gifts, yet Humans sought to take away my throne, my family, my right to rule my people and Country as I wished."

"Weren't you at war with the Turks?" Gillian asked, hoping now that he wasn't influencing her mind that she had her Romanian history correct.

"Everyone was at war with the Turks, not simply my kingdom. They were a rampaging presence across the land, taking slaves, demanding tribute, slaughtering everything in their path."

"So you did what you believed needed to be done to protect your people," she ventured, knowing that before he went over the edge into Megalomania Land, Vlad Dracula had been revered as a hero in his homeland.

"I did that and much more," he agreed.

"You still haven't shared with me what it was that changed your opinion. Humans and Paramortals have always been suspicious of each other until the Compact and Legalization. What caused your level of hatred? Why advocate a superior/inferior structure of existence?"

Once again, he'd told her of his parents' deaths at the hands of Humans. He talked about raising armies to defend his Country and being betrayed by both the Human clergy and some of his nobles. When he got to his own wife's death, something dark and terrifying crossed his features.

"Long before my involvement with the mistress I killed, I was married to my own Elizabeta. Make no mistake, Gillian, I was truly and deeply in love with my wife. In their determination to rid themselves of the monster who ruled them, the Humans betrayed her. She had done nothing but be my wife. She was not even Reborn, just a beautiful, gentle presence who loved her Prince, his homeland and her children."

"They betrayed her? How?" Gillian asked softly.

"She was sent word that I had been butchered during a battle and that the Turks were on their way to sack the city. Knowing that they routinely rounded up entire towns for slavery, and that they generally killed the ruling family—or worse—my beloved chose death over captivity or torture."

"She committed suicide?"

"Indeed she did. If we had established a blood bond, I would have been able to tell her I lived. She died because she was frail. She died because Humans are easily deceived. She died because she was not a Vampire. I failed her in that." His voice was barely a whisper, but his rage made the air around Gillian vibrate.

Beneath the anger, her empathy registered a depth of despair, loss, loneliness and hopelessness that even Perrin had been unable to achieve. Her Gestalt-therapist self couldn't stand it. Vlad Dracula was a monster, a megalomaniac, the cause of a thousand nightmares and deaths. But he was also a man. A man who had mourned the loss of his beloved due to the duplicity and fortunes of war and what he believed to be a disability: being Human.

She reached out with her empathy and her hand. Grasping his forearm gently, she radiated sympathy and acknowledgment of his loss. "I am truly sorry that your wife killed herself because of lies, but I think it is more about the lies than about her being Human and fragile. I can't imagine what it must be like to love someone like that and then learn that you've lost her forever."

Vlad regarded the small hand on his arm, then lifted his eyes to meet hers. She was genuinely sympathetic, he noted to himself with some surprise. The loss of Elizabeta was still an open wound in his soul; he was not lying or exaggerating how deeply her death had affected him. Despite knowing what he was, in spite of being his captive, Gillian was focused on *his* pain, not her own; not the plight of every Human he'd ordered killed or converted. His pain.

"Why do you care, Dr. Key?"

Gill looked at him as though he'd grown another head. "I'm not sure what you mean. You are a Being who is in deep pain. I am sorry that you've had to feel that pain."

"You are Human. Why do you care what a Vampire feels or thinks?"

"It's my job." Her mouth quirked into a slight smile.

"I do not think so," Vlad replied. "I believe you truly cannot tolerate another's emotional pain."

"Maybe," she admitted grudgingly. "It's still my job to pay attention to what you tell me and to understand what you're feeling."

He settled back a little in his chair but didn't remove her hand from his arm. "Gillian, you are an interesting Human."

Gillian pulled her hand back, slowly, mirroring his seated position. "Not really. I'm like most of my species, if you would look a little deeper and consider us as more than a food source."

"Indeed. Then have a look at this and tell me what you think." He grasped a large leather-bound tome and flipped it open to a full-page drawing of a room with many unusual items in it. He wanted her opinion, but he also wanted to deflect her attention away from the roiling emotions clawing inside his chest.

Gillian studied the picture. The book was called *Museum Wormianum*, published in 1655. The room depicted was called Musei Wormiani Historia, representing Ole Worm's cabinet of curiosities.

"If my memory is correct, a cabinet of curiosities was actually a room, like a miniature museum, which held unusual, rare and scientifically uncategorized items. They were most popular back in the seventeenth century."

"Very good." Vlad smiled at her. "I am impressed. What you probably do not realize is that there are a number of these still in existence, with all their creatures, devices, automatons, gadgets and artwork, scattered around the world."

"And what does that have to do with what you're after?"

"A great deal, as you will see."

Gillian continued looking at the picture and flipped through some of the pages of the book. It was written in Latin, of course, and other than rudimentary psychological and medical terms, she didn't have the language base to translate.

"So . . . we're going to one of these cabinets . . . because you believe it contains something that can help you in your quest." It was a shot in the dark, but she took it.

"No, I have already found what I was after in one of them. I have a device with me that can literally call the Beings of Light down from the heavens. We are simply traveling to where I intend to use it."

"Beings of Light?" Gillian repeated. "You mean Angels?"

"*Nephilim* is what they were called in Hebrew, I believe," he replied.

"The Nephilim were thought to be the 'sons of god, who bred with the daughters of men,' according to the Torah," Gill stated for the sake of argument and because she thought she remembered enough Hebrew from her Midrasha school. "I still don't understand what that has to do with this trip, or how I'm going to be able to help you."

"There are allegedly three types of lesser Nephilim Giants who were bred from those unions, Gillian. 'Giant' referring not just to their physical size but to their powers as well. You have heard of them before in various Hebrew texts. The Anakim—those with graceful necks; the Emim—those who frighten; and the Rephaim—the dead ones.

"I believe that Osiris; Dionysus; Odin, who is Lord of the North; myself and a very few others are directly descended from the Rephaim: the resurrected dead Giants of legend. The first Vampires."

Gillian was thinking her way through everything he was saying. She was absolutely certain he was no longer trying to influence her mind. What was boggling her brain at the moment was that what he was saying made complete sense.

There had been tales and legends of Vampires being the children of Cain, Adam's son. No one had gone back further in their research than that. Vlad's theory predated any form of religion or religious pantheons, and would certainly take into account that nearly every single culture worldwide had legends, stories and variations of Vampires.

"You believe one of these Beings made you. You want to contact them through an ancient device you have on board this plane . . . then what? What is it exactly you think is going to happen?" she asked as levelly as she could.

"I have told you, I want answers. I want to know why I was chosen, why I was given no guidance and allowed to go mad. As you probably know, one of the possible Hebraic translations for Nephilim is 'those who cause men to fall.' I want to know why I was chosen to fall."

At Gillian's surprised look, he smiled. "I am aware that I was quite insane and did very despicable things, my dear."

"What am I here for?" she asked, her mouth going dry.

"You are a virgin," he said matter-of-factly, as if that explained everything.

"I know I'm not going to like this, but what does my physical state have to do with it?" She frowned at him, her entire body tensing up in anticipation of his response.

"You are my gift, of course. I shall be purified and forgiven, after my questions are answered, by offering you to the Rephaim as a sacrifice."

"Shit, I knew you were going to say that." Gillian slumped in her seat. Better and better. Yup.

CHAPTER

7

"DRACULA is interested in his origins. He was looking through at least the Torah and probably other Hebrew texts. His plane took off toward the West . . . We have to look further back." Tanis handed another ancient book down to Aleksei from his position on one of the library's ladders.

"He cannot possibly believe we are descended from Cain." Aleksei was shaking his head. There was no rational thought process for it. Dracula wanted to confront his maker. Cain was eons dead and there was no known Bloodline.

The Romanian Lord raked his hand through his hair. It had to be simpler. They were missing something obvious.

"Rephaim. Aleksei, Vlad believes the Rephaim made him and the others. Gotta go."

Gillian's short-lived burst of thought in his mind was a golden wash of shimmering sunlight. He felt his heart literally leap with joy at her brief message.

" 'Rephaim.' Does anyone know the term?" Aleksei's deep velvet voice brought everyone in the room to a standstill. They were all digging through texts, maps and documents, trying to determine Gillian's location and Dracula's intent.

"The Rephaim are known as the unliving ones," Osiris informed them. "Where did you hear that name?"

"Gillian sent word to me, saying that Dracula believes that we are descended from these Rephaim," Aleksei said.

Osiris closed the volume he was holding. "That would make complete sense. Now I understand."

"I do not." Aleksei was too shaken by worry to think straight. Gillian was obviously alive, which was comforting, but why had she referred to his former Master as Vlad? No one in his memory was on a first-name basis with the Dark Prince . . . except Gillian. What the hell?

"Before the Gods, before us, there were Angels." Isis came to stand next to her mate. Sapphire eyes glowed in a face too young, too delicate, to contain all the wisdom harbored in those blue orbs.

"The Nephilim were believed by the ancient Hebrews to be a variety of Angel that crossbred with descendants of man. Three races of Beings were only some of their progeny. They were the Emim, which were mistranslated as 'fearful' but were actually 'the ones who caused ravening fear.' There is some belief that these are the ones who caused the Shifter lines.

"The Anakim were 'those with graceful necks' but were actually 'the noble ones,' those who retained most of their true divinity in their appearance. They were beautiful, aristocratic, part of the nobility of the Angels themselves."

"And the Rephaim," Helmut finished for her. "The dead ones, or rather those who were dead yet lived on."

"Precisely." Isis graced them all with a spectacular smile.

"Then how do we find these Rephaim, and hopefully Gillian?" Aleksei asked.

"He must believe he has a way to get to them, or at least contact them." Tehuti was deep in thought over several books with pictographs of old tablets. As the Egyptian God of wisdom, science, writing and magic, he was putting his considerable knowledge to the test.

"Here." A long, elegant finger pointed to an indecipherable excerpt of ancient Greek. There was a drawing on the page of some sort of device.

"The Antikythera mechanism." Tehuti's eyes glowed with excitement over his discovery.

"Really?" Helmut moved to read over the Vampire's shoulder. "I thought that device was used to plot the positions of the planets and stars."

"That is the common thought, yes, but it was so much more than just a simple, primitive computer," Tehuti assured him.

"But it was made thousands of years after the time of the Rephaim," Helmut insisted.

"It was, yes," Tehuti continued, "but its purpose was to determine locations in time rather than in the physical world.

"This tablet"—he pointed to another drawing in another ancient text—"tells how to use the Antikythera mechanism."

"The Phaistos Disk?" Osiris had moved over to see what his son was reading.

"Someone wanted an encrypted record of how to use the mechanism. It was created a thousand years later and has never been deciphered. I believe I can figure out the language."

"So you are saying that the Antikythera mechanism is for some sort of . . . what? Time travel? And that plaque is the instructions for how to run it?" Daed was very interested in anything having to do with antiquities, especially Greek ones.

"Not precisely time travel, more of a . . . communication device for any time period." Tehuti kept scribbling notes, never looking up from his work.

"I believe I can help in that case." Trocar's velvety voice came from the corner. Everyone turned toward the Dark Elf. He'd been uncharacteristically quiet during the entire discussion. He was peering intently at the screen of Gillian's laptop.

"If it is indeed both a 'where' and 'when' question, the Elves can help with this," Trocar informed them. "I have sent out a call to look for Gillian, Dracula or any large gatherings of Paramortals. With luck, we should receive a response."

Elves of all types had the ability to straddle both space and time, opening portals to other worlds, dimensions and time frames at will. The Doorways were generally used as portals of swift travel, for information gathering and history observance. The First People believed in the acquisition of knowledge for knowledge's sake. If anyone could find Gillian quickly, they could.

"Why large gatherings?" Kimber asked.

"Because if he has broken his cover by kidnapping a high-profile Human like Gillian, then he has everything prepared and this is the final keystroke," Trocar replied.

That bit of information didn't sit well with anyone in the room. "Let's hope he keeps her alive long enough for us to get to wherever they are, then." Daed sighed and rubbed his forehead.

"He had better." Aleksei turned and walked out of the room, down the hall and through the front door of the castle. He had to do something, even if it was pacing around the compound, or he would lose his mind.

He didn't know how long he walked, but a mental call from Tanis sent him back to the castle in a swift stream of mist.

"Where are they?" Aleksei materialized next to Trocar, startling several Brownies perched on the chair behind the Elf.

"Here." Trocar's long, ebony finger pointed to a map on the computer's screen.

"Egypt?" Isis asked. "Right under our noses?"

"Impossible." Osiris stood to see where Trocar was pointing.

"Akabat: the land of many obstacles. It is remote; there is little life off the main road. Nothing but chalk and pyrite deposits. It would be the one place we would not think to look." The anger in Osiris's voice made the walls tremble. The Egyptian God seemed to fill the room with his fury. He was completely in control yet scary as hell even for the other Vampires in the room.

"Hey, Osiris, tone it down a little." Even Daed looked a little pale from the force of the Lord's power.

The Egyptian Lord ignored him. "My plane has been refueled and is ready to leave. Make whatever preparations are necessary and let us go rescue your lady. I will have a contingent of my people there, waiting for us."

"I have also put out a call to those loyal to me," Dionysus added.

"There will be Elves, as well," Trocar mentioned quietly to anyone who was listening.

Daed punched speed dial on his cell phone. "General Riven? Daed Aristophanes here. I need a crack outfit of Marines . . . Yes, sir, a mixed group would be fine or just Paras . . . In Western Egypt. Yes, sir, Akabat . . . Immediately would be best . . . Press coverage would be great. Thank you, sir."

There was a long pause as he listened intently, then repeated, "Thank you, sir. I will take all precautions with my group here."

He snapped the phone shut. Everyone was staring at him. "What?"

"I swear to the Great Spirit, Daed, if this is yet another goddamn photo op for you, Gill isn't going to get to kill you, because I will." Kimber casually examined her fingernails, then stared him down.

"Look, all hell is literally about to break loose. What you don't know is that there is a small but very vocal resistance to the recognition of Paramortals as sentient Beings and to the Osiris Doctrine. Religious nuts of all flavors have cropped up and are calling for a reckoning. Don't you people ever watch BBC news?" Daed's black eyes locked with the eyes of everyone in the room in turn.

"And you were going to tell us this when?" Helmut's normally warm Austrian accent was suddenly chilly.

"I wasn't going to tell you at all. Most of the talk was just that: talk. Intelligence on both sides indicated that there wasn't any real reason for concern, so nobody bothered organizing any structured procedure. We've just been keeping an eye on the situation.

"Word has now spread through Dracula's people that Armageddon is virtually at hand. This isn't just about Dracula and his nutty plans anymore. There are going to be all different factions, some pro-Human, some pro-Paramortal, en route to Akabat as we speak. There's going to be a showdown of 'us versus them' that no one had counted on ever occurring."

"Daedelus, if I had known this 'unimportant' information, Osiris, Dionysus and I could have found out much more than your spies and informants. Our focus has been on the wrong problem, based on what you are now telling us." Aleksei was not a happy Lord and the room shimmered with his anger. Daed managed not to flinch under his icy stare.

"Aleksei, there was nothing you could have done to prevent this. It seemed to be coming; we just didn't know the time or the place. Everyone assumed it would be later rather than sooner. Gillian and this Institute have done so much to shed new light on the realities of cooperative living. Lately the intelligence reports have been much more favorable overall on the side of positive Human-Paramortal relationships. Everything has appeared to be calmer than it has been in centuries."

"The quiet breath before the hammer falls," Osiris mused.

"Yes . . . No!" Daed said emphatically. "No one expected the hammer *to* fall. Everything I've observed here, every contact I've had from Eastern Europe, has been positive. Positive about the Rachlav Institute, the Rachlavs themselves, about Gillian . . . There have been no negative reports or threats . . . Except for one, and we didn't believe the threat was serious enough to consider at the time."

"Wait a minute, chico." Luis spoke up for the first time. "What do you mean, everything you've observed? Are you here spying on us? On Gillian?"

This time, Daed did visibly flinch when literally every eye in the room pinned him where he stood. "I'm here as medical director of this Institute."

"With a little cloak-and-dagger on the side, Major?" Trocar rose with deadly grace and moved toward Daed like a stalking panther. Daed had enough sense to back up, realizing he was completely on his own.

"Just a minute, Lieutenant . . ."

"I am not your lieutenant, and even if I were, if you have endangered my Captain, there will be consequences." The Dark Elf's melodiously beautiful voice echoed everyone's thoughts. He wasn't kidding, and Daed knew it.

"Trocar . . . I give you my word I have not put Gillian or any of you in jeopardy."

"Really? Why, thank you, Major. That means so much." His tone was condescending; the dagger that materialized in his hand was not. Methodically, he produced a silken blue square of material from one of his hidden pockets and polished the blade with it.

"What else do you find not important enough to share?" Trocar leaned one hip on the back of the couch and breathed on the blade, scrubbing off his breath with the cloth. He was inches away from skewering Daed, who was backed up nearly against the wall.

"Aleksei? Helmut? Will one of you call off your attack Elf? I will explain everything." Daed was looking decidedly nervous.

It was interesting watching a shape-shifting Minotaur being rattled by a tall, slender but very lethal Elf. Two thousand pounds of Minotaur versus a one-hundred-eighty-five-pound Grael would be a pretty fair fight. If Daed shifted, he would have the advantage of size and strength, but Trocar's dagger was fourteen inches of pure Elven silver covered with arcane runes. The Elf had three thousand years of assassination practice and Wizard-level magical skills, and was blindingly fast. Not quite Vampire speed but enough to take on a Shifter bovine . . . unless the beef got in a lucky shot.

"I do not believe it is my place to 'call off' Trocar." Aleksei wasn't smiling. "He is a guest in my home and free to do whatever he believes in his heart is right."

Trocar's crystalline-faceted eyes flicked to Aleksei's for an instant, then back to Daed. For Trocar, it was both an acknowledgment that Aleksei wouldn't interfere and a look of gratitude.

Helmut was sure his blood pressure was off the charts.

He was pissed at Daed too, but Trocar was absolutely not joking. They didn't need the publicity that would result from a psychiatric medical director and a highly decorated retired major in the USMC being dissected by a Grael in the library of the Rachlav Institute.

"Trocar, wait. Let Daedelus tell us what he knows. *All* he knows."

"Very well." The dagger vanished as quickly as it had appeared. Ebony hands folded and came to rest on a sleek thigh.

"Daed? Is there anything else you should share?" Trocar's frothy white hair shifted in an invisible breeze as he cocked his head and stared down his former superior officer.

Poor Daed. He visibly blanched, and his upper lip was damp. He knew what the consequences of an actual throwdown with Trocar would be. Truth seemed an excellent choice.

"As I said, there has not been anything concrete since the original Compact, and definitely not much since Osiris wrote that Doctrine. There has been so little information that we thought things had finally settled down. Yes, there were occasional threats or public blustering from one group or another, but nothing we could arrest or detain someone for."

"However?" Trocar prompted.

"However . . . recently there have been a number of small religious groups, largely from Christian and Muslim backgrounds, who have been gaining some momentum with their negative outlook on Paramortals, particularly Vampires. Interestingly enough, most Christians, Muslims, Jews, Buddhists, Hindus, Native Americans, Aboriginals and Inuit believers are overall squarely on the Paramortal side of the fence. Sort of a live-and-let-live thing, assuming that if the Almighty created it and allowed it, it's supposed to be here."

"So we are being targeted by two major monotheistic groups?" Tehuti asked.

"No, just very small fanatical segments of their populations. Most are subscribing to the belief that it is not their place to judge, and they actually support the Compact and the Doctrine. Straw polls indicate that only the more separatist of their members are hostile."

"Hooray for good PR," Kimber said dryly.

"Exactly," Daed agreed. He sounded surprised that she hadn't noticed. "Why do you think I've been insisting on all these so-called photo ops? I want to highlight all the good we do together. To show that there is no reason for antiquated fears. It's really not about me, Kimber; it's about how we all function together for the greater good."

"Gillian hates it," Aleksei said softly. "The publicity, I mean. She would prefer to just do her job, know she has done it well and be satisfied with that."

"I know, Aleksei." Daed smiled at him. "She has always done her job extremely well. Gill understands that the spotlight is sometimes necessary to sway public opinion. I know she didn't approve of the cameras being around in Russia, but we garnered a lot of positive feedback and public interest from that mission."

"That mission was supposed to be impromptu and secret," Kimber mused. "She didn't like sensationalizing the drama and agony those children and families were going through from that situation."

Daed looked at her. "The public response and sympathy has ensured that an organized task force will stay on top of the child traffickers. Even with our prior intelligence, it took Gillian and the team to zero in on the pick-up site. You saw what we went through there."

"Wait a minute." Kimber's eyes narrowed. "What prior intelligence? We spent weeks there, gathering intel . . . and yet . . ." Her voice trailed off as she thought about the circumstances.

"And yet," Trocar chimed in, "how interesting that you managed to lead us almost directly to their base of operations in the forest."

"You knew." Kimber's accusing tone matched the glare she was giving Daed. "You already knew, before we got there, where those asshats would be. You took us right to them."

"No, I didn't. We tracked them back to their base solely due to the intelligence you gathered." Daed's face reddened just enough.

"That is a lie," Aleksei said flatly. "Your blood pressure has been steadily increasing and your scent has altered. You took them out there, knowing what they would run into, Daed. You set them all up: the pedophile ring, the local authorities and Gillian's team."

"Why would you do that?" Helmut faced off with his medical counterpart. "Why not just tell Gillian that you already had the place pinpointed? Why waste time having the team track down leads that you already knew?"

"It wasn't like that," Daed argued, clearly embarrassed. "We wanted to capitalize on the efficiency with which she and her team worked."

"By leaving those captive children directly in harm's way longer than they should have been?" Helmut had gone from amiable to livid.

"We had people in the area checking on the kids," Daed snapped back.

"Is that an excuse or an explanation?" Aleksei was equally infuriated. "The simple fact is that you used Gillian and her friends for publicity while endangering those children."

Daed had the decency to look uncomfortable, but was unbowed. "I don't expect you to understand, but it really was for the greater good."

"She is going to kill you," Kimber muttered. "Yup. Plain and simple, kill you."

He paled a little. "If someone tells her, that is."

"Oh, I assure you, I will tell her," Aleksei stated.

"And if she is reluctant, I am not." Trocar didn't elaborate, but Daed got the point.

Daed looked positively ill, but he had to get them off this subject and back on track. "What's done is done. I can't change what happened, and the kids are safe. We have a more pressing issue right now."

"This issue is not over, I promise you," Aleksei said.

"I'm sure it isn't." Daed sighed. He was going to pay

the piper at some point in the future, and Kimber was right. Gill would probably kill him. He wasn't looking forward to that conversation, but what was done couldn't be changed now.

"I screwed up. I will take the consequences, but I need to catch you all up on what *is* a very large, current problem. I was telling you about these fanatic factions before we got sidetracked."

He ignored Kimber's derisive snort behind him. "One man in particular is a self-proclaimed evangelist with his own little television network. He's been supplying his viewers with a constant stream of rhetoric about the dangers of cross-species mingling. He's managed to gather a fairly large number of followers who are as fanatical as he is."

"Who's that?" Kimber asked. "I don't watch religious programming of any kind."

"He calls himself Father Bartholomew Daily. He is, in fact, a Vampire who is actually a defrocked Jesuit priest. According to his unauthorized bio, he was excommunicated for inappropriate relationships with female parishioners.

"One of his dalliances was Reborn and Turned him shortly before his case went before the Vatican. He associates his loss of Faith, loss of humanity and loss of vocation with a skewed version of the facts. Sort of a fraternization with the enemy type of theory."

"Well, he was the one who violated his own vows," Helmut interjected.

"Exactly. But he insists that if he had not chosen an 'unnaturally beautiful' Vampire as his target, he would have overcome his base passions and been absolved instead of being damned. Unfortunately he has a lot of people who agree with him."

"He's still a Vampire. Who the hell is he feeding on if he thinks it's so bad?" Kimber asked.

"That's the best part. He actually sets up what he calls 'sacrifices' on live TV, where he demonstrates the 'seductive allure' of a Vampire—himself—over Humans who believe they can withstand his enticement."

"Isn't that rather self-defeating? He's preaching about the evils of mingling species, then partaking of the very thing he's ranting about?" Helmut pointed out.

"Dichotomy in acts and deeds has always been glaringly obvious from the more vocal proponents of various belief systems," Osiris added.

"Gives organized religion a bad name, in my opinion," Kimber said.

"But it hasn't damaged his credibility with his own flock," Daed said.

"How is this man a concern for us?" Aleksei asked.

"Because he wants to redeem Gillian."

"Redeem her?"

"Redeem, reclaim . . . Get her to see the error of her ways: her affiliation with her profession and her relationship with you." Daed stared at Aleksei.

"He intends to harm her?" The Romanian Lord's eyes went platinum with fury.

"I don't know what he intends, but it's in Gillian's best interest to find out. What I am afraid of is that Father Daily and others like him will get wind of what Dracula is doing and show up in Akabat to meet her. We need to have an equal show of strength, if we do nothing else," Daed finished.

Aleksei took the hint and gathered his thoughts. Wordlessly he sent out a plea to any Vampire loyal to him. He was surprised when he felt the instantaneous responses of all those who had pledged their loyalty.

It was Teo, the first Vampire to take his Oath during the great healing, who answered initially. *"We will be there, Lord Aleksei."*

"All I want to know is who and what do I need to blow to hell?" Kimber's voice interrupted his thoughts. She was standing next to him, hands on her hips and looking pissed off.

"I am not certain that where they are is a place for Humans, little sister." Tanis gripped her shoulder, gently.

"Bullshit," Kimber announced. "Gill's Human, and she's in the middle of this. I'm going."

"Count me in," Pavel said, stepping up beside his lady love.

"And me." Luis flanked Kimber on the other side.

"I am going." Trocar's voice was flat and angry.

"We leave no one behind, folks. You are just going to have to put up with Humans and Shifters on whatever rescue mission you're planning." Daed's Southern drawl had thickened, a sure sign he wasn't going to back down. "Gill is one of us, and no Marine would ever leave another one behind, even if she does decide to shoot me."

"There will be no dissuading you, I see." Aleksei was tremendously proud of Gillian's friends and of her.

"Nope. If you all leave without us, we'll get there ourselves. We are resourceful, you know." Kimber shot a grin that would have melted butter.

CHAPTER
8

A quick phone call from Aleksei to Ivan, Cezar's police chief brother, procured them enough additional vehicles to get them all to the airport in Brasov. Gillian's personal car and the Institute's van were already filled to capacity by their small but mighty group.

The flight to Egypt would take a few hours and land them in Cairo close to Daybreak. Fortunately, despite Dracula's power, not even a Vampire Lord could tolerate the full force of the Egyptian sun at midday. He would be forced to wait until at least late afternoon or dusk, as the sun was falling, to exit whatever shelter he would have for himself and his own Vampires. The playing field was level at the moment, and they intended to use it to their advantage.

After a quick discussion with Helmut, Cassiopeia agreed to stay at the Institute and arrange for some temporary staff to come in while everyone else was away, so the remaining clientele's therapy would not be interrupted. Meanwhile, Daedelus ordered a UH-1 Huey cargo chopper to pick everyone up at the Cairo airport and transport them to Akabat. There was room enough for everyone, plus the Vampire's containers, and it gave them the maneuverability to thoroughly search the area.

There was an intense argument with the Brownies, who insisted on going. Aleksei finally managed to convince them that they would be a much bigger help if they stayed at home to look after things until Gillian got back.

Cezar selected a number of Wolves to accompany the group to Egypt, leaving the balance of his pack to watch over the castle grounds and village since he and Pavel were going with Aleksei. Besides, Galahad Upchurch, the Interpol officer, would need help keeping Gill's newest patient, Chester, under control and under wraps.

The aforementioned officer was brought into the conversation by Daed and Helmut, who explained what had occurred and promised to bring Gillian back, safe and sound, very soon. Galahad in turn contacted his office and requested additional officers to help the pack with extra security at the Institute. No one argued with him. Even with the main focus on Gillian's recovery, client safety was still paramount.

"We'll get her back, Aleksei," Helmut quietly said to the tall Vampire as they slid into Gillian's car, with Trocar at the wheel.

"We have to," Aleksei responded, turning to grace Helmut with eyes gone platinum. "I cannot imagine life without her."

"You will not have to," Trocar interjected as he barreled out of the driveway and rapidly shifted into high gear. "You must have your lady and I must have my Captain and my friend back. It shall be so."

There was a chill in the Dark Elf's musical voice that everyone in the car noticed. Aleksei was furious that Gillian had been taken, but Trocar was absolutely seething with the ruthless rage his race was feared and famous for.

"Damn, I'm glad you're on our side, brother." Daed grinned and patted Trocar's leather-clad shoulder.

"As am I," Trocar responded, never taking his eyes off the road.

"Just where the hell are we going?" Gillian was peering into the pre-dawn dark surrounding the plane.

"I supposed it does not matter if I tell you now. We are headed toward the Western desert in Egypt," Vlad's supremely marvelous voice purred.

"How exactly do you know where to go?" She turned away from the window to look at him.

Smiling, he rose and went to an overhead bin. He removed a very bedraggled leather satchel and brought it to the table. Opening it, he gingerly removed two objects and placed them in front of Gillian.

"This"—he pointed to the first one, a flat, clay disk with concentric circles of some type of ancient hieroglyphs—"is known as the Phaistos Disk."

Gillian frowned as she examined it. "I don't recognize these glyphs. They're not traditional Egyptian."

"This language predates Egyptian writing. It is a ritual, religious hymn. I was not able to translate anything in it except the word *Akabat*, which is where we are going."

He moved to the other device, a bronze box mounted with various gears, wheels and dials. "This is an intact Antikythera mechanism, unlike the one found in the Aegean by divers. I managed to locate both of these after searching among the collections of a number of cabinets of curiosity."

"And what does this do?" Gillian asked.

"It will call the Rephaim to us."

"How do you know that these devices are related?" She locked eyes with him.

"What do you mean?" Another frown creased his perfect brow.

"If I understand you correctly, these two devices were created thousands of years apart. What evidence do you have that one has anything to do with the other?" She was careful to keep her voice soft and level. She wanted answers, not a fight. At least not right now.

"Gillian, I have spent centuries researching this. I have accessed and invaded the best scientific and religious minds of both Human and Paramortal. I assure you, while these artifacts were centuries removed from each other, they are indeed related. They were intended to be kept separate in order to prevent someone from doing exactly what I am going to attempt."

"Opening a proverbial stairway to Heaven?"

"In the most basic of terms, yes."

This was *so* not a good idea. She watched as he carefully, almost lovingly, replaced the two relics back in their case.

"Vlad . . ."

"Yes, my dear?"

"Do you think that your humanity might be more self-evident if you didn't offer up a Human sacrifice? I hear the Gods in general really frown on that."

His laughter, as always, was light, musical and very enthralling. "We shall see what the Rephaim deem to be necessary."

"Fabulous." She turned back toward the window. The sky was noticeably lighter.

"It's getting light out. Shouldn't you be skulking off to your casket?"

He seemed noticeably surprised. "Has your time with Rachlav and, I am assuming, Osiris not shown you that the ancients are immune to the effects of everything but the strongest sunlight?"

"I'm usually asleep myself by then."

"That is very close to a lie, Gillian. I am certain you noticed. No matter. I shall retire in due time. I have those in my employ who will watch over you until dusk. While I am indisposed, I suggest you get some rest yourself. If you are hungry or thirsty, we do have food and drink for those who need it aboard the aircraft. You have only to ask."

"Aren't you concerned that I might just try to escape while you and your fanged friends are asleep?" Gillian was dead serious. If she could get out, she would.

"My dear . . . where would you go? We will be landing shortly in the middle of one of the most hostile desert environments on the planet. You may leave the plane, but if you run, you will not get far." His grin was a little too smug for her liking.

"So, you'd let me just wander off?"

"Not hardly. If you wish to leave the plane to stretch your legs, that is your prerogative. You will be guarded at all times and no harm will come to you."

He rose, picked up the cases containing the relics, then came to stand next to her. In an uncharacteristic gesture, he took her head in his hands, bent down and kissed her lightly on the forehead.

"Thank you," he said softly.

"For what?"

"For not judging me."

After Vlad and the artifacts left her area of the plane, Gillian took the opportunity to pace and fume. Not judging him? She couldn't level any judgment as his therapist, but she sure as hell could as his captive, prisoner, pawn, bargaining chip . . . or whatever the hell else she could be considered. Asshole Vampire. No wonder the son of a bitch got what he wanted most of the time. He was a pushy, egomaniacal know-it-all.

She shot Aleksei a brief thought so he'd know she was still alive, but curtailed any ideas of an extended mental conversation. It was Vlad's plane, Vlad's rules. He could have any number of individuals on the aircraft who might intrude on her thoughts.

Strange, though . . . She couldn't feel any real animosity from him toward her. She could sense Vlad and Elizabeta, the cockpit crew and several other people aboard, but not the large entourage she assumed came with a Vampire Lord. Dionysus traveled light, but Osiris generally had a small herd of folks around him. Either Vlad was even more of a megalomaniac than she thought, or he knew there would be reinforcements when they arrived in Akabat.

The pilot's very Human voice came over the intercom with instructions to fasten seat belts and get ready for landing. *Great, a thrall,* Gill thought to herself. Conventional wisdom about Vampires was that most Masters had a Human or two who were loyal to the death. If they weren't the Vampire's lover or true servant, they were people who were enamored of the particular Vampire but who had little use outside of a very specific purpose or skill. A trusted Human pilot made sense. Easy to control, easy to seduce. Blech.

The plane's landing gear unfolded and the engine noise shifted to a protesting whine as the captain throttled back in preparation for landing. The back tires caught the ground first, then the nose dropped a split second after. It was all familiar to her, yet anticipation of what was to come made her stomach lurch.

"Dr. Key?" An unexpected voice made her twitch.

She turned to find an attractive Human woman, wearing desert combat fatigues and a helmet, and who was heavily armed. The M-16 rifle was pointed casually in Gill's direction. Not exactly a threat, but almost.

Gillian's eyes narrowed. "You are . . . ?"

"Lieutenant Bausch." The woman's sharp tone matched her features. Hazel eyes regarded Gillian suspiciously.

"And?" Gill prompted her.

"Lord Dracula has asked that you be monitored if you would like to leave the plane."

The cockpit door opened and, as she had surmised, a Human pilot and copilot stepped out, both dressed in fatigues similar to Lt. Bausch, and both with Ruger 9mm sidearms. The taller of the two men spoke. "Please don't get overconfident, Dr. Key. We are under orders to let you walk around the immediate area and to keep you from harm."

"Does keeping me from harm include not shooting me?" Gillian was getting irritated.

"We don't have to shoot you to restrain you." That was from Lt. Bausch.

A chilly smile crept over Gillian's mouth as she sized up her captors. Anyone with any sense would have run, but Bausch and the pilots weren't up to speed on irritated ex-Marines. Bausch may actually be a real soldier, but these two guys were obviously civilians. Their guns were too low on their hips, and the holsters were not in position for a fast draw. She was betting the safeties were on.

"Really." Her response was flat, cold and matter-of-fact.

The shorter pilot popped open the front exterior door. Through the hatch's opening, Gillian could see an aircraft boarding bridge being rolled into place. The taller pilot moved to kneel and secure it at the gangway. She had a gun in her pants pocket, but it wasn't as accessible as the three weapons currently in the cabin. Figuring it would take Lt. Bausch at least two to three seconds to orient the rifle on her in the enclosed space, she moved.

Her first kick landed against the shorter pilot's knee. There was an audible crack. He screamed and went down, and Gill had his sidearm. A second kick to the jaw of the kneeling taller man knocked him over. Gill grabbed his gun as he fell. She spun, weapons in both hands, to smack the rifle's stock up and away from her, then planted her foot in Lt. Bausch's midsection. As the other woman doubled over, Gillian yanked the M-16 away from her and ran the few steps to the door.

She didn't bother with the stairs, just jumped the railing, rolling as she landed to absorb the twelve-foot drop. Coming to her feet, Gill slung the rifle over her shoulder, unlocked the ambidextrous safety on both of the handguns and glanced around for the first time since procuring her freedom.

Oops was the only coherent thought she could come up with.

The plane, the landing strip, the landscape and Gillian herself were literally surrounded with Beings of various species. The sun was up. The sky was slightly overcast due to the time of year. There were rock formations but no underbrush, no plants, no trees, not even a dry twig to hide the fact that there were thousands of people around her. This was Vlad's army, or at least part of it. Humans, Shifters, Sidhe, magical Beings of all varieties. She was certain there were Vampires and other Nightwalkers around too, but they would be in the ground, secured away on the plane, as Vlad and his friends were, or hidden away nearby. She had run from the proverbial frying pan into the fire and was totally screwed.

"Um . . . hi?" She tried for what she hoped was a friendly smile, despite holding two Ruger SR9 9mm pistols and an M-16 rifle on her back.

"It's *her*" and "Look . . . he brought *her*!" seemed to be the predominant whispers and mutterings echoing through the throng.

Gillian frowned as the crowd pressed closer. There was no direct threat . . . yet. But she wasn't taking any chances.

"Okay, that's close enough." She didn't exactly brandish the two pistols, but she did raise them just a little. The crowd obliged and moved back a notch.

"Just back up and let me have some space. All I want to do is to look around at the area. I'm not going anywhere, and I'm not going to shoot anybody unless I have to." Her voice was clear, level and commanding as she looked as many of the frontrunners in the eyes as she could manage.

Lt. Bausch came scrambling down the gangway at that point, apparently recovered enough to move and speak. "Give me my weapon back, Dr. Key."

"No."

Bausch started toward her. Gill casually pointed a gun at the woman's midsection and Bausch stopped short. "I don't think so, Lieutenant. Now, piss off and go find something to do, like taking care of the pilots."

"I'm supposed to watch you," Bausch hissed back.

"I don't care. I can watch myself, and these folks aren't going to let me run off and get bitten by a cobra. Don't force me to make an example out of you." Gill's eyes became very green and very chilly.

To her credit, the lieutenant appeared to have some reasonable self-preservation skills. Her face whitened, but she backed up and then retreated to the stairs.

Definitely not regular Army, Gillian thought to herself. *A real soldier would have at least tried for the weapon.*

Tentatively she reached out her empathy and consciousness. The mood around her wasn't overtly hostile, but it wasn't exactly friendly either. Since everyone appeared to be watching her, she yelled to anyone listening: "I have permission to be outside the plane. I am not going to run off into the desert, nor am I going to harm myself or any of you unless someone tries to hurt me first. We have a long time before darkness falls and Vlad wakes up . . ."

"*Lord* Dracula!" Emphasis on the self-proclaimed title came from a smattering of voices in the crowd around her. They sounded pissed off. Oh well.

"You call him what you like. He asked me to call him Vlad, so that's what I'm going to do." Her comment was met with shocked silence.

"Now, Vlad does not want me to leave, and he does not want me to get hurt. So everyone just give me space, let me move around and look the area over, and I promise I will be here when he wakes up. I don't want to have to tell him that I spent all day hunkered down by the plane and afraid for my life." There was a little edge of sarcasm in her tone, but her point was taken. Everyone moved farther back.

She kept her senses cranked up on high and took a moment to look at the landscape. Naturally formed squat obelisks of reddish orange stone dotted the otherwise flat, tan-colored ground. It wasn't so much sand as it was packed, solid earth. White patches of gypsum painted frost-like patterns over the ground and the monuments. There were black geometrically shaped stones scattered randomly around, which Gillian supposed were pyrite. There was nothing as far as she could see in any direction but the white-dusted earth and rock formations. It was starkly beautiful, but at the moment, vastly outnumbered and probably outgunned, she couldn't take the time to appreciate it. This sucked.

Aleksei. An empty void greeted her probing thoughts. If he'd maintained any amount of consciousness, he would have responded to her feelings of defeat. She wanted to reach out to him; let him know she was still alive. But he was hours from waking. Then again, so was Vlad. Great.

Gingerly she moved away from the group. They mirrored her and moved a little farther back. Lowering the guns to her sides, she continued to move, putting space between herself, the plane and the people. Nobody was behind her;

she would have felt them. She didn't want to trigger a mob scene if she fled, so she kept her movements deliberate, assured and confident.

One of the monuments close to her was roughly seven or eight feet tall, and had a circumference of about twenty feet. The surface was ringed and eroded enough to make climbing easy. Jamming the guns in her pockets, she scrambled up to the top of it like a squirrel. From her higher vantage point, she could ascertain that there was indeed Jack Shit in the way of shelter or civilization in any direction. Fabulous.

The rock was fairly flat and level. Gill unslung the rifle from her back and laid it down. Every movement was deliberate and slow, not to be misinterpreted. She retrieved the guns from her pockets, shoving one into the front waistband of her cargo pants, the other in the small of her back. Her own gun she laid next to the rifle, and sat down in full view of the throng.

She reached back into her pocket to feel around. The cargo pants were a little loose and the pockets were deep. Her cell phone was there, down at the bottom. She was pretty sure no one was going to willingly let her make a call, at least not an obvious call. Praying silently to whatever Gods were listening that she had all the beeps and bells turned off, she slid the cover open. Kimber's number was hot keyed to the number two on the keypad.

On Osiris's jet, everyone was either locked securely away from the daylight or napping. Osiris, his mate, Isis, their son, Tehuti, Sekhmet and Anubis had a private sealed chamber directly behind the main cabin. Dionysus and his Vampires, Hades, Thetis, Nyx and Persephone, were safely ensconced in the opulent cargo hold. The Lions, Wolves, Cheetahs and Humans were all together in the main cabin. There was a larger group of Osiris's Vampires who were standing by, waiting for sunset and word on where to meet them. Daed had his platoon of Marines in Akabat already doing recon work, trying to determine exactly where Gillian had been taken.

Since there wasn't much to do except wait until they arrived in Akabat, Kimber had snuggled up with Pavel on one of the couches in the lounge. She was beginning to think life as a Vampire might not suck too badly after all. Castles, private jets and, from Gillian's description of Osiris's underground palace, pretty stylish living conditions.

Her phone vibrated and she jumped. Pavel's blue eyes fluttered open as she dug in her jeans for the phone. Gillian. Holy shit. Helmut was dozing across from her and Pavel. She kicked him in the leg to wake him up. "Gill's on the phone. Don't say anything; just be quiet."

Years of knowing her friend, serving with her friend, and she instinctively knew to do nothing but flip open the cover and engage the call. All the Shifters, Daed and Helmut gathered around her. Putting it on speaker, she waited.

Silence.

Back in Akabat, Gillian mentally calculated the time it would take Kimber to get the phone out of her pants or pack and answer. When she judged it to be sufficient, she stood up again.

"How many of you are here?" Gillian called out to those closest to her.

"Thousands," came a voice from the group.

"Thousands?" Gillian repeated, hoping like hell Kimber could hear her through her pants material and the wind that was whistling through the desert.

"Enough to make our Lord's plans come true." That was from a closer male voice.

Gillian spun around, drew the front Ruger and leveled it at the group flanking her on the right. "I said get back away from me, and I meant it. Any closer and he's gonna have one less follower."

The man in front registered as a Shifter on her radar. He smiled a very unfriendly smile, which spoiled the effect of his handsome face, but he motioned the rest of them back.

She returned his smile, just as coldly. "You'll be first, slick. You may heal up, but I'll just shoot you again. Understand?"

That time he moved back with the group. The look he shot her wasn't pleasant, but he did move.

"What's your name?" Gillian asked him.

Dark eyes glittered up at her. "Samir."

"Okay, Samir, all we're going to do today is leave me alone and wait for nightfall. I've already explained Vlad's wishes, and I don't intend to keep repeating myself. I will shoot the next person who is stupid enough to threaten me. I am absolutely serious that your Lord will be extremely pissed off if you so much as tweak a hair on my head."

"Understood." He wasn't pleased about her bravado, but he motioned the others away and followed them.

When they were far enough away, she palmed the cell phone and brought it out of her pocket. It slid a little back into her sleeve, allowing her to raise her arm as if to look over the horizon, and whisper to Kimber.

"Kimmy, I don't know how you're going to get me out of this. There is no cover except rock obelisks, no shelter except the plane. We're so far out in the desert the Gila monsters have set up a lemonade stand. If you guys need to call it a day, no hard feelings and I understand."

She couldn't hold the phone to her ear or her mouth, so she might have imaged it, but Kimber's indistinct voice seemed to say, "No one gets left behind."

Gill chewed on her lower lip and returned the phone to her pocket. She slid the cover shut, cutting the connection. Bless Daed if he could pull a GPS tracker out of his ass to lead them directly to her.

Kimber relayed everything she had heard and what Pavel's preternatural hearing had picked up to those who were awake. Gill was in a world of shit; that was a given. She didn't want them to attempt a rescue if it was too dangerous; that was also a given. Any of them in the same situation would have said the same thing. The response would have been exactly the same. No one was left behind. There was nothing to do but wait until Egypt; until nightfall.

On Gillian's end, she had a high-ground vantage point and weapons, and she wasn't the least bit sleepy with all the adrenaline coursing through her system. Inexplicably, she didn't feel terribly afraid for her own safety. She was already resolved to the fact that she may not live through tonight. What worried her was that one of her friends or Aleksei might get hurt or die.

Aleksei. This was her proverbial last stand and she was taking stock. Did she love him? No! Her mental bitch kicked her in the spleen. Well . . . yeah. Yes, she did. Helluva time to realize that. Too bad she couldn't tell him. The problem was, did she want to tell him? Hell no.

And why not? Why didn't she want him to know? Because it would tie him to her more than he already was? He loved her; that was the truth. He'd proven it, come through for her and stood by her every step of the way. He'd respected her boundaries, her quirks, the more questionable aspects of her job, with only a minor digression into Fanged Fossil World . . . and he had apologized. Not just with words but with his actions.

One thing Gillian knew for certain was that in any relationship—friend, foe, lover or patient—it was more important to pay attention to what someone did rather than to listen to what they said. Aleksei said he loved her, but he had gone beyond that and shown her, time after time.

Now . . . carefully . . . without scaring the absolute shit out of herself, she slowly opened the one remaining door of denial in her own mind. Aleksei. Did she want him and everything he had represented and promised? Yeah. She did. She wanted to stay with him and see where this all would wind up. It really was that simple.

A deep, shuddering exhalation of breath was the only outward sign that she'd come to a decision. Immediately she noticed a release of tension that she didn't realize she'd been harboring. Was this how love was supposed to feel? It didn't seem to hurt or make her panicky, she realized with a jolt.

How did she feel? Giddy and stupid? Nope. Sort of relaxed, calm and at peace? More like . . . secure. Like a homecoming. Home was with Aleksei, wherever they were together. It felt good. It felt right. It felt safe. Too bad she was probably going to die before she could tell him.

CHAPTER

9

GILLIAN snapped out of her daydreams to notice the shadows around the obelisks were longer. What time was it? She checked her phone and was amazed to find it was late in the afternoon. Four fifteen. Where the hell had the time gone? Had she been sitting there lost in her thoughts, mooning about life with Aleksei and musing the day away? Apparently she had.

Great Ganesh, if she was that inattentive, she was lucky to still be in one piece with all the unfriendly bodies in close proximity to her rock. Mentally shaking herself, she stretched, stood up, then stretched some more. She was used to long, involved stakeouts and sniper's nests, so enforced inactivity wasn't something new. The fact that she was out of practice was a problem. She felt stiff, thirsty and a little nauseated. Probably would have been a good idea to escape the plane with a bottle of water and a sandwich instead of just guns.

Dehydration was a real dilemma. She'd been sitting outside for hours. Even though she'd been inactive and it was a lower level of heat this time of year, her body was still being leeched of moisture. When the sun fell it would become chilly. The desert was a contrast of environments and temperatures. It might be blazing hot during the day, then cold at night. Since it was winter, the days were already cooler. Eight hours in the heat of an Egyptian summer with no water or shade would have given her heat stroke. Her body wasn't used to the hard life of a Marine officer anymore. Bummer.

She called out toward the plane: "Bausch! If you want to be helpful, I could use some bottled water and a granola bar!"

To her surprise, Bausch appeared in the open doorway of the plane and waved, then disappeared again. She hadn't really expected an answer to her request, so it was nice to know they were being attentive. Right.

A few minutes later Bausch, minus her helmet, clambered down the gangway and headed toward Gillian's rock. She wasn't armed, from what Gill could see, but was carrying several water bottles and a satchel.

"Here, I brought you some food and your water."

"Thank you. Just toss it up, please."

Bausch obeyed, throwing the satchel up first, then the four individual liters of water. "You really shouldn't be outside without a hat or some shade, Dr. Key. Even with the clouds, the sun out here is strong. If you hadn't called out, I was going to check on you soon anyway."

"I'm fine, thanks," Gillian replied, rummaging in the satchel. There was a sandwich, the granola bar, a pear, a container of strawberries, aloe vera gel and a brownie.

"What's all this?" She stared down at Bausch suspiciously.

"You need to eat and drink. Don't worry; it's not poisoned or drugged. We're under orders to keep you alive and well, remember?" Bausch tossed her a glare, then walked back to the plane.

Gillian took a moment and weighed the possibilities. She hadn't felt any duplicity from Bausch, and she was really hungry. The hell with it. Why bring her out in the middle of literal bumfuck Egypt, then poison her? It didn't make sense. Besides, the food smelled good and the water bottles were commercial brands with the seals intact.

She cracked open the seal on one of the liters of water immediately, drained the bottle, then sat back down to enjoy the sandwich. After she demolished the sandwich, the strawberries and another bottle of water and began munching on the pear, she felt more like herself. Eyeing the brownie, she felt a jolt of queasiness. Normally she considered chocolate a separate food group, but today wasn't one of those days. She'd save it for later. If there was a later.

The sun was starting its early winter descent toward the horizon and the temperature was dropping. Gillian slathered the aloe vera gel over her face, neck and hands. It was for post-sun-exposure and she figured she might have a slight burn.

Aleksei would be waking soon; but then, so would Vlad. Older Vampires could stand everything but the direct glare of the sun, depending on the time of year and weather conditions. They could be up and around in the early morning and early evening if they wanted to, and could remain conscious longer during winter weather or heavy storms when clouds dissipated the intense golden rays.

A familiar uncomfortable feeling interrupted her thoughts. Two liters of water and now she had to pee. Fabulous. That would mean going back into the plane. There was no way she was hiding behind a rock and dropping trou out here with all the wandering people around. She shrugged on the rifle, tucked the guns back in her pants and yelled at the plane again. "Bausch! I'm coming back into the plane for a minute. Make sure you and those pilots are well away from the door."

Kimber, Helmut and Pavel were seeing to the unloading of Osiris's plane. Daed was off commandeering a vehicle large enough to move the Vampire's containers, the Lions, the Wolves and the Cheetahs to where they were headed. Trocar was off God knew where, probably stocking up on Grael assassin articles. Gill had thoughtfully left her phone on, so whatever transportation Daed came up with needed a GPS system in it.

The noise of a rotor blade in the distance grew louder. Kimber looked up to see a helicopter headed toward their vicinity. From what she could tell it looked like a Huey but it wasn't a Slick. Gun turrets and missile launchers bristled from the front. Apparently someone was expecting trouble. Great. This was just getting better and better.

Cezar, the Alpha Wolf, piled out of the airplane with a dozen of his handpicked Wolves. Aleksei had insisted he stay at the castle since Pavel was already coming, but Cezar had vetoed that idea, saying that Gillian was his friend too and he'd be damned if he was staying back home minding the store while everyone else was rescuing her. Aleksei rather suspected that Cezar's admiration was at least partly due to Gillian calling him an "overgrown Rottweiler" to his face shortly after they'd met. No matter; Cezar had decided and that was that.

Gill managed to get in the plane, to the head and back out again without incident. Bausch wisely stayed back, her hands in full view. Both pilots were nursing their injuries and greeted her with frightened eyes and empty holsters. Part of her felt a little remorse for kicking the shit out of them, but she dismissed it. This had been a hostage situation and she had simply freed the hostage.

Growing bolder since no one was actually challenging her, she kept the rifle in her hands and walked a perimeter around the plane and most of the crowd. Since she was assuming that the majority of the gathering wasn't on her and Aleksei's side, she had to admit it was an awfully peaceful assembly.

Other than assorted whispers and glares from the folks who could actually see where she was, no one was aggressive on any level. That fact concerned her more than comforted her. Yeah, she was supposed to be untouched and kept safe, but she was expecting some sort of indirect hostility at least. All she was picking up from her empathy was tension and a deep, underlying fear that was definitely not directed at her.

If they were really that afraid of repercussions from Vlad, she had seriously underestimated his power, his authority and the genuine depth of his psychosis. Jack had been a prime example of a powerful underling with a personal agenda; surely someone in this mob had it in for her just on principle. Then again, Jack was dead and she was still very much alive, and if that wasn't a glaringly obvious indicator of her importance to Vlad's plan of the moment, she didn't know what was.

Frowning, she circled back to the plane. None of this felt right or natural. That thought unsettled her as well. Since her total immersion into Fangland, few things struck her as odd or unnatural anymore. This did, and that in itself was scary as hell.

The sun dipped farther and the haze created by the lowered rays and swirls of dust darkened the landscape. Gripping the rifle more firmly, she edged closer to the gangway of the plane. Her senses were tingling in a very bad way. It was like being catapulted into the ocean, knowing without a doubt that there were great white sharks swimming beneath you in the water but being powerless to stop going in the direction you were headed. Something was there, but she couldn't pinpoint it yet.

"Good evening, Dr. Key."

An unknown dulcet female voice, lightly accented with Hungarian, sounded at the top of the stairs. Shit. Now what?

Gill flinched at the greeting, slowly turning to look up. A Vampire stood framed in the doorway of the plane in all her glory. Glory was not an exaggeration in this case. Gillian had never seen anyone so strikingly beautiful who wasn't an Elf, except Dracula himself.

Long chestnut hair was artfully arranged in rich waves, framing a delicate porcelain face. The eyes that were leveled on Gillian were the color of amber overlaid with gold leaf and framed by dark, thick lashes. Her mouth was a perfect, plump cupid's bow, graced by the same delicate shell pink on her cheeks.

She wore an extraordinary clinging, midnight blue velvet cocktail dress and matching skimmers, showing off her slender curves and décolletage to perfection. The vision of loveliness rendered Gillian completely incapable of speaking for a moment, but she recovered swiftly.

"You are?"

"Erzsébet Báthory."

Oh, that was just fucking lovely. The infamous Blood Countess, and here she was, impersonating a virgin. What next?

The woman descended the stairs and extended a hand to Gillian. "Vlad has told me so much about you."

"I'm thrilled."

Nevertheless, she took the proffered hand and shook it briefly. The Vampire's hand was warm and dry to the touch; her grip brief and polite. She wasn't much taller than Gillian, but was a good bit more slender. Gillian didn't even think of assaulting her as she had the pilots and the unfortunate Lieutenant Bausch. This woman could rip Gillian's head off with no effort whatsoever, despite looking like a soft cream puff in comparison to Gill's Marine Corps muscles.

Erzsébet wasn't registering as a normal Vampire on Gillian's radar. Her power was contained but still swirling around them both. She felt . . . beyond Master level, more like Vlad when he wasn't covering his true nature up. More like . . . Aleksei or Osiris. Shit, shit, shit. She was another Lord.

"I can see it in your eyes, Dr. Key. You are surprised to find another Vampire with a Lord's level of power which was unknown to your friends."

"Well . . . yes, it is a little bit of a shock." That was an understatement. There was no point in denying it; Countess Báthory would have known she was lying before she'd formed the words.

Sweet, bubbling laughter came from those perfect lips. "I think you and your profession have been somewhat misinformed about the more highly evolved of our species."

"I think you are absolutely right." Gillian smiled wryly. Again, no point in denying the obvious. She was going to track down and kill the author of *Using Your Empathy to Your Advantage* when she got back home. Sometimes it really was better not to know things.

"Um . . . I assume you are here to help Vlad with whatever it is we're going to do?" Lame, Gillian. Very lame.

Cold steel with a very sharp edge was abruptly placed against the side of her throat, and a slender, powerful arm snaked around her chest. Gillian had an intense moment of absolute flashback panic, thinking Jack had somehow found her again. Then she remembered that Jack was dead and it couldn't possibly be him pressing a knife or scalpel against her carotid artery.

"Oh, you'll help us, all right, love. You will indeed." The voice was midrange, lower-class British. Not quite Cockney, but almost. Jack's voice had definitely been uppercrust. No clue there.

"Stop it, Sweeney. Let her go. You are supposed to help me keep an eye on her and keep her safe. We are all behaving with civility for Lord Dracula's benefit." Erzsébet waved her hand in a dismissive gesture, but her eyes drilled holes in the person behind Gillian.

"Very well. If you insist," the deceptively soft tenor voice said as the blade was removed from her throat area.

He moved around in front of Gillian and kissed Erzsébet's hand. Another Vampire, naturally, but without even a Master's level of power. The son of a bitch shouldn't have been able to sneak up on her. Of course, she and her screaming empathy had been completely distracted by Erzsébet's beauty . . . At least that was what Gill was telling herself.

This was a very bad time to allow her mind to wander for any reason. She had definitely lost her edge for field work. That inexplicably irritated her more than anything else.

The male turned toward Gillian. "Sweeney Todd, miss . . . I am told that I am at your service."

"Er . . . nice to meet you?" Gillian wanted to bang her head on the side of the plane, but she took his hand in a faux friendship greeting.

"Pleasure is all mine, pigeon."

Sweeney Todd evidently wasn't a made-up story after all. Note to self: don't believe for a moment when someone tells you a legend really is not based in fact. Lies. All of it.

He flashed sharp, small white teeth at her, dramatically bowing at the waist and snapping shut the straight-edged razor he'd held at her throat. His hair was tousled, black and wavy, but streaked liberally with gray. Gillian noticed right away that he looked more disheveled than any Vampire she knew on a personal level. His clothing was rumpled and his fingernails were bitten back and dirty. There were dark circles around his equally dark eyes. He looked more like a drunk recovering from a weeklong bender than a preternatural Being with virally enhanced powers.

"Now what? Do we just wait here for Vlad or are you going to tell me what exactly is going on?"

Gillian slung the rifle over her shoulder and straightened to her full height. Since no one had attempted to kill her yet, or even shown any threat—well, except for Sweeney, but he was obviously off his nut—there was no point in false bravado or waving guns around.

"All I can do is confirm what you already know, Gillian." Erzsébet smiled. "Lord Dracula has the same plan he has had all along. The ascension of the Vampire to the pinnacle of influence. After this night, Humans, the Fey, the Elves—everyone will answer to us."

"I'm not sure how he plans to accomplish that." Gillian swept her arm around, indicating the nearby crowd. "There aren't enough people here, or enough Vampires on his side, for that matter, to stage a literal world takeover."

"I can only tell you what he has shared with me," Erzsébet said. "He is more calculating and meticulous than anyone gives him credit for."

"Why hasn't anyone tried to attack or kill me?" Gill said, with a pointed glance at Sweeney, who had the grace to drop his eyes and actually blush.

"Because you were not to be harmed, for any reason."

"So says Vlad?"

"So says Lord Dracula."

Great Ganesh, were any of Vlad's affiliates capable of giving a completely straight answer? Apparently not. She'd have to wait until he deigned to make an appearance to ask him.

It would also be nice to have some inkling of when her rescue party was planning on showing up. The thought slipped out before she could stop it. *"Aleksei, where the hell are you?"*

"Nearby, piccola." His deep, velvet baritone rumbled through her mind, stirring her senses. The unexpected response nearly made her jump out of her skin. Years of schooling her responses and her face kept all suspicion away from the two Vampires who stood less than three feet from her.

"Sorry for breaking mental radio silence, but you guys need to get here now."

He chuckled, sending her warmth and the sensation of his arms enfolding her. *"Very soon, cara. We will defeat this monster together. All of us."*

The brief contact was cut and Gill was alone again in her own head. It was enough to reassure her and confirmed that just hearing his voice and feeling his love for her made a huge difference in her outlook on the immediate future. She was damn well going to live through this and start enjoying her relationship for a change.

"Good evening, my dear." Vlad was up and about. Oh boy!

Gillian didn't need to look at him to recognize the sultry tones of that voice. "Stop saying that. Why does almost every antique Vampire say that?"

Hearty laughter emitted from Vlad's chest as he strode down the stairs to greet her with a light, one-armed hug and an unwelcome kiss on the forehead. "You continue to be a source of delight, Gillian."

"I'm overjoyed. Look, I'd really like to know what the hell is going on. This is making less sense as time goes on. Who are all these people? Why am I still in one piece? Why have I been allowed to keep my weapons? And what's

that? Are those the items you showed me on the plane?"
She pointed to the cloth-wrapped object under the arm he
hadn't hugged her with.

"So many questions." Vlad gently laid a finger against
her lips. "Everything will be answered for you, right now."

He gently turned her around to face the crowd. She had
to look down because everyone who had been standing was
now on their knees. Any question she had about the overall
loyalty of the huddled masses was now moot.

"My loyal followers!"

Gillian jumped as his melodiously beautiful voice thundered across the expanse without benefit of electronic en-
hancement. There was a dramatic pause for effect, then he
continued.

"This is the night I have promised for so long. Tonight
will be recorded in history as the true Masters of this world
ascend to their rightful place. Tonight is the revolutionary
rise of the Vampire. The Humans will fall from their unnatural domination of this earth and serve us, as they were
meant to do. You will hear this not only from me but also
from the Angels themselves. The Vampire is not a cursed
Being but a blessing from the Almighty! We are the true
descendants of the Angels!"

There was a thunderous cheer from all around them.
Gillian wasn't sure whether it was Vlad's charismatic ora-
torical skills at work or his pure, unrivaled seductive power,
which was spilling everywhere, commanding everyone's
attention. She half believed him herself, even with rational
and educated knowledge of just what he was: a megalomaniacal, sociopathic monster.

CHAPTER

10

THE helicopter carrying Aleksei and the rest landed just in time to see thousands upon thousands of Paramortal Beings and Humans rising to their feet and turning as one body. Trocar was off the transport first, followed by Aleksei, Kimber, Luis, Pavel, Helmut and Daed, then the Egyptian and Greek contingencies and finally Cezar and the rest of his wolves.

Arriving immediately afterward were other land vehicles, military transports and another smaller aircraft, all rallied by Osiris and Dionysus. The new influx of individuals stopped behind an imaginary line started by the original helicopter that had flown in. It had all the timing of an action-adventure movie with none of the glitz.

Aleksei surveyed the area, instantly pinpointing Vlad and Gillian as the living mass covering the desert turned, opening a corridor to allow passage, then closing the gap behind. He didn't need visual confirmation to know Vlad was at the head of the procession or that Gillian was with him. He could feel his archrival's power beating at him. Gillian's own retreating scent and empathic touch were like a cool, clear breath of wind on his senses.

"We are here, cara. *I swear that you will be safe."* He sent a brief thought to Gillian, to reassure her.

There was a fleeting, happy surge of emotion from her, then barriers were slammed down, cutting him off. Aleksei felt her attention shift to the Vampire who stood next to her.

"He is beginning his ritual," Osiris observed.

"We are going to get her out of there," Kimber stated.

"Why would you do that?" a new voice said, off to their right.

Everyone spun around to face the new arrival, mouths collectively dropping open. Gillian's doppelganger stood smiling nearby, head cocked to one side, a chilly smile on her soft mouth.

"Hello, Aleksei. Did you miss me?"

"Elizabeta? How is it possible?" Aleksei's shock and surprise were apparent.

"Lord Dracula gave me the gift of Rebirth when you refused me. Did you never wonder for even a moment what happened to your . . . fiancée?" She spat the last word at him.

Aleksei's eyes melted from icy gray to platinum as he recovered from his initial astonishment. "I was told you married another and were happy, Elizabeta. There was no reason to seek you out. When I was later told you'd died in childbirth, I mourned your loss along with your family. You were my fiancée for only a brief time before my Rebirth. You made it clear that you wanted my powers as a Vampire more than you wanted me as a man. There was nothing left to wonder about."

Kimber, Trocar, Helmut, Daed and Luis were staring at the Vampire who might have been Gillian's twin. The resemblance was astonishing. Thoughts of transference and countertransference whirled through Daed's psychiatric sensibilities. Was this why Aleksei loved Gillian? Did he still harbor love or guilt for this woman he believed to be long dead?

Helmut was thinking the same thing, until Aleksei finished his sentence. Whatever Aleksei had felt for this woman was long past. The hostility in his voice radiated around them all. Helmut glanced over to Daed, locking eyes for a brief moment. No, Aleksei's love for Gillian had nothing to do with her strong resemblance to this woman. Guilt and depression might have brought Aleksei to Gillian's therapeutic couch, but love and trust kept him by her side.

"You harbored guilt over my 'death' for centuries, Aleksei." Elizabeta was not willing to drop the issue and sneered at him. "The entire region talked about it. Do not try to deny that you loved me. I know you loved me. You even sought therapy because you loved me."

"I deny nothing." Aleksei's power swelled, sending tingles over everyone near him. "I did love you, but you are wrong about the reason I wanted a therapist. I felt undeserving as a man. I knew that your attachment and desire for me increased tenfold when you discovered my newfound abilities.

"You did not see me through the changes, Elizabeta. You wailed and cried when Tanis brought my drained body back to the castle, then ran when you found I had been attacked by Vampires. Tanis is the one who helped me keep my sanity. My family and my village are the ones who sheltered me and kept me safe. You only returned when you learned of the powers I received after being Reborn, and because the Vampire virus was the only way to ensure you kept your youth and beauty. You wanted my power, my gifts, my money, my lands. I was simply part of the package."

"You love her because she looks like me." Elizabeta gestured in the direction Vlad and Gillian had gone.

"I love her because she is completely unlike you," Aleksei shot back. "Gillian is honorable, trustworthy and intelligent. She is the most courageous person I have ever known. She is so utterly different from you, Elizabeta, that I cannot help loving her."

Elizabeta awarded him with a stinging slap. "Liar!"

Aleksei stood rock still, then caught her hand as she moved to strike him again. "You were an unfortunate lapse in judgment, Elizabeta. I was young, unsophisticated and arrogant. My guilt was because I believed I had allowed you to die, calling my name. My anxiety was from learning what a lie our relationship was. My shame and depression were from wasting so much time and feeling on worrying about an empty shell of a woman like you.

"I have changed personally because I wanted to change. You, however, are still the same. Vain, selfish, petty and empty inside. Even if I had Turned you, I would have left you when I learned just how shallow you are. If you call that monster 'Lord' and do not realize that he has used you, just as you tried to use me, then you are also naïve and ignorant."

"Ooh . . . that was good, Aleksei." Kimber flanked him, a flamethrower in her hands. Her sparkling green gold eyes locked with the other woman's. "Look, bitch, we are going to rescue Gillian now, so back off if you don't want me to fry your pretty hair, understand?"

Elizabeta's lip curled into a snarl as she jerked away from Aleksei's grasp. "This does not concern you, Human."

"You heard her." Aleksei stepped between them. "Leave us. You have no place here, and I have more important things to attend to."

It looked like Elizabeta might press the matter when she edged around Aleksei to square off with Kimber again. Aleksei frowned, stretched out a hand and mentally pushed. Elizabeta stumbled backward as if he'd physically shoved her. Her eyes widened in fear.

"That is not possible. You do not have his level of power!"

"It is possible. I have evolved," Aleksei informed her, then turned back to his group and hustled through the crowd after Vlad and Gillian. The throng parted again, the power of three Vampire Lords pushing everyone aside, enveloping their entourage in a protective envelope.

———◆———

Vlad didn't lead them very far from the plane. There was a natural ring of sorts formed by the rock obelisks, stretching almost twenty yards in diameter. It was an uneven circle, but there was room for the assembled masses to gather round. Some were on the ground; some climbed or levitated to the tops of the small monuments. The local population of Akabat had swelled further since the sun had fallen. The Vampires had risen, both those loyal to Dracula and those on Osiris's side of the proverbial fence. There was an increase in the mumblings and mutterings from the ever-growing crowd around them as the different factions intermingled and voiced individual opinions.

Gillian's position was unenviable. She was two feet away from Dracula, armed to the teeth, but with Erzsébet and Sweeney flanking her, and thousands of Dracula fans inches away, there was absolutely nothing she could do. There might be a chance of a lucky head shot before Sweeney cut her throat or the Blood Countess broke her neck . . . or the mob literally tore her apart. Resistance was indeed futile. She'd have to ride this one out and gauge her responses on what happened next.

"Now, Gillian, we will call down the Heavens," Vlad said to her.

He knelt on the gypsum-frosted ground and removed the Antikythera mechanism and the Phaistos Disk from the covered box. Adjusting the mechanism carefully, he spread the cover on the ground and laid the object on top of the dark, coffee-colored cloth. Gillian could see there were glyphs, hieroglyphs and runes embroidered around the edges of the rich-looking fabric.

Lifting the disk high so that everyone could see, he spoke. "Now is the time for our redemption! Now is the time for our justice! Join with me now, my friends, my fellows and even my enemies . . . Tonight the barriers fall and you will serve a new, enlightened Master!"

There was a deafening cheer from everywhere around them. The noise filled the bleak, barren desert of Akabat, causing the very ground to tremble as countless Paramortal voices signaled their approval. The much smaller number of dissenting cries were drowned out in the din. When the noise faded, there were shouts of anger and rebellion. From all directions, the crowds parted as Aleksei, Osiris, Dionysus and their entourages stepped forward to join Gillian, Dracula, Erzsébet and Sweeney in the circle.

"Stop it, Csangal . . . or whatever you are calling yourself this night." Aleksei stepped up to Dracula, reached past him and pulled Gillian to relative safety at his side.

"Rachlav, I have centuries on you in power. Do not think you will deny me my right or my prize." Vlad's beautifully toned voice turned scornful.

"I will deny you," Osiris said simply. His hand came up and Vlad literally flew through the air to slam against an obelisk. Utter silence reigned as Vlad shook his head and painfully climbed to his feet. He wasted but a moment on a contemptuous look at Osiris.

"Kill them. Kill all of them except Dr. Key." All hell broke loose as the crowds surged forward toward them and against one another. Saying chaos ensued was a drastic understatement.

Osiris, Aleksei and Dionysus ringed Gillian, facing outward as the fighting began. Helmut, Trocar, Luis, Daed, Oscar, Pavel, Cezar and Kimber were literally plucked out of the crowds by the three Lords and deposited in their crudely constructed circle with Gillian. Isis, Tehuti, Anubis, Sekhmet and the Greek Vampires, Hades, Thetis, Nyx and Persephone formed another ring surrounding the Shifters and Humans. The Barbary Lions, Cheetahs and Wolves were already fighting in front of Osiris, Aleksei and Dionysus. There was no time for greetings, thank-yous or reunion statements. This was the moment where they would live or die.

Vlad was protected for the time being by Gillian's proximity, the Vampires protecting her and the bubble of fighting around him. He raised the Phaistos Disk where he stood and screamed out words in a dialect and language no one could understand. His voice pierced the cacophony of noise in a thunderous, poetic diatribe.

Abruptly there was a tremendous crackling sound, then an enormous *boom* as if lightning had struck right at their feet. The noise brought all activity to a standstill. The landscape shimmered near where Gillian's group stood as a metaphysical Doorway formed. A heartbeat later, hundreds upon hundreds of heavily armed Elves poured from the Door, pushing back the crowds from the defenders in the circle.

At the head of the Elves was one familiar face, then another. Prince Mirrin Everwood, Gillian's former lieutenant and High Elf regent, stepped forward and greeted his ex–commanding officer with an eons-old salute: right arm across his body and a slight bow. It was a gesture of respect that Gill returned before grasping his forearms in greeting, warrior to warrior. Hierlon, Mirrin's friend and right-hand man, moved into view to greet Gillian, Trocar and Kimber as well.

"I don't know how or why you're here, but I'm glad to see you." Gillian was delighted that the cavalry had shown up in the nick of time.

"Trocar's message was of concern to us all, Mellina." Mirrin's turquoise eyes swept around, missing nothing. He noted that Gillian stepped back toward a tall, handsome Vampire with ghostly pale eyes.

"Aleksei, this is Mirrin. He was in my Special Ops unit in the Corps. We've known each other for years." Gillian realized she was babbling nervously and clamped her mouth shut. Now was not the time to explain everything. And why hadn't anyone shut Vlad up? He was still bellowing in an archaic language.

"I can see that," Aleksei said dryly.

"The platoon has got this area sealed off. No one gets in or out. Oh, and the press is filming everything," Daed informed anyone listening. No one had noticed him screaming into his cell phone over the ruckus that had been going on.

"Stop him! You must stop him!" a new, bombastic voice called out.

Everyone stared in surprise as a literal knight in authentic shining armor rode through the multitude and into the middle of the circle on an enormous gray draft horse. He leapt to the ground, drawing a massive two-handed sword from a scabbard slung across his back. In the space of a breath, he reached Dracula and neatly flipped the clay disk out of his hands and onto the hard ground. It shattered into a hundred crumbled pieces. The sword was then pressed against Vlad's throat. When Sweeney and Erzsébet tried to stop him, they were slammed backward by an unseen hand.

"I swear by God above that I will stop you!" the stranger yelled in Vlad's face.

Since everyone was virtually pressed together with no room to maneuver, Gillian handed her rifle to Kimber, drew two of the pistols, then pushed her way through the press of bodies to see what was going on. Aleksei was right on her heels.

"No, Gillian . . ." He put out a hand to stop her, but she brushed him off, still moving forward.

"Aleksei, that new guy . . . He's registering to me as a Vampire. He's very old . . . Master level . . . but not hostile toward us."

"I know, *piccola*. I can sense him and so can everyone else with your abilities or mine." He pushed his way around to stand slightly in front of her. She might not like it, or even notice, but he was going to protect her.

"Well, who the hell is he?"

Before Aleksei could answer her, the new Vampire knight spoke up, loud enough for everyone to hear. "I am Sir Georg Frankenstein. I fought against this monster long ago and have hunted him through the centuries. He made me what I am, and I am bound to kill him before he completes his task."

"You are too late, Georg. It has already begun," Vlad informed him, his crystal green eyes raised to the sky.

Everyone looked up. A pinpoint of light shone down, illuminating Dracula's forehead, then his face, then his body. He looked like he was standing in a Broadway spotlight.

There was no sound of trumpets, no heraldic chorus, just the literal opening of a Gate to whatever dimension or supernatural place that Angels come from. The entire desert was suddenly lit by a blinding flash of light. The less

courageous Vampires and dwellers of the dark shrieked in
terror, expecting to be evaporated.

Gillian was absurdly proud of her friends. Not one of
them flinched, from what she could feel. Her empathy was
on overload, swamping itself with conflicting messages
and responses. She felt flushed, giddy, terrified and secure
all at once.

The arrival of the Elves and this strange knight seemed
to bring a sense of solidarity and strength. He was still
brandishing his sword at Vlad's neck, but he too was looking skyward with the rest of them.

Beings, seemingly made of the light itself, materialized
on the obelisks and pillars around them. They glowed so
brightly that a full view of the mob and landscape was possible. In truth, they were so spectacular, everyone's eyes
welled up from the piercing light and from their sheer
beauty. Tall, aristocratic, noble . . . There weren't enough
words or the right words to describe them.

"You have called us for a less than righteous purpose,
Vlad Dracula, but we are still compelled to answer. Speak,
so that all may know what you desire."

Gillian clapped her hands over her ears, nearly knocking herself out when she forgot she had guns in both hands.
The tone was so pure, so lovely, like heavenly bells. But it
tore through her like a flood. Out of the corner of her eye,
she could see everyone else was cringing and squinting too.
The night was actually cold, but the Beings brought with
them a fragrant, balmy breeze in the wake of their arrival.

"Do not look at them directly, any of you." Osiris's voice
was expansive, his words clearly stated. "It is forbidden to
look upon an Angel's face. Even for an immortal, it would
be devastating."

No one wanted to point out that his advice was unnec-
essary. No one could see shit because the visitors were
glowing like the surface of the sun. Everyone's eyes were
downcast against the glare, and all were covering their ears
in case the Being spoke again. Vlad managed to recover
first.

"Holy Nephilim, it is your blood, your power, which

brought us into your glory. I do not regret the Gift you have given, but I ask why I was left alone with no mentor, no teacher. I might have truly done great deeds, brought the Vampire into the light long before now. Instead I went mad. I committed many foul and unforgivable acts. My very soul is stained with my deeds."

Before anyone could react, he blurred forward, knocking the ancient knight's sword away, grabbing Gillian from Aleksei's side and locking her against him. She struggled but Vlad wrapped his fingers around her neck as Aleksei and Georg started toward him.

"Do not try to take her from me, Rachlav. Get back, Frankenstein! I will crush her throat." Vlad's normally beautiful voice moved into an ominous lower range, setting everyone's teeth on edge.

"She cannot help you." Aleksei's eyes were full of fear and fury. He couldn't remember ever feeling so completely powerless.

"Yes . . . she can." Vlad never moved his hand from Gillian's neck, pulling her backward with him, closer to one of the pillars. "She is my savior, Holy Ones. My redemption and your justice. Take her for your own. She is as pure as I was stained; she is as redeemed as I wish to be. Release me from my acts and exploits. Forgive me all the sins that I have committed while blessed with your power."

"I can't save you, Vlad. Only you can do that." Gillian spoke as loudly as she could against the press of his fingers on her throat. Gingerly, she lowered both of her weapons. Shooting him would only piss him off at this point.

"I am damned! I have already spent part of eternity in hell," he declared with his voice breaking.

Gillian's stomach lurched. Vlad's eyes were wild and unfocused. His whole aura felt brittle . . . disjointed, shattering. He had truly gone over the edge into madness.

"No one is damned for eternity, Vlad, if they truly ask for forgiveness. But you have to forgive yourself as well. Let it go. Let go of all the hate, all the resentment. What happened to you originally wasn't your fault. The actions you took afterward are your responsibility. Justice is served if you admit to what you did, ask forgiveness and make restitution somehow."

Gillian prayed she wasn't being too blunt, but she honestly couldn't think of a single diplomatic thing to say. She knew they were at an impasse. If she couldn't get him to listen, to accept what he needed to do for himself, to get past his egomaniacal intent, he'd surely kill her.

The Nephilim were staying the hell out of this, the giant, glowing light fixtures. She couldn't blame them, and she thought she understood their reasons. They weren't supposed to interfere in the first place, way back at the beginning of time, yet they had . . . And now they were only spectators watching her being nearly strangled in front of them. Prime directive, her ass.

There was no way Aleksei or any of her friends could get to her in time before Vlad broke her neck. Yeah, she was screwed. Unless . . .

"Vlad, listen to me. You have seen past your hatred and your grandiose plans. I'm not an actual virgin. It was just a side effect of a healing we did. That purity you are searching for . . . well, it's not me. You can't put the genie back in the bottle. I wasn't a virgin, and I can't be again. Not officially, anyway.

"I can't redeem you. I can't save you, and unless you let go of me, I can't help you. If you kill me, you will never make it out of here alive and neither will your followers."

She could see Helmut out of the corner of her eye. He was nodding in agreement and motioning with his hands for her to keep talking. Great, because she was rapidly running out of things to say and starting to panic. Vlad's fingers were ever so slightly tighter on her throat.

He looked down at her. "I do not wish to kill you. I am offering you to them as a sacrifice. An even exchange: your soul for mine."

"Believe me, they don't want mine either." She forced a smile up at him. "Good doesn't make deals, Vlad. Only evil makes deals. These Beings are only messengers and observers. Some of them screwed up by Turning you and the others. You may have gotten a bad batch of First Blood, but the bad things you eventually did, you did on your own. You have to accept that and forgive yourself for it before you can make restitution for your actions."

To her surprise, he released her neck and turned her to face him. "You believe this? You believe I can be forgiven? Do you think they will go back to their God and speak for me? Gillian, do you honestly know all that I have done?"

She opened her mouth, but one of the Nephilim spoke first. "She is correct; only evil seeks to make bargains. Those of you who were given the First Gifts—Osiris, Dionysus, Odin, Shiva, Quetzalquatal, yourself . . . there are others—you were given the Gift irresponsibly by a few rogue Rephaim. Those you call Lycanthrope, or Shifter, have the Emim to thank for their existence.

"We, the Anakim, were sent with the Rephaim and the Emim merely to breed. We were to strengthen the Human race so it might coexist more freely with the First People." It seemed to radiate warmth and love toward the assembled Elves, who looked as if they were alternatively resonating joy and disbelief.

The Nephilim continued. "To show them Free Will was a glorious gift to use to their advantage. The Anakim have failed in our efforts, in our one task. We were to monitor breeding. That is all we were to do.

"When we saw what had been done, we returned to our fold, disgraced. The Gift, once given, cannot be taken back, but we had done the unthinkable. We had essentially allowed the evolution of new races to compete with Humans. Free Will was given as a Gift to every sentient creature . . . and so it was abused, even by those you call Angels.

"Some of us were so shamed by their catastrophic interference that they willingly Fell, living out disastrous lives here on Earth, yet continuing to wreak havoc on their own. The damage they have done by Gifting those such as yourself, Vlad Dracula, Erzsébet, Dong Zhuo, Uesugi Kenshin, Ghengis Khan, Attila and many others is incalculable. Some, like you, went mad, but some overcame their madness and rose to great power and stature. Who is to say that they would have achieved so much without our Gifts?"

The glowing Being paused in its speech and looked over the entire crowd. "We cannot grant absolution, salvation or redemption. That is not within our realm of authority. We will not allow nor accept sacrifice. That is forbidden. That is not justice, nor is it just."

Sir Georg spoke up at that point. "This one"—he pointed his sword at Vlad—"wishes a new order to arise. One which will enslave part of God's own children. He has earned his death many times over."

One of the Nephilim pointed a radiant limb toward Vlad, who was facing the pointy end of Sir Georg's sword. Gillian wisely backed away while she had the chance, putting some distance between herself and her patient. "The disk is destroyed, and so must the mechanism be. It is not for you or anyone to abuse the right to call down the Nephilim. What you have done should never have been done.

"Georg Frankenstein, you say you want his death. There are others here who also wish it. Which of you has earned the right to be his executioner? Which of you will sacrifice yourself for vengeance? It is not justice you seek, Knight, but revenge. We cannot and will not kill him, nor will we interfere with your Free Will. That is also forbidden. Who among you will take this life, if it is to be taken?"

Gillian was watching Vlad, who was now absolutely white with terror. Not from Georg's sword at his throat, but from the words the Nephilim was speaking. His megalomaniacal illusions and delusions had just been dashed against some very big rocks. She wanted to kill him herself, in a lot of different ways, but now he was only a patient in crisis, his mind on the verge of truly shattering. His need as a seriously troubled patient overrode her desire to blow his face off.

"I will kill him. I do not answer to a Human concept of God." Trocar's timing was impeccable as always.

"You will answer in your own Halls of Justice, Elf," the Being spoke gently. "He is incapable of defending himself now."

Trocar looked at Gillian, who nodded. "The Angel . . . or whatever it is, is right. Look at him. He's having a psychotic break. You can't kill him like this. That isn't justice, Trocar; that's murder. I can't let you do it. It's dishonorable."

She motioned to Daed, who hurried over with a field medical kit. "He's catatonic. Waxy flexibility . . ." She gingerly reached out, lifted Vlad's unresisting arm and let go. It stayed where she left it. "Can you chemically restrain him?"

"I don't know," Daed admitted. "I've never had to do this for a Vampire before. I don't know what to give him or how he would react to it."

"Well, whatever you give him, it can't kill him. Just make sure you don't give him a stimulant or agitate him, or we're all going to die." She looked around. The crowd was pressing closer to see what was going on with their leader. Diversion time.

She rose and, without directly looking toward the Nephilim's face, spoke up. "He wants his humanity back. He wants to be who he once was."

"That cannot be, Gillian." The Being's voice was gentle but still shook the foundations of the Earth. "He holds the key to his own humanity. He turned his back on the man he was."

"Forgiveness lies within?" she asked, thinking she might already know the answer.

"Forgiveness lies in word, deed and within," was the reply.

"Gillian . . ." Aleksei was standing behind her, but with the massive input of stimulus and shutting her own defenses down, she hadn't felt him.

"Aleksei, I know this is hard for you to understand, but I can't let him be killed like this. He . . ."

". . . is your patient, first and foremost," Aleksei finished for her. He reached over to tuck an errant strand of golden hair behind her ear.

"I'm sorry," was all she could think of to say.

"Do not be," he countered and pulled her against his chest in a tight hug.

"We're not going to blow anyone up?" Kimber sauntered forward.

"Not today, Whitecloud." Gillian grinned at her around Aleksei's flexor muscles.

"I do not forgive!" Sir Georg was apparently a feisty Vampire in any era. "In the name of God, of St. Michael, of St. George, in the name of all you have slaughtered, used, abused and abandoned, I condemn you, Vlad Dracula, to death."

CHAPTER

11

"No, wait!" Gillian shot forward, heedless of Aleksei's and Trocar's attempts to stop her. She stepped in front of Georg as he lifted the massive sword over his head for a killing stroke. With Vlad frozen in place behind her, she lifted both hands in a supplicant gesture to the knight, hoping like hell he would hear her out before bringing the blade down.

Gillian's mind was frantically whirling. Her senses were overblown from the tremendous sense of goodness she felt from the visiting Nephilim, the fury and hatred radiating from Sir Georg, the antagonism from half the crowd, the sheer terror from the other half, Aleksei's love and worry . . . She snapped shut every mental wall she'd ever had.

Now she could think. Closed off inside her own mind, she could filter through what was happening and reason. Georg had an old grudge, a self-righteous one. He was stuck in his own era, like many of the older Vampires, and believed that as a knight he could be judge, jury and executioner.

Vlad had threatened all of them. He had just kidnapped her, kidnapped Tanis soon after she'd arrived in Romania, ordered Tanis's and Aleksei's executions four hundred years ago, sent Jack the Ripper after her after they'd rescued Tanis from London and had been planning for years to create a Vampiric Utopia at the expense of every other creature on the planet. What was she arguing about? Why was she arguing? Why couldn't she just shut up and let events play out, or kill Vlad herself? She had more than enough reason, and no one would blame her.

She sighed. She knew why. Because right now he was helpless and sick, incapable of putting up resistance or objections. In Marine terms, she was about to screw the pooch, but she couldn't watch Georg execute him. It wasn't even a remotely fair fight, and it would be dishonorable.

"I know, better than most, exactly what he's done. But right now he's sick. He needs help. Look at him! What kind of justice allows you to kill him in that condition? He needs to be well enough to answer for his crimes, not slaughtered here because he happens to be helpless and you have the opportunity."

She didn't know why the hell she was arguing for Vlad's life, but there she was. Hooray for impulsivity. The good news was that Sir Georg lowered his sword and his eyes, then backed away.

"He came to use you." Osiris's rich baritone rumbled over her. "He came to force all the Lords into a confrontation, just like this; to cause a literal war between Humans and Paramortals. His intention was to force every Being who is not a Vampire into servitude. He is beyond your help or even the Nephilim's capabilities, Gillian. Why do you argue for his life?"

"Because he . . . If we kill him . . . If we remove him and his threat because he's helpless and it's the easiest thing to do right now . . ." She looked helplessly at Osiris, trying to find the right words. "Then wouldn't we be just like him?"

She realized there was a camera in her face at that point, and shoved its operator away from her with one hand. Sneaky CNN guy.

The Egyptian Lord smiled down at her. "It is a wonderful thing to witness one so young gaining such wisdom. It is even more wonderful to hear that wisdom shared."

"I think I learned that from you, back in Egypt." She grinned up at him.

"I am proud of you, *piccola*, for so many reasons, but most of all because you are absolutely right." Aleksei's eyes were glowing with love and pride.

"Mercy and forgiveness are both divine gifts," the Nephilim spoke again. "Be merciful to one another. Forgive so that you are also forgiven." There was a sudden shard of white energy that blasted down from somewhere and destroyed the Antikythera mechanism at their feet.

"Do not seek to call down the Angels again," it said in parting. All of the Nephilim shimmered, then whisked upward and away, back to where they came from. It was a rather anticlimactic departure from Gill's viewpoint.

Now they had another problem: there were less-than-friendly shouts coming from the assembled crowd now that the Heavenly Hall Monitors had gone. "I've called for a vehicle," Daed said quietly. "We have to get him out of here."

"We have to get *us* out of here." Gillian retrieved her guns and looked around. The mass of people was pressing closer, curious.

"Lord Osiris . . ." Another new voice. Oh boy.

A tall, platinum blond man with piercing sky blue eyes walked through the crowd toward them. He too had what could only be described as a big-ass sword, and was wearing what looked like very primitive garb. As he came closer, Gillian could see that his clothing was very dated. He looked like a Viking, felt like a Vampire . . . or like . . .

"Odin?" Osiris asked before she could.

The blond giant bowed with respect to Osiris and nodded in acknowledgment to the rest of the Lords, Elves, Shifters and Vampires in the inner circle. "I am Odin. I must ask forgiveness myself from my own kind for hiding away in my own lands all this time.

"I thought to keep my flock and my own lands from his grasp. I succeeded, yet by segregating us from the rest of you, by not being visible or engaged, I may have inadvertently helped him succeed in this psychotic plan."

"None of us could have predicted this, my friend," Dionysus said.

"No, no one would have believed such a thing was possible," Osiris added.

"Could we please do this later?" Gillian butted in. "Have you all noticed that we have an angry mob about ten feet away, and that they're not pleased with their spiritual guru going down without a fight?"

"I will be in contact, I give you my word." Odin gave a slight bow, then misted off into the night.

"She is correct. We will assist you in your escape." Mirrin barked a few words in High Elven, and his troops snapped into two perfect lines, opening a path for them through the undulating former followers of Dracula and straight back to the Marine vehicles . . . and the Associated Press, Reuters and CNN vans. Great, just great.

Gillian shot Daed a look that would have melted metal. He shrugged weakly, then scooped an unresisting Vlad up in his arms and headed for the caravan.

"Go, Mellina. We will hold them away from you until you are safe."

"Thanks, Mirrin. I owe you a big one." She hugged her friend in gratitude, grinning at her Elven nickname. "Come back to Romania with us. We all need some comrade-in-arms downtime."

"We shall. Now, go." He shooed her toward Aleksei, who was waiting for her. They hurried off toward the safety of the Marine Corps escort. Due to the recent chain of events, it didn't occur to her or anyone else that Erzsébet, Elizabeta and Sweeney had vanished from the area and were now unaccounted for.

The Elves waited until everyone in Gillian's party had been located and counted off. Some of the Shifters were a little rumpled from tussling with the crowd and keeping them off Gillian, the Vampires and Dracula.

"That was an extremely courageous thing you did, Gillian," a delicate-looking Vampire seated next to Osiris spoke in a voice like silvery bells.

"Isis?" *Great Ganesh, please let me be right.*

The lovely woman affirmed her identity, then introduced Gillian to all the new fanged friends she'd acquired during her stint as a temporary hostage. Instead of using the planes, the Marines were driving them as far away as they could to avoid any entanglements. The press vans were hot on their trail for a few miles, until a strategically placed roadblock let Gill's party through, then stopped the newshounds in their tracks.

Gillian was uncharacteristically snuggled up against Aleksei. He felt warm and safe, and he smelled good. Cardamom and nutmeg, a clean, masculine aroma. She'd missed his scent. Hell, she'd missed him. Her mind turned back to the conversation she'd had with herself on the obelisk. Shit, hell, damn and fuck. She was going to have to have a repeat of that conversation with him sooner or later. He deserved to know how she felt. She could feel the heat rising to her face in anticipation of that little chat.

"Is anything wrong, *carissima*?" Aleksei's voice rubbed through her skull like the finest chinchilla.

"No, I'm just glad this is finally over."

"Then why are you blushing?"

"What? I'm not blushing, you idiot. I'm tired, I'm hungry, I have to pee and I want to go home." Gill shoved at his ribs, but he didn't budge.

"Your face is pink, your blood pressure is rising, you do have to . . . " He stopped before he made an indelicate statement.

"Pee. I have to pee. It's a normal biological function and we're all adults; you can say *pee*, for Crissakes."

Aleksei scooped her up into his lap and nearly squeezed the life out of her in a hug. He threw back his head and laughed harder than he could ever remember laughing in his life. The entire populace of the Hummer joined him. Even the normally stoic Trocar, who was seated on the other side of Gillian, started to chuckle.

"All of you suck." Gillian scowled.

"Some of them more than others," Kimber piped up.

"Shut. Up."

Once the hilarity had died down, everyone settled in for

the ride. The driver, a Human named Corporal Hennessey, assured his passengers that they had arranged for the chopper to meet them farther out, away from the nosy press and any of Vlad's potential hangers-on.

That suited Gillian just fine. The faster they got out of there, the faster she could get her sense of security back. Suddenly, the bouncing, rocking vehicle began to make its presence known to her stomach. She'd been on battleships, in a submarine, in dozens of types of aircraft and countless motor vehicles. Not once had she ever been seasick or experienced motion sickness. Right now, though, she felt positively ill.

"Pull over!" She gasped, clamping a hand over her mouth.

Hennessey complied immediately, bringing the caravan to a dusty, rapid halt. Gill had the door open and was retching by the side of the Hummer before he had the parking brake on. Seconds later, Kimber was next to her, barfing and gagging.

"What's wrong with you?" Kimber managed, with heaving breaths.

"What's wrong with *you*?" Gill countered. "I've had a shitty day and not enough to eat, apparently. The bouncing around in that thing got to me, is all."

"You can't barf around me and not have two sick people. You know that," Kimber groused, leaning against the Hummer and wiping sweat off her forehead.

Daed ran up from the van behind them. "What happened?"

"Where's Vlad?" Gillian looked past him toward the van.

"Drugged and boxed up. I gave him enough medication to stop a charging T. rex, then locked him in one of those Vampire travel cases. He'll keep. Now, what's wrong with you two?"

"Motion sickness." Gill gasped before heaving again.

That set Kimber off and she too was hurling what was left of her stomach contents onto the hard ground. "Fuck off, Daed. We'll be fine in a minute."

They missed Daed's quizzical look at Aleksei, Trocar and Luis, who was huddled in the backseat with Oscar, Osiris and Isis. "She didn't eat anything in the Hummer? Neither of them?" Everyone confirmed that all was well until a few moments ago.

"I have to pee. I'll be right back." Gillian staggered toward the darkness and out of the glare of the vehicular light sources.

"I'm coming too," Kimber wheezed, wobbling off after Gillian.

"This isn't a sorority. I can go by myself!" Gill's voice carried back to the Hummer in the night.

"I have to go too, you dumbshit!" Kimber yelled back.

"Well, go over there!"

"What if there are cobras and shit over there?"

"What makes you think they won't be over here too?"

"Because there are two of us; that's why. It's a rule: snakes can't bite you in the ass if there are two of you."

"Oh, for hell's sake, Kimber, shut up!"

"Shut up? Don't tell me to shut up. I'm not going to shut up because snakes and scorpions and shit don't like noise. I watch the Discovery Channel too, you know. They say to make noise while you're walking because it will drive the snakes away, and you're telling me to shut up. What's wrong with you?"

"I hope you barf on a cobra!" Gill's stomach took over again and she dry heaved onto the barren ground.

———◆———

Aleksei wrenched his focus off Gillian for a moment to give her some privacy. Out of the blue it occurred to him that Daed was a doctor. "What is wrong with her . . . them?"

Daed looked up at Aleksei's icy gray eyes. "It probably is just motion sickness compounded by stress. Gillian was hostage to a psychopath, and Kimber's her best friend. I'm sure a lot of it is about anxiety. I'll look over them both when we get back to the Institute to be certain. I'm sure it's nothing serious."

"What is wrong with Kimber?" Pavel ran up from one of the other transports.

"Daed says it is motion sickness," Aleksei told him.

"It's been a long day for everyone and I know she hasn't eaten today." Daed smiled and patted the Wolf's arm.

When the women came back, they were still arguing amiably, but were arm in arm, supporting each other to the Hummer. "Look, call the helicopter. I am not getting back in the amusement park ride again. My stomach can't take it," Gillian ordered Hennessey.

"Yes, ma'am." He complied and radioed for the chopper.

Soon they were all settled in on the Huey. Daed had had the foresight to order extra shielded shipping crates in case there was a larger rescue of post-Dracula Vampires. Osiris's and Dionysus's Vampires were loaded up for the brief trip to Cairo. Osiris had plenty of people to meet them there and escort them safely back to his headquarters. Dionysus would stay in Egypt for a brief visit, then take his crew back to Greece where Maeti awaited him. The Shifters didn't need shielding, but sat in the back with their respective Lords.

There was a brief argument over what to do with Dracula. It was getting to be very early in the morning. The sun was still hours away, but no one wanted to leave that particular detail unattended. Osiris offered to take him. He thought an infusion of his own blood might bring their former enemy out of his present unresponsive state and might actually heal some of the damage done when his mind overloaded. Once his mind was intact again, they could decide what to do with him.

Gillian wanted to secure him somewhere other than right under the Egyptian Lord's feet, or, for that matter, under hers. "We have an Interpol agent at the Institute. He's more than capable of making arrangements for Vlad's confinement and care."

"Where would we send him, Schatzi?" Helmut asked her, gently. "In the brief history of our profession, we have never had a Vampire, or any other Paramortal, for that matter, with this type of complete psychotic break. Who will treat him? The foremost experts in the field are us and our staff at Rachlav Institute. We have no place to keep him, no known way to reverse the process. There are no books or reference materials for this."

"Helmut's right, pumpkin. Osiris is probably the best bet for helping him recover," Daed said.

"Stop calling me that," Gill snapped at him, then relented. "All right, fine. You win. You're probably right. There's nothing I could do to help him the way he is now."

Aleksei suppressed a sigh of relief. He didn't want Vlad lodged at the castle, no matter what the circumstances. He understood Gillian's dedication to her patient and her concern, but was glad when the others made it clear that Vlad's best hope for recovery was with their most powerful: Osiris. She knew that Osiris would take his responsibility seriously and was honorable enough to trust with her charge.

"If I didn't believe that Vlad would be in the best possible place, I would not try to talk you into this. Osiris really is his best chance for recovery, based on what we know." Helmut hugged her with one arm.

"I understand that. I just don't like feeling as though I'm taking the easy route by letting him go there," Gill grumbled.

"He needs more help than we can give or know how to give," Daed assured her again.

"Let's just go home."

Daed gave the order and the powerful rotors of the chopper started up. Soon they were airborne, on their way back to the familiar sights, smells and environment they all loved. Daed briefed Gillian on the situation with the newly vocal factions who didn't approve of her or the Institute. He switched on a laptop, pulled up CNN's website and played a video of the coverage in Akabat.

A tall, darkly handsome Vampire in a priest's frock was one of the people interviewed. "Gillian Key has jeopardized all of us with this rash act! She has opened a literal door to the Heavens, yet instead of asking for the redemption of our kind, she bargained for the soul of one man: her lover, Vlad Dracula!

"We cannot let this dereliction of her duty as a psychologist or a soldier stand! We will oppose her and her kind until people listen to reason! Vampires and Humans do not belong together! I am living proof of the seductive power they wield. I have been a tireless crusader against the creatures that made me. I offer absolution to those who will renounce their evil and Face The Sun. Redemption is possible! Retribution is at hand!"

Daed switched the broadcast off. "That is Father Bartholomew Daily. He is someone we will definitely have to contend with at some point in time."

"Fabulous. Right now I want dinner and a hot bath, and to sleep for several days." Gillian rubbed her forehead. The headache that had been threatening during the video clip was moving in full force.

"Soon, *cara mia*." Aleksei kissed her head and smoothed her hair. "We will be home soon and you shall have whatever you desire."

"Aleksei, you do know Vlad is just another patient to me, right?"

"I know, *piccola*. Believe me, I know."

"Good." She leaned her head against his hard chest and let him stroke her hair, taking the tension of the headache away.

CHAPTER
12

THE USMC platoon flew back to Romania with them.
They were under orders to stay in the vicinity of the Rachlav Institute, so they bivouacked in the village and were
having a hell of a time.

Esi, the coffee shop owner, was beside herself making
beverages and beignets for the lot and yelling at them to
pick up after themselves. She threw more than one dish
towel at more than one Marine, and banged more than one
head with her coffeepot. Samuel, happy and content at her
side, was in seventh heaven helping out his lady love in
her shop and fielding friendly ribald comments from the
platoon.

All things considered, the soldiers were a respectful,
well-behaved group. They had their fun, told their jokes,
but were spot on time for their duty watches, and showed
the village they were solid professionals who were the
best people for the job. After a night or two, Sacele took
them into its rhythm and they became part of the extended
family.

Gillian was actually happy to have them there. Cezar's
Wolves were on duty, as were the Vampire Watch Group
that Teo was in charge of. Aleksei had been impressed

that the younger Vampire had kept his word and brought a good-sized group of Rachlav loyal Vampires to Akabat. They'd gotten into an altercation or two, but hadn't drawn undue attention to themselves even though they'd won the fight. He'd done Aleksei proud. Still, it felt familiar to her, having the mixed bag of USMCs striding around town day and night. It reminded her of her own tour of duty and it felt good.

She had wound up with a crappy sunburn, despite the aloe vera application in Akabat. Daed assured her the nausea, dizziness and general shit-tastic feeling were likely due to dehydration and overexposing her fair complexion to the desert sun for so long.

Since she felt better within two days of returning to Romania and the sunburn faded into a healthy glow, she was inclined to agree with him. Cassiopeia was delighted to have her friend back, and spent time reading and watching over Gillian in a motherly fashion, shooing Aleksei out so Gill could rest.

Kimber, on the other hand, felt lousy. In view of the fact that she hadn't been a virgin-sacrifice hostage who was out in the sun for hours, Daed chalked it up to her picking up a stomach bug and prescribed bed rest and clear liquids. Pavel delighted in making her homemade chicken soup and spoon-feeding it to her. Kimber gave up arguing with him and let him dote.

Aleksei let Gillian have her time to rest and rejuvenate. He was anxious to have some quiet time alone to talk with her, but she was frazzled about the situation with Father Daily. Her patient Chester was also driving everyone in the castle nuts.

Galahad spent several hours with her, Helmut, Cassiopeia and Daed, catching them up on Chester's latest activities and outbursts. The four of them put their heads together and came up with what seemed like a workable treatment plan for him, and Daed finished researching a medication regime they all prayed would stabilize his mercurial moods.

Father Daily wasn't the only vocal dissenter getting face

time on television. There were a number of others who had taken up the banner and were parroting back what he had already stated: Gillian had been doing the horizontal mambo with the Devil himself and had missed out on an opportunity to put an end to bloodsuckers forever.

That pissed her off more than anything. Gillian was like most women: Accuse her of something she actually did and she'd deal with it. Lie about her, especially on international television, and you were bound to find out where the expression "hell hath no fury like a woman scorned" came from. After a few days of being greeted with Father Daily's face every time she turned on network news, she'd had enough.

"All right. That's it. Daed! Get some of your buddies from the BBC out here. I'm doing an interview." She stomped off to write up some notes. Brownies scampered after her, bringing her a fresh ashtray, tea and their delightful little sandwiches.

"Do you think that is wise?" Aleksei asked their resident psychiatrist/Minotaur.

"You want to try and talk her out of it?" Daed's raised eyebrows convinced Aleksei that he should really let someone else handle that conversation.

"No . . . I think I will go find something to paint."

"Gillian is right. You are a smart Vampire."

———◆———

Gillian put together a scathing but polite rebuttal that would have made a diplomatic attaché proud. She met the news crew at the front gate. Evidently her reputation for having a low tolerance level for bullshit had preceded her. Instead of sending a second-stringer who might have said the wrong thing and gotten a light meter broken over his head, they sent her Arthur Kent, formerly known as the Scud Stud. He was completely professional and sympathetic to her situation, and he had done his homework. The interview took more than two hours, but he promised to show her the result before it aired later that evening.

True to his word, Arthur had Gillian look over the taping

and got her okay to air it. Ten minutes later, they had a special news bulletin go out: "Arthur Kent's exclusive interview with Dr. Gillian Key. Forgiveness, Faith and Sacrifice, after these messages."

He had taken their entire interview and boiled it down to just three specific questions: "Dr. Key, the rumor mill is apparently working overtime with you and your colleagues these days. Is it true that Vlad Dracula is a patient of yours and that you were also lovers?"

"Please, call me Gillian. I cannot confirm or deny anyone as being my patient or not. To do so would be a breach of confidentiality and privacy. I also will not comment on my personal life for the same reason. Next question."

"Very well, Gillian . . . Is it true that you accompanied Vlad Dracula to Akabat in hopes of making contact with . . . Angels?"

"That part is partially true. He had an idea that he had extensively researched and wanted to try an experiment. As you gathered, it was successful. However, the Beings were not actually Angels but rather Nephilim. They gave us specific information, which I'm certain you or one of your colleagues caught on tape.

"He was after the same information Father Daily claims to know. As you can tell, if you review that unedited tape sequence, you will hear straight from the horse's mouth, as it were, that Father Daily has it completely *wrong*. We are all responsible for our own forgiveness. We are all called upon to be merciful to each other. I think that speaks to every race or type of Being on the planet. If we're going to coexist, we have to learn to work together."

"Do you really believe that Humans and Vampires can coexist without serious problems?"

"I do, Arthur, for two reasons. First, the highest courts of our world and the Paramortals' world all agreed that we are all sentient and equal Beings. The Paramortals have always been among us, they were simply never treated as people with real feelings, needs or desires before. The Compact changed that; the Osiris Doctrine took it a few steps further and laid out some specific expected behaviors and repercussions.

"There will always be pot stirrers on both sides of the fence. These sorts of people live for the attention they receive. It's much like a schoolyard bully. They can't get along with people in a normal manner, so they act out and get the attention they're craving. It's just not always the right kind of attention. The world will always have Father Dailys and those like him, Arthur. I simply thank the Gods that there will also be Vampire Lords like Aleksei Rachlav, Osiris, Dionysus and Odin; Elves such as Prince Mirrin and his Kin; Lycanthropes like Cezar and his pack; representatives of the Fey like Lord Dalton and Lord Finian; and the Brownies . . . in fact, all the Courts of the Fey, all of whom absolutely disprove those arguments simply by being the honorable Beings they are."

"I'm sure everyone will agree that it is awfully lucky to have individuals like yourself and your team: Dr. Gerhardt, Dr. Aristophanes, Dr. Delphi and all the rest you mentioned on our side. Everyone I have personally spoken with in Romania or connected with the Rachlav Institute itself seems to be an individual case in point of remarkable coexistence."

"Thank you, Arthur. That truly means a great deal to all of us."

"Thank you for your time, Gillian. Well, you have heard it directly from the lady herself, and I use that term with all the positive connotations it is meant to have.

"It seems that the generators of prejudice, bigotry and intolerance will always be around. Thank heaven there are those like Dr. Key and her team, who are demonstrating that it is possible to overcome those barriers as well, making the world a better place for all of us. This is Arthur Kent reporting for the BBC. Good night."

The interview was a success. The switchboard at the network was lit up like Times Square for several days after her spot was aired. They ran it again, every half hour, for the next three days, as a lead story. Father Daily's rant was edged out, and more proponents of Gill and her group came forward with positive *atta-girl* statements.

The Brownies were absolutely ecstatic about being

mentioned specifically in Gillian's interview. They went on a mad cleaning and cooking spree, making the castle, guesthouse, grounds and village into a Disney-esque portrait of beauty, tranquility and amazing food.

The IPPA and the USMC issued their own pro-Gillian announcements, backing her 100 percent in all her endeavors and coining the phrase "Paranormal Partners for Peaceful Coexistence" as their tagline. They had never doubted her intent or her skill. No one had anticipated the level of shit that was stirred up by Father Daily and his offshoot cronies. This was just damage control, but they were happy to do it.

Aleksei finally cornered Gillian long enough to take her hand and, with every ounce of genteel decorum, ask her for a date. Gill stared at him for a minute, then got his meaning perfectly clear. She opened her mind just a crack to let him know that all was well and he was definitely her number-one guy.

"Sure thing, hot stuff . . . What should I wear? Or are you going to be ripping it off the first chance you get?"

Aleksei actually blushed, then laughed uproariously. "Not at the first chance, certainly, but do not wear anything you are terribly fond of."

Now it was Gillian's turn to blush. The white-hot heat radiating from his eyes was enough to turn her legs to Jell-O and other parts of her to liquid.

"I have made dinner arrangements in Radu's restaurant. I understand you are particularly fond of the steak there."

"I love his steak! Goddess above, I wish you could still eat food, Aleksei. I don't know what he does to it, but it is amazing."

"I am glad you approve of my choice." He smiled down at her. His little powerhouse of a woman. Well, she wasn't his yet, but soon, with any luck . . .

"Of course I do. You always have impeccable taste."

He leaned down and brushed a kiss against her neck. "So do you, *bellissima* . . . so do you."

"I have to go." She pushed him away and ran up the stairs, blushing again. Dammit, how did he do that? He made her feel like a virgin . . . Oh wait. She skidded into her room and shut the door, slid down it and laughed herself silly.

Later, after a shower and some primping, she was ready for her night on the town with her favorite Vampire. It was after eight, but even with dinner they would have plenty of time to progress to other activities if they chose. Gillian checked herself a final time in the full-length mirror.

Hair, check . . . makeup, check . . . clothes, yup. Car keys, cell phone, purse, gun . . . oops. She wasn't planning on shooting anyone tonight, so she removed her Glock from her clutch and started to lay it on the bedside table, then put it back in her bag. She still felt naked going around without at least one weapon on her. Her back-sheathed dagger was out. It wouldn't do to get a spinal injury if Aleksei got a little overenthusiastic. The gun and her little cleavage dagger went with her. Hopefully she wouldn't have to use them.

She made it downstairs to find Aleksei talking with Cass, Trocar and Helmut. Daed was thankfully elsewhere. She didn't need his twisted brand of Southern humor tonight. Just looking at Aleksei sent warm tingles through her central nervous system. He looked stunning in black velvet pants that were laced both up the outer sides and in the groin. His matching jacket was cut in a bolero style, accentuating his lean hips and perfectly flat stomach. They were so tight they left very little to the imagination, but she didn't care.

His shirt was an amazing silvery blue silk, with a flat front and pearl buttons, open at the neck, which brought a glow to his skin, and gave a hint of blue cast to his eyes when he raised them to meet hers. His hair fell in its usual thick, black waves past his shoulders. Yeah, he made her mouth water.

The smile he gave her was for her, and her alone. Gillian couldn't remember who else was in the room when she experienced the full force of that smile. It wasn't Vampire foo; it was just him.

Aleksei looked her up and down appreciatively. She'd left her hair down from its usual French braid and it spilled in golden waves over her shoulders and chest. He didn't know where she'd found her outfit, but he made a mental note to tell her that brown was definitely her color. The dress was one she'd had stashed away for ages, bought but never worn. She'd been saving it for a special occasion, and this was about as special as they came.

The dress was a nutmeg brown silk blend with long sleeves, a deep décolletage and an appropriately short skirt. Three gold buttons held the shirred waistband together and matched the ones on her cuffs. Her legs were bare and lightly tanned, from what he could see of them. The lower halves of her legs were covered in brown suede flat-soled boots that looked painted on. She looked like a dryad; delicate, sweet and oh so very alluring.

He walked to her without a word, bent and brushed a kiss across her shell pink mouth. "Breathtaking, Gillian. Simply breathtaking."

She blushed again at his appraisal, and muttered, "Thank you."

Tucking her hand under his arm, he escorted them from then hall and into the Transylvanian night. It was cool, clear and vibrant outside. Gillian felt invigorated by the fresh, crisp air, and very proud to be accompanied by such a stunning date.

"You look really handsome tonight, Aleksei."

"Thank you, *dolcezza*. I am glad you approve."

As they got to the parking lot, he waited until she unlocked the Opel and then opened her door for her. Once she was seated, he walked around to the passenger side.

"We are quite the gentleman tonight," Gillian teased him.

"I would always treat you that way, if you would let me." He grinned back at her.

It was a short drive to the village, but they were much more relaxed with each other by the time they arrived. Over dinner, Gillian told him a few stories of her adventures with the Marines. The topic had come up because several of her comrades were off duty and in the bar, and they saluted and toasted her as she and Aleksei came in. He was intrigued by her tales, amused by her animated recounting of several near disasters in the field and altogether charmed by her company.

On Gillian's part, she realized she felt more comfortable with him than she had with anyone else in a long time. Kimber, Helmut, Trocar, Daed and Luis didn't count. They were family to her and she'd known them for eons. Aleksei was still relatively new to her circle, but she had no qualms about sharing more than just a few bits and pieces of her life with him.

"You told me about your family, but I still do not know where you grew up," Aleksei prompted her while she was munching on a bite of Radu's superb steak.

"Well . . . I grew up in northeastern Oklahoma. We had some land, a few horses, like I told you. I went to school, to college and enlisted in the Marines from there."

"Is it a nice area?"

"It's gorgeous. There's the prairie, the foothills of the Ozark Mountains; out West there are plateaus and desert; down in the Southeast, there's swamp. It's everything really, in one state."

"Do you miss it?"

She looked up at him and thought about it. "No, not really. I love the countryside; in fact, I love the whole area—cities too. Oklahoma people are the nicest you'll ever meet anywhere. I had a lot of friends. I just had a not-so-close family, like I told you already."

"Are you still in contact with them?" His question took her off guard.

"Like . . . do we send holiday cards and stuff like that? Yeah, we e-mail a little bit. As you know, I haven't been anywhere except here for the past few years, so no, we're not close and we don't have big happy Rockwell-type family get-togethers."

"I apologize, Gillian. I did not mean to bring up bad thoughts or memories."

She realized she'd sounded a little harsher than she'd

intended, so she smiled and squeezed his hand. "It's fine. You didn't know."

He relaxed under her grip. Either he was imagining things or she was getting less reactionary about her personal life. A year ago she would have bitten his head off if he'd asked her about herself. Interesting. Very interesting.

"I feel really badly eating in front of you, you know," she laughed.

"Please do not worry about it. I have no desire or craving for food. I enjoy watching you take pleasure in your meal. It is enough that we actually have time alone together."

"Thanks, Aleksei. I'm having a good time with you too."

After dinner, he gave her directions out of the village, away from the castle. They drove for about ten minutes, then he pointed out a turnoff into the forest. It was a dirt-and-gravel road leading up the side of a mountain. The only illumination was from the headlights on the car. They drove in relative silence, with Gillian's commentary on the lunar landscape of the road they were driving on and Aleksei chuckling over her swearing and griping.

There was another turnoff and another dirt road, this one even more rustic than the first. It curved around the mountain to the right, then leveled off. In the glare of the headlights, Gillian could make out an absolutely lovely log cabin.

"This? This is it?" She was all smiles as they pulled up and she hopped out of the car.

Aleksei's long legs took him quickly to the door. He opened it with a key, then flipped on the light, making an inviting golden glow for them to walk into. He went back to take Gillian's hand and lead her into his surprise.

"Oh . . . wow. Aleksei, it's beautiful." She meant it; it was stunning.

Unlike the little guesthouse she'd stayed in long ago, this cabin really was a cabin. The walls were burnished logs, set together with perfectly spaced and level mortar. A stone fireplace filled one corner. The huge prow front windows were hung with traditional Romanian-design curtains. He showed her the fully stocked kitchen and open dining area. A whimsical loft with a sitting area, plate glass windows and another bathroom were up a flight of stairs. The furniture was rustic, solid, charming old-world pieces. All of it was antique and in perfect condition.

He led her off to the side of the living room, showing her where yet another bathroom, the extra bedrooms and finally the master suite were in the open floor plan. The cabin hadn't looked that large from the outside. Inside, however, Gillian was mentally totaling up the square footage, and it had to be over three thousand square feet.

"This is the first home my father built for my mother," Aleksei told her. "I had it remodeled a little to hopefully reflect a more modern style. He wrapped his arms around her as she took in the master bedroom. The log walls were strategically interspersed with drywall to allow for a soft cream-colored paint, while the furniture and bed were golden oak, decorated in soft peach and golden yellow hues. Despite the lack of windows, the entire room seemed suffused with light. She was betting the bedspread was real honest-to-God damask silk. The bare floor was wooden and had several reindeer pelts and bearskins strategically placed on it. It was a perfect blend of luxurious rustic décor.

The full bath carried the light-colored theme from the bedroom. There was a shower, a tub with a spa system, a toilet concealed behind another door and a white marble countertop with a clear glass bowl for the sink. The entire place looked like it was straight out of *Architectural Digest*.

CHAPTER

13

"HOLY shit, Aleksei. When the hell did you have time to pull this off?" She stared at him.

"I've been wanting to redecorate it for a long time." He smiled down at her. "This used to be a place I came to so I could be alone with my thoughts. There are paintings in the middle bedroom, from the time I spent up here. Finally, I decided that I would like to eventually share this with you, so I hired a decorator and architect, gave them a free hand, and this is what they came up with."

"Well, it's beautiful." Gillian pulled away and wandered around the room. "I love the colors in here."

"I am very glad." He settled into a large wing-backed chair to watch her as she moved around the room.

Gillian was admiring one of the gorgeous Egyptian-themed paintings on the wall. Her eyes widened when she saw *A. Rachlav* in the lower left-hand corner. Aleksei had painted this. She'd seen only this painting and the painting he'd done of her that hung in the hallway of the castle, but based on her limited knowledge of art, she had to admit he was extremely talented.

She stiffened, remembering her promise to herself. Deliberately, she put her purse on a chair, then turned back to where he sat waiting across the room. He was staring at her, so she dropped her eyes to avoid another blush.

"Aleksei . . . I had some time to think while I was in Akabat, before you got there."

He frowned a little. Her demeanor had completely changed from open and warm to very guarded. What was on her mind to make her shut down so quickly?

"Yes, *cara*? Tell me."

She looked up at him, this time meeting his gaze squarely, and walked to where he sat. To his utter amazement, she knelt at his feet and took his hand in both of her smaller ones.

"What I thought about was you. I thought about all the things we've been through together, about how our relationship just evolved naturally to where it is now. I know I tend to overanalyze things, but that's not what I was doing. I was really looking inside myself. I wanted to know what was holding me back."

He reached out his other hand and stroked his knuckles down the side of her cheek, then cupped her chin. "Holding you back from what?" His voice was almost a whisper.

She shivered at his touch, but didn't falter. "From loving you the way you say you love me."

"Oh, Gillian . . ." He started to lean forward to kiss her, but she stopped him with a hand on his chest.

"No, let me say this or I might chicken out again. I realized I had no reason not to trust you. You've been there for me. You've put your faith in me. Even when it went against your nature, you trusted me and let me do what I had to do . . . with a minimum of bitching." She grinned at him and he returned her smile.

"All this time, you let me be who I am and didn't push me for more than I was ready to give you. That means a lot to me, Aleksei. You don't know how much.

"I realized that none of this experience was painful, scary or restricting. I wasn't feeling anything but happy, warm and safe when I was with you. I realized . . . that I do love you. I guess I have for a while but was too stubborn to let myself know it."

Aleksei let out the breath he didn't realize he was holding. He wanted to scoop her up and spin her around the room. He wanted to laugh, cry . . . make love to her and return her declaration with his own. Instead he kept his mouth shut and let her finish.

"I love you, Aleksei. I know you love me; you've told me a dozen times. I just wanted you to know that I love you back."

Her clear green eyes were shining and not with tears. The smile she gave him was from the bottom of her chickenshit little heart. He couldn't stand it anymore; he gathered her up and lifted her to him.

"That was the best gift you could have ever given me, Gillian." His voice was low and sensual. "I love you and I am not going to let you out of this cabin until I have shown you, over and over again."

His mouth closed on hers with a singular purpose. When she opened to receive his kiss, she felt his love, his passion and his need pour through her. There was no more discussion as he tenderly laid her on the bed, disarmed her, then undressed her small form.

When Gill tried to help him with his clothes, he stopped her, removing his own clothing, piece by piece, never taking his eyes off her as she reclined against the pillows. The supple mouth tissue holding his hidden fangs snapped them down into place as his groin filled with longing for her. For a Vampire, sex and blood were closely bound as exciting stimuli. Sexual excitement or blood anticipation meant fangs were involved whether the Vampire intended to combine the two activities or not. Aleksei definitely intended to combine the two if she was willing. Gillian's appreciative gaze beckoned him like a magnet as he impatiently shed the remainder of his clothing.

Both of them completely forgot about her present state of being. When he moved over her, she opened to him automatically, wrapping her arms and legs around him and pulling him in tightly. It was the gesture of one familiar lover to another when trust and love have already been established. His first thrust brought them both back to reality instantly.

He felt her forgotten barrier give, then he was seated inside her. Gillian felt a sharp, brief pain, then a deep, stinging fulfillment as he came to rest against her cervix.

"*Dios mio!* Dear God, Gillian, I am sorry!" Aleksei was horrified that he might have hurt her.

"Don't be," she gasped up at him. "I'm fine. Just don't stop."

She pulled his mouth down to hers and deliberately nicked her tongue across his razor-sharp canine. The blood hit his tongue and drove him into a near frenzy. He forgot about the near mistake. It had been so long without her. All the worry he had gone through, all the need he had suppressed, all the love he had held at bay . . . None of it mattered. The only thing he could think of was the woman beneath him who loved him for what he was and what they could be together.

As they strained together, he raised his head, looking into the perfect Nile green eyes he loved. Gillian saw the question there, and nodded. The dark head dipped down, nuzzling her hair out of the way. In perfect timing with a thrust from his hips, his teeth penetrated her neck. Gill bucked beneath him. The sheer pleasure from the dual entry nearly caused her to black out.

Aleksei moaned against her throat. Her blood was like no other. The taste of her in his mouth, the feeling she was producing as his perfect sheath, was overwhelming. He opened his mind to her and found a welcoming touch in return. In that moment, they each gave everything they had to the other. Trust, love and the sheer pleasure from the act they were sharing brought them both to a shattering release. He poured into her as she poured into his mouth. He stopped before he took too much blood, but she pulled him in deeper, milking him and locking him as tightly as she could against her core.

"I love you," she said breathlessly, and immediately regretted her Marilyn Monroe vocal inflection.

"I love you too, *cara*. With all my heart." He opened a tiny cut in his own throat, then pressed her willing mouth against it. His mind took over, making it pleasurable and fulfilling for her. The pulsing suction of her lips on his throat brought him fully erect again. He stopped her, closed the small wound, then kissed the blood off her mouth. This time he made love to her slowly, deliberately. Every touch, every stroke, every glance and every kiss were seared into her memory and into his.

When they lay panting and sweaty in each other's arms for the second time, he whispered sweet nothings in her ear in Romanian and Italian while he stroked her hair and face. She didn't care what he said, as long as he kept talking. Finally, exhausted but relieved, they both slept.

Gillian woke hours later with an intense need to empty her bladder. Aleksei was dead to the world, and would be until dusk. Since there were no windows in the room and the door was shut to any outside light, she didn't worry about his aboveground safety. Hopping out of bed, she headed for the bathroom. Dizziness hit her on her way there, had her grabbing for a wall. They just might have gotten a little carried away with the blood exchange. She smiled at the recent memory. It didn't matter. The blood exchange was a rare thing between them. Aleksei didn't want to make her into anything she didn't want to be, and Gill enjoyed being Human. She wouldn't mention it to him or he'd be filled with self-recriminations for weeks.

After she'd relieved herself and washed her hands, she padded naked into the kitchen to find something to eat. Looking in the refrigerator, she realized he had been paying attention for longer than she had believed. Everything she loved to eat and drink was in there. She made herself a light meal, then lay down again on the living room couch to rest, wrapping herself in a soft handmade quilt draped over the couch back. He'd really outdone himself last night. She was still wiped out.

When she woke again, it wasn't for her bladder's benefit. She felt crappy, nauseous and out of sorts. Shit. Kimber had probably passed on whatever stomach flu she had to Gill. Lovely. She'd see if Daed could bring something to the cabin for her. Driving down to the castle would definitely not be a good idea right now.

She retrieved her phone from her purse and dialed Daed's cell. "Hey, Daed?"

"Hello, pumpkin. Have a good date?"

"Stop calling me that. Yes, it was a good date. Aleksei brought us to this cabin down the road and up the mountain. I feel really shitty, though."

"What's wrong?" Daed was suddenly all doctor.

"Well, for starters, I'm really tired, I'm dizzy when I get up too fast . . ."

"Did he take too much blood?" He wasn't being funny or intrusive; it was a legitimate question, so she bit back a sharp retort.

"No, he is really careful about that. I just feel rotten. I ate, but I still feel nauseated."

"Any vomiting? Diarrhea?"

"No and no. Just sort of an off feeling. Can you run something up to me? Like something for nausea or a B12 shot? Aleksei worked really hard to make this special, and I don't want to screw it up by barfing on the furniture."

There was silence for a minute and Gillian thought the call had been dropped. "Tell you what. I'll be up in a few minutes. I'm assuming someone knows how to get where you are. I'll bring my bag and we'll take a look at you."

"How's Kimber?"

"She's still under the weather as well. I'm going to run some tests on both of you and see what's going on."

"Okay, thanks, Daed."

"See you soon." He hung up and Gill lay back on the couch.

Dammit. This was not the time to get sick. She couldn't remember the last time she'd had the flu. Generally she had an iron constitution and didn't have to worry about trivial things like viruses and colds.

She curled up on the couch under her quilt and a comforter she located in the guest bedroom closet and went back to sleep. Daed found her there when he arrived some twenty minutes later. She didn't look pale, or flushed, for that matter.

He woke her gently. "Gill? Honey, sit up and let's look you over."

About that time Gillian remembered that she was stark naked under the covers. "Um . . . I'm not dressed."

"I'm a doctor, remember? I've seen it. If you're squeamish, keep the ta-tas covered." He rummaged through his bag and took out a length of tubing and a syringe while Gill tucked the quilt around herself like a bath towel.

"What the hell is that for?" She eyed the apparatus in his hands.

"I'm going to take some blood and run it along with Kimber's down to the lab at the police station. They've got a good enough setup for me to test this and see what kind of bug you two have contracted."

"Well, shit, Daed. What do you think it is?"

"Probably just a weird flu strain. You've been under stress for a long time, you were just kidnapped and we had the meeting with pseudo-Angels. I'm guessing that you and our lovely Count have come to some understanding—all of those are stressors, and after extended periods of time, it can run hell over your immune system. I just want to be sure."

"Fine." She stuck out her arm for him.

After he drew a vial of her blood, he took her temperature, blood pressure and a urine sample and prodded her appendix. Gillian was getting supremely tired of it by the time he was done.

"All right, I'm going to run these down to town. Stay lying down if you can. If you have to eat, you know the drill."

"Clear liquids, nothing fancy and rest," Gill said firmly.

"You've got it. See you later."

As soon as he left, Gillian was curled back up under the cover. She could go back and sleep next to Aleksei, or at least get dressed, but she didn't want to go through the trouble. The couch was so comfortable and she was just so tired. Maybe after a while she'd call Kimber so they could share moral support.

Much later in the day, Aleksei awoke. He had a brief, overwhelming panicky moment when he couldn't find Gillian right away. After he located her on the couch and saw that she was still asleep, he got dressed, then popped out of the cabin to find a donor.

When Gillian woke, she got herself something to drink and felt well enough to get dressed. Aleksei had thought of everything. She found an armoire with soft, comfy loungy-type clothing just for her. She slipped into a dove gray brushed-cotton tunic and some matching pants. She noticed Aleksei's absence and figured that he'd gone out for a bite.

Where the hell was Daed? She checked the time. He'd had plenty of time to get to Sacele and back. There was some soda in the fridge so she fixed herself a drink and went outside for a smoke. Shortly thereafter, she heard a car coming up the drive.

Daed, Kimber, Pavel, Helmut and Trocar piled out. Kimber looked a little wobbly, so Pavel scooped her up and carried her inside. Daed glared at her. "Put that thing out, will you? The nicotine is not going to help right now. Where's Aleksei?"

"He stepped out for a bite . . . er . . . a minute. Just tell me what's wrong with me."

"I will, as soon as Aleksei gets back."

"What the hell does Aleksei have to do with it?"

"Gill, don't argue. This is something everyone needs to hear at the same time." Daed brushed past her and went into the cabin.

"Helmut? Trocar? What's going on?"

"I don't know, but I'm sure Daed will enlighten us shortly." Helmut shook his head and went inside.

"We do not know, Petal. Daed asked us all to come." Trocar looked at her gravely, squeezed her shoulder and then went inside too.

Aleksei misted in about that time and swept Gillian up in a bear hug. "I missed you."

She giggled and snuggled against him. "I missed you too."

"We have company?"

"Yup. Daed ran some tests on me and Kimber while you were asleep. He's back with the gang to tell us what's going on."

Aleksei's happiness immediately turned to concern. "What kind of tests?"

"Blood tests, pee, you know, a full physical, basically."

"Did I hurt you last night?" His lovely platinum eyes were full of apprehension as he set her on her feet and looked her up and down.

"No, of course you didn't. I think Kimber and I are just passing a stomach bug back and forth. Let's go in."

Wordlessly he followed her inside, nodding a greeting to the others. His throat was so tight he doubted if he could speak anyway. If anything happened to her . . .

"You both had better sit down," Daed instructed them. "Kimber, Pavel, you as well." The tone in his voice was completely serious, without the usual lighthearted banter.

Gill and Kimber looked at each other, then at Aleksei and Pavel. Unconsciously, Gillian reached for Aleksei's hand. He took it, led her to the couch, then seated himself on the arm rest next to her. Pavel picked Kimber up and plunked her in his lap.

"Well?" Gillian asked. She couldn't stand the suspense.

Daed looked at her. "You're pregnant."

"What?"

"You heard me. You're pregnant." He wasn't smiling.

Kimber snorted from her vantage point on Pavel's lap.

"Don't you laugh either, missy. You're knocked up as well." Daed still wasn't smiling.

"There has to be some mistake . . ." Gill tried to wrap her mind around what he'd just said, while arguing him out of it.

"No mistake. The lab here wasn't sufficient to run all the tests so I drove everything to Brasov. They've got a hospital there, so I was able to check for everything: diabetes, the flu, food poisoning, everything. It all came back negative except the pregnancy test. That was positive. I ran it twice on both of you."

"Oh my God." Kimber looked like she might faint.

"Oh shit." Gillian was pretty sure she was going to either throw up or faint.

"Pregnant?" Aleksei felt a thousand-pound weight lift off his shoulders. He threw back his head and laughed for joy and in relief.

"Laughing? This is not funny, you fertile old fossil!" Gillian slugged him in the arm.

"How?" Helmut asked. "I know both of you are responsible . . . How can you be pregnant?"

Something pinged in Gillian's mind. "The healing! Perrin's stupid healing must have . . ."

She stopped herself, realizing that she might be oversharing about her and Kimber's little former problem.

"Of course!" Aleksei wasn't as demure, apparently. "It must have done much more than just heal physically. It must have overridden your birth control pills."

"Shit. What are we going to do?" Gillian felt ridiculous. She'd just worked out how she felt about Aleksei, last night had been amazing and now this. A baby. Good Goddess.

"I will tell you what we are going to do," Aleksei stated. He rose from the couch, reached into his pocked and dropped to one knee in front of Gillian.

"This was not the way or the time I envisioned proposing, *piccola*, but what is more important is that I do this now."

"Aleksei . . ." Gillian could see where this was going and wasn't sure she liked the cause and effect. She didn't want a commitment because she was pregnant; she wanted a commitment simply because they wanted one.

"Gillian, you have to marry me now. The baby needs a father. Make an honest man out of me." Icy gray eyes that should have been chilly burned into her soul. He loved her. That was a fact. The baby was another fact.

"I had planned to ask you tonight, but now I want you to know, in front of all these people, that I am in this for the rest of our lives. I cannot imagine my life without you in it."

He slid the ring onto the third finger of her left hand. "Marry me, Gillian."

She stared at the ring. It was a large bezel-set diamond in an obviously very heavy, very old yellow gold setting. It must have cost a fortune.

Aleksei read her easily. "It was my mother's. It has never been on another hand but hers. I want you to have it because I know it will never leave our family."

Gill looked up at him. "Your mother's ring?" Her voice sounded shaky.

"Now it is your ring. Elizabeta never even saw it." That simple assurance from him gave her the courage to answer.

"Okay." Gillian's voice cracked.

"Excuse me, *piccola*, what was that?" Aleksei cocked his head at her, grinning from ear to ear.

"I said okay."

" 'Okay' what, my love?" he teased her.

"Okay, I'll marry you."

He didn't give her a chance to say anything else, but lifted her off the couch and set her on his knee. The look in his eyes told her everything she needed to know. The kiss he gave her made her come up gasping for breath.

"It will be all right, sweetling," Aleksei breathed into her hair.

"I hope you're right." Gillian sighed.

"We are stronger together than apart. We will do this together."

"I do love you, you old fossil."

"I know you do, *piccola*."

"I'm going to suck as a parent."

"No, you will not. You will be remarkable." Aleksei grinned at her.

"You do have to quit smoking, as of right now," Daed informed her.

"What?" Gillian stared at him. "Oh, that's just fabulous. I'm pregnant, I have patients to see, a wedding to plan, and I have to give up nicotine."

"And drinking too. No arguments. It's bad for the baby and isn't doing you any good either. Doctor's orders." Daed's normally playful countenance was gone, replaced by Dr. Know-It-All.

"Why couldn't you just have been an antiques dealer like the rest of your family?"

Kimber was giggling into Pavel's shoulder.

"And you're laughing why?" Daed shifted his black eyes to her. "You're in the same boat. No cigarettes, no booze for you either."

"Aw, dammit!"

"Aleksei, you and Pavel make sure these two get plenty of rest, fluids and food. I've ordered some prenatal vitamins, which should arrive sometime tomorrow. Make sure they take them before they go to sleep. Less nausea that way."

Aleksei's face was completely serious. "Of course, Doctor. Anything else?"

"Make sure they go easy on any big adventures for the next nine months."

"Oh, come on!" Gillian was exasperated. "We're pregnant, not terminal!"

"You will be pampered, cherished and looked after, *cara mia*." Aleksei kissed her on the nose.

"That's what I'm afraid of." Gill sighed.

"And what I am looking forward to." Aleksei hugged her tightly. She was having his child and was officially almost his. Life was indeed good.

"Babies?" Trocar's astonishment cut through the warm, fuzzy blanket of feeling everyone was luxuriating under. "The two most deadly females I know, of any species, are having babies?"

All eyes turned to the Dark Elf. He raised an eyebrow and looked from Kimber to Gillian, grinning the most wicked grin either of them had ever seen.

"So . . . sperm happened?"

CHAPTER
14

AFTER the initial shock of discovering her impending motherhood, Gillian, with true Marine discipline and adaptability, settled in to the reality of the situation. Her routine of cigarettes and coffee upon waking gave way to hot tea and toast. Kimber bitched a bit more than Gill did, but she too adjusted to life at the Institute as a walking womb.

There were one or two almost blowups between the women and their respective males. Aleksei at first flatly refused to allow either of them to leave the interior of the castle without a literal platoon of soldiers, Wolves, Vampires and Elves surrounding them. Pavel was in complete agreement with his Lord.

This was unacceptable to both Gillian and Kimber. First they tried reasoning with their men, then they tried diplomacy. When none of the above worked out as well as they hoped, Gillian went straight for *bitch*.

All she wanted to do was go outside, sit in the fading, late-afternoon sun and enjoy the crisp mountain air. She didn't want to talk, eat, sleep or be coddled. Just a few moments alone with herself and her thoughts as night fell.

Slipping down the stairs was the easy part. Getting out the front door or any other exit was next to impossible. There were just too damn many people around. The Brownies insisted on packing her a snack to take with her. They were tickled to pieces about being part of the extended family and were determined to be the best little caregivers in their Paramortal Paradise. Their tiny voices and scurrying feet brought Aleksei to the hallway. Without asking Gillian, he sent a wordless command to Cezar, who summoned a few of his Wolves and the Marines who were hanging out with them.

Gill was greeted with a group of twenty-five heavily armed individuals who stood parade style on either side of the hall leading to the door. Her eyes narrowed as she turned back toward the sounds of Aleksei's booted feet on the flagstones.

"What the hell is this?"

"They are simply going with you, *cara*. I want someone with you at all times outside of the castle."

"No."

"Gillian . . ."

"You heard me. I said no."

"I am afraid this is not optional." Aleksei tried staring her down. "I will not compromise your safety."

Gillian stared right back, her bright green eyes hardened into shards of glass, the fingers of her gun hand twitching.

"Aleksei, I am not going to have this goddamn conversation every time I want to go outside for a walk or a drive. I am not—repeat, *not*—going to tolerate a bazillion people following me around to the bathroom, outside or down to the village. I'm pregnant, not an invalid."

"*Piccola*, I am not going to allow anything to happen to you or our baby." Aleksei's eyes were just as cold, just as hard.

"If you persist in this and continue to piss me off, I am going to start shooting members of your 'escort.' Then see how many volunteers you get to tag along after me," she snapped in response.

The small army of Marines and various Paramortals standing behind her at the castle doors collectively moved back and away from her.

"Then I will accompany you myself."

"No, you will not. I want to be alone for a few minutes. There are at least a hundred Shifters, Elves, Brownies, Fairies, Ghosts and Sluagh patrolling the boundaries of the castle, the village, the county and the province. I couldn't be safer if I were in Fort Knox. Now, I am going to go outside. I am going to go alone. If I see one Being, just one, I swear by all the Gods I will shoot it. That includes you."

She stepped forward and poked him in the chest with her finger. "I am telling you for the last time, stop all this bullshit, treat me the way you normally do, remember that I am capable of taking care of myself and we'll get along just fine."

He looked a bit stricken by her vehement declaration. "I mean it, Aleksei. I know you love me and I appreciate you wanting to keep me safe, but if you drive me crazy, I will take you with me."

She reached up and slid a hand under his hair and behind his neck and pulled him down to her. A brief kiss across his mouth and she was headed for the door.

"Don't even think about following me," she announced to the group as she breezed past. The door slammed and she was gone.

"Kimber said as much to me a few minutes ago." Pavel stepped up from the hallway behind Aleksei with a heavy sigh.

The Vampire Lord looked down at the young Wolf. "I suppose we are going to have to accept it, Pavel. We are completely in over our heads with these two."

"They are just so different from ordinary women." Pavel looked wistfully out the window to watch Kimber as she strolled the grounds, stopping to stretch.

"That is true." Aleksei smiled. "They are the most extraordinary women."

Later that night, their quarrel forgotten, Gillian was typing her notes on her latest session with Chester. He was proving a little less difficult since Daed had been playing chemist with the pharmacy in Brasov. He and the pharmacist there had concocted a new medication that kept his proverbial dark side from experiencing serious impulse control issues, while allowing for expression of thought.

Gill was able to listen to both sides of her conflicted patient and make determinations and suggestions based on their collective needs. If the drug continued to work, then Daed would see to it that it was tested as a legitimate aid for Beings with Chester's extreme variation of Paramortal dissociative disorder.

Chester would never be a completely free man again. Nobody could come to a consensus that he was 100 percent responsible for his actions since taking the potion. His "good" side was forever arguing and attempting to thwart the intentions and actions of the "bad" side, so in a manner of speaking, he was being responsible. However, the "good" side had to sleep sometime, and that was generally when the Hyde portion of their collective Being pushed forward and did naughty things.

Since there was no other option or governing body to make the decision, Scotland Yard poked its head in and said they'd help Interpol and Special Agent Upchurch with permanent quarters and supervision. Chester was legally a British citizen, so that made the most sense. Gillian was perversely hoping that her old pal Inspector Brant McNeil got stuck with "Chester Watch," then realized his ever-patient partner, Claire Jardin, whom she genuinely liked, would be pulled into the mess as well, and dismissed her thoughts. *Water under the bridge,* she reminded herself.

Nobody had heard from Jenna Blake, Gill and Kimber's airheaded lieutenant and friend. The last anyone had contact with Gillian's bubbly pyromaniac friend was when Tanis and she had parted company in Egypt. Gill, Kimber and Trocar were a bit surprised she hadn't appeared during the fiasco with Vlad and Akabat. While it was characteristic of her to disappear for periods of time, it wasn't typical for her to miss a giant multi-Being free-for-all. Especially if it involved her friends' safety. Daed put out feelers of his own, hoping the military channels would provide some clue as to her whereabouts.

Their question was answered one evening some weeks later when the Brownies were watching CNN. A special report came on about a growing movement of protestors who were objecting to the Osiris Doctrine, among other things. The Brownies began shrieking and pointing at the television, bringing everyone to the library.

As the reporter talked, the camera panned over a crowd of people facing a stage with a podium and royal purple velvet curtains. The two figures on the platform were recognizable: Jenna and, next to her with his arm draped around her shoulders, Father Bartholomew Daily, who wasn't stopping in his attempts to discredit Gillian after the Akabat incident.

"He seems to be hell-bent on casting a dim light on our fair heroine . . . almost a religious determination," Trocar quipped to no one in particular.

"Oh, ha-ha," Gillian bit back. "What disturbs me is seeing Jenna there with him."

Kimber was peering at the television screen, her green gold eyes narrowing as she stared at their friend. "She doesn't look like herself, Gill. Look at her eyes."

Gillian leaned in to examine Jenna's face as closely as she could. "You're right. She looks . . . It's not drugged . . . That's not pharmacological . . . That's something else."

"She is enthralled." Leave it to Aleksei. Damned Vampire vision.

"Enthralled? Like hypnotized?" Gill asked.

"More like bespelled," Trocar informed them.

"Agreed." Aleksei moved closer to the television. "Very much like a spell. That is how a Vampire who is powerful enough can make a slave."

Gill poked him in the arm. "Slave? Like Renfield?"

"Not so melodramatic, but yes. The concept of Renfield is most likely something which Bram Stoker witnessed to a degree between a Vampire and servant, then added to the drama of Dracula's pseudohistory for his book."

"Care to explain further?"

Aleksei smiled down at her. She had the cutest crinkle over the bridge of her nose when she frowned.

"Aleksei, I'm getting old here." Now her eyes were truly sparkling.

"Apparently not only Vampires can bespell people, but pregnant Human females as well." Trocar draped himself artistically across the couch and out of Gillian's reach before she could elbow him in the sternum.

"My apologies, *cara*, but you do look most adorable when you are trying to delve into the mysteries of Vampire magic."

"I am pregnant, nicotine deprived and getting pissed off. Are you going to answer the question or not?"

To her irritation, he hugged her tightly and kissed the end of her nose. "Of course, my dear. I will schedule my admiration for a later time."

She shoved him away. "Dammit, Aleksei!"

Chuckling, he answered her. "Remember long ago when we discussed what it took to make a servant? The blood exchanges?"

"I do."

"Those exchanges are generally reserved for a willing partner, one whom the Vampire is literally eternally committed to. It can also happen covertly or by coercion."

"So he could have lied to her or forced her?"

"Precisely. It is not in exact parlance a rape, but it is very close." His expression darkened. "It is most certainly forbidden by our Laws, and is punishable by death."

Gillian turned back to the television. Father Daily was still talking and Jenna was still gazing at him with those empty, adoring eyes.

"We have to get her away from him."

"Gill, we don't know what the circumstances are. She might be with him voluntarily," Kimber said as gently as she could.

"Jenna has never, ever consented to being just arm candy for anyone, and she sure as hell wouldn't consent to being a mindless drone," Gillian argued.

"She is not necessarily a mindless drone," Aleksei

pointed out. "As Kimber suggests, she may have initially been with him of her own accord, and has subsequently been seduced into believing what he is advocating."

"I don't care which one it is; she has a right to make her own decisions with her *own* mind," Gill insisted.

"I am not arguing that point, *piccola.* I am simply pointing out that your friend may not appreciate you interfering with her personal life if she did indeed at least begin their relationship by her own volition."

Gillian scowled at him, then at the television. "I do see your point. All I want to know is that she's not being forced to be with him or to stay with him."

In an eerie echo to her statement, Father Daily pulled Jenna closer to him at the microphone.

"Gillian Key was Jenna's friend. They served together, had many adventures together, fought side by side together. Gillian Key was her commanding officer, confidant and sister in arms." Father Daily's eyes were piercing, while Jenna's eyes remained vacant and glassy.

"I have helped her see her life clearly," Daily continued. "She now understands that her lifestyle as directed by Gillian Key was detrimental to her well-being and to her very soul. She has repented and come into the presence of my light."

"I'm going to knock that shithead out," Kimber snarled.

"Listen first; knock out later," Gillian shushed her friend.

"Jenna was trapped in a lie. She believed the lies Gillian told her. She believed that Vampires and Paramortals can live peaceably with Humans. She believed the lies in the Osiris Doctrine; that there would be justice for those who broke the Laws. When we met, she was reluctant at first to hear the truth. Now Jenna is redeemed. She understands that she was a victim all along. A victim of lies and deception brought about by Gillian's lover, Vlad Dracula. The same lies and deception that have been told to all of you.

"I have a plan. A plan that will allow Vampire and Humans to coexist. A plan that will truly bring the freedom that the Osiris Doctrine promises but does not deliver. A plan that begins with the lawfully ordered death of Vlad Dracula, and brings justice to Gillian Key and her half-breed bastard child!"

There was a collective gasp around the room. Helmut, Daed, Cassiopeia and Pavel had joined the group as Daily's speech continued.

"Now I'm gonna knock him out." Kimber slapped the television off.

"How the hell did he find out I was pregnant, and what the hell did I do to piss him off like that?" Gillian was pale. Her hand reflexively went to her abdomen. "I don't know this guy! The first I heard of him was when Daed mentioned him in Akabat."

"You did nothing, *cara mia*." Aleksei drew her close. "He is clearly delusional, but with very powerful spies and friends. This is not your fault."

"I know, Aleksei, but . . . damn." She pulled away from him and went to sit in one of the large, overstuffed wing-back chairs.

Her eyes shifted upward to see Kimber glaring at her. "What?"

"Since when do you give a shit about what anyone else thinks? Now you're all worried about what some raggedy-ass, used-to-be-priest is conniving? What's wrong with you?" Kimber kicked Gill's foot off the arm of the chair.

Gillian glared at her and readjusted her legs, tucking her feet up next to her. "I don't care. I'm worried about him stirring up shit about the baby."

"Calling bullshit on that one, Captain." Kimber poked her in the shoulder with a single finger. "You are upset that after all we've been through on this, he might really be damaging everything we've worked for."

"Okay, fine. You're right . . . sort of," Gillian admitted. "It's not about me, Kimmy. I don't give a shit what anyone thinks about me. This is my life and I'll live it the way I choose. I don't like the fact that he is using a seemingly personal vendetta with me to orchestrate this 'rage ma-chine' against Paramortals in general. That's what worries me. We've got to figure out a way to rescue Jenna and do some really stellar damage control, fast."

"Gillian, this is beyond damage control now," Helmut pointed out. "It's true that the opinion of one disgruntled Vampire is irrelevant, as are the opinions of most bullies. However, this is reaching beyond opinion. Underneath all that venom, he's specifically targeting you and your baby."

"Helmut's right. That was an express threat to the safety of you and your baby." Daed's usually smiling face was grim. "Not to mention a direct threat on Vlad's life. We need to contact Osiris. He needs to know that some of these zealots who are following Daily may know of Vlad's whereabouts. Particularly if news of Gillian's pregnancy has already been leaked somehow."

"I will contact Osiris," Aleksei said. "Cezar, Teo and the others will step up security around the castle, the grounds and the village."

"I'll take care of the military aspect. This province will be locked up tighter than a mouse's ass within five minutes. Also I'll put out feelers to see where the hell this asshole is hiding. If we're going to attempt a rescue, we need to know where we're headed." Daed was already headed for the door and dialing his cell.

"We've got to get Jenna out of there." Gill looked to Kimber and Trocar. "I don't believe for a minute that she is with him voluntarily, especially after that speech."

"I do not believe it either," Trocar agreed.

"Jenna didn't even know we were knocked up." Kimber was pacing back and forth. "None of us has talked to her; she hasn't even spoken to Tanis that I know of. I wanted to tell her myself and watch her shriek."

Gillian ignored that and was tapping her front teeth with her fingernail. "He's attractive, charismatic . . . Jenna might have approached him or allowed him to flirt with her initially, but she isn't any more prepared than any other Human to resist a Master-level Vampire. He has to be holding her against her will, or would be if she knew she was being held."

Aleksei was frowning at her. "Gillian . . . I do not wish to appear insensitive but you cannot be thinking of rescuing Jenna yourself."

Twin green orbs snapped up to pin him with her glare. "Aleksei, I am not going to argue this point with you or anyone else. We leave no one behind. I am going to investigate this and, if need be, I am going to get her away from that phony priest, at least long enough for her to either punch me in the nose for interfering or to thank me for getting her the hell out of there. I am not going to deliberately put myself or the baby in danger, but I am completely capable of doing what I need to do. Don't make this an issue between us."

He stared at her a long time. The silence was overwhelming as two iron wills locked eyes.

"All right, *cara*. I know better than to fight you over something when you have made up your mind. However, understand this: I will be with you every step of the way this time." He shook his head and held up his hand when she opened her mouth.

"No, I will not argue this point with you. You may be the superior soldier, but I am the man who loves you. You will not take on this situation alone. I do not care how many Marines you bring with you. There will be a specific Vampire at your side at all times: me."

Her frown slowly melted into a smile. He was so honorable and earnest. He didn't like it, but he wasn't going to go all Victorian chauvinist on her either. In fact, he was willing to risk his life for her and her friend. She knew then more than at any other time why she loved him.

"All right. You've got a deal." She rose and went to hug him.

"Hear that, Pavel? You're either in or you're out, but we're going on another Jenna rescue." Kimber poked the handsome Shifter in his ribs.

"I hear you. I am at your side as always." Pavel hugged her to him.

"Do I have anything to say about this?" Trocar smirked.

"No!" Gill, Aleksei, Pavel and Kimber chorused.

"But you can help us talk Daed into it when he gets back." Gill grinned at him over Aleksei's arm.

"Gladly." The Dark Elf was loyal to the core. No questions, no discussions, just there if he was needed.

"Gillian . . . Schatzi . . . this really is not a reasonable idea," Helmut tut-tutted.

"My fiancée has never been particularly reasonable, Helmut, but whatever she needs, we will support her." Aleksei chuckled at Helmut and was rewarded by an enthusiastic kiss from Gillian.

"I do love you," she whispered in his ear.

"I know." He hugged her tightly.

Later, when Daed returned, and after he did his predictable blowing up over the suggestion that two pregnant women tangle with a very public Fangland figure who happened to hate Gillian's guts, they got a commitment from him to use his media connections to instigate their own public relations blitz and contradict Father Daily's claims and statements. He was still swearing in a unique mixture of Southern anecdotes and Greek when he shooed them out and barricaded himself in the library for a video conference with the IPPA to discuss what to do.

While checking in with their Egyptian allies, Osiris let Aleksei know that Vlad was still catatonic but safely guarded. Unless Daily had a Lord's power or extremely adept allies, there was no way anyone was getting near the former Dark Prince during his current convalescence.

The Marine and Elf presence was immediately doubled in the province and around Sacele. Cezar's pack spent more and more time in Wolf form, patrolling the area surrounding the castle. Aleksei's lieutenant, Teo, had arranged for some local public service announcements about Aleksei's ongoing campaign to keep Romania safe, as a whole. One of the recent responders was a clan of Lynxes in Northern Romania who expressed interest in being associated with Aleksei's retinue. Another was Odin.

CHAPTER
15

ODIN arrived at the castle somewhat unceremoniously that night, setting off a flurry of aggression from the pack and the Elves who patrolled the grounds. The fur-and-arrow police had no idea they were expecting visitors, nor did anyone else at the Institute.

The Norse Lord had vanished after Akabat, as had Elizabeta, Erzsébet and Sweeney. Aleksei and Gillian were looking forward to Odin's arrival. Privately, Aleksei was concerned about where the hell Elizabeta was and why he couldn't seem to locate her, despite an elaborate network of informants and his own personal abilities. Gill was moderately worried about what had happened to Erzsébet and Sweeney, but not enough to mention it to Aleksei.

Pavel and Trocar interceded during the commotion of Odin's arrival, managing to prevent any accidental deaths or dismemberment. Odin and his company were shown into the library by Trocar and one of the Wolves, an Irish girl named Ariel.

"Lord Aleksei, Lord Odin is here to see you." Ariel waved at Trocar with a twinkle in her eye, then scampered off.

Gillian's eyebrows rose. She cocked an eyebrow at Trocar. "Really?"

Trocar smiled enigmatically, then went back to deliberately sharpening one of his runed knives. Gillian rolled her eyes at him, turning back in time for Aleksei's reintroduction of Odin. There was no point in pondering Trocar's love life. He was as secretive in matters of love as he was in the rest of his life. She hoped he wasn't working his way through the pack. Aisling Crosswind, the Wood Elf he'd been keeping company with, might decide she wanted a Wolf pelt coat threaded with Grael hair.

"Nice to see you again, Odin." She smiled at the blond giant and took his proffered hand in a firm grip.

"And you as well, little sister." Odin's pale blue eyes were guileless and inviting.

Like most Vampires, the Norse Lord was breathtakingly lovely. He had apparently been older when he was Turned. There were laugh lines at the corners of his eyes, and silvery threads among the shimmering blond in his long hair.

"May I introduce my company. This is Freya, Thor and Baldr. My Wolves, Garm and Sigundr. My Bears, Bodvar and Helgi."

Freya was tall, with strawberry blonde hair, freckles and penetrating eyes of a frosty blue. She smiled with an easy warmth before settling herself near the fireplace.

Thor and Baldr bowed to Aleksei, then Gillian, and shadowed Freya on opposite sides of the hearth. Thor's hair was a darker gold than his Lord's, and was braided back against his head on either side, resembling an Elf warrior's braid. His eyes were a piercing robin's-egg blue, darker than either Freya's or Odin's.

Baldr was extraordinary. His hair was unexpectedly dark brown. It curled over his broad shoulders and down his back in loose waves. His eyes were a crystal-clear violet that made his expression at once vulnerable and poignant. God of light and beauty indeed.

The Wolves were a mated pair. Garm was massive in height, build and sheer presence. His thick blond hair was wind tossed and tousled. It fell in heavy locks around his bulky neck and shoulders. He simply looked dangerous, even standing casually behind Odin. There was something in those green eyes that made even Gillian shiver, though she could detect no animosity from him.

Sigundr, the female, was as tall as her mate but nowhere near as massively built. Her own hair was darker blonde and her blue eyes were more friendly.

Bodvar was an impressively sized redhead. He was tall and thickly muscled, and sported a goatee that matched his flame-colored locks. No freckles on this one. His skin was sun darkened, making his sapphire eyes blaze.

Helgi was smaller, more delicately built. Her pale blonde hair was in two thick braids down her back. Loose tendrils of her hair framed a pixie face with very blue eyes.

There was a different feel to the Norse group than Gillian had experienced before. Odin's power seemed almost on a level with Osiris's. The Bears' Shifter aura was denser, heavier than what she normally felt from the local group of Bears who patrolled the province.

Two of the Brownies scurried in at that point, chattering excitedly. "There are more visitors! We let them in. They say they are friends of the Viking."

Everyone except Odin and his group tensed for a second, not knowing what or whom to expect.

Odin turned back to the door with a smile. "May I also present my longtime comrade, Thane Hreidmar of the Dwarven lands, and his Lady Kelda."

Like the Dwarves of legend, a short, stocky, compact, perfectly proportioned man with a long, flowing red beard, braided and beaded to match his long, flowing red braided and beaded hair, strode into the room holding hands with an equally stocky, compact, perfectly proportioned woman. Both were wearing intricately etched metal-and-leather breastplates. Her hair was just as red, just as flowing, but with no braids or golden beads, and she had no beard on her pretty face.

Trocar swore in some obscure Elven dialect, staring at Kelda. "By the Gods, you are certainly not ugly nor are you bearded." He circled the pair, looking them both up and down. "You are real."

Kelda giggled. "Indeed I am, Elf. Or are you given to believing those old Fairy stories?"

Trocar blushed, if it was possible. "I . . . I . . . Forgive me. I am just astonished that in all my years I have never seen a female of your species. Moreover, that those legends and stories are quite wrong."

Gillian was flabbergasted first of all by the crack in Trocar's unshakeable demeanor, and second because she'd heard the legends too. No one in any recorded history had ever laid eyes on a female Dwarf. They were supposed to be ugly and hairy and kept underground. Kelda was the antithesis of that description.

She was small, yes, but obviously muscular, quite pretty, and if the twin daggers at her sides were any indication, she didn't need to be locked away and protected by anybody. Hreidmar had a heavy, disproportionately large axe on his own hip; his hands were calloused and scarred. He didn't look like he needing protecting either.

Hreidmar guffawed and everyone jumped. The little man literally held his belly and chortled heartily. "Kelda was my bodyguard, Elf. She is now my lady and my mate, lucky bastard that I am. One day I will tell you the story of why our women are so reclusive, but not tonight. Tonight is for forming alliances and making new friends."

"Welcome, then, Thane Hreidmar." Aleksei had no composure to recover and stepped forward to shake hands with the Dwarven King.

"Just 'Hreidmar,' my friend. My title is only valid among my own people. I am here because your reputation and your own lady's status demand it."

"What do you mean?" Gillian was taken aback.

"You truly do not know?" Hreidmar frowned at her.

"Know what?" Gillian frowned back.

"My dear girl, you and your intended have caused quite an upheaval amongst magical folk. We all heard your words before, witnessed your actions. There were those who rushed to ally themselves with anyone who opposed the Dark Prince, and those of us who preferred to wait."

"Why did you wait?" Gillian interrupted, her frown deepening. "If you were against Dracula from the beginning, why not come forward then? Or were you waiting to ally yourself to the victorious side?"

"I can assure you, Hreidmar is of the highest integrity." Odin moved to his friend's side. The look he gave Gillian was less friendly than before.

"Quite all right, Odin. She had a right to ask and I would have been disappointed if she did not. She is a soldier, after all." Hreidmar chuckled. Gillian didn't find it funny.

She couldn't feel anything duplicitous about the Dwarf; his timing was just a bit odd, but so was Odin's. Her mind whirled. Being pregnant was evidently slowing down her synapses. She should have noticed something was off right away. Maybe she just needed food. When had she eaten last? She shook herself mentally. Focus, Gillian. Ascertain the situation. Brownie goodies later.

She cleared her throat and reached down for a little sandwich off the tray the Brownies had thoughtfully brought in. "In fact, why are you all here? Odin, you showed up at Akabat and now are here with your little friends in tow. Next we hear from a group of Lynxes who have been in Romania all along and now want to make nice. What's going on?" She fixed each of them with a chilly look.

"*Cara*, what are you doing?" Aleksei was following her reasoning and understood her questions, but was puzzled by her forthright manner when greeting potential allies.

"I am finding out why every one is picking *now* to appear when we could have used the help long before Akabat and possibly avoided that whole situation with Dracula." Gillian's empathy was warring with itself. She could feel nothing that would normally arouse any concern, but her tactical mind was demanding answers. "This whole state of affairs is too convenient." Gillian paused to take a bite out of the sandwich and grab a glass of soda off the tray.

To their credit, Odin, his company and both Dwarves blushed, appearing rather uncomfortable. "You are correct, Gillian. It is not as innocent as it appears," Odin acquiesced.

"Then explain it, please," Gillian said around a mouthful of sandwich.

"We were not, as you believe, waiting for the clear victor to emerge in the conflict. We have no love for Dracula and his like. We believed that no matter who emerged as the winner, our lives would not truly change."

"And now?" she pressed him.

"Since Akabat and Dracula's defeat, despite that Father Daily creature's vitriolic speeches, we have seen the difference in our own acceptance among Humans. In my own lands the atmosphere has shifted. My people . . . the Humans who live there . . . they have come to me, offering treaties, allegiance . . . a pact." Odin's eyes sparkled with humility and unshed tears.

"In my prior arrogance, I assumed they kept our secrets and kept us safe out of love, when it was actually for fear of reprisal. That is a shame I shall have to learn to live down. Since witnessing the events at Akabat, they realize that the true goal of yourself, Osiris, Gillian and the others who had already joined you was to unite us all, to give true laws and a true relationship between our species.

"We are here to offer our friendship and our alliance, Aleksei. We existed on the foundation of legend which has proved to be brittle. Now we want to forge a relationship that will last through suspicion, doubt and turmoil, as you have done with your own people. We want to be part of everything you have tried to build."

"What do you want in return?" Gillian asked. She didn't realize she had moved closer to Aleksei during Odin's dialogue. He noticed, bringing a hand up to softly massage her shoulder.

"Nothing, little sister. We want only to learn." Odin smiled down at her. "Aleksei is truly an enviable man to command such loyalty from such a woman."

Aleksei echoed Odin's smile to Gillian. "I thank you, Odin. While I know you intended a compliment, I command nothing from her. She is here out of choice, not obligation."

"Then I am even more impressed." Odin bowed slightly to Aleksei and to Gillian.

"Let me offer my praise as well," Hreidmar said. "My people have been content to live apart from most Beings. We are not ignorant of the world, simply removed from it. Prince Everwood travels far and wide in our lands. It was from him that I first heard of a Human commander who had earned his respect. Odin and I have long been acquainted, and consequently, when he heard of your Institute, your accomplishments and your agenda, he discussed his thoughts with me.

"Kelda and I talked with our people. The consensus is that we can be of help to you, if you will allow us into your coalition and let us also learn from your people. So, my dear Lord Aleksei and Gillian, we are yours in word and deed, if you will have us as your friends and partners."

Aleksei was surprised. This was not at all what he expected. It was his turn to blush. Gillian felt his discomfort and squeezed his hand unobtrusively. When he could trust his voice, he spoke to all of them.

"I will ask Gillian to send thanks to Prince Everwood for gaining us such allies. I am flattered but I believe you misunderstand. I am not the Lord of anyone except those who have expressed their loyalty in my own lands. You owe me no allegiance.

"We are a compact; a unit. We work together, but if that is impossible, we at least do not work against each other. There will always be Father Dailys and Draculas in the world. We cannot silence them, nor do we have a right to, lest we become what we hate. All who are with us want only long-term, peaceful coexistence. That is the single goal." Aleksei's voice grew stronger as he spoke. His personal feelings were very clear. He believed in his cause. That in itself was enough for all of them.

"Every movement needs a leader, Aleksei." Odin grinned. "We are willing to follow you."

"As are we," Hreidmar agreed.

For the second time since she'd known him, Gillian felt the powerful surge of humility and astonishment as Aleksei realized the level of loyalty they were offering. The first time had been when the village of Sacele had come to him, offering their literal life's blood in support of him and Tanis. That had been a long time ago, but she still remembered the pride she had felt in him then.

"I . . . I . . . do not know what to say," Aleksei stammered.

"Say yes. That's what they want you to do." Gillian dropped his hand and slid her arm around his waist.

He stared down at her. She poked him in the ribs. "*Yes*. It's a simple, three-letter word."

"Yes?" He didn't mean it to come out as a question.

"He will do it?" Odin asked.

"He'll do it," Gillian confirmed.

"Let us celebrate!" Hreidmar bellowed. "Where is the beer?" The Brownies had been listening at the door, as usual, and scurried off to find refreshment for the group.

Later, after the Rachlav Institute staff, personnel and occupants had been introduced to their guests, Gillian insisted the focus turn to a more serious subject: finding Jenna. It took Gillian less than fifteen minutes to organize a team, a route, transportation, supplies and additional muscle. Through Daed's frenzied, exhaustive search, they had a fairly good idea of where Father Daily might be holed up. Wherever Daily was, Jenna was bound to be. Destination: Prague, Czech Republic.

Aleksei was in awe of her ability to orchestrate a rescue. He insisted on going with them, over her objections. In her eyes, he was a great and powerful Vampire; however, he was still green in the field and in direct combat if it came to that. She didn't want him getting hurt.

Finally they came to a consensus. Gillian, Kimber, Aleksei, Pavel, Trocar, Daed, Odin and his group, plus Hreidmar and Kelda, would go. Helmut, Cassiopeia, Cezar, Teo, the Brownies and the Marine platoon would stay. It was a given that the Sluagh, the Sidhe and most of the Elves who had settled in to the area would remain. Tanis wanted to go, owing to his former relationship with Jenna, but Aleksei

wanted him at the castle to oversee things while he was doing what he could to keep Gillian out of harm's way. Tanis
didn't like it, but finally relented.

Trocar did come to Gillian with three Elf volunteers
who wanted to come along. Gunner and Aisling Crosswind,
she knew. The brother and sister Wood Elves had been a
wonderful addition during the incidents with Perrin and
Dracula. Aisling had become good friends with Gill and
Kimber, plus she was Trocar's off-and-on date of the moment. Gunner was simply a good, steady, loyal friend. The
third Elf was one Gillian hadn't met personally before.

He was tall, as heartrendingly lovely as his fellows with
almost blindingly golden hair and starlit blue eyes. He introduced himself as Dagr Hawthorne and explained that
he was the Captain of Mirrin Everwood's personal guard.
Then he dropped a bombshell on their little party by in-
forming Gillian that Mirrin himself and his lady would be
joining them on their adventure.

Gillian was very surprised. Mirrin was a titled Prince
who normally didn't leave his beloved homeland for any
reason. Seeing him at Akabat had been a welcome shock;
having him accompany them to find Jenna was an appreciated gesture.

On cue, Mirrin strode in, hand in hand with a tall,
auburn-haired, gray-eyed woman. At first glance she appeared Human, but her sheer beauty and lightly pointed
ears were testament to her mixed heritage.

Mirrin spoke first. "My friends, may I present my Lady,
Dorian Leganth."

"Welcome, Mirrin and Dorian. Thank you both for
coming, but I am a bit surprised that you're here." Gillian
greeted them both warrior to warrior: clasping forearms
with each of them in turn.

"Once a Marine, always a Marine." Mirrin grinned at
her. "We leave no one behind. Elves do not either."

Dorian stepped forward. "I am glad to finally meet you,
Gillian. My husband has told me a great deal about you and
your friends." Dorian's voice was as lovely as she was. Gillian didn't miss the slight inflection on the word *husband*.

"It is a pleasure to finally meet you as well. Mirrin spoke of you often and with the highest regard when he served in our company." Gillian smiled and radiated good will. She couldn't explain it, but she wanted Dorian to feel secure and welcomed.

"This is my fiancé, Aleksei Rachlav. He met Mirrin previously at Akabat."

Aleksei took the hint and grasped Dorian's hand, all the while keeping his other hand on Gillian's shoulder. He greeted Mirrin much the same.

"I am pleased to see you again, Mirrin, and happy you have brought your wife to meet us as well."

"It has been a long time since I have been on an adventure with Gillian, Kimber and Trocar. All that is missing is Luis, and of course Jenna."

Gill laughed. "Well, Luis is involved with a new love. They're back in England for the moment, sort of cleaning up Oscar's house after some unsavory occupants vacated."

Mirrin's eyebrows shot up. "Oscar?"

"Oscar . . . er . . . Gray. Really nice guy. You'd like him. Plus Luis is happier than I've ever seen him." Gillian was happy for her friend.

"Then I am happy for Luis." Mirrin smiled back. "And for you and Kimber. It is truly magical to find love."

Gillian ignored that remark despite Aleksei squeezing her shoulders. *"Uncomfortable, piccola?"* His rich, deep tones vibrated through her mind.

"Stop that! And no, I am just getting used to the idea myself, while everyone else seems to think it's fairly obvious that I love you."

Aleksei laughed, making everyone jump, then kissed her head. He didn't care how he heard it; it warmed him every time to hear her say it.

They waited until the crack of dusk the following evening to depart. Tanis, Helmut, Cassiopeia, Cezar and the Brownies were at the door to see everyone off.

"Farewell, Aleksei." Tanis embraced his brother.

"I trust my lands and home will be intact when I return. I do not want to have to stage a coup against my own brother," Aleksei said sternly, then broke into a smile.

Tanis looked at him incredulously, then grinned at Gillian. "You are a bad influence on the Lord of these lands, little sister. There was a time when he was grim and humorless. I think I liked him better that way."

Gillian mirrored his smile. "Well, tough shitsky. He's funny now and I'm not changing him back."

Everyone chuckled at the exchange. Aleksei had indeed changed for the better in a number of ways. Gillian didn't realize yet how much she too had evolved, nor that they were also chortling in appreciation of her own metamorphosis.

She found herself in a group hug, squished between the two brothers. "Hey, hey, *hey*! Lady with a baby! Don't squeeze!"

She whacked each of them on the back of the head. "Put me down, dammit!"

Tanis tossed her in the air, then hugged her. "Go with care, my friend. The rest of your family here will miss you."

"Thanks, Tanis." Gillian hugged him back.

Good-byes were said all around; final waves were given as Mirrin led them all toward the far end of the glade, away from the castle. He had a little surprise with him besides Dorian. Near the edge of the forest there was a group of Elven steeds milling around.

"Retro travel?" Gillian asked. "I thought we had our travel plans covered, Daed." She held out a hand to the nearest animal, a brilliant blood bay stallion, approaching him slowly.

"Mirrin?" Daed was confused. "I thought we would go through the woods, then over to the next highway and pick up a convoy there to Brasov."

Mirrin shook his head. "This will keep you off any travel or communication grid. We will ride East toward the coast where you and Aleksei will be seen at the Eforie Nord resort. It is a well-known spa area known to cater to a number of different health situations, including women with gynecological problems."

Gillian's eyes widened. "I don't have . . . gynecological problems, Mirrin."

To her surprise, the Elf Prince laughed. "I am aware of that, Captain, but your enemy is not. He does, however, know you are pregnant. If you are visible at that resort, he will speculate that you are having problems related to your pregnancy. It will assuredly bring him out for another speech against you and keep him where he is currently located."

"Damn, he's bright. Why did we let him quit the Corps, pumpkin?" Daed was beaming.

Gillian threw a nearby rock at Daed, who ducked it casually. Stupid Shifter reflexes. "Stop calling me that! And I didn't let him quit; his time was up and he had obligations elsewhere."

"Too bad. I would have loved to have coerced him to stay." Daed was teasing about his prior strong-arm techniques with Gillian, Kimber, Trocar and the missing Jenna. The three of them threw rocks that time. He couldn't dodge three simultaneous projectiles from three different directions.

"Ow!"

"Stop complaining. We might have thrown knives instead," Trocar said dryly as he moved toward the animal next to Gillian.

The Elven steeds were lovely. They would have resembled normal horses, except for their unnatural beauty, regal bearing and preternatural speed. They also had the ability to port their rider through a Doorway. Elven Doorways were the portals between time and space that all Elves had the ability to manifest. Doorways were seldom used, as Elves generally preferred to remain in their own realms unless they were observing and researching a specific time and place.

"So we make an appearance there, then we go to Prague?" Kimber asked.

"Correct. Dorian and I look enough like Aleksei and

Gillian from a distance. We will remain there, allowing the press to have glimpses of us during our stay," Mirrin informed her.

Kimber pointed to Dorian's blazing red hair, then back to Gillian's golden blonde. "Really?"

Dorian pulled a vial out of her pack. "Elven women do not dye their hair; we simply take a temporary potion."

"Nice!" Kimber was impressed. "Where can I get some of that? Does it come in a lot of different colors? Can you combine potions?"

"Can we discuss Elven beauty implements later?" Gill interrupted. She was patting the horse she had approached and was securing her things in one of the bags on its saddle.

"Mount up," Mirrin called out.

Everyone but the Elves followed Gillian's example and approached individual horses. Once the animal sniffed them and established a relationship, they were safe to approach and mount. The Elves already had their own personal steeds tethered away from the rest of the group.

Trocar selected a black mare, her coat so dark that it shimmered with blue highlights. Aleksei's mount was a golden palomino stallion. The horse's mane and tail were a frothy fantasy of pure white, while his coat actually shimmered in the moonlight like beaten brass. Kimber took a blood bay mare, a mirror to Gillian's own mount. Daed selected a pure white giant with massive hooves that stood at least a hand above the rest of the horses.

Hreidmar and Kelda chose matching sorrels whose hair blazed golden red, with shimmering manes and tails. Odin and his lot selected a group of primitively marked buckskins that ranged in shade from light gold to an almost deep red. All had black manes, tails, socks and a black stripe down their backs. Gillian had to admit, they were an impressive, dangerous-looking group.

Pavel was stroking a liver chestnut with a flaxen mane and tail. "I cannot believe these animals stand still for a Shifter."

Mirrin's friend Dagr spoke. "Our mounts are well

trained and very intelligent. They understand the spoken word very well and have incredible sensibilities as to who is hostile and who is not."

"In fact, Pavel, these horses are only wearing tack because we are in a mixed party. Elves normally have at least one horse in their individual stables that is so well trained that there is no need for reins or saddle," Trocar spoke up.

"This one reminds me of a horse I had long ago, at least in coloring." He stroked the silken neck of his mount gently, sounding almost wistful.

"Tinechor. I remember him well, Trocar," Dagr said as he mounted his own golden palomino mare.

"I had forgotten that," Trocar responded, then turned his horse East and started off into the trees.

"You two knew each other?" Gillian asked the other Elf.

"Long ago, yes. I was not certain if Trocar remembered or not," Dagr replied.

"Curiouser and curiouser, Alice," Gillian muttered.

"Someday he might tell you." Dagr smiled.

Dorian, Aisling and Gunner all mounted up on black, gray and white horses respectively, and the party was complete.

"East. And quietly," Mirrin instructed. He started off after Trocar with the rest of them trailing.

CHAPTER
16

THE trek to the coast was uneventful. There were a few expected details to contend with, such as getting across highways and roads, and around small villages in the Romanian countryside. They moved at an unnerving pace. Once outside of the area around Sacele, Mirrin simply took off at breakneck speed. The other mounts leaped forward, nearly unseating a few of the group. These were magical animals, not normal horses. Their hooves seemed not to touch the ground during the extraordinary ride.

Kimber pulled up next to Gillian, who was dodging the occasional tree limb that would appear in her line of vision a split second before it would have whacked her in the face.

"Didn't you use to ride back in that backwoods area you grew up in?" She ducked her own branch, but not fast enough, and wound up with leaves in her hair.

"Normal horses, yes. I've never been on anything remotely like this." Gillian gritted her teeth and leaned lower over the horse's neck. It gave her the advantage of missing most of the foliage.

"Smooth ride, though."

"That's true. I've never heard of anything going this

fast or this smoothly." Gillian's horse flicked his ears and nickered.

"I think he's laughing at us." Gill grinned and patted his neck.

"At least we won't be saddle sore. This is like riding a couch." Kimber laughed.

"Are you all right, Gillian?" Aleksei's deep voice vibrated from her right. He knew perfectly well she was all right; his hearing was outstanding.

"You know I am." Gillian risked a glance his direction.

Damn. He looked good on that horse. All noble and aristocratic and . . . mouthwatering. *Stop it!* she told herself. This was not the time to be drooling over her intended. This was the time to . . . *smack*.

The branch she hadn't seen caught her in the shoulder. It would have unseated her, resulting in a nasty fall, considering the speed they were traveling. However, her wonderful horse felt the shift in her weight and compensated, getting himself beneath her before she came off his back.

"Shit!" Gillian was amazed to find herself still on the horse and in one piece.

"Okay, no more distracting me, Aleksei. Just ride over there." She pointed decisively away from her.

His heart had nearly stopped when she was hit with the branch. Seeing her still on the horse and surly was enough to reassure him.

"As you wish, *cara*." He chuckled and pulled away from her. Knowing that her near fall was due to her being enchanted with him was a rare gift, one he did not take lightly. Gillian had lived with him and among his kind for quite a while, but was no more immune to Vampire magic than anyone else. Normally she was more careful, more barricaded, particularly since his transformation. There was too much on her mind and too much at stake for him to distract her.

The amount of ground they covered during the night was astonishing. They made it from the Institute to the outskirts of Eforie Nord just before dawn. Dorian drank her potion, which turned her hair to Gillian's shade of blonde. Mirrin took his midnight black hair down from its traditional warrior braid and shook it free. A quick change of clothes for both of them: Mirrin into an open-neck silken shirt, boots and very tight laced pants, and Dorian into some khaki cargo pants and a T-shirt. Even close up, with their height difference, they made a fair "Aleksei and Gillian." From a distance, it would be extremely hard to distinguish.

There was some discussion about who would remain to guard the Elf Prince and his Lady. Aleksei argued that he did not normally travel with bodyguards, nor did he employ them for himself around the castle.

Pavel looked sheepish, prompting a question or two. "I am sorry, Aleksei, but Cezar and Tanis made me promise that you would never be out of earshot from a trusted sentry."

Aleksei frowned. He was uncharacteristically annoyed. "Am I the appointed Lord of these lands or not?"

"Yes, of course . . ." Pavel stammered.

"Then why has my request been disregarded?" Aleksei was more concerned that someone was guarding him when they ought to be guarding Gillian instead.

"Because if anything happens to you, the rest of us really are dead meat." Gillian stepped in to rescue Pavel.

"You knew about this?" Aleksei stared at her.

"I had an idea. Nothing definite, but an idea. Tanis, Teo and Cezar wouldn't be doing their job if you were unprotected, Aleksei. Don't blame Pavel. He's just following orders. I think it's a compliment to you that your people are determined to protect you, whether you want it or not." She grinned up at him.

"And if someone comes after you while they are looking after me so diligently?" Aleksei felt his irritation draining away. He couldn't help it. She was just cute.

"There are enough guns, claws and teeth to protect all of us. Just learn to deal with it. I had to. Under your orders, I might add." Gill poked him in the arm for emphasis. "You made certain I was shadowed day and night when I first came here. Get used to it. You're too valuable for any of us to lose."

It was finally determined that Aisling and Gunner, along with some local Fey that Mirrin had contacted ahead of time, would watch over the Prince and Dorian while they were impersonating Aleksei and Gillian. Dagr assured them that there was a group of Elves waiting for them near Prague to help with any situation that might arise.

Their stand-ins strolled down toward the main entrance to the resort, flanked by their bodyguards. Aleksei contacted Teo via Vampire Mind Net and directed him to get in touch with their new allies, the Lynxes, for the purpose of extra security for the pair.

"Aleksei," Odin spoke softly. "Thor, Freya, Sigundr and Bodvar will stay as well. There needs to be a show of strength here if the Lord of Romania is visiting this resort."

Aleksei grudgingly agreed. "I thank you for your offer. I am hopeful that they will not be needed, but the gesture is very much appreciated."

"Thank you, Odin," Gillian said earnestly. She was concerned about her friend and his wife remaining safe if Father Daily's threat toward her extended out this far.

"You are welcome." Odin smiled down her.

"Any chance of a Portal?" Hreidmar spoke up, startling the group. The Dwarves had been quiet companions in the group, and everyone but the Elves had nearly forgotten they were there.

"Did you enjoy the ride?" Dagr asked.

"Indeed. Normally we have our own ponies, but this was an unforeseen pleasure." Hreidmar patted his horse. It nuzzled him in return.

"Dwarven ponies are bred for a life under and above the ground. They are swift, but not as swift as these." Kelda stroked her own mount.

"I would like to see your lands sometime," Dagr said. "Our people have had little communication during this past age. I, for one, would like to remedy that."

"That can very well be arranged." Hreidmar nodded. "I believe my folk have been denied the beauty of the Elf lands and your culture. Perhaps after this is done, we can arrange a détente between our realms."

"The Portal," Trocar reminded them. He waved a hand and the forest shimmered in front of them.

"Mount up and let your horse take you through," Dagr told them.

They all obeyed him, letting the horses choose the moment to step through. Trocar went first, Gillian following him. Aleksei's heart wrenched as he watched them literally vanish before his eyes.

Gillian felt an almost nauseating, displacing twist, then she was through. Trocar was there, mounted on his horse and looking at her expectantly.

"Over here, Gillyflower," Trocar beckoned her. "Are you all right?"

She did as he asked and moved to his side. "I'm fine, I think." She shook her head a moment.

"It takes some getting used to." Trocar smiled.

"Evidently. That was probably the weirdest thing I've ever felt."

Aleksei, Kimber, the Dwarves and Odin's people popped through. Trocar directed them all out of the way of the next rider. Pavel was next to last, and finally Dagr. The Elf closed the Portal behind them.

"How far is Prague from where we are?" Gillian asked.

"Follow me to the top of that ridge," Dagr told her.

They all rode after their blond leader to the designated spot. Beneath them, thousands of bright lights announced the picturesque city of Prague, or *Praha*, as it was known in the Czech language.

"It's really beautiful," Gillian stated. Even with years spent in Eastern Europe, she hadn't had the time to do any pleasure traveling. She made a mental note that when things eased off a bit, she was going to have to take some leisure time and explore the surrounding Countries. With Aleksei, of course.

"Of course, bellissima. *I would be honored to escort you around and see the sights,"* Aleksei murmured in her head.

"I really hate it when you eavesdrop," Gillian snapped back at him. Making an effort to soften her response, she

continued: *"I would like that too; just please stop randomly monitoring my thoughts, will you? It's very annoying to have you suddenly pop up inside my mind."*

He chuckled and moved his horse closer to hers. "The dawn is breaking. Odin, Baldr and I will find our own shelter. I will contact Gillian late this afternoon when it is safe for us to rise."

"We'll go into town and find a hotel and some food," Gillian informed him.

"What about the horses?" Kimber asked. She found she really liked both riding and her mount.

"They will return when we need them. Our horses need no stable or fenced field. They are one of our great joys and return to us freely," Dagr told her.

Aleksei stroked his hand down Gillian's hair as she looked down over the valley. "I am sorry I have to leave you, *piccola*. Please take care while I rest. I will join you as soon as it is possible for me to do so."

She turned and looked up at him. "Just make certain you all go to ground in a safe place. I don't want to find out you've been ratted out and staked during the night."

"I promise." He smiled that meltingly magical smile at her that always made her knees weak.

"Good. Then I'll try my best not to break too many heads while you're getting your beauty rest." Impulsively, she hugged him tightly.

"I'll be fine. I've got a veritable herd of armed and dangerous people with me. You go on and get hidden before the sun gets any stronger. I swear to the Goddess, if you turn into a crispy critter, the engagement is over," she added with a grin.

The first rays of light were indeed streaming across the sky. The bright golden rays were pushing back the dark velvet of the night. As ancient Vampires, Aleksei, Odin and Baldr were not as susceptible as newer ones would be. Aleksei and Odin had the additional benefit of a Lord's power, allowing them to remain conscious and active far longer than their fellows. Baldr was only a Master level, but he was old. Very old. None of them had anything really to fear except danger to their loved ones. They could have easily remained aboveground for hours yet, but they needed to be in the earth and well hidden before any potential Daywalking allies of Father Daily began roaming the hills.

Aleksei kissed her quickly. He didn't want to linger or let his worry for her safety show through.

In respect for her wishes, Aleksei didn't pry into her thoughts. It never occurred to him that she watched him intently as he misted out and vanished into the deep woods with their two friends. Gillian's attentiveness and protectiveness toward him hadn't yet registered on his radar. He was too busy being worried about her to notice.

***

After the parting kiss between Aleksei and Gillian, the rest of the party gave a final wistful pat to their lovely steeds and began to trudge down the mountainside. The Dwarves went first. Kelda literally vanished before everyone's eyes. Trocar and Dagr exchanged an incredulous look. Evidently even the Elves, with their spectacular visual skills, couldn't see where she'd gone.

"No wonder we never see the females. Can they all do that?" Trocar asked Hreidmar, who was stomping down the makeshift trail after his wife.

"Aye. They can all do that. It is maddening, I tell you." Hreidmar huffed as he scurried in the direction Kelda had started.

"I cannot scent them either," Pavel said to no one in particular. "That is truly amazing."

"Nor can I," agreed Helgi, Odin's remaining Bear.

"None can," Garm concurred. "That truly is interesting."

Three of the Shifters opted to change form. Pavel was his usually Shetland pony–sized blond Wolf with playful blue eyes. Garm, however, dwarfed him. The stunning Viking shifted into what looked to Gillian like a Dire Wolf. His body was stockier than Pavel's, heavier. Overall he was more compact but with much more muscle mass than her friend's appearance. Golden fur, lighter than Pavel's, covered him, fading to a cream color on his chest, underbelly and legs. The green eyes were unmistakable, however. There was something so primal, so alien, about them. Combined with the oversized canines of a Dire Wolf, Garm ought to scare the hell out of anything they might encounter.

Helgi's form was surprising. Once, long ago, there were legends of the Ghost Bears: a subspecies of grizzly that tended to have light-colored or white fur. Helgi's fur echoed her own pale, nearly platinum hair. The blue eyes were softly disconcerting in her newly formed ursine face, but she looked formidable enough.

Daed elected to stay in Human form. Gillian wasn't certain if it was due to vanity or if he thought the sight of a Minotaur walking the streets of Prague might cause a fuss. Shifters, like other Paramortals, were becoming more open in major cities ever since the original legislation that recognized them as sentient Beings. Her other thought was that he might be saving his ability as a surprise should they need it later. Yeah, she'd go with that. A surprise.

"Do you have any contacts here?" she whispered to Daed.

"Nope. You?" He glanced over to her, then continued navigating his way down the path Hreidmar had made.

"Nope. Well, shit. Scouting around town is all right, but staying in the city is probably a bad idea unless we split up," Gillian suggested.

"Splitting up is definitely a bad idea," Daed replied.

"True. Hmmm. Prague is a major tourist destination these days. What if we mingle in with a tour group?" Gill said as she hopped over a fallen log.

"Gillyflower . . ." Trocar's dulcet tones whispered over their party. "Stop where you are and stay very still."

Gillian stopped instantly. If Trocar said stop, something was amiss. "What's up?"

"The Dwarves have stopped. Or at least Hreidmar has. I cannot tell where Kelda is." The Grael suddenly appeared at her elbow.

Daed was next to Gillian, frozen in midstride. He scented the air. "There is a faint scent . . ."

Gillian's blood ran cold in the next instant as Vlad Dracula misted out of the coming dawn to stand by her side.

"Good . . . morning, Dr. Key." Vlad's voice was no less
beautiful than she remembered. At the moment, it was no
less chilling.

Trocar's reaction was instantaneous. He pinned the
Vampire against a nearby oak's trunk. That would have
been fine except he had literally pinned him. Vlad's arms
and legs were abruptly bristling with four of Trocar's runed
knives. It was difficult to say who was more surprised: Vlad,
Gillian, Daed, the Shifters, the Dwarves, Kimber or Dagr,
who came sprinting up, bow drawn and ready to fire.

"What the hell are you doing here? Better yet . . . how
the hell did you get here?" Gillian was alternating between
mad, astonished, mad, scared, mad . . . Mad seemed to be
winning.

Just as suddenly, Osiris appeared next to the group. Vlad
was busy writhing against his impromptu bounds, making
inarticulate noises but not bleeding very much. Trocar was
good at his job. He'd intentionally avoided the major arter-
ies in Vlad's limbs. Points for Trocar.

The Egyptian Lord gave a slight bow to Gillian before
he spoke. "I am sorry for the sudden intrusion, Gillian.
Aleksei? Could you join us?" Osiris's incredible voice
resonated around them.

The request was both vocal and sent from Osiris's powerful mind. Aleksei appeared within the space of a breath.
He inserted himself between Vlad and Gillian, platinum
eyes blazing at Osiris.

"Why has this monster been released from your care and
why have you brought him here, to confront her?" Aleksei's normally lovely voice carried undertones of fury.

"I apologize again, to both of you. This is a most unusual
situation and not meant as a confrontation. He awoke, literally minutes ago, from his catatonia. I have been giving
him transfusions of my own blood since we all parted in
Akabat." Osiris waved a hand and Vlad froze against the
tree. Even his dripping blood slowed, then stopped.

"It is near dawn. Why would you bring him here *now*,

whatever the reason?" Aleksei was clearly annoyed with his friend.

"He awoke within the space of a heartbeat. His eyes became focused; his first words were that Gillian was in mortal danger and that I must accompany him to her immediately. Aleksei, I cannot detect any of his former dark taint. I examined his mind fully before bringing him here. There is none of the madness or the evil that had resided within him," Osiris informed them.

"Trocar, wait." Gillian had one eye on Osiris and the other on her friend. She wanted to hear the details before Trocar did bad things to the former Dark Prince. The Dark Elf was lazily spinning a wicked-looking blade near Vlad's nose.

Aleksei was still frowning but the fury was melting from his voice. "You drained him completely before the infusions?"

"Yes. It was my thought that since my blood was First Blood of the Nephilim as his was, it might undo the damage in his soul and bring him back in order for him to stand trial for his crimes. I had no idea if it was successful. He has been as he became at Akabat until minutes ago."

Osiris studied the myriad emotions sweeping across Aleksei's face. "Scan him yourself, Aleksei. You have a Lord's power. See if you can detect anything I may have missed."

Aleksei closed his eyes, casting his powerful, intelligent mind outward. Osiris waved a hand, releasing Vlad from his unmoving state.

The first word from Vlad's mouth shocked everyone. "Please, Elf. Please release me. I mean neither her nor any of you harm. Gillian . . . you are in terrible danger. Father Daily . . . We must destroy him."

Aleksei's eyes flew wide. He and Osiris exchanged a glance. Neither of them had ever heard Vlad Dracula say *please* for any reason.

Gillian was stunned as well. She moved closer to Vlad, drawing her Glock and pointing it at his head. "How do you know about Father Daily?"

Vlad met her gaze unflinchingly. "Because I made him."

Silence reigned. A squirrel in a nearby oak dropped an acorn, nearly giving everyone a heart attack.

"You . . . made him," Gillian repeated, hoping she'd heard him wrong.

"Over four hundred years ago. He was a protégé, much like Jack. The connection between Lord and servant remains. I am both grateful and ashamed of that." Vlad shook his head. The movement made Trocar's knives bounce. It looked very surreal.

"I'm confused," Kimber said, lowering her rifle. Gillian noted it was a modified Kalashnikov. Where the hell had Kimber hidden that?

Aleksei stared at both of them, then at Trocar. He hadn't realized any of them were armed.

"Join the party," Gillian said. "I'm still not clear on this, Vlad. You tried to kill me . . . Hell, you tried to kill all of us in Akabat, not to mention that 'taking over the world' thing. Now you're here essentially saying that you're concerned about my safety from one of your . . ."

"Progeny," Osiris filled in for her.

"Have you two got this?" Gillian asked Osiris and Aleksei. "I mean, if Trocar lets him down, can you heal him enough and talk quickly enough before the three of you become charcoal briquettes to determine if he is telling the truth? And can you kill him quickly enough if he isn't?"

Osiris glanced at the sky. It was fully dawn now, yet they were deep in the forest and sheltered well enough by the trees. "We already have determined that he is being truthful, but yes, we could kill him and still obtain shelter quickly enough."

"Aleksei?" Gillian turned to him. "I trust Osiris's judgment, but I trust yours more."

The bottom line was, she trusted her own empathy above all, and it was in overdrive trying to determine something, anything, from her former enemy. She was getting nothing from Vlad that triggered any unease. That in itself made her uncomfortable. He felt different. On her name-that-

Vampire meter . . . he almost felt like Osiris, Dionysus . . . even Aleksei, in terms of his intent.

"He is telling the truth; of that I am certain. I also cannot detect any of his former evil." Aleksei wanted to embrace her for her admission of trust, but knew her well enough to realize that touching her right now was not what she wanted.

"All right. Trocar, release him." Gill gave the order.

"As you wish." Trocar didn't hesitate. She knew the Vampires better than he did. However, after spending so much time in Aleksei's company and observing his treatment of Gillian, he was willing to take his word as well, though he dearly wanted to carve Vlad's heart out.

Once Vlad was released, Osiris offered him his wrist. Vlad's eyes closed in seeming ecstasy as he took in the powerful blood. Like magic, the wounds in his arms and legs closed. When he released Osiris's wrist, even his color was brighter, his skin more alabaster.

He thanked Osiris, turning back to Aleksei and Gillian. "Bartholomew was one of my most vocal detractors in Walachia when I was a living Prince. I did not want to kill him outright for political reasons, but I needed to stop him and his poisonous diatribe.

"Our nation had been decimated by Turk raiders. Since I did not have enough personal wealth, I wanted the Church's treasuries to donate enough to buy seeds, grain and live-stock to be distributed around our province. Bartholomew opposed all of it.

"His viewpoints alienated my people from their Faith. They already had nothing, and he took away more so that they had no hope. At that point, I realized I had waited too long. I had to act."

"I hate to interrupt but we are sitting ducks out here in the woods like this in daylight," Daed interjected.

"Shush. Let him talk," Gillian rebuked him.

Vlad continued. "I had not realized the extent of my powers until then. I was able to approach him, seduce him and eventually Turn him over the course of a few nights.

When he rose, he was as a Master. I stayed with him, taught him, used my influence over him. He became a faithful servant."

"He did mention you in his speech," Gillian said dryly.

"What speech?" Now it was Vlad's turn to look confused.

"While you were . . . away, he got himself some press coverage and was talking up a storm about how Gillian had interfered with your master plan involving the Angels." Daed was happy to enlighten him.

"He also has my friend as a hostage," Gillian told him.

"Then we must act immediately." Vlad sounded almost panicked.

He looked around the forest for a moment. "Where are we? Near Prague?"

"Yup." Gill nodded.

"How did he know that?" Kimber asked Gill.

"Because he's older than dirt and probably has been here a million times." Gillian snorted.

"We must get to ground. We can discuss everything this evening," Aleksei reminded them.

"I will secure Vlad for now. We will rejoin the rest of you when it is safe to do so." Osiris clapped a large hand on Vlad's shoulder and vanished with his charge.

"Be careful, *cara*." Aleksei kissed Gillian quickly, then he too misted out.

"Should we camp here or closer to the city?" Daed asked.

"Let's go into the city. We can do some legwork, see if anyone has seen Daily or has knowledge of him. That way when they get back we'll have something to go on." Gillian put her gun away and brushed the hair back from her face.

"Is that safe? We don't want to draw too much attention to ourselves." Daed wasn't certain about marching into Prague as a group.

"I think Kelda will be enough of a distraction if she and Hreidmar go into town looking for a honeymoon suite." Gillian winked at the Dwarves.

Hreidmar laughed uproariously. "Aye. That is indeed

a plan. Kelda, my love, are you up for being a bit of a diversion?"

"Does it involve danger, subterfuge and perhaps a fight?" She winked at him.

"Of course. Do you think I would take you someplace where you would be bored?" Hreidmar bellowed.

"Then I am ready." Kelda took his proffered hand and cuddled against his shoulder.

"This is going to be exciting." Trocar's ever-present sarcasm was a sure sign he felt everything was in order.

He flipped his cape over his shoulder and melted into the woods again. He allowed them to catch glimpses of him through the trees ahead. Everyone followed his path and began the long hike down the slope toward Prague.

CHAPTER
17

"Why are we in Prague again?" Kimber was dragging ass down the street. Her backpack shifted over to one hip and her energy level was sagging. Pavel trotted along beside her, still in Wolf form.

"To rescue Jenna." Gillian was no better off. Her steps were slower and she was feeling more than a little bit shitty. Currently light-headedness, nausea and thirst were hammering at her.

"Why is Jenna in Prague?"

Gillian stopped and stared at her. "Are you serious?"

"Oh fuck. Father Daily. That's right. Pregnancy fog. Jesus, Gill, I forgot all about Jenna for a minute. Does that make me a bad friend?" Kimber's green gold eyes misted for a moment.

"No. It makes you pregnant and going on fourteen hours without food, just like me. Let's find a pub or something. I'm starving."

The truth was Gillian had never felt less like eating in her life. She was worried about her friend and pissed off at Daily, Vlad and Osiris at the moment. Well, sort of. She wasn't as much pissed off at Osiris himself as she was at his timing. Who brings a recently catatonic, recovering megalomaniac, paranoid schizophrenic Vampire to a knife fight? That was what this was going to boil down to: an old-fashioned knife fight. No rules, just people kicking ass and taking names, and hopefully no casualties on her side of the disagreement.

"I can carry one or both of you," Garm interrupted her thoughts. He had shifted back into his Human form and was walking arm in arm with Helgi, who had also abandoned her animal shape at the edge of the forest.

"Or I can as well," Helgi added.

"Did Aleksei or Pavel put you up to this?" Gillian stopped in her tracks. "Just ignore anything they might have told you. If I need help, I'll ask for it."

Both Norse Shifters looked confused. "No . . . no, no one gave us instructions. We were only trying to help. No offense was meant, Gillian," Helgi soothed.

"Fine," she said, turning back to the city and scanning the streets for somewhere with food.

"Really, Gillian, we meant no harm." Helgi's eyes were wide.

"I said fine. Let's keep moving."

To have Garm, the scariest-looking Wolf any of them had ever seen, and Helgi, white Bear extraordinaire, both squirming under Gillian's level glare made Pavel laugh. Unfortunately, it came out as more of a choking cough from his canine larynx. Kimber pounded him on the back.

"You'd better watch yourself too. I might get a hankering for a Wolf pelt for my bed." She scowled at him.

"Don't underestimate the power of a hungry, pregnant Marine." Daed laughed. "They need food and probably a little rest."

Gillian was too distracted thinking about where the hell Jenna was in Prague to argue with him or to appreciate the beauty of the city they were stomping through. She figured they'd all feel better after having something to eat. Even Daed's step was less than springy.

Prague was a crown jewel in the cities of Eastern Europe. It was a thriving metropolis with pristine streets, remarkable history, friendly people and amazing sights. A modern city with its roots firmly in the past. Cobblestones and automobiles, horse-drawn carriages and cell phones: all were a welcome sight after trudging through the woods for several hours.

Trocar had vanished at the edge of town, promising to keep within shouting distance. The Grael was too well-known as one of Gillian's regular companions and didn't want to attract unwanted attention to their escapade by parading through the streets. He planned on joining them for food, but for now he'd scout ahead with Dagr.

Dagr stayed as close as possible to the unseen Grael. He was there more as an intermediary between the party's two locations than anything. The Elves had their own methods of communication and didn't need visual aids to keep in touch. Dagr took a few moments outside town to activate his contacts with the Sidhe and the Elves in the area. Arrangements were being made to accommodate any number of possibilities. He also put the word out about locating Father Daily's current retreat.

Hreidmar and Kelda had stolen, or rather commandeered, a horse and wagon from a farm on the edge of the forest. Gill wasn't happy about it until they left a sizable bag of gold for the owners and a note that promised the return of their property. The Dwarves drove into the Old Town section of Prague, near Josefov, the Old Jewish section of the city, causing quite a stir as Kelda smiled and waved at the gawkers. With a female Dwarf casually driving through town in a horse-drawn carriage, a crowd of local press soon gathered, jogging after the cart as Hreidmar moved leisurely around the city. Bless the Dwarves. They were true to their word, creating a distraction any political figure or public personality would envy.

With the majority of the city's attention elsewhere, Gillian felt remaining in the Old Town area might be the safest way for them to avoid Bartholomew Daily and his friends. She didn't know why. It was just a feeling that abruptly started when they entered the area. Years of dealing with weird shit and situations had taught her to rely heavily on those feelings.

Hopefully they could locate Jenna's whereabouts without arousing too much suspicion, and hopefully she was safely secured away from wherever her puppet master was located. The sector had less vehicle traffic to contend with, and a smashing open-air market. Josefov was glorious with old synagogues, a world-famous astrological clock and a beautifully kept ancient cemetery. There were dozens of eateries around the area as well. She was following her nose and her stomach.

"Look!" Gill pointed and veered off diagonally from their current path.

"It's perfect!" Kimber took off after her at a dead limp.

Daed followed closely, trotting after the two women as they headed for a place called Bed Lounge Bar and Restaurant. He rolled his eyes. Two gorgeous women, neither of whom was interested in him romantically, and they were headed for a place to eat with beds. It figured.

He caught up with the women in the doorway of the café. Gillian was following the hostess to the continuous bed wrapping around the walls of the restaurant. The interior was lit with soothing sea green lights. An entire wall of white linen covered a huge bed that curved around the dimensions of the restaurant. White acrylic trays were strategically placed at the foot of the beds. Gill and Kimber scrambled up on the huge linen expanse and fluffed their pillows. Pavel curled up next to Kimber.

"Only you could find a restaurant like this," Daed groused. He still sank gratefully down onto the softer-than-it-should-be mattress and leaned back against the pillows, mirroring Gillian and Kimber. Garm and Helgi took places across from the rest of the group so they could keep an eye on things.

"Are you bitching?" Gill accepted the menu from the hostess.

"Nope. Just making a statement."

"Jenna would love this place," Gillian mused. She wanted to eat just enough to fuel up and then get moving. Feeling crappy was not helping her mood. She was going to have to learn how to balance her lifestyle with her hormones.

"They have shrimp!" Kimber squealed.

"So they do," a silky voice said next to Gillian's feet. The approaching waitress nearly jumped out of her skin.

"Dammit, Trocar. Cut that out. We're starving and this is the most perfect restaurant idea in the world." Gillian shoved the Dark Elf as he seemingly materialized out of thin air.

"If food is inevitable, lay back and enjoy it." Trocar wriggled in between the two women, putting his arms around both of them.

"You're not staying."

"Yes, I am. Your Vampire would kill me if I let anything happen to you. I will order lunch, let you eat your food and I will be here with Daed, Garm and Helgi to watch over you. Tonight will be a busy night, make no mistake."

The waitress, who looked to be fully Human, was practically drooling on Trocar's boots. He turned on the high beams, smiling at her. Gillian watched with amusement as the woman's eyes predictably glazed over. Trocar translated their orders and made arrangements for them to eat and rest undisturbed.

"I didn't know you spoke Czech."

"I have many skills. Besides, what would our relationship be without a little mystery, Petal?" He grinned at her.

"You're an ass," Gill said affably.

"You love me."

"Occasionally, yes." She scrunched around to get more comfortable, removing Trocar's arm from across her shoulders. "Hands to yourself. I remember what happened last time we were in bed together."

"Ah, yes, our British adventure."

"What happened again?" Kimber mumbled from her side of the Elf.

"He grabbed my boob when Aleksei came in—that's what. It was a magical moment. Wait a minute, you were there in the next room with our token Wolf."

Gillian's tone would have been more biting if she hadn't been so exhausted. Who knew being pregnant and walking seven or eight miles could wipe her out? She mentally kicked herself for being a slack-ass.

"Shit, that's right. I forgot." Kimber sighed.

"You're just hungry. Your brain cells are starving."

Gillian hoped the traditional levity they kept up would help them keep from thinking about what could possibly be happening to Jenna.

Once a Marine, always a Marine. The standard operating procedure was that the more dire the situation, the more jokes and bullshit were flying around. She figured they were doing so well needling each other that Jenna had to be in one hell of a mess. Gallows humor, for the win.

The waitress appeared again, with two more waitstaff behind her. All were carrying loaded trays. Trocar had ordered enough food for a small army. There were platters of Kimber's requested shrimp; two types of soup: broccoli and chicken; lamb chops with mashed potatoes; gallons of water and tea; and a dessert platter so beautiful, it nearly made Gillian cry.

For a time, the only sound from the group was chewing and making happy noises as they ate. Kimber was shoveling food in as fast as she could chew and swallow without choking on the large pieces. Gillian forced herself to eat, knowing that keeping her strength up was good for both the baby and her own survival. Since Pavel was still in Wolf form, they all tossed him choice bits off their plates.

After eating and making herself catnap, Gillian suggested they split up and see what kind of information they could gather individually on Bartholomew Daily. She was vetoed immediately by Trocar, Kimber and Daed.

"There is no way I am letting you go off on your own, Captain." Trocar's normally smooth brow furrowed slightly.

"It was bad enough following you for your Ripper suicide mission in Sacele, but I am not going to explain to your Vampire why I let his pregnant fiancée get mangled in Prague because she insisted on individual data acquisition."

"And I'm not sewing you up again. There is a limit to

the types of anesthesia I can use on pregnant women. We'd have to risk exposure in the hospital if you get yourself seriously wounded." Daed scowled.

"Oh, hell no! I am not going through a pregnancy on my own if you get yourself killed. Besides, it's your fault that I'm pregnant in the first place," Kimber griped.

Pavel's lupine face registered shock. If his eyebrows had been as mobile in Wolf form as they were in Human form, they'd have been up in his hairline.

Gillian laughed. "She means because of the healing, Pavel. Don't worry; your stud status is intact."

He panted happily and licked Kimber's face. She pushed him off impatiently. "Ew! Dog germs!"

"All right, you guys win," Gillian conceded. "We'll stay together."

"You stay together, and I will continue shadowing you as before. Dagr has his own network looking for Daily's lair and for Jenna, in case she's being kept separately. He will meet us in Old Town shortly, hopefully with a guide." Trocar gave another mock salute, paid the waitress as she handed him the bill, then walked out into the bright sunlight of Prague and vanished.

"How does he do that?" Helgi gasped.

"I have no idea. I've seen him do it for years and I still can't figure it out. He told me once that people only see what they are expecting to see and that Elves generally take advantage of that." Gillian shrugged.

"It's still unsettling whenever he does it." Kimber nodded.

"Will you please get over to Old Town and into the Old Jewish Sector?" Trocar purred next to Gillian's ear.

Everyone jumped, including Pavel. He had the decency to look embarrassed. A Shifter in Wolf form who couldn't detect a well-known companion ought to be discomfited.

"Shit! Dammit, Trocar. I've told you not to do that." Gill punched the suddenly visible Grael in the arm.

"And I have asked you not to look so delicious. I think we are even." Trocar blew her a kiss and sauntered off with a flip of his cape, remaining fully visible this time.

"I really hate him sometimes," Gillian grumbled. She

shifted her pack to a more comfortable position on her shoulder and marched off after the Dark Elf.

Daed was still laughing after Trocar's quip and nearly tripped over Pavel. The Wolf was sitting directly in the doorway of the restaurant, doing the lupine version of giggles with Kimber leaning on him, snorting back her own laughter.

"Come on; let's follow pumpkin before she dismembers Trocar in the street."

"I heard that!" Gillian called back. She scratched the back of her head with her middle finger, knowing that Daed would catch it.

"I can see that!"

"Good! It means your vision hasn't gone to hell yet!"

The Dark Elf led them deep into the Josefov section of Old Town. Here some of the buildings dated back to the tenth century. Six ancient synagogues, a Jewish cemetery, an old ceremonial hall and what was known as the Old Jewish Town Hall were located here.

Gillian stopped and looked upward. She pointed to a clock high on the top of the Old Town Hall.

"That's the Astronomical Clock. I've read about this. It's a representation of the Earth, but the local view of the sky. See the Zodiac ring? It moves counterclockwise from the rest of the clock with the Sun on it. The Moon ring goes much faster. The outer ring shows Czech lettering for a twenty-four-hour clock. This is so cool! I've always wanted to see that."

They all took a moment to admire the clock, hoping to look like tourists. It was indeed beautiful and fun to watch. The ancient engineering feat was a strong tourist draw, and soon the little group found themselves surrounded by fellow travelers taking pictures.

Fueled by a little rest and wonderful food, Gillian's brain clicked on.

"Wait a minute. I know this area. I studied it in Midrasha," she announced.

"In where?" Kimber asked.

"It's a Jewish educational program for teenagers to teach us about our heritage."

"Do you speak Hebrew?" Daed wanted to know. Some of the signs around the area were in both Hebrew and Czech.

"Just the prayers. I'm Reform, not Orthodox." Gill was tapping her finger against her teeth, thinking.

"There's the Old Jewish Town Hall, so there should be a cemetery nearby, plus several old synagogues. Look, there's a ticket stand over there. Do you guys mind if we continue to look around a little bit . . . like in a tour group?"

Joining a tour would give them better anonymity before their rendezvous with Aleksei, Osiris and Vlad. Plus, they needed to reconnect with Hreidmar and Kelda. Daed went to get tickets. He asked the vendor if they could be kept together in a private tour group. Something on a newspaper lying on the counter of the booth caught his eye.

"Pumpkin!" Daed called and beckoned to Gillian.

She repressed the desire to kill him on the spot when she realized he wouldn't call out her real name when they were trying to be covert.

"Coming, sugar!" She waved cheerfully and walked to where he was.

Daed pointed to the paper, paid the vendor and handed Gill one of the tickets. "Looks like things are going well in Romania."

On the front page of the paper was a distance shot of Mirrin and Dorian, walking hand in hand on a moonlit beach. The caption was in Czech, of course, but the names Aleksei Rachlav and Gillian Key were easy to make out. The press coverage they'd been after and the establishment of their alibi was working as planned. Good. Hopefully Father Daily would be privy to the local media and believe that Gillian and Aleksei were safely at a resort in their home Country.

Dagr soon came striding up out of the maze of streets. Hreidmar and Kelda scurried along in his wake. Evidently Elves had excellent homing beacons. Finding them in even this section of the city couldn't have been easy. After welcoming back their friends and congratulating them on a marvelous distraction, a local Sidhe named Evzen joined them. He was sporting a name tag from the tour vendor.

"Good afternoon, my friends. I will be honored to point out some of the more fascinating sites of our fair city." Evzen was tall and lovely, but with the wiry muscles of a Fey warrior underneath his tightly fitted shirt and jeans. His hair was an interesting mix of dark rust and bright orange, complementing his deep violet eyes.

Soon they were roaming through one spectacular synagogue after another. Evzen was very enthusiastic about his knowledge of Prague, leading them around the larger crowds via back alleyways and narrow passages.

Dagr waited until Gillian stopped to look at an ancient flag displayed in the Old New Synagogue. He whispered as discreetly as he could, "Evzen is a friend."

"I figured that. But thanks for telling me," Gillian whispered back.

Dagr smiled and went back to admiring the artifacts around the synagogue. Gillian continued her rounds as well, her empathy twitching madly at her. Some "Thing" was making it twitch. It wasn't Jenna and it wasn't a nearby unknown Vampire . . . or Shifter . . . or Fey. The feeling was strongest here, in this very synagogue. It felt . . . off, in some way. Her mind was whirling, trying to sort through her feelings, thoughts and memories while she listened to Evzen.

There was a story . . . something that happened in Prague a long time ago. Something she should remember. Damn pregnancy hormones. She felt like she was riding the little bus to combat school. What the hell did she need to remember? Bah!

"This way, everyone." Evzen waited for his charges to follow him outside. He led them around through an alleyway to an extremely old cemetery, stopping at one of the ancient graves. The tombstone was made of salmon-colored granite and was covered with weathered Hebraic script.

"Here is the most famous grave in the cemetery. Rabbi Judah Loew is credited with saving the city of Prague, or at least this section of it, during a pogrom initiated by the emperor in the sixteenth century." Evzen's English was flawless and his voice soothing and musical.

Something clicked in Gillian's mind as she listened. She remembered! It gave her hope that she wasn't going to be spending her pregnancy blathering due to exhaustion, lack of caffeine and permanent nicotine deprivation.

"The Golem! I remember that story!" she said louder than she meant to.

Evzen laughed. "You are correct! The Golem indeed is a permanent inhabitant of the Old New Synagogue. It remains in the Genizah, ready to defend again, if invoked."

"Golem? You mean a literal Creature made from clay?" Daed asked him.

"Yes, I do." Evzen nodded. "Should I tell him the legend, or would you like to, Gillian?"

"No, you go right ahead. They're all probably sick of hearing my voice anyway." Gillian grinned. She was terribly pleased with herself that she had funneled a memory from her teen years into the reality of what she was feeling. No wonder she was getting odd vibes inside the synagogue. The Creature was deactivated, but Its latent power was definitely still present.

Evzen recounted the tale of how Rabbi Loew, in an effort to protect the Jewish population from a vicious anti-Semitic army, had created the Golem. He called It to life and unleashed It on the unsuspecting enemy. The Creature had devastated the army, protecting the synagogue and the rabbi's people. Eventually the emperor appealed to Rabbi Loew to destroy the Creature.

The rabbi agreed, providing the persecution of the Jews in Prague would stop. Instead of destroying It, the rabbi deactivated It and stored It in the synagogue's attic, or Genizah. There It remained among old Hebrew-language books, papers and scrolls, ready to rise again, should there be need.

"That is so cool!" Kimber squeaked.

"You're really getting on my nerves with the overenthusiasm, perky girl." Gillian grinned as she poked her friend in the ribs.

Kimber jumped and tried to put on a frowny face. "Shit, I know. I'm getting on my own nerves. I feel like an extra from *The Brady Bunch*."

Gillian sighed. "It's not a problem. I'm sorry I'm all glum and bitchy, but I really feel shitty. Plus my sensory net is giving me fits over that damn Golem."

"No worries, Kemo Sabe." Kimber spontaneously hugged her.

"You're just a happier incubator than I am. Don't sweat it. I'll get used to it."

"When we get out of this alive and with Jenna, you'll be all sunshine and flowers too," Kimber assured her.

"That would be bad, with Aleksei being a Vampire and all."

Kimber frowned. Pavel bumped her with his head. "Oh right! Vampire . . . sunshine. I get it!" She was very pleased with herself to have put it together without further explanation.

Gillian had to laugh. Her friends were her family, and Kimber, more than any of them, was as close as she'd ever come to having a sister.

"We're going to get through this, Tonto. You, me, Fluffy over there and Fang." Gillian slung her arm over Kimber's shoulder. No small feat, since her friend was several inches taller than she was.

Pavel growled at her dubbing him *Fluffy*. He was fairly certain Aleksei would have objected to *Fang* as well.

"Have you two rested enough?" Trocar's silky voice reached them. He was perched on one of the bed-shaped tombs.

"Get off of there. That's disrespectful," Gillian ordered him.

"I doubt if the occupant minds," Trocar countered, but he got off anyway.

Gillian shot him a look that would have put anyone else firmly in their place. "Okay . . . let's caucus, since we seem to be alone for the moment. Dagr, have you found anything out?"

"Indeed I have. Bartholomew Daily is registered at the International Hotel. However, the room has remained unoccupied since the date of registration. Local intelligence has it that he is in New Town, which is the next district over, and he has Jenna with him."

"Thanks, Dagr. Evzen? Got any ideas about where the hell Daily is? I would like to try a daylight rescue, if that's possible."

Gillian's mind was racing, the hormonal fog and former fatigue retreating into memory. If they could get in now, get Jenna safely and summarily get the hell out of the area, that would suit her just fine. There had to be a way.

"What about Daily? According to Vlad's affirmation, that phony priest is after you specifically," Daed interjected.

"I don't give a shit about Daily. Vlad can arrange a throwdown with him on his own time, if he really is recovered and not on some other goddamn delusional mission. I'm only interested in getting my friend out of there." Gillian's tone took on the edge her former Marine colleagues knew only too well.

"You know how I hate to contradict you, Gillyflower, but there is the matter of your pregnancy."

Trocar. She'd forgotten he had appointed himself Elf Voice of Reason in Complicated Situations.

"If I'm safe, then the baby is safe, Trocar. Jenna's well-being is the issue here. In a few months, after this baby is born, we can all storm Bart Daily's battlements and call him out. Right now, I'm not grandstanding because some Vampire Lord wannabe is being snarky on TV about not liking my choices. I don't remember asking for his opinion, and I care exactly balls about it now. We can rescue Jenna and be back up on that ridge before Aleksei and Vlad are up and running."

Kimber nodded. "Remember, Trocar? We sneaked into Oscar's house and rescued Tanis out from under Jack's nose."

"Yes, and remember what happened next?" Trocar circled them both. "The little visit Jack paid to us in Romania?"

"Yeah, we were there. What's your point?" Gillian crossed her arms and went toe-to-toe with the Dark Elf.

"All of you were nearly killed; that is my point. You may be able to survive that kind of fight again, Petal, but you both are carrying children now." He wasn't backing down, but neither was she.

"And?"

"If you are hit in the abdomen, or sustain the type of beating Jack delivered to you on that night, or manage to become an unwilling donor for that radical priest, you may lose your baby."

There. He had said it.

"I'm not planning on getting injured at all, and I will slit my own throat before I let him make me into his thrall," Gillian said firmly. Well, at least she wasn't yelling.

"Gill . . . maybe we should wait until Aleksei gets here." Kimber was wavering. Both of her friends were making sense. She just couldn't decide who was making more sense at the moment.

"What the hell does Aleksei being here have to do with when we rescue Jenna?" Now she was yelling.

"Because it's his baby too, Gillian," Daed reminded her.

CHAPTER
18

DAMMIT. She hated it when her friends were right and she was w . . . wr . . . wro . . . er . . . mistaken.

"Fine. We'll wait until dusk."

"Gill . . ." Daed was prepared to continue the argument.

"I said *fine.*"

She marched over to a nearby sausage vendor and ordered the Prague equivalent of a hot dog. Kimber dashed over to join her. The others lined up behind. Soon all of them were happily munching away on mustard-covered sausages cleverly inserted into appropriately sized baguettes. The ones who weren't pregnant were sipping the mulled wine the vendor sold, while Gillian and Kimber satisfied their thirst with soda.

"Didn't we just eat?" Daed knew he was treading dangerous ground but couldn't help himself.

"When *you* grow a uterus and can comment intelligently on pregnancy, hunger, hormones and patience levels, we'll talk," Gill said around a mouthful of hot dog.

Daed laughed heartily. Both the women were far from being overweight. He watched as Gillian paid for another two and handed one to Kimber, who devoured it with great enjoyment.

"These are really wonderful," Kelda stated.

"Indeed they are." Hreidmar gently wiped a smudge of mustard off his wife's mouth with a paper napkin.

"We will introduce you to Dwarven cooking when we accomplish our mission here." Kelda winked at Gillian.

"Thank you, Kelda. I'll look forward to that!" Gillian was enthusiastic about her offer. It was very generous, for starters; secondly, it would give her a chance to observe something about Dwarven culture that no Human in recorded history had been able to do.

"It's getting toward dark; we need to decide where we're meeting up. Aleksei can track Gillian anywhere, so it doesn't matter where we are as long as it's a safe area to talk," Daed reminded them.

"Not to be macabre, but the cemetery is pretty isolated," Gillian suggested.

"True. And the last place an insane Vampire would think to look for anyone is in a cemetery," Trocar quipped dryly.

"Dammit, my mind is going to hell," Gill grumbled. "All right, how about the Old New Synagogue?"

"Do Jewish artifacts affect Vampires?" Kimber asked.

"No," Gillian replied, her shoulders slumping.

She suddenly brightened again. "Wait a minute . . . Daily is a defrocked priest. He may be excommunicated and crazy, but he is still a Catholic and he obviously thinks he's superior to everyone. Evzen, I know Prague has a cathedral. Where is it?"

"St. Vitus Cathedral is within the Prague castle complex across the city from here. There is also a basilica and several chapels," Evzen replied.

"He won't be able to enter the cathedral or the basilica . . . probably not the chapels either." Gill was pacing, tapping her thumbnail against her teeth. "That leaves the castle itself. Are there any other buildings, crypts or structures up there where a Vampire can hide out and be fairly secure?"

"The basilica now serves as a concert hall," Evzen responded.

"That would make sense. If it's been converted, in his

mind, it would be safe for him to enter. He has a stage, seating for an audience and room for a film crew. Remember, guys? He's been broadcasting his tirades from a stage with a podium," Gillian reminded them.

"That's right. He had Jenna in front of purple velvet curtains." Kimber nodded.

"The concert hall has royal purple curtains and they are indeed velvet," Evzen confirmed.

"Let's get across town, then. Any way over there without attracting attention to our bunch?" Gillian asked.

"The metro or a tram would draw the least attention. Locals of all types use them frequently. We would blend in easily," Evzen said.

"Except her." Gillian pointed toward Kelda.

"True," Kelda agreed. "Hreidmar and I can get there on our own. We will meet you outside the castle complex in the space of an hour."

The Dwarves scurried off in the direction Evzen indicated without waiting for confirmation. They were promptly lost in the gathering crowds. It was getting late. More and more street vendors were opening their stalls, turning on lights and beginning to display their wares or cook their offerings.

"Let's take the tram, then. It's almost dusk, and the more powerful Vampires in the area will be able to be up and mobile about the same time as Aleksei and Osiris. Other lesser Vamps might be up, but they will restrict themselves to the metro since it's protected underground," Gillian suggested.

"Don't forget Vlad and Odin. Odin may not realize that we have company," Daed reminded her.

"Odin almost certainly knew the minute Osiris blew into our area. He's two years younger than God as it is. I doubt much would get past him."

"Then why didn't he pop back over when we were discussing things with Vlad?" Kimber asked.

"Probably because he knew Osiris and Aleksei were there and weren't dismembering him," Gillian said. "Or maybe he's just not that nosy. I'm sure they filled him in before they all conked out for the day. I'm still getting used to their whole concept of blood bonds and telepathy and Lord versus Master power."

They all hustled to a tram stop and bought tickets. The tram arrived shortly thereafter. Everyone climbed aboard, spreading out on the vehicle. The former Marines, Trocar, Daed, Kimber and Gillian, took vantage points at all of the steps. Dagr, Pavel, Helgi, Garm and Evzen remained in the middle of the car.

Gillian thanked the Gods for the millionth time that her empathy was serving her well. Her friends were mere blips on her metaphysical radar screen. Their familiarity didn't spark any concern. The surrounding crowd on the tram and in the area registered, but again, there did not seem to be anyone or anything in the area that was a direct threat to her party.

The trip to the castle complex took about fifteen minutes. Seeing Prague in the magic of twilight was quite an experience. She found herself musing what it would be like to be enjoying it with Aleksei. When the conductor called for everyone to disembark, it shook her out of her daydream. She stomped off the tram more forcefully than she meant to, irritated with herself that she could lose focus so quickly when her friend might very well be in life-threatening circumstances. Okay, she loved the guy and she was going to marry him. That was no excuse for forgetting what she was doing.

"I am very flattered and moved that I can turn your thoughts away from anything, after all this time, piccola.*"*

Gillian jumped when Aleksei's black velvet voice poured across her brain cells.

"Dammit! Stop doing that!" she said aloud. She spun and whacked him in the arm as he materialized next to her. Hearing him before seeing him was still taking some getting used to. Ah, love.

"Where's Osiris and—*mmph!*"

Her words were lost against Aleksei's amazing chest as he hugged her tightly. He had been secretly terrified that she might attempt to orchestrate a rescue before he'd risen.

"Here, little sister." The Egyptian Lord walked toward

their group, with Vlad and Odin close behind him. Everyone at least had the sense to dress like Aleksei. A former Egyptian God in a linen kilt, a Viking in fur and leather, plus Vlad's overstated Prince gear would have been a glaring flag that their Vampire cluster was out of the ordinary. Now at least they blended in with the older Vampires already cruising the area.

Gillian couldn't remember ever seeing a more noble-looking group. She had to admit, the high boots, tight pants and billowy shirts made them all shoot to a ten on her Hot-o-Meter. Okay, so Aleksei was a twelve. Once again she found herself unintentionally ruminating over her intended's scrumptious factor. Aforementioned tall hotness interrupted her thoughts again.

"Gillian, we do not have much time. Daily will be rising now, or has already risen, since he is probably sheltered underground. Vlad has explained his fears to Odin, Osiris and myself. I cannot explain it, *cara*, but none of us can find reason to doubt him. Not in his mind, at least. It is for you to say if there is anything in his heart to be concerned with, but please hurry. If we are going to find your friend, it must be very soon." Aleksei held her away from him, looking solidly into her eyes.

She stared back at him. With a monumental effort it never occurred to her she would have to make, she dropped her last bastion of doubt about Aleksei, his motives, his intentions and his love for her. She trusted him. Completely, irrevocably, she trusted him in the same manner she trusted Kimber, Trocar . . . or Jenna. It was an unexpected but relieving epiphany. He was Family, as much as her Corps partners were. Shit.

Well . . . their relationship really was falling together with almost no effort and very few emotional speed bumps. With that thought, her fear of a real commitment vanished into the fading twilight.

"Okay."

Turning away from him, she beckoned to Vlad, who approached her willingly. Addressing her past patient and former captor in the middle of a castle courtyard in Prague was a little weird, but hey, she'd go with it. Since she'd come to Romania over three years ago, every other goddamn thing had come out on the weird side as well.

"I am not a telepath. I can't probe your mind the way they can. What I feel from you right now is concern and urgency. I have no reason to trust you and every reason to kill you, but for the moment I believe you." There, that was definite.

"Thank you, Gillian. After this is over, I will tell you how much you helped me, even when I was still gripped with madness. I do not remember much of what happened at Akabat, except dimly hearing you arguing for my life. I give you my word that I will not betray you." To her surprise and utter horror, he took her right hand and kissed her wrist.

Vlad let go of her hand and knelt on the cobblestones before Aleksei. "Before these witnesses, I pledge my loyalty to you and yours . . . my Lord."

Aleksei looked even more shocked than Gillian was. Seconds rambled by as he contemplated his ex-Master and archenemy. Finally he spoke.

"I accept your offer."

He held out his wrist to the former Dark Prince. Vlad took it, sinking his fangs into Aleksei's wrist briefly.

Aleksei gently removed his arm and closed the marks himself with a quick swipe of his tongue. "There is no time for formalities now. If we survive, I will take your formal oath later."

"I have a blood bond with him. He can go nowhere without my knowledge," Osiris added.

Gillian stepped up to the kneeling Vampire, partially drawing her Glock out of her pocket and allowing a discreet amount of the gun to show. The metal grip flashed in the glare of the streetlamps that had just turned on.

"Let me emphasize one thing. If at any time during our search you give me reason to suspect that you are a traitor, I will put a bullet through your skull with no further discussion. Understand?"

"I understand, Gillian. I will give you no reason to destroy me." He rose gracefully from the ground and bowed to her.

"All right, then. Let's go."

Evzen started off, leading them toward the basilica. The complex was enormous. The buildings were labeled in Czech and English, but it would have taken them longer without a guide. He led them in a roundabout loop, skirting the most heavily trafficked areas. Dagr and Trocar had disappeared from the time they exited the tram. No surprise there. Gillian knew Trocar in particular was not far away. Dagr would be at least within shouting distance.

The Sidhe stopped between the back of a building and the outer wall of the castle. Gillian couldn't tell where the hell they were since there were no signs in sight. Darkening shadows loomed on either side of them and around the corner of the structure.

"We are close to where we need to enter the basilica. I suggest you arm yourselves in whatever manner you have." Evzen produced twin blades similar to ones Gillian had seen Trocar wield on occasion.

Kimber dropped her pack, rummaged around and brought out a Velcro armband with several throwing knives sheathed in it. She wrapped it around her upper left arm, then reached back into the pack. Next out was a shotgun-flamethrower combination. After shouldering the gun, she kicked the bag over against the wall.

Gillian had her Glock in one hand and a spare gun at the small of her back and was affixing a knife to an ankle sheath when she noticed Kimber's arsenal.

"Where the hell did that come from?"

"I had some spare time, so I made something new. Like it?" Kimber grinned, flicking on the small blue flame that would power the flamethrower's lethal fire.

"How many shells?" Daed asked. He walked over to admire Kimber's handiwork.

"It's a dual magazine that holds twelve. I figured out how to jack two shells in at once; plus I made a couple of extras," Kimber said proudly, patting her thigh pocket.

"Can we discuss this later? She knows what she's doing, so the damn thing will work." Gill was getting impatient.

"Here, I brought these just in case." Daed tossed them both high-grade military flashlights. "It has a UV feature on it. Flip the blue switch and instant sunlight. Just be careful where you point it. We don't want to take out one of our own."

"Also, let's be very clear on this," Gillian began. "We are here to get Jenna. Nothing else. I don't intend to tangle with Daily right now. This is his turf and we can take up issues with him later on a more level playing field. I just want her out of there. If she is with him voluntarily and isn't bespelled, then fine. She's entitled to her own opinion and choices. If she's not, then we're getting all of us out of there, pronto." Gillian said it more for Vlad's benefit than the rest.

"Gillian . . ." Aleksei's senses tingled. He reached out, yanking her behind him at the exact moment that Garm and Helgi sensed an intruder and shifted.

The gigantic Wolf leaped ahead of Evzen, followed by the great white Bear. Pavel was a heartbeat behind them. Together they formed a furry, living wall between their party and the female Vampire who materialized a few yards from where the Fey warrior was standing.

"Hello, Gillian." Erzsébet Báthory stood there in all her jaw-dropping glory.

"Do not move." Trocar melted out of the shadow behind her. He had a crossbow shoved up against her back. It was loaded with a silver-tipped ash-wood bolt.

"Yes, do not move." Kelda also seemed to solidify out of the gloom. She only came up to Erzsébet's waist. The two wicked-looking knives she held were pressed against the Vampire's abdomen and kidney, front and back respectively.

Gillian didn't respond to the greeting. Instead she queried Osiris and Aleksei, her own weapon trained on Erzsébet's head. "Well? Do we kill her or listen to her? I can't feel anything resembling a threat, which is weird because back in Egypt she and her sidekick Sweeney were thinking of cutting my throat."

Before they could answer, a new but familiar voice butted into the conversation. She'd heard it only once before, but still . . .

"No! Do not harm my Lady!"

"Sir Georg?" Gillian turned to see if she was right.

The ancient Vampire knight was hurrying toward them with Hreidmar in front of him at sword point. How he kept his armor from clanking was anyone's guess.

Kelda's lovely little face became suffused with pure fury. "If my husband is harmed in any way, she dies, Knight."

"Wait a minute. No one is killing anyone yet. Everyone just stop." Gillian took command of the situation before someone really got killed. Great Ganesh, they hadn't even begun to look for Jenna yet and all hell was already breaking loose.

"Georg, stop where you are. Let Hreidmar go. Kelda isn't going to ventilate Erzsébet . . . Wait . . . Did you say *your* lady? Erzsébet is your . . . girlfriend now?" Gillian was getting supremely confused.

"At last count, you two were on opposite sides of the Vlad fence. What's going on?"

Gill hastily moved in front of Georg as he released Hreidmar and beaded in on Vlad. "No, you're not killing him either. He's helping us for the moment. You need to calm down and someone needs to explain really fast what the fuck is going on."

Aleksei grabbed Georg's shoulder in case he didn't listen to Gillian. "Do not move, Sir Georg. If you harm her in trying to get to Vlad, I will destroy you."

Georg's surprised look was all the reassurance he needed that the newcomer Vampire wasn't going to try anything. Aleksei shot a look at Gillian that wasn't friendly. Stepping out in front of a Reborn armored fanatic with a sword wasn't his idea of bravery.

She ignored his reaction and turned back to Trocar and Kelda. "Put the pointy things away so she can talk."

They reluctantly stepped back from Erzsébet and gave

her some space. Hreidmar went to Kelda's side, his axe in his hands. Trocar backed up but he didn't lower his crossbow.

Erzsébet laughed. "I do not blame you for being suspicious, Gillian. Georg and I found each other not long after the incident at Akabat. After an incredibly protracted discussion during several enduring meetings, we discovered that we are not so very different, he and I."

"I would disagree with that statement. If I remember my limited knowledge of Vampire history correctly, Sir Georg never murdered more than six hundred women. He was a victim of Vlad's psychotic behavior, same as Aleksei." Gillian hadn't lowered her gun or moved since Erzsébet had appeared.

Unexpectedly, Erzsébet's eyes sparkled with tears in the moonlight. She lowered them immediately, but crystalline flashes of color reflected from her dark lashes.

"I believe I was subjected to the same madness that affected Vlad. I am First Blood, just as he is. I do not know how or when I was Turned. I have no memory of the event except awakening in my family crypt. The memories I have of my life before, prior to that moment, are very disjointed and muddled. I was riding my horse through a high mountain pass; it was beginning to snow. My horse spooked . . . That is all I remember until waking among the dead."

"Is she lying?" Gillian asked. She couldn't feel any deception from Erzsébet, but right now her normal Spidey senses were a bit skewed.

Osiris frowned. "No, she is not. Her description is very like my own experience, and that of Dionysus."

"And of mine, with the exception that the rest of us did not suffer from madness as you and Vlad have," Odin chimed in.

"I remember my full life before and after I was Reborn," Aleksei commented. "Perhaps the madness within the two of you springs from the same Source."

"You are the only Lord in our history not to be a direct progeny of the First Blood," Erzsébet reminded him. "Neither you nor your brother suffered insanity from Vlad's

Bloodline. In fact, the two of you went to great lengths to reestablish your own Line after your Ascension to Lord."

"Then Vampires are evolving," Gillian stated.

"Daily may then be one who has also evolved. That would make this even more concerning than it already is." Aleksei raked his hand through his long, thick hair.

Daed interjected. "No, what she means is that every species that can breed true will evolve. Humans have changed dramatically from their first creation. Even in the space of recorded history, people have shown increases in natural adaptations, abilities and powers. Gillian, for instance, would have been considered a sorceress in bygone days for her empathic abilities alone. Now she is still an anomaly, but those gifts are accepted as being special instead of something dark and frightening."

"Hell, in the old days, she would have been burned at the stake or sacrificed to the old Gods." Kimber snickered.

"Have to be a virgin for that," Gill quipped back.

"Aleksei? You get anything from her?" Gillian asked him. Her eyes never left Erzsébet.

"She is telling the truth. That is all I can confirm," Aleksei said.

"I find nothing duplicitous in her, Gillian. However, if Aleksei has evolved, then it is entirely plausible other Masters have come into a Lord's power. Daily may in fact be one," Odin offered.

"I understand that, but even among you, your power levels differ, don't they?" she asked him.

"Correct. Osiris is truly the most powerful Vampire I have ever seen or felt."

"Then even if Daily has a Lord's power . . . he could be at either end of the power scale. Sorry, Erzsébet. I do recognize you are at a Lord's level as well . . . I am not certain what to call the female version without sounding sexist. I can feel how strong you are compared to the others. There is definitely a difference."

Gillian felt a bit kinder toward the woman, knowing that her former madness may have come from the same source as Vlad's. Which brought her down another path of thought. If Erzsébet and Vlad came from the same line, then Erzsébet's progeny, like Vlad's, wouldn't necessarily be psychotic.

Aleksei was a perfect example, as was Tanis. They were both of Vlad's direct Bloodline, but neither of them was nuts. On Erzsébet's side, however . . .

"Erzsébet . . . where is Sweeney?" Gillian felt icy cold sweep down her spine with her revelation that the woman's Akabat companion was noticeably missing.

This time, the woman's eyes swept upward to meet Gillian's hard stare squarely. "He is in league with the priest who hides here. After Akabat, we had an opportunity to witness one of Father Daily's broadcasts. With all his ranting, I knew he was a madman. Sweeney was always a zealot of sorts, easily led by powerful figures. I think that is why he stayed with me and Vlad all those years. He changed from a broken shell of a man into a pathologically faithful companion during our time together."

"Did either of you coerce him to Turn?" Gillian's gun and eye never wavered.

"On the contrary, he begged Vlad for Rebirth. At first he was in love with power, with the infatuation that all Humans first feel in a relationship with a Vampire. When Vlad saw his fascination had become worship, he Turned him."

She turned to Vlad. "So your being dead to the world, so to speak, allowed Sweeney to run free?"

"That is correct, Gillian. Without me as a direct threat to keep him harnessed, and with his separation from Erzsébet, Sweeney would gravitate to the next Vampire he perceived as being all-powerful. Father Daily is very charismatic, from what I have observed."

"Fair enough. Why are you here, Erzsébet? This is the second coincidence in the span of one day. I don't like coincidences." Gillian's stance didn't change, but she lowered the gun just a little.

"Since Vlad has been gone, since Akabat, there has been more and more acceptance of us in the real world. You all are isolated in your little corner of Romania. The rest of us have to exist within the Humans' parameters at all times.

What was accomplished in Egypt, Father Daily is trying to destroy.

"I will not go back to that existence again. Daily needs to be silenced. If he will not see reason, then we will have a problem. I have discovered I need others in my life very much . . . and Georg wants a life with me." The beautiful Vampire smiled tenderly at the knight who had frozen at Aleksei's threat.

"We are not here to kill Daily," Gillian enlightened her.

Georg managed a scowl on his handsome face. He had frozen at Aleksei's command, and had been observing the situation. "Then why are you here?"

"I have a friend who is with him. I just want to make certain she's all right and isn't being kept against her will," Gill said.

"If Daily has her, and she is your friend, it is not due to her free will," Erzsébet informed them.

"Then Jenna is going to be minus one fangy captor," Gillian said flatly.

CHAPTER
19

LOCATING a back entrance to the basilica would have been difficult if not for Evzen. The Fey warrior had been in the area when the structure had been built in the year 920, and when the entire basilica was rebuilt following a fire in 1142. He knew the foundation layout and where unscrupulous workers had left secret passageways into the crypts to allow for more lucrative grave robbing.

Using one of his fancy knives, Evzen pried loose mortar away, allowing him to ease a brick out of its niche. Behind it was a lever, which he triggered. Rusty pulleys moved with a deep grinding sound as a panel of bricks moved back and to the inside of a darkened corridor.

"Wait a minute." Daed raised a hand to stop anyone from entering.

"Pavel, can you scent anything? Gill? Any feelings we should know about?"

She shook her head. "I got nothing. It's just another building. I can feel Humans and Paramortals everywhere around us, but there is no threat."

Pavel gingerly stepped into the passage, went in about twenty feet, then returned to them on the outside. He shook his lupine head, indicating that no, he hadn't smelled anything of consequence.

Gillian glowered at the opening. The wheels in her mind were spinning so fast, her mental hamster was reaching for oxygen. She and Daed exchanged a look. Something was wrong. She knew it intuitively; she could almost taste it. This wasn't her empathy firing; this was instinct forged through combat and a few too many covert missions. Out of the corner of her eye she could see the ancient knight approaching the entrance.

"Something is fucked-up about this. No, Pavel. Georg, get back over here. Everyone stay out of the passage for a minute." Gillian shooed everyone away from the door. She crouched down and stared into the recently hidden entrance.

"I do not understand." Evzen's angelic face didn't do anything remotely resembling a frown, but he did look puzzled.

"It's not you, Evzen. I know you're on our side. I know that you believe this passage is safe or you wouldn't have brought us here. It's not the passage. We should not have made it this far through Prague, up here to the castle area, without some kind of altercation from Daily's followers or entourage. There should have been some kind of alarm raised, or at least notice taken of our presence. We are a large group consisting mostly of powerful Beings, excluding Kimber and myself—"

"Hey! I am not some weak-assed bitch and neither are you!" Kimber interjected.

"No offense, Kimber, but you and I are the weak links in this chain. We've got Vampire Lords, ancient Viking Shifters, Grael, Sidhe, a closeted Minotaur, a knight and a female Dwarf, for hell's sake . . . Sorry, Hreidmar, but she's the novelty. Why is no one paying attention to us? Shit, if I wasn't with us, *I* would gawk."

Now it was Aleksei's turn to frown. Gillian's empathy was a powerful benefit to her survival and was usually right on target. She was not picking up any threat in the very place where there should be danger. He and the other Vampires were not registering any hazard either on their own radar grids. The Shifters seemed to be unable to scent any risk. Without a doubt, something was not right.

He asked everyone, to be certain. "Do any of you sense or smell anything wrong?"

Gillian locked eyes with every Being standing there. Negative responses from all around. Shit.

"Either Daily has an incredible dampening shield that none of us can penetrate, an army inside that is so bad-assed he doesn't need to post guards . . . or . . ."

"Or what?" That was from Kimber.

"I don't know. But just thinking of all the possibilities makes my trigger finger twitch."

Gillian stood up. "Okay . . . we are not going to solve this one out here. Let's go find Jenna. Pavel, come up here and take point. I'll be right behind you."

The Wolf obeyed her, trotting past her into the passageway, then continuing on at a brisk pace. Gillian was next, followed by Aleksei, Garm, Helgi, Hreidmar, Kelda, Dagr, Georg, Erzsébet, Evzen, Osiris and Daed. Trocar and Kimber brought up the rear of the group in case anyone sneaked up on them from behind.

Traveling through the corridor was rather uneventful. Dipping down and under the basilica, it wove through the crypts, storerooms and subbasements of the building. The farther they went inside, the more the tension of the group spiraled. Everyone was waiting for the proverbial big bad "something" to leap out of the dusty recesses at them.

"He has to have moved his base." Gillian spoke more to herself than the rest.

"We knew that we might be wrong about his location," Daed reminded her.

"Yeah, but he did use this place. I can't explain how I know; I just know that he's been here very recently. He can't be far. The Fey intelligence network would have alerted Dagr or Evzen if they knew Daily had shifted locations, so it has been literally within the hour that he moved."

"I do not understand either. We were told specifically that Daily's lair was here." Dagr was frustrated and perplexed.

"At the castle or the basilica?" The annoyance was plain in Gillian's tone.

"The basilica, Gillian. Neither Evzen, myself or any of our Kin would make such a glaring mistake with our facts," Dagr retorted, his vocal pitch matching her own.

"I understand that, Dagr. I'm not blaming you or your friends. If Daily is here, he's moved to another part of the complex, or he was only here in this section temporarily and leaked misinformation of his whereabouts to your people. Crafty bastard. We need to start checking the other buildings."

Evzen pushed through to the front of the line. "I will lead you up, then."

"Pavel will go first. Just tell him which way is out." Gillian backed up to follow the Sidhe.

"That way." Evzen pointed.

Pavel complied and headed for a door on the opposite side of the room they were in. Gillian opened it for him, then pushed Evzen back as she followed the Wolf. They traipsed up a set of stairs, down a long, carpeted hallway, into the main chapel, then out the front doors. Tourists who were visiting and taking pictures of the interior whispered and pointed at the group, mostly at Kelda, who smiled and waved at them.

Outside, Evzen pointed to a bigger building near the basilica. The sign read ST. VITUS CATHEDRAL. It was much larger than the church they'd left. The baroque exterior of the buildings had obviously been added long after they were originally built.

They filed across the courtyard, everyone's senses on full alert for any undue attention or aggressive behavior from the state-employed, uniformed sentries patrolling the grounds or the groups of tourists enjoying the sights. Nothing seemed out of the ordinary. Several of the sentries even waved to their bunch.

Gillian paused at the entrance to the cathedral. "Wait a second. Daily is a real priest, right?"

"*Was* a real priest. After he went crazy he was defrocked, excommunicated and defamed," Daed confirmed.

"You mean after he was Turned," Gillian corrected him.

"Nope. I mean after he went crazy. The Church doesn't excommunicate Paramortals. There are a number of non-Human priests. They're not particularly famous, but they are definitely ordained priests. When Daily got political and started talking insanity, the Church took the position that hatemongering against the newfound peace wasn't an ideal they wanted promoted by one of their own, so they told him to knock it off. When he refused to comply and even escalated, they booted him."

"Points for them, then." Gillian nodded.

She addressed the others and clarified her own thoughts all at once. "All right, since Daily was a genuine priest, he's not going to have his lair in a church.

"Evzen and Dagr, I'm afraid either your sources really were misinformed or Daily's putting out crap to lead us in circles. I should have thought of that before I wasted our time here."

Gillian's tone was angry. She wasn't mad at the Sidhe; she was mad at herself. Venus on a biscuit, she needed to get her head out of her ass and start paying attention or they were going to die. She stopped walking and started scanning the area around where they stood with total concentration.

"This is not your fault, Gillian. You only went where we told you." Dagr tried to soothe the obviously angry Human.

"It is my fault. My mommy-fied brain is in a fog of pregnancy-induced giddiness, and my thinking processes are in hormone hell. Either way, I need to get my game together. We should never have gone through a church's catacombs looking for a Vampire pseudopriest. We had already discussed this before we went in, but my dumb ass didn't register it fully.

"All we accomplished was leaving a dandy scent trail any Shifter that Daily has in his retinue could track. I'm a soldier, a goddamn United States Marine Captain, and I know better than to do what we just did. I am really sorry for wasting everyone's time just now and for possibly making our mission more difficult."

"Should we buy crosses or holy water or something? There's a vendor over there selling religious articles." Kimber pointed to a stall several yards away, interrupting Gillian's self-recriminations.

"Religious objects like a cross or holy water will only work against certain Paramortals if the wielder is a devoted follower of their own Faith or the Vampire is a staunch follower of his own Faith. I tossed a gold cross into a Catholic Vampire's face once. Worked really well. He's still got a scar, from what I've been told." Gillian grinned.

"I'm Catholic. Greek Orthodox even," Daed offered.

"I said *devout*. You're not a devout anything."

"Point taken."

He grinned at her. She glared back.

"You got your Star of David on you?" Kimber asked Gillian, half seriously.

"I already told you, I'm not Orthodox. I was raised in both the Temple and in the Unitarian Church, neither of which uses religious icons to be worshipped or prayed to. A so-called sacred symbol of any kind is not going to work for me, nor is a Star of David going to work on Daily," Gillian said.

"I thought you were Pagan," Daed stated.

"That too. There's a concept in all religions about treating others as you want to be treated. The 'do unto others' rule is the single common thread in every Faith. That's why I read other theologies and consider anyone's prayers genuine when they come from the heart and soul of the person praying, no matter what their personal God or Gods may be."

"Daily is Catholic," Aleksei reminded them.

"Yes, but he was also excommunicated, so the core of his Faith isn't intact anymore. The Church kicked him out. That would shake his beliefs to the bone. Anything with Catholic connotations that we wave, throw or sprinkle at him isn't going to work," Gillian explained.

She didn't want to be standing there discussing religious philosophy at the moment, but it was giving her time to think. Another Human sentry walked by and gave her what looked like a friendly wave. Not the group, just her.

There was something akin to recognition in his face, which made it weird. She'd never been to Prague, and while her face had been splashed all over the news recently and on various magazine covers over the years, she didn't consider herself notable enough to garner much public recognition.

Jenna's safety and rescue was foremost in her mind, but this entire situation was playing hell with her instincts versus what her empathy and other senses were telling her. The light dialogue that she wasn't really paying attention to was giving her time to better process her thoughts. The entire situation was so wrong to her, yet she still couldn't put her finger on it.

"Gillian, do you know that man who just walked by?" Aleksei asked her.

"No, but you saw that too, right?" She looked up at her tall, scrumptious fiancé.

"I did notice, yes. He seemed to recognize you."

Aleksei was protective by nature. He was also definitely observant. He hadn't stayed alive for nearly four hundred years by being a dumbass. If Gillian was uneasy, he was uneasy. She was correct about too many things not adding up since they'd arrived. Now he was certain the waves and friendly greetings they had been receiving from the castle sentries were not necessarily directed at the group as a whole. They were for Gillian. Very odd, without a doubt.

"She is fairly well-known, you know." Daed beamed at her.

"Not enough for city guards in Prague to recognize me from across a courtyard, Daed." Gillian fluffed it off, embarrassed. She didn't like notoriety of any sort.

Trocar spoke up from the back of the group. Everyone jumped. The Grael had been so silent, they'd almost forgotten he was there. "Aleksei, what happened to your former lover after Akabat?"

The handsome Vampire stared at the equally stunning Elf, perplexed. "I do not know. I have not seen Elizabeta since that night and for nearly four hundred years before. Why would you ask something like that?"

"She looks very similar to Gillian, does she not? Someone who did not know both of the women very well might mistake one for the other."

"Are you saying you think she's here?" Gillian asked him.

"Why would Elizabeta be here?" Now Aleksei really was confused.

"Because she hates you, Aleksei; Gillian too. Teaming up with Daily on a mission to get back at you both would be logical." Trocar filled in the thoughts that he'd instigated.

"That would also explain why Jenna might have originally been involved," Daed mused.

"For Crissakes, Daed, Jenna could pick me out of a mud-filled mosh pit. Plus, she's never seen Elizabeta that any of us know of, nor did she even know about her," Gillian pointed out.

Daed persisted. "No, hear me out. Think about it for a moment. Trocar may be right. Jenna leaves Tanis in Cairo to go discover herself. Cairo is a safe place. Too safe for Jenna, with her attention span of a rabid squirrel. So she starts looking for something to do, maybe hears about a job . . . as a bodyguard, attaché, something exciting . . . and figures she'll hit the soldier-of-fortune trail again.

"She's flitted off to points unknown on a regular basis for one half-assed reason or another since you all left the service. Meanwhile, Daily and Elizabeta have hooked up. Daily knows what you look like. He's done his homework."

"That's how he found out that I was pregnant! Elizabeta was at Akabat," Gillian interrupted.

"Of course! Any Vampire would have noticed that you were pregnant," Aleksei said.

Gill frowned. "You didn't notice. Nor did Osiris or any of the other big guns. Erzsébet and Sweeney didn't notice. Neither did Vlad or Sir Georg."

"I am afraid all of us were distracted by the unfolding events of that night and by fear for your safety, *cara*. I apologize. I should have noticed." Aleksei smoothed a gentle hand down her back.

"That is not true. I simply did not mention it. Sweeney was probably too enthralled with his own position in Vlad's entourage to have noticed, and he is not a Master." Erzsébet shook her head, smiling.

"I was too preoccupied with revenge that night." Sir Georg hung his head.

"I apologize as well, Gillian. I was drunk with power and my own insanity. My belated congratulations to you and Aleksei on my unforgivable breach of propriety." Vlad was clearly mortified. He looked embarrassed; her empathy was even registering his self-consciousness. In fact, he was turning a delicate shade of shell pink. Good grief.

Gillian stared at him. Was he kidding? Psycho Vlad apologizing for not noticing she was preggers during an attempted world-species takeover? Apparently he was still riding the post–catatonic megalomania crazy train. Cured, her ass. She'd have to watch him closely.

"I think most of us had our minds on other issues that night, but I did notice. Dionysus did as well," Osiris enlightened them.

"As did I," Odin said.

"Well, son of a bitch, why didn't any of you say anything?" Gillian scowled at all the confessors.

"We are all . . . slightly younger than God and from a time period which is more discreet?"

Oh, ha-ha, Osiris. Well, that was just lovely. The Lord of the Egyptian Vampires was making jokes. Gillian made a mental note to talk to him about his timing. Oops. Daed was saying something.

"Sorry, Daed. I got distracted for a second. Go on . . . Jenna, Elizabeta, Daily . . . I was paying attention." Gillian waved her hand at him to continue.

Daed laughed. "No worries, pumpkin. It's to be expected in your condition."

Ignoring her glare, he continued. "As I said, Daily's no fool. He would have noticed the resemblance immediately. Elizabeta has had four hundred years to nurture her anger and resentment. Think about it: four hundred years with Vlad, his megalomania and paranoia. Daily would have exploited that after Vlad's failure at Akabat, maybe even offered her a deal."

Vlad nodded at Daed's assessment. "I am embarrassed to admit that he is correct. I did encourage Elizabeta's vengeful fantasies while keeping her in check until I was ready."

"What better way to take out you and Aleksei together? Defame you and your relationship, kidnap your friend; force you into a rescue mission while you're pregnant. Aleksei would surely not allow you to go alone. One, two, three. Elizabeta gets her revenge; Daily gets what he wants and proves his imaginary point; the world goes back to a segregated environment with everyone distrusting one another; Daily cleans up as the new 'spiritual leader.'"

"Gillian is right, then. Even without any obvious danger or threat, the reason we sense that something is wrong is because this is a trap." Aleksei felt his chest tighten.

"Without a doubt," Daed agreed.

"I don't care. Forewarned is forearmed. This isn't chess, people. This is a good, old-fashioned game of checkers. Daily is telegraphing his punches. If what Daed speculates is true, he knows we're coming. It's all on the table, and depending on which moves we make, we'll either be kinged or taken. We've been in situations like this before; at least my team has. We can do this."

"Evzen? Back to the original question. Which of these buildings is not a church?" Gillian asked him.

Evzen pointed diagonally from where they were standing. "That one, known as the Daliborka; that one, the royal palace; and that one, the castle itself. There is an art gallery in the stables, but I do not believe Daily would be there. It is too open."

"What's the Daliborka, besides a tower?"

"The old prison."

"That's where Jenna will be," Gill said firmly.

"How do you know?" Evzen asked.

"I just do. Daily's using her as a lure on camera. Off-screen, she's just a toy."

No one could think of a reason to dispute her thoughts.

They set off toward the tower. On the way, Evzen explained that the tower had been named after its first prisoner, Dalibor of Kozojedy. He had been a knight of the realm and sort of a Robin Hood in his day. His crime had been to shelter some serfs who were rebelling against the emperor.

During his incarceration he learned to play the violin, and his music was heard by passersby. The joke among his captors was that a "violin" was also the name of a torture device. The music made by his executioners was a far cry from the sweet sounds Dalibor made during his sentence. Legend has it that the sounds of soft violin music can still be heard coming from the tower. The story made everyone even more uneasy. Gillian supremely hoped they wouldn't have a pissy ghost to deal with on top of everything else.

When they reached the door, Trocar checked it for any nasty surprises. Suspicions were high that their party was in for an attack at any moment. Things had been going way too smoothly for anyone's taste.

Not surprisingly, Gillian halted everyone right after Trocar declared the entrance safe. "Look, we can split up and cover more ground. We have more than enough people to search all these buildings quickly. If anyone finds anything, just fire a shot or give a shout-out. The rest of us will come running."

"I don't think that's a good idea. There are too many tourists around. We might hit a civilian." Daed frowned at her.

"Definitely not a good plan to split us up, Petal. Especially if you or Aleksei or both are the main targets. We can protect you better within the safety of the group." Trocar shook his frothy white hair in negation of her idea.

"Seriously? You want to collectively sneak through every one of these remaining buildings?" Gillian was incredulous.

Kimber snorted. "You don't watch many slasher movies, do you?"

"What does that mean?" Gillian's eyes narrowed at her friend.

"Everyone knows when you split up the party, people start getting killed. Especially the naughty girls and their lovers. They're always first to die," Kimber said with a completely straight face.

Gillian whacked her on the back of the head with her free hand. "Are you kidding me? You're taking cues on what to do next from slasher-movie rules? You suck, you know that? We'll just stay together, then. Jesus H. Christ. I have never seen such a whiny bunch of overpowered candy-asses in my life."

Gillian huffed and opened the door to the tower, still grumbling to herself as she went in. She'd gotten about six steps when it dawned on her that Kimber had aggravated her on purpose. Her thought processes were back online and in full kick-your-ass combat mode. Part of her was grateful. At least she hadn't gone too soft. The other part was planning ways to exasperate her best friend right back. Later. Get even later.

"Bellissima, *you never cease to lighten my heart.*" Aleksei chuckled in her mind.

"*Shut up, you. Domestic accidents can happen.*" She sent him a very clear thought of her "accidentally" shooting him. Her reward was more of his deep, velvet laughter smoothing over her synapses.

There was untoward tittering behind her as she navigated the front part of the castle. No one was quaking in their boots anymore from her infrequent outbursts of temper. She really was losing her touch. Dammit.

"Up or down?" Osiris pointed to the stairs leading to the tower, then the stairs leading down to the dungeon area.

"Down. Daily wouldn't risk us taking Jenna during a daylight rescue."

Odin, Evzen, Georg and Hreidmar volunteered to remain on the ground floor by the doorway in case they really had been followed or tracked. Everyone else followed Gillian downstairs, with Pavel taking point again. His senses were more attuned than even Gillian's empathy. If Jenna really was drugged or bespelled, there was a chance that she wouldn't register any alarm or concern at being held captive, making it impossible for Gillian to home in on her location.

"Gillian . . ." Though she was two feet in front of him, Aleksei's voice barely carried to her.

"What?" she whispered back. It irritated her unreasonably that he would speak out loud at all when they were on a covert undertaking.

"I trust your abilities but will protect you if necessary."

Gillian thought briefly about being annoyed, then let it go. "Ditto."

She reached back, caught his hand and squeezed it. The warm wash of affection from him was her reward. The stairs wound down to a large round room. A fire pit glowed in the center, illuminating the pale stones that comprised the walls and the dark slate slabs on the floor. There were various niches and doors at intervals along the circular walls. In between were instruments of torture. Some were carefully spaced on customized racks or hung on the wall. A brazier, tongs, thumbscrews and knives were on their own raised platform.

Pavel had his nose to the ground, trotting around the perimeter of the room. He stopped at a split door inserted flush with the curved wall. Both the top and bottom were affixed with iron hinges and locks.

"In there?" Gillian whispered.

Pavel nodded and backed away. Kimber rummaged in her pack and removed a set of lock picks. When she went to the door, Aleksei stopped her, shaking his head. The Vampire simply reached out and pulled the hinges off, catching the two halves of the door. He laid them carefully against the stones.

Inside was a crumpled female form in a tattered yellow gown. The chocolate brown hair was unmistakable. The fire-engine red streaks were gone, but Gillian could recognize her friend. She went in, gently touching an exposed shoulder.

"Jenna?"

CHAPTER
20

THE figure turned slightly. Gillian's eyes widened but she gave no other outward reaction. Jenna had definitely been abused. Whether by Daily or one of his pals, she couldn't tell. Small, nonlethal cuts covered most of Jenna's body. The front of the fitted yellow dress was dark with drying and fresh blood. They had spared her face; however, the sheer amount of slices on the rest of her body would scar her for life.

"Gill?" Jenna's voice was raspy. "Is that really you?"

"Of course. Kimber, Trocar, Daed and Aleksei too. We brought a few more friends along as well."

"How do I know it's you?"

"What are you asking?"

"Tell me something we both know. Only us." Jenna rallied enough to scoot away from Gillian and the open door.

"Captain, they are coming," Trocar warned. His superior hearing alerted him to an alarming number of creatures headed their way.

"Shit, Jenna, you see me here with Kimber and everybody. I can't tell you something private that only we know with a group of people around. I'm not Elizabeta. Is that who you're afraid of?"

Noises of fighting upstairs interrupted any response Jenna might have made.

"The trap is sprung," Osiris added unnecessarily.

"Everyone up against the wall, away from the door," Gillian ordered.

"Garm, you shift with Pavel; we'll keep Helgi and Daed as a surprise. It's too damn small in here for two Wolves and a Bear, plus giant Vampires and, dear God, a Minotaur."

Garm obeyed her, taking position with Pavel in front of Jenna's tiny room. Gillian stepped around them and in front of Aleksei.

"No, *piccola*. Behind me." He tried to move her out of the way, but she balked.

"I'm armed. You get back. I will move when I need help. In fact, everyone without a projectile weapon, move behind us."

She pointed toward the wall, indicating they move right now, then leveled her guns at the stairwell. Daed mirrored her with his own two sidearms. Kimber was slightly out in front with her shotgun-flamethrower combo. Trocar, Dagr and Kelda all held ornate short bows. Behind them, Osiris, Aleksei, Vlad and Erzsébet waited to pull them out of the way, if necessary, and to take over the fight when needed.

"Erzsébet, fight fairly. We do not want to become what Daily is," Osiris reminded her.

"Or what I was," Vlad said under his breath. No one contradicted him.

The fighting was coming closer. Odin's battle cry reached their ears. Both Garm and Helgi tensed up.

"Not yet, guys. They won't kill him. They probably have sheer numbers in their favor if a lot of Vlad's former army joined up with Daily. I can almost guarantee you that their goal is to capture, not to kill," Gillian said softly.

Aleksei stared at her in surprise. Outwardly she was perfectly calm. The guns she had pointed at the doorway were level and straight. Inwardly, he felt only a cold void from where her natural warmth should be. Her composed stance was putting everyone around her at ease. No one was tense; no one was anxious except, apparently, himself.

The first group of their adversaries boiled down the stairs and into the room. Kimber lit them up with her flame gun, while Gill, Daed, Trocar, Dagr and Kelda peppered them with bullets and arrows. Pavel and Garm slashed with jaws and teeth at any body part that came into their range after being charbroiled or ventilated. Enemy Vampire, Shifter and Fey went down under the ex-Marines' initial onslaught.

"I thought we weren't killing," Erzsébet called out over the din.

"I said *they* weren't. I didn't say anything about us not killing them first," Gillian yelled over her shoulder.

Abruptly the onslaught stopped. Gillian signaled for everyone to stay put and still, then waited a silent count of ten before nodding toward the stairs. Trocar, Kelda and Dagr stashed their bows, then pulled out all kinds of daggers and knives. Together they melted up the stairs ahead of the rest of the party.

Gill caught Osiris's eye and jerked her head toward Jenna's room. He moved in a blur, scooped Jenna up in his arms and waited to go up last.

Mentally she reached for Aleksei. *"I don't want you carrying Jen if Elizabeta is anywhere around. She'll go for you or me first, and your hands need to be free."*

He nodded to her. *"I understand. Thank you for protecting me."*

She ignored his attempt at sarcasm, moving forward, pushing Pavel and Garm out of the way. Kimber balanced the barrel of her gun on Gill's shoulder as they crept up the stairs.

"If you fire that thing next to my ear . . ." Gillian warned.

"Bite me. I'm using you as a bipod," Kimber snapped back.

"Come up, Captain," Trocar called.

They all hustled up. Odin was alive, literally staked to the floor, not with wood but with metal spikes driven deeply into the flagstones. Hreidmar was elaborately tied up and suspended from an iron wall sconce. He was bleeding from a dozen wounds, alive and cursing heartily. His axe lay nearby. Evzen and Georg were nowhere to be found.

"Too many of them. They took Evzen and the knight," Odin gasped.

He would have been strong enough to get himself loose if they hadn't hit every segment of his arms, hands, feet and legs. With the spikes between his shoulder blades and hips, there was no leverage to push from. The Norse Lord looked a little like Gulliver, but pinned down by a dozen spikes rather than hundreds of tiny ropes.

"I will free Odin if someone will help Hreidmar down." Aleksei knelt by the Viking and began yanking out spikes, cauterizing each of the wounds with his saliva. It wasn't pretty, but it was efficient.

"Absolutely not. He was inept enough to get himself hung up like that; he can stay there." Kelda stood beneath her husband with her hands on her hips. Knives bristled like spines from her hands.

"Woman, this is not the time for grandstanding." Hreidmar struggled, causing him to bounce against the wall.

"Aye, it is, ya daft git. How is it that a royal of the Dwarves is hanging up like a smoked ham? Were there too many of them for you? By Vulcan's forge, what have I married?" Kelda turned away, shaking her head.

"Get. Me. Down!" Hreidmar bellowed at her.

"All right, then. Stop being cross or I will be referring to you as 'Oldfather.'"

Almost nonchalantly, she flicked her wrist, sending a dagger through the rope that held him suspended.

"No!" Hreidmar yelled.

The blade struck home, the rope severed and Hreidmar plunged to the ground. Evidently Dwarves bounce. He sprang back to his feet, shoving the ropes off himself. With a scathing glare at Kelda, who grinned at him, he retrieved his axe and stomped toward the door, swearing under his breath.

Aleksei had finished freeing and healing Odin in the meantime. He held out his hands helplessly to Hreidmar.

"Will you let me . . . Hreidmar? Your wounds should be attended to . . ."

"Piss off, lad; we have fighting to do," Hreidmar growled at him, then yanked the door open.

There was a soft giggle from the bundle of cloth in Osiris's arms. The giggling got louder until full-throated guffaws ensued. The irrepressible Jenna was laughing.

Her ex–comrades in arms joined her, leaving the rest of the party who weren't former United States Marines ogling the sight of a badly wounded woman, a Grael Elf, two Humans and a Greek Shifter laughing their asses off.

Gillian snorted, wiping her eyes. She ejected the spent magazines from her guns and reloaded. "Oh shit, that was funny. Glad to see you're feeling better, Jenna. Let's try to get out of here."

"Gallows humor," Daed coughed out in explanation as he passed Aleksei.

"I do not understand any of you," Aleksei grumbled, following Daed out the door.

Hreidmar gave a war whoop and ran forward, swinging his great axe. Gillian started firing almost immediately, pivoting around the corner of the doorway to make room for the rest of them.

As predicted, there were more of Daily's friends outside. The enemy formed a fighting gauntlet, pressing Gillian's bunch between two groups, angled toward the Golden Lane, a tight row of small houses leading to the Old Royal Palace. Ages ago, craftsmen and artists lived here. Now it was a crowded aisle of shops and food vendors.

Tourists were still wandering everywhere. Apparently most assumed this was some sort of planned, staged fight. They were smiling and taking pictures as they scattered out of the way of the attacking Paramortals. Gillian's group was applauded as they were herded through the tiny alleyway.

"Fight! Open up a hole in their ranks; they're taking us to Daily!" Gillian yelled over the ruckus.

She backed up to fight as close to Osiris as she could. He was still dangerously hampered, carrying Jenna the way he was.

"Gilly, I can walk," Jenna informed her.

Gillian kicked a Vampire in the face who ventured too close, then shot him point-blank through the eye. "You might be able to walk but you're in no shape to fight. Let him carry you."

Things were definitely not going their way. The Old Royal Palace loomed closer and closer. If Daily had reinforcements beyond what they had already seen, he'd unleash them soon.

"Trocar, Kelda, it's magic time!" she yelled at the top of her lungs.

Trocar was busy being an Elven Vegamatic: a whirling, black-clad blur with silvery knives. He heard her, finished killing the Shifter he was engaged with and vanished in plain sight. Kelda was confused until she saw Trocar's disappearing act. She tossed a nod to Gillian and also vanished. Gillian knew her own people would recognize what was going on and act accordingly. They'd worked together long enough to understand subtle and no-so-subtle instructions.

Gillian sent a frantic thought to Aleksei. *"Pass it on to the other Vampires. If they swarm us like I think they're going to, just surrender. Trocar and Kelda are loose. Hopefully they'll get us out before we're in real trouble."*

"Understood," Aleksei confirmed.

Within a few minutes another large group descended on them, as Gillian had predicted. The sheer numbers were overwhelming. Their group was quickly captured; guns and bows were handed over. Hreidmar put up the most resistance until he noticed Kelda was missing. He relaxed and quietly handed over his axe. Gillian gave him what she hoped was a reassuring glance when he looked her way.

They were marched into the Old Royal Palace, where Father Bartholomew Daily awaited them from his position on an ornate throne. Next to him, seated on an overstuffed footstool, was a smiling Elizabeta.

"Gillian Key, we finally meet." Daily smiled as she was dragged up to the front.

"I'm sure it's a real thrill for you," Gillian replied dryly.

She was scanning the room, looking for exits and possible entrances for more of his cronies. What she found interesting was the level of nervousness emanating from the little army behind him. Why were they nervous? Her group was certainly outnumbered and outgunned at the moment. Daily had the upper hand for the time being . . . Why the lack of faith in their boss?

"You have no idea how thrilling it is." Daily smirked at her.

"What exactly did I do to you personally that has put a burr under your saddle?" Gill cocked her head at him.

From where she stood and where he sat, she could tell he wasn't particularly tall for a Master Vampire. At least, she was assuming he was a Master. A lesser Vampire wouldn't have the level of charisma or glamour to attract followers from Vlad's retinue. He was as attractive as most Vampires she'd seen, but something more was going on.

Daily's hair was dark brown, wavy and cut in a shoulder-length, fashionable manner. His eyes were deep, dark brown. It wasn't the color but the fanatical gleam in them that concerned her. This was another Vlad Dracula: grandiose delusions, narcissistic. What made Daily dangerous, however, was completely different from Vlad's paranoia. Daily's problem came from his fanaticism. He was little more than a religious zealot, only now he had a Vampire's magic to enhance his cause.

Aleksei murmured to her mind, then cut off contact almost immediately. *"You are correct,* cara. *He is a lesser Vampire than we are."*

She was grateful for the knowledge but annoyed that it did nothing to improve their predicament. All of the Lords in her party—with the exception of Georg, who was only a Master—could kill Daily and Elizabeta with a single thought, though absolutely none of them would.

Well, Vlad might, but based on his history, he probably wouldn't either. He had liked toying with his prey too much. What good was having Lords, psychotics and vindictive knights around if they wouldn't fight dirty once in a while?

Scratch that thought, she reprimanded herself. None of her friends was that dishonorable.

Daily's voice butted into her thinking process as he wagged a bejeweled finger at her. "You have done nothing to me; however, your flagrant disregard of propriety between Humans and Vampires is a terrible example for everyone."

"Says who? You? I don't remember asking your opinion nor needing your advice on how to conduct my life. If you have morality issues, Bart, work them out with your own therapist . . . or your own God."

"Bart" visibly flinched at her abbreviated use of his name. "You will not address me in that manner. My given name is Bartholomew. Father Daily is also acceptable."

"Then you will address me as either Captain Key or Dr. Key, Bartholomew. You sure as hell are not my father or even a priest. You lost the right to use that title when you decided required celibacy and obedience to your Church wasn't your thing. There are men out there who have earned it through great personal sacrifice, diligent study and works of Faith."

Bartholomew turned absolutely purple. Gillian wondered for a brief moment if it were possible for a Vampire to keel over from apoplexy.

"I am still a priest!" he managed to choke out.

"Your Church says you're not. I think I'll go with their opinion."

"The Church." He practically spat the word. "I've built my own Church. My followers are loyal to me. Only me. They recognize that the current Church is flawed. We are doing what we can to bring the flock over to right thinking again."

She decided that despite the overabundance of Vampire glamour, he was an aggrandizing little prick, no matter how attractive and brilliant he thought he was. Her eyes flicked to Elizabeta, who obviously thought her new boyfriend was pretty hot. The woman was positively drooling on his gaudy robes.

"We?" Gillian asked sweetly.

"Elizabeta and myself. She is proving most invaluable to me."

He favored the aforementioned woman with a leering glance, stroking a fingertip down her jawline. She practically swooned with adoration. Gillian wanted to barf.

"Elizabeta in particular is happy to see you, Dracula and Aleksei. Now we have all the betrayers in one place. I honestly did not believe you would be quite so stupid or easily led, Captain Key."

"That's your mistake, then, Bartholomew, believing we were lured here or tricked. We came for Jenna and we are leaving with her. You want to take this meeting beyond that and you will die."

Gillian was tired and pissed off, and she had to pee. Stating facts seemed the most efficient way to get through this quickly. She was not in the mood for a taunting contest with a Vampire, even if he was dressed up in pretty purple robes.

Immediately after she said it, she realized her stupid hormones were instigating her temper to a new and exciting level. She hadn't been this blunt since she was a raw recruit. Shit. Probably wasn't a good idea to mention dying in a room full of fanatical Paramortals with their Grand Poobah sitting ten feet away. Oops.

Now she was certain Daily was going to have an apoplectic fit. She'd never seen anyone turn that particular color and live.

Daily's Vampire command voice rang out. "Samir, kill her."

Samir? The same Shifter who had been snotty with her in Akabat? She felt a ripple across her empathy and spun to the left. Yup. It was the same Samir. She faced him squarely as he shifted into a man-sized, lean, powerful desert Lynx. He snarled at her and gathered himself for a pounce.

"Hiya, Samir. Thought I told you to fuck off in Egypt."

As he leaped, Gillian moved, drawing the silver blade they hadn't found from her boot and flicking it straight into Samir's face. He dropped like a stone as it tore through his eye socket and into his brain. He lay twitching on the ground inches from her booted foot.

"Seems your right-hand Kitty has a terminal condition, Bartholomew."

Gillian finally got it. Bartholomew Daily was a big fat Master Vampire chickenshit. The coward didn't have the stomach for fighting. He wanted someone else to do it. If she had pissed Vlad off like that, he'd have torn her head off, patient or not. Vlad had been a lot of things in his day; "coward" wasn't one of them.

"Yeah, he's got a big silver dagger stuck in his face."

Bless Kimber. She'd caught on as well.

Daily went from purple to white in the space of a heart-beat. Elizabeta had her dainty hand up at her throat and was staring at Gillian in wide-eyed shock. She was as pale as Daily.

"I'm going to kill that bitch."

Gillian whipped around to see Jenna on her feet next to her, breathing heavily.

"Someone grab her before she hurts herself," Gillian ordered.

"No, Gill. I'm done. He seduced me, then kept me with him. I thought it was that Vampire thing . . . you know . . ."

"Glamour?"

"Yeah, glamour. But when I fought him, he drugged me. He sent her to me, and in the state I was in, I thought it was you torturing me every night. Oh, Gillian, I'm so sorry." Jenna's chocolate brown eyes were anguished.

"Don't worry about it. We're here to get you out. If you were here of your own free will, I'd have let you be. Seeing you cut up in that room, I knew you were his prisoner."

"I want to kill her . . . and him." Jenna turned back to the recoiling pair on the dais.

"You may get your chance, but not now. We need to leave get you healed up, then we'll talk about what to do next." Gillian put a hand gently on her friend's shoulder.

"Burn her! Burn the witch!" Daily screamed.

Behind them, the packed group of his followers sprang into action. There were dozens of braziers, candles, sconces and torches all around the throne room. Suddenly everyone in the room but them was holding something flaming. This was bad. Very, very bad.

"Um . . . guys . . ." Gillian didn't finish her sentence.

Steel, flesh, bone and muscle collided with each other as her group formed a semicircle to defend herself, Kimber and Jenna. Shouts, snarls and growls of aggression overwhelmed the screams, sizzles and gurgles of death.

"Hello, love," a voice said right before a hand clawed for her throat.

Sweeney. Shit. Where the hell had he come from? It was only honed instinct that saved her from instantly having her throat ripped out. Gillian found herself in the absolute last place she ever wanted to be: locked in hand-to-hand combat with a razor-wielding Vampire.

For one brief, shining moment, she flashed back to a moonlit night in Sacele when she had tangled with Jack the Ripper. He'd had a scalpel; Sweeney had a straight razor. Knowing she couldn't hope to beat him by strength, she opted for speed, weaving and dodging around the combatants in the room, praying she'd stay alive long enough for someone to kill him.

"Gillian! The holy Grael is here!" Daed shouted at her.

"The Grail? The witch has *the* Grail?" Bartholomew heard him as well and was now very confused. Point for Daed. Confusion among one's enemies was a legitimate battle strategy.

Trocar was indeed there. The doors to the throne room slammed open. There stood Trocar and behind him was . . . dear, sweet Ganesh, what the hell was It? Her mind made sense of It after a moment. She didn't know how the hell he'd done it, but somehow Trocar had activated the Golem of Prague.

"Kill everything in this room," the Grael ordered It.

The Golem was over ten feet tall. It looked like a rotting man-shaped mound of swamp debris onto which someone had etched a rudimentary face. There was Hebrew written across Its forehead, but from the distance, with bad lighting and the Golem's color of muck brown, Gillian couldn't read it from where she was.

Bipedal, thick-girthed, genderless and powerful, the Thing swept Its foot through a knot of fighting bodies. Beings flew in every direction. Some splatted against walls; others were impaled on sconces.

"Get away from It!" Gillian warned. "Don't get in Its way. It's like a robot: no emotion, no feeling. Once It's turned on, It's going to keep killing."

The order was for her own people, but she couldn't help shouting. None of them but Aleksei would have heard her otherwise, and she doubted any of them would have noticed until too late. The damn Thing blended into the walls and floor like a chameleon except when It lurched. There wasn't time for relayed messages.

"Move, move, move!"

Gillian backed up and the others followed suit. Unfortunately the only direction open at the moment was toward Daily and Elizabeta. Where the hell had Sweeney gone again? Sneaky-ass Vampire.

The Golem was tearing through the packed group inside, with more and more trying to get in from the outside. How and where had Daily recruited them all? That was the question of the day. It would have to wait to be answered.

"Gill!"

Now what? She turned to see Jenna launch a solo blitz attack on Elizabeta. The Vampire was so shocked that she forgot to fight back until Jenna jerked her off the stool, tossed her against the nearest wall and landed a few serious blows to her pretty face.

"Goddammit, Jenna."

Gillian grabbed the nearest weapon she could, which happened to be a fallen torch from a wall sconce. The damn thing seemed to weigh fifty pounds.

She ran at the two of them. Jenna was quickly losing ground as Elizabeta recovered from her surprise and got down to the business of trying to dismember Gillian's friend.

A crack from the torch against the side of Elizabeta's head knocked her away. Gillian grabbed Jenna and yanked her back. They overbalanced and fell together. Sweeney's razor was instantly at her throat. Devious son of a bitch.

"Sorry, love. Got to do what I got to do."

Gillian didn't have time to react before Sweeney was knocked on his ass. She watched, stunned, as he skidded across the floor on his butt, grabbing his own throat. The dark red fountain pouring from it gave her incentive to move. She scrambled to her feet, pulling Jenna with her, and backed straight into Aleksei.

"Are you all right, *cara*?"

"Yeah . . . thanks. Did you do that?"

"He will not touch you again." Aleksei's eyes were platinum disks of rage. She'd never seen him like that before. Actually, she had, except the anger had been directed at her.

"Nice going. We'll make a Marine out of you yet." She grinned at him and then shoved Jenna into his arms.

"Get her out of here. She's still wounded."

"Gillian, watch out!" His warning almost came too late.

Elizabeta had a jeweled knife and was bearing down on Gillian. She would have moved faster if she'd used her nifty Vampire foo skills. Instead she was fighting the heavy skirt of her antique gown complete with petticoats to limp purposely toward Gillian. She was probably pissed off at having her hairdo wrecked by the conk to her head.

Gillian's life might have ended just then if not for the sound of a heavy blade swishing through the air. Georg was free. He stood behind Elizabeta as her body took a step farther before crumpling to the paving stones. Her head rolled gently away. The ancient knight lifted a section of her skirt and wiped his blade clean. The manacles that had bound him dangled broken from his wrists.

"I managed to free myself and Evzen," Georg said apologetically.

"I can see that. You're awesome." Gillian gave him a quick smile, then turned back to shoo Aleksei and Jenna out of the room.

The quiet, familiar voice in her ear made her freeze.

"I am so sorry for this, Gillian. I am sorry because you truly did care about me as your patient, despite my resistance to getting better. You did more to help me than you will ever know. You must know that, at least. 'Thank you' is not enough. Not nearly enough," Vlad said softly behind her.

"Not. A. Good. Time. Vlad," she hissed over her shoulder. *"Bartholomew Daily!"*

Vlad's voice thundered through the throne room. He shoved Gillian to the floor in front of him and leaped over her to stand before Daily.

By the time his voice stopped reverberating, everyone except Osiris, Aleksei, Erzsébet, Odin and the Golem was shaking in their boots. Those that weren't quivering in fear were already dead. Most of Daily's group were literally scattered on the floor, some in fetal positions. Gillian's friends were less embarrassingly indisposed, with the exception of Jenna, who was disheveled and shuddering against Aleksei's shirt.

Clearly there were only five Vampire Lords in the room and one Creature who had been inexorably sent on a mission of destruction by a certain Grael Elf. Holy shit. Things were getting more exciting by the moment.

Way to separate the chaff from the wheat, Vlad, Gillian thought to herself as soon as she could collect her wits.

Vlad backhanded Daily across the face, knocking him and the throne over. The former priest scrambled to his feet and wiped the blood from the corner of his mouth. His liquid brown eyes widened in alarm, giving him a passing resemblance to a deer in headlights, except Vlad Dracula was the headlight.

"You dare set yourself above the laws of this land and our own code."

Vlad had the Vampire Lord thing turned up full throttle. His voice reverberated through Gillian's body, sending cold chills down the spine of every sentient Being in the room. She couldn't speak for anyone else, but it was a crappy feeling. The Golem didn't give a shit. It casually lumbered through the area, demolishing Paramortals left and right. Golem awake. Golem smash.

"Heretic!" Daily shrieked.

"Happily so," Vlad replied.

"I am the law of the land!" Daily declared.

Vlad smacked him again, sending him reeling. Daily tried to back away, but Vlad's booted foot stomped on the hem of the purple robes, pinning him in place.

"You are insane. You have threatened my therapist, her beloved and her child. You are threatening the peaceful existence we have all enjoyed. You have lived too long."

"So have you," Daily hissed. He reached for a jeweled hilt in his belt but wasn't quite fast enough.

CHAPTER
21

VLAD grabbed Daily's shoulders, hauling the smaller Vampire against his chest. Fangs descended in his mouth as he pulled Bartholomew to him. The phony priest made choking, protesting sounds as Vlad drove his fangs into the other's throat. Testosterone superiority exhibitions within the Vampire community. Oh, boy.

"Vlad, no!" Osiris yelled.

The difference of timbre in his tone compared to Vlad's was remarkable. The Egyptian Lord's voice echoed at the same volume but invoked much different feelings. Pure, absolute power resonated from that voice. That voice could command armies, people, even nations, with ideas of hope, growth and solidarity. Vlad's people had served him out of terror; Osiris's people had followed him for thousands of years out of sheer adoration and trust.

Gillian was vaguely aware that the Golem had systematically decimated Daily's army. The remaining Beings who weren't dead, mortally injured or shitting themselves were scattering to the four corners of Prague and the landscape beyond. Out of the corner of her eye, she could see Georg, Evzen, Hreidmar, Daed and Kelda rounding up the ones who were still mobile.

Jenna was sitting in the middle of the room; Kimber and Pavel were beside her. Aleksei, Odin, Dagr and Erzsébet were dispatching the last few nasties with fight in them that the Golem had missed. Garm and Helgi had shifted during the fight and were chasing stragglers off into the night.

Trocar was suddenly at her side. "We have to stop It, Gillyflower."

"Stop what? The Golem? What do you mean, 'stop It'? You mean you don't know how to turn that Thing off?"

"No, I do not. I merely asked the rabbi how one would activate It if a certain Jewish heroine were in serious trouble. It turns out he is a fan of yours."

Gillian stared at him. She pointed at the Golem, who was methodically stomping bodies into goo.

"You told a rabbi . . . an Orthodox rabbi, that I . . . *we* needed help from that?"

"Did you need help?"

"Are you kidding me? Look around! Of course we needed help." She slapped a palm against her forehead.

"Then do shut up, Petal. Just say, 'Thank you, Trocar, for saving everyone,' and help me figure out how to deactivate It. But do it quickly. I ordered It to kill everything in this room, and we are still in this room, need I remind you."

She gritted her teeth and fought not to yell. "Thank you, Trocar. Now tell me how you activated It before It notices us."

"Hence my urgency in seeking your help." The insufferable shit grinned at her.

"How did you turn It on?" Now she was yelling.

"The rabbi had me draw a Hebraic letter on Its face. He said if I was to control It, I had to do the drawing."

"What letter? It's hard to see from here."

"I believe he called it . . . *aleph*."

"Just the one letter? It has more than one letter on Its forehead. I could see that when you came in with It."

"Just one. The rest were already there."

"Aleph . . . aleph . . . okay, that makes sense." Gillian's mind was whirling, putting things together that she'd learned years ago.

"Because . . . ?" Trocar gestured impatiently.

"The Hebrew word for truth is *Emet*. It is literally one letter away from being *Met*, the word for death. If we rub out the aleph, we should be able to stop It."

"What do you mean, 'we,' Gillyflower?" Trocar backed away from her toward the door.

"Oh, no, you don't, you pointy-eared arrow twanger. Get back here. We are doing this together." Gillian grabbed his cloak and hauled him back to stand next to her.

Unfortunately the Golem picked that time to turn. It finally realized It was doing nothing more than getting squishy stuff between Its toes and began looking for more active prey. The massive shoulders turned as It squared Its body toward Gillian and Trocar.

"Gillian, run!" Aleksei ordered her.

His heart nearly stopped as the Creature fixed on his fiancée and her friend.

Osiris echoed him. "Vlad, let him go and get out of there!"

Shit. Vlad. They'd all forgotten about him, except Osiris, apparently. He still had Daily in a death grip. The purple-robed Vampire was struggling mightily but was still pinned against Vlad's chest.

Vlad's entire body jerked and abruptly he let Daily free. The other Vampire scuttled back, his right hand covered in blood as Vlad's legs slowly buckled.

"All that power and still at the mercy of a wooden stake." Daily was sheet white, trembling, almost stumbling away from Vlad but with an eerie, sardonic grin on his face.

"Vlad!" Osiris, Aleksei and Gillian chorused. They ran as one toward their fallen companion.

Aleksei got to him first and was cradling him as Osiris and Gillian skidded up. Vlad lay in Aleksei's arms, the hilt of a jeweled wooden dagger between his ribs.

Daily was chuckling to himself over how clever he had been to think about using wooden weapons against those of his own kind. He turned to run and bumped into the leg of the Golem.

The Creature reached down, picked him up and promptly

tore him in half. Almost casually It dropped the truncated body and began stomping it into unrecognizable chunks.

Aleksei scooped Vlad up as they all ran for the door. Once everyone was outside, Gillian called for them to stop.

"We're okay now. It's inside; we're out here. Trocar told It to kill everything in the room. It should stop at the door."

She was breathing heavily as she sank down next to Vlad. Aleksei had laid him on the cobblestones away from the door and was still cradling his former enemy's head. Daed was beside them, a medical pack in his hand.

"The rest of you, do some crowd control. Keep those tourists away from here and make sure there are no wannabe heroes from Daily's bunch around. Dagr, Evzen, see if you can handle the local authorities. We don't want this in the papers tomorrow."

Gillian turned her attention back to Vlad, whose eyes were fluttering. Daed was giving him a shot of some kind. Her gaze flicked upward to meet Aleksei's eyes. He shook his head at her, sadly. A glance at Daed confirmed it. Her friend was a doctor but he could do nothing for the mortally wounded Vampire.

"Can any of you save him?" Gillian asked helplessly.

"No . . . there are limits to our powers, Gillian. You know that perhaps better than anyone," Osiris told her kindly.

Daed looked up at her, lifting the broken, shattered hilt and what remained of the bloody wooden blade that Daily had stabbed Vlad with. "The dagger . . . It was wood, all right, but it was brittle, old wood and it hit a rib going in. There are splinters all over the inside of his chest and heart, Gill. Think of what a .45-caliber hollow-point slug can do to the inside of a Human. This effect is pretty similar."

"So . . . just making him comfortable is all we can do?" she asked.

"I am comfortable, Gillian."

Vlad's eyes had opened, coinciding with his ability to speak. The ice green crystalline color was becoming hazy as his life ebbed. He lifted a hand to her and she took it. His grasp was weak.

"I have lived long enough, as Daily said," he began.

"Daily's an asshole, and Daily is dead, by the way. Trocar's new pet Golem made certain of that," Gillian told him.

"No, please listen. I have done a multitude of terrible things in my unnatural lifetime. My shame for deceiving you was more poignant after knowing how much you wanted me to get better." He was speaking quickly, knowing he had little time left.

"Aleksei, I can never make it right for Turning you and Tanis. I hope someday I might earn your forgiveness."

"If I had not been Reborn, I would have never met Gillian. I forgive you, freely," Aleksei stated with absolute conviction.

Gillian was shocked. Aleksei had been desperately depressed about being a Vampire when she'd first met him. To hear him forgive Dracula for that transgression was remarkable.

"Osiris, you worked a miracle with me in your care. I regret that we might have been friends but for my madness." Vlad coughed, pumping blood from his chest wound. A small trickle of blood formed at the edges of his mouth.

"Don't talk; just rest," Gillian told him.

"I will rest soon. Have to talk now." Vlad struggled to sit up more. Aleksei propped him up farther. His breathing was becoming more labored.

"I would have killed Daily myself except for this." He gestured almost imperceptibly toward the dagger Daed still held.

"We know," Odin said.

He knelt by the fallen Vampire and clamped a hand on his shoulder. "You helped save us . . . all of us. Soon you will be in the Halls of Valhalla, where the dead may live forever. Say hello to my forefathers on my behalf."

"Good-bye, my old friend." Erzsébet stood hand in hand with Sir Georg.

Vlad shuddered a final time. "Justice is finally served." The ice green eyes closed forever.

The Dark Prince of Romania, Vlad Tsepes—the Bogeyman of lesser Vampires everywhere—died in the arms of his former servant, surrounded by his temporary comrades in arms.

"Gillyflower?" Trocar's voice insinuated itself into the somber scene.

Gill looked up. Her eyes were completely dry. She laid the hand she'd been holding across Vlad's still chest.

"Yeah?"

"Are you all right?"

"I'm fine. I'm confused, but fine. I'm sorry, guys. I am unhappy we lost anyone during this venture, but better him than one of you."

She searched for and locked eyes with Jenna, Kimber, Pavel, Daed, Aleksei and Osiris.

"He said 'justice is served' as he died. I think he had no intention of living through this. I think his going after Daily was his way of redeeming himself back to some semblance of the hero he once was when he was Prince of Walachia. I also think he honestly, really felt remorse at the end. At least I hope so."

"I believe you are correct, *cara mia*. I am not particularly sorry he is dead, but I am not particularly happy either. He had a great deal to atone for," Aleksei told her.

"At least he apologized for Turning you and Tanis," Gillian reminded him.

"Yes, but as I said, if he had not, I would have missed meeting you." His smile to her was wondrous.

Daed butted in. "What do we do with him?"

"We will return him to our homeland. He will be given a hero's burial. I believe that is what he ultimately would have wanted," Aleksei said firmly as he laid Vlad fully on the ground and stood up.

Daed reached into his pocket, pulling out two gold coins. He placed them on Vlad's closed eyes. "For the ferryman."

"For the Halls of Justice." Trocar placed one of his runed daggers in Vlad's hands, arranging them over his chest.

Odin took off his fur cape and covered the body with it. "For Valhalla; I hear it is cold there."

They all stood in a communal moment of silence and contemplation.

"What about this lot?" Kelda called over to them.

Gillian's head jerked up. She'd completely forgotten the large group of prisoners they'd rounded up.

"Leave them to us. Our people will sort it out," Dagr told her.

He and Evzen started herding the group out of the complex.

"Thanks for everything, guys," Gillian called after them.

"We will meet again, I am certain." Evzen gave a cheery wave. One hand was bandaged against his chest and he was as bloody, dusty and disheveled as the rest of them, but still lovely as only a Sidhe could be.

Soon, only their original party minus one and plus Erzsébet and Georg remained. Erzsébet spoke up.

"Lord Aleksei, do you have any unfinished business with myself and Georg?"

"I am not your Lord, Erzsébet. You have that title in your own right," Aleksei responded.

"Gillian? What about you?" The gloriously beautiful woman smiled at her.

"You never hurt me or mine that I know of. It's all good." Gillian returned the smile, surprised that she actually felt like smiling.

"Like Vlad, I have a lot to atone for. I would like to remain here, in Prague, as an ally . . . and Lord of this region, if no one objects. I would like to begin my penance by making restitution in some manner to those I wronged long ago. Later, I will focus on raising an army of Vampires and Shifters loyal to the Compact," Erzsébet stated.

"Our own laws say that you may insert yourself into an area devoid of another Lord if you are strong enough to take on the challenge. Prague is closest to Aleksei's territory. If he has no objections, no one else should either," Osiris told her.

"Aleksei? What are your thoughts?" Erzsébet prompted him.

"By our laws, he could claim this territory for his own.

What will you do if that is the case?" Odin asked. He waved to Aleksei to keep from speaking yet.

Erzsébet managed a mischievous-looking grin. "I would not like it, but I am on a quest to save a soul . . . my own. Therefore, if Aleksei wishes this territory, it is his. He will gain two loyal followers who will still raise that army to serve Romania's needs.

"What say you, Georg? Shall we bow to this Romanian Vampire who has steadfastly ruled through kindness?" She looked at her lover, waiting for an answer.

Georg looked blank for a moment, then recovered himself. "I will swear fealty to anyone who is our friend, Erzsébet, whether it is in his territory or yours; wherever we will be safe."

"Well spoken." She bowed a little toward the knight.

"Again, I ask. Aleksei, what are your thoughts?"

Aleksei, for once, didn't look to Osiris for confirmation about Vampiric Laws and Customs. "You are welcome to these lands, Erzsébet, if it is your wish to have them. I would welcome an ally so close by."

Erzsébet did bow then, to both Aleksei and Gillian. "I will not disappoint you. My first act will be to clean up this mess. My second will be to track down the descendants of the families of the girls I brutalized and attempt to make amends. I will also make certain Vlad's body is returned to you in Romania immediately. You need not worry. I will treat him with respect and dignity."

Jenna whispered to Gillian, "Who is that again?"

"Erzsébet Báthory."

"No shit, the Blood Countess?"

"The very one."

"Didn't she slaughter, like, six hundred girls?"

"Shhh. Later. She did but I'll explain later."

Trocar cleared his throat. They all turned to look at him. He was standing in front of the open doors to the throne room.

"I so hate to interrupt such touching displays of mutual admiration, but we still have a problem."

He pointed back over his shoulder at the Golem who was

standing motionless in the shadows of the archway. "Our friend here needs to go back to the Old New Synagogue."

"Is It shut off?" Gillian walked around Aleksei to peer at the Giant.

"No, It is not. We were discussing this before Vlad's heroic death."

"Oh, for hell's sake, I'll shut It off."

"If you deactivate It here, we will never get It back to the synagogue."

"Shit, that's right." She thought for a moment.

"Got an idea. Y'all watch this."

Kimber's eyes widened. "Oh, hell no. Anytime anybody says 'y'all watch this,' shit is going to go down."

Gillian ignored her, limping over to the doorway. She was rumpled, dusty, bloody and extremely thirsty. Every muscle in her body ached, her back was killing her and she still had to pee. No overgrown Pillsbury mud-boy was going to interfere with them leaving and her going to the ladies' room.

Aleksei's heart leaped in his chest, and not in a good way. "Gillian . . . that Thing has no mind. It cannot recognize friend from foe."

Gill waved him off and addressed the Golem.

"*Shalom*, Golem."

The Thing actually inclined Its head toward her, as if It were listening as she bid It *peace* in Hebrew.

She beckoned to It, backing up away from the doorway as she did so. To her surprise, It followed her docilely.

Pleased with her idea, she took a few experimental steps away from the building, then beckoned again. It lumbered after her with no aggression.

Aleksei let out the breath he'd been holding. "Brilliant, *piccola*, just brilliant."

"Thank you! Okay, let's go. Trocar, you brought It from the synagogue. I need you to lead us back, please."

He applauded her slowly, then gave a mock bow. "I am duly impressed, Petal."

"Good. I'm rather pleased myself. So pleased that I won't shoot you for calling me *Petal*."

Gillian extended her arm toward the gates of the complex. "After you, Sir Elf."

Trocar sighed and turned toward the gate. "All of you, try to keep up."

Gill waved back to the new Lord of Prague. "See you, Erzsébet and Georg! Good luck with everything."

"Thank you, Gillian. You as well. We will come for a visit after the baby's birth." Erzsébet waved back from Georg's arms.

Jenna hobbled up to Gillian as they prepared to start the long walk with the Golem. "You're really pregnant?"

"Yup."

"Me too," Kimber admitted.

"Holy shit, what happened while I was gone?"

"We'll tell you everything after we've eaten, showered and found a bathroom," Gillian said. She caught Aleksei's hand as he moved up beside her.

"I'm going to deliver the babies," Daed said brightly.

"Like hell you are," Gill and Kimber chorused.

"I am a real medical doctor, you know. I just happen to like psychiatry best," Daed grumbled.

"Our kids aren't going to need analysis, so get over yourself. We'll find a nice midwife in the village."

Gillian was baiting him and she knew it.

"A midwife? I don't think so. You two are going to get the best medical care possible," Daed declared.

Gillian started to argue, but Aleksei interrupted her.

"My fiancée will choose her own care, as she wishes. Thank you very much for your offer, but I think we will be fine."

Gillian stared up at him, then cracked up laughing.

"This whole trip has done wonders for your confidence. I'm impressed."

Aleksei realized she was joking with him. His face formed into the most wicked grin she had ever seen.

"You should have already been impressed. I am Lord of my own realm, you know."

"Yeah, well, we'll just see about that." She scooted away before he could swat her bum.

Laughing, he scooped her up in his arms and kissed her thoroughly. He was happy to be alive, happy to have her safe in his arms, happy they had all come through their ordeal with little more than a few minor injuries.

"Gillian!" Osiris called to her.

"What?" She looked back from over Aleksei's shoulder.

"You forgot something." Osiris pointed to the Golem.

"Oh shit! Aleksei, put me down!"

CHAPTER
22

IT was a long, slow, exciting walk through Prague back to the synagogue, where the Golem would sleep once more. On the way, Gillian stopped to buy vast quantities of the wonderful hot dogs they'd had earlier for everyone in the group who could eat actual food. She was happy the vendor accepted plastic. Werewolves and Werebears could eat a great deal, as it turned out. So could two pregnant women, which was evidently a surprise to the Vampires.

"Great Ra, I did not realize Human women could eat so much at one time." Osiris scratched his head in disbelief.

"If you don't want to go back to Isis with a boot up your ass, I'd be careful with your commentary if I were you," Gillian said before taking another bite.

Kimber wasn't so polite. She kicked him in the ankle.

"Starting shit with hungry pregnant women is really not a good plan there, King Tut."

Osiris laughed heartily. "Feisty little things. They remind me of Isis."

Odin was chortling away. "And of my dear Frigga."

"I wouldn't have her any other way," Aleksei said proudly.

Pavel shifted to express his agreement with them on

Kimber's behalf, then realized he was naked due to the clothes-shredding-during-shifting thing, and was now on the corner of a very busy street. He also found he was choking on the hot dog he'd been bolting down in Wolf form while trying to hide behind the vendor's stall. The vendor didn't appreciate a large naked man ducking back among the meat cooler and stacks of buns. He started soundly swearing at Pavel in Czech.

Kimber began pounding him on the back, laughing uproariously. Gillian and Jenna were no help at all. Both were sliding down the sides of the stall, laughing themselves silly.

Garm and Helgi were yelling, "Shift! Shift back!"

Of course, poor Pavel couldn't concentrate while he was trying to dislodge the chunk of hot dog from his windpipe. As a result, furry feet appeared and disappeared, then lupine ears and a snout, followed by a tail that he couldn't seem to get to vanish. Kimber gave up trying to pound on his back after the tail hit her in the face, and surrendered to hilarity.

Osiris, Odin, Hreidmar and Kelda were nearly doubled over with mirth. Trocar covered his eyes, shook his head and opted for walking away from the lot of them while grinning like a fiend and pretending to look at the sights. Aleksei got himself under control long enough to remove his cloak and flick it over the squatting, coughing man.

"Forgive me, Pavel, but that is the best thing I have seen happen in a long while." Aleksei laughed.

Pavel finally coughed up the sausage and wiped his eyes and mouth. A quick twist of Aleksei's cloak and a bit of Shifter magic, and he recovered his dignity, his voice and a backside unencumbered by a tail. "It is fine, Aleksei. I am certain that was quite the sight."

"Not as much as that one." Gillian pointed across the alley. The Golem waited where they'd parked It. Silent, eternally patient; a mute witness to their revelry.

The sight of the giant earthen man just standing there while tourists pointed, taking pictures, sent them into another paroxysm of laughter. Gillian frantically grabbed at Kimber's arm.

"Bathroom. Where is a bathroom?"

"I don't know, but I have got to go!"

The vendor pointed diagonally across the street in the other direction. The women bolted for the indicated route.

"Back in a sec!" Gillian called out.

When the women returned with their composure intact, they continued on their way to the synagogue. Fortunately it wasn't far from where they were. Soon they were among the now-familiar streets of the Old Jewish Quarter of Prague, amid the buildings that offered so much beauty and history.

At the door of the synagogue, Trocar rang the bell respectfully. Gillian was busy beckoning the Golem the last twenty yards to Its home. The rabbi answered the door. He was an old, frail-looking man with deep, penetrating eyes, a salt-and-pepper beard and a beautifully embroidered yarmulke.

"Good evening, Rabbi Loew. We are returning your property, as promised." Trocar gave a slight bow.

The rabbi chuckled as he watched the behemoth lumber over to stand before the door. Gillian turned to greet him.

"Rabbi . . . Did he say, 'Rabbi Loew'? As in the Maharal of Prague?"

"He did indeed. I am a descendant of that very same Rabbi Loew. That is very good, Dr. Key. You remember your Midrasha classes."

Gillian could have sworn his eyes were twinkling. To her horror, she found herself blushing.

"Er . . . Rabbi Loew, I'm Reform, not Orthodox, and to be honest with you, I don't remember a damn thing from Midrasha classes. Oops. Sorry. I didn't mean to say *damn*. And please call me Gillian." Forgetting for a moment she was speaking to an Orthodox rabbi, she stuck out her hand, then immediately realized her mistake. He couldn't take her hand for any reason. She was female and he was married.

Kill me. Kill me now, she thought to herself.

Rabbi Loew chuckled heartily. "Forgive me, but I cannot shake your hand, Gillian. Please allow me to offer you my services as the rabbi of this place. After you put the Golem back in the Genizah, of course."

Gillian was confused. "Your services?"

"May I meet your friends as well?" the rabbi asked her, dismissing her immediate question.

"Oh! Of course. Please forgive me. This is Aleksei Rachlav, Trocar—well, you already met Trocar—Daedelus, Osiris, Odin, Garm, Helgi, Hreidmar, Kelda, Pavel, Kimber and, um . . . that's Jenna back there."

Gillian's voice had suddenly taken on a very meek timbre. Everyone who wasn't the rabbi stared at her.

"Are you all right?" Aleksei's voice being in her mind suddenly made her jump.

"I'm fine. Dammit, I've asked you to stop doing that. This is just . . . Well, he's an Orthodox rabbi, and I don't want to accidentally offend him, which I almost did by offering to shake his hand. Evidently he has a sense of humor, since he let Trocar borrow the shambling mound here."

She was getting better at the mind-to-mind thing, she decided, when she didn't yell at him out loud. As unobtrusively as she could, she straightened her shirt and brushed some caked blood off her sleeve.

"Sorry about our appearance, Rabbi Loew. We . . . well, we wanted to thank you very much for allowing us to use the Golem. You literally saved our lives. So . . . thank you. Thank you very much."

He nodded to her, bowing slightly. "You are quite welcome. I was glad to help. May I say, Gillian, that you and your group are favorites of mine on the news. It is always good to see a young woman distinguish herself as you have, and your adventures always make me laugh."

"Oh God . . . I mean . . . you've watched stories about us?"

"Of course! You are an Eshet Hayyil; a very good example and very entertaining, if I say so myself." He chuckled heartily as she blushed again.

"Oh no, no, sir, I'm not. I'm really not, trust me." Gillian wondered if she had any spare bullets in her gun. She could shoot herself and end this humiliation.

"Not a chance, bellissima. *You are not getting out of marrying me that easily."*

Aleksei was practically chortling. He put his arm around her shoulders and smiled proudly at her.

"Thank you, Rabbi. She is indeed a woman of valor. At least, I think she is."

Gillian poked him in the arm. "Since when do you speak Hebrew?"

"I believe the expression is 'I have many skills.'" The twinkle in his expressive ice gray eyes was new to her. She was glad to see it. Sort of.

This time she said it out loud. "Kill me now. Okay, look, enough already. Let me just put the Golem back where It goes, and we can get out of Rabbi Loew's hair. Rabbi? Is that all right with you?"

Rabbi Loew threw back his head and laughed until he clutched his sides. "My dear girl, you are even more entertaining in person."

Gillian covered her face with both hands and muttered, "I'm putting the Golem back now."

She beckoned the Thing forward, through the doors of the synagogue. As carefully as she could, she guided It through the chamber, up the stairs and into the attic. There was a thick layer of dust on the wooden floor, so it was easy to see where the Golem had stood for so long.

Positioning It took longer than she liked, but finally It was standing in Its original footprints in the dust.

"There. Okay, Golem. I know you can't respond and you're just programmed, or whatever you call it, to do what you're told, but I would like to thank you for saving us."

She reached out and patted Its lump of a hand. Curiously, after all the carnage It had done, not a trace of blood, tissue or body fluid remained on It anywhere. Evidently that was just part and parcel of Its magic.

Looking around, she found a ladder, which she leaned against the wall next to It. Climbing up, she could just reach Its face by leaning as far as she dared.

"Sleep well. I hope you are not needed anytime soon."

With that, she briskly rubbed off the aleph, and the Golem stiffened almost imperceptibly into the statue It always had been. Gillian climbed down from the ladder, put it back where she'd found it and dusted off her hands.

"Golem." She backed a little away and beckoned It.

Nothing happened. It was slumbering, or whatever unneeded inanimate objects did when they weren't required for an impromptu rescue mission.

Gillian returned to her group. As she approached, she could see they were all chatting merrily with Rabbi Loew. Trocar came in through the synagogue doors carrying tea in a porcelain cup. God only knew where he'd gotten it. He handed it to the rabbi, who thanked him, then continued the discussion he was evidently having with Osiris.

"Ah, there you are," Rabbi Loew greeted her as she returned. "Shall we go out into the garden, then?"

Aleksei took her hand as they followed the old man out past the cemetery to an area that was just barely lit by streetlights. It was dark enough on the outskirts of town for the stars to be twinkling brightly in the sky. Ahead of them, a *chuppah* or canopy was set up amid a patch of wildflowers.

Rabbi Loew stood under it and pulled a small black book from his robes. "Come, children. The Golem is back where It belongs, and it is very late for an old man."

Gillian balked as she took in the scene. "Wait a minute . . . What's going on?"

"You are engaged and pregnant, correct?" the rabbi asked her.

"Well . . . yeah." Oh hell, she was blushing again.

"Generally people do it the other way around, you know. Engaged, married, then pregnant, but this is not the time to discuss the way love has arranged itself in your life. Come here, my dear. Stand here by your young man."

There was some snickering from Kimber and Jenna when he referred to Aleksei as a young man. They weren't certain if the rabbi realized Aleksei was at least three hundred and fifty years older than he himself was. Gillian shot them a glare to shut them up.

"Do you have a ring?" he asked Aleksei.

Aleksei had been grinning from ear to ear until the question. His face became more serious, but he couldn't seem to stop smiling. "No, sir, I do not."

"You have to have a ring . . . and a wedding glass."

"I was not expecting this . . . and neither was Gillian. I am very sorry." Aleksei wasn't smiling now.

"We are not getting married now." Gillian backed up.

Rabbi Loew smiled at her. "Of course you are. You are worried that you are not in a beautiful dress, but your fiancé seems to think you are lovely just as you are."

"But I'm not Orthodox, Rabbi Loew, and I don't want to be disrespectful or make you do something you're not supposed to do. Aleksei isn't Jewish, and I really don't want to get married with blood all over our clothes."

"What better way seal your commitment than to wed after fighting side by side against great opposition? You should be married. Your baby needs two parents."

"I do not know what you people would do without me." Trocar reappeared next to the rabbi. No one had noticed him disappearing, which made his reemergence that much more of a feat.

He handed the rabbi a soft red pouch and a smaller blue pouch. "I believe those things will suffice."

The rabbi looked in both pouches and laughed. He shook a finger at Kimber. "He has thoughtfully made arrangements for you as well."

Kimber was flabbergasted. "What? Wait a minute. I will pick out my own ring and arrange my own wedding, thank you . . . Oh my God, is that it?"

Rabbi Loew handed Pavel a ring. He was still dressed in Aleksei's cloak, which he had tied like a toga around his naked form. Pavel held it out to Kimber, who squealed like a starstruck schoolgirl.

"Is that a diamond? Is that a ring made out of a diamond?"

Aleksei was handed the second ring in the pouch for Gillian. He gave it to her for her inspection.

"They're made out of diamonds? How . . . ? Trocar, where did you get these and what's in the other bag?"

She turned it over and over in her hands. It was a perfect crystalline circle. Brilliant colors of yellow-white, blue-white and white flashed from the jewel, sparkling under the light of the moon.

Trocar managed a rare smile. "They are diamonds, but they are from another realm. They have no internal flaws and will not break, scratch or shatter. We call them rings of the sun, moon and stars. They are highly prized and often given as friendship or love gifts. I give them to Aleksei and Pavel, whom I consider my friends. They may bestow them as they wish."

Gillian didn't know if she was more surprised by the rings or by Trocar's admission that he considered Aleksei his friend. She knew he and Pavel had become close, but he had past issues with Aleksei's archaic attitude where she was concerned. Right now, she had other problems. This just wasn't right, no matter how well-intentioned the rabbi was.

"Rabbi Loew, I appreciate what you're trying to do. There are just so many of your own traditions you'd be bending to accommodate us. I just don't feel comfortable letting you do this. I give you my word that Aleksei and I will be married as soon as possible, and I promise I'll be married under a chuppah in your honor. Is that all right?"

The old man looked at her for a long time. Finally he spoke. "I don't mind bending the rules a little for someone who is in need, Gillian, but I understand your feelings. You are concerned that I might be compromising my principles. I can assure you that is not the case, but I won't press the matter. I must admit, I am a fan of yours and wanted to do something for you."

"You already did. You saved our lives tonight. You're a good man, Rabbi Loew." She smiled at him.

"I know I can't hug you, but I want you to know you'll always be thought of in our household with great affection." Impulsively she gave him a little bow.

"You cannot embrace him, but I can." Aleksei leaned down, took the rabbi's shoulders and kissed him on both cheeks. To his surprise, the gesture was returned.

"Thank you, sir, for your kind heart." The handsome Vampire was clearly moved.

Rabbi Loew chuckled again. He was a holy man, but undoubtedly a man who saw the joy in everyday life and in everyday things.

"It is time for this old man and his kind heart to be asleep. Please take care, all of you. Thank you for bringing a great deal of fun to my evening." He gave the remaining bag back to Trocar turned and walked away, back to his home near the synagogue. They watched until he disappeared around a corner.

Kimber spoke up, breaking the silence. "Trocar? Can we keep the rings?"

"Of course. I gave them to your men and they have given them to you. They are yours."

"What's in the other bag?" Gill wanted to know.

"Wedding glasses."

"For breaking after the ceremony?"

"Correct."

"Where did you get those in the 'other realm'?" Gillian narrowed her eyes at him.

Trocar managed to look sheepish. "Fine. I took them from a vendor's stall, but I assure you, I left more than enough money to cover their cost."

"You shoplifted wedding glasses?" Gillian asked.

"I did not shoplift. I already told you, I left money."

Their banter was interrupted by Jenna, who was trying not to laugh and failing. "You guys . . . I've really missed you guys."

"Let us go home." Aleksei hugged Gillian to him.

"Trocar? If you would be so kind?" Gillian's voice was muffled in Aleksei's embrace.

"Certainly."

There was a low rumble as the Grael opened a portal Doorway. "Step through and we will be right outside the Rachlav Institute."

"I must communicate more with the Elves in my realm. That is a very convenient thing," Odin admitted.

He was the first to go through, followed by Garm

and Helgi. Hreidmar and Kelda were next. They agreed to come back to the Institute in order to formally sign the Osiris Doctrine. Osiris went through, then Pavel and Kimber, and Jenna. Aleksei and Gillian were after that, with Trocar being last since he had to close the Doorway after them.

They all hurried into the warm light of the castle. Everyone was excited to be home. There were tales to tell, reminiscing to do and old friends to visit with.

The moment they stepped through the doors, Gillian knew she was going to have to put her foot down on Institute duties after hours. Helmut and Cassiopeia greeted them in the Great Hall. After the hugging and welcoming home was finished, Helmut handed her a folder, almost apologetically.

"I'm sorry, Schatzi, but I wanted you to see this before you were surprised with it tomorrow."

"Shit, Helmut, can't this wait?" Gillian was tired and filthy, and Aleksei was beckoning to her from the stairs leading up to their room.

"This will only take a moment. Aleksei? Do you mind if I steal her briefly?"

"Don't ask him. Ask me." Gill clomped on Helmut's instep.

"Ow! I'm sorry, Gillian. I should have asked you, but I was only trying to be polite to Aleksei as well." Helmut sounded so remorseful while hopping on one foot that she gave in.

"All right, shit. Give me a minute to look at the damn file."

"We should probably go to the library."

"What or who is in the library?"

"The patient."

"Helmut, I don't want to meet anyone right now. You said just to look at the file."

"I know, I know, but he won't expect any therapy tonight. Cass and I will handle the full intakes. We know you're tired." Now he looked sheepish.

Gillian rolled her eyes and sighed. "All right! I know

better than to stand here arguing with you. You're going to get your way anyway."

Helmut brightened immediately. "Thank you so much, Schatzi. You'll find this very interesting, I must tell you."

"Be right there, Aleksei. Don't start without me." Her grin was infectious. He smiled back at her from his position on the stairs.

Helmut walked her down the hallway to the library. Gillian opened the great doors, shoving the file under her arm so she could grasp both handles at once.

She started inside, then stopped. She gave Helmut an incredulous look. "Are you serious?"

"Yes, well . . . it's a little hard to explain." Helmut scooted her fully into the room.

"I bet." Gillian turned back to the room and extended her hand to the person walking up to them.

The new guy would have been well over six feet tall . . . if he'd had a head on his shoulders. Ornately sculpted black leather armor covered the wiry, powerful frame. A heavy black wool cloak fluttered behind him and was held at shoulder height by an elaborate iron chain. A sword swung at his left hip, while a short-hilted battle-axe rode his right side.

Gillian's proffered hand was taken in a firm grasp by a dusty black leather gauntlet. The glove was obviously old, the leather nicked and scarred from many confrontations. His handshake was icy cold. It took everything she had not to jerk back in surprise.

A Ghost? Surely not. He was much too corporeal. Zombie? They were infernally stupid. She'd try talking to him and see what happened.

"The Headless Horseman, I presume?" Gillian took a shot at it. She couldn't be that wrong. How many headless Paramortals could there be anyway, dressed like that?

"Guten Abend, Ma' morgens," he responded in a deep, eloquent, sepulchral voice.

Gillian's eyebrows shot up in amazement that he could answer her at all. She searched her protesting brain for the few German phrases Helmut had taught her. *"Wie geht es Ihnen?"*

"Nicht so gut, wirklich." He sighed.

"All right, Helmut, out of my element here," she admitted to her friend as she gently extracted her hand from the Horseman's freezing grip. He hadn't let go since they started speaking.

"Well, that's the interesting part. He can speak, as you have heard. He is corporeal, so by definition not actually a Ghost . . ."

"He's not a Zombie or Revenant either. In fact, I can't read him at all . . . It's like a blank feeling where he should be. And why are you speaking as though he weren't right here?"

She turned back to their new guest. "My apologies . . . Sorry—I don't know your name."

"Leopold." Helmut provided everything in English for Gillian, then translated everything back to the Horseman so he would feel part of the dialogue. "His name is Leopold Drachenberg. He was indeed a Hessian mercenary who was killed by soldiers of the Continental Army during your Revolutionary War. He is only fluent in German, I'm afraid."

"Leopold? Would you excuse us for a moment. It's very nice to meet you by the way. I'm Gillian. Gillian Key." Steeling herself, she shook his hand again, waited for Helmut to translate, then shooed Helmut out the door, closing it behind them.

"That's just great, Helmut. You take him as a patient, then. I can't speak German. No, don't start. You taught me a few phrases, but most of it was swear words. What do you expect me to do with him? Record the sessions for you to translate? I'd have to wait for hours to find out what he said. This is not going to work." She folded her arms and glared at her former teacher and mentor.

"But Schatzi, you really are the best at what we do. I'm much more effective in the academic and administrative arena . . ." Helmut protested.

"I'm calling shenanigans on that one, Helmut. You just don't want to get back into the trenches again and do actual therapy. I am not going to counsel somebody I can't communicate with directly. It's not fair to him. Not to mention the fact that it is very disconcerting to try to look into someone's eyes when there aren't any to look into. Blank air does not provide visual information." She folded her arms across her chest, trying to ignore the stiff feel of her blood-spattered sleeves.

Helmut chattered on as if she hadn't spoken. "He says his main problem is that now that the wars are over and he has taken his revenge, he's grown tired of haunting upstate New York and wants to find a new purpose in life. Oh yes, and his head is still missing, but that's another issue."

"Revenge? Missing head? You really have gone completely insane. He may have been a mercenary, but he killed a lot of innocent people too, according to the stories I've heard about him. Do you know about the Hessians, Helmut? You should, being as you're sort of from his original neck of the woods. If you can't remember, let me refresh your memory. They were butchers. Guns for hire, so to speak, for the British Army during the Revolutionary War. The Hessians slaughtered a lot of people, and not in very nice ways. He is also still armed; did you happen to notice that?" She was yelling again. Note to self to work on her volume control.

"Of course I noticed. That sword of his is an extraordinary artifact." Helmut took on the faraway look he often got when confronted with an interesting historical antique.

"Artifact? He beheaded people with that sword, Helmut. He is a hired killer and he should have surrendered his weapons when he stepped over the threshold. This is supposed to be a therapeutic Institute, not *Antiques Roadshow*! Goddammit, I leave for a couple of days and everything goes to hell. What is wrong with you people?"

Deep, rich laughter floated down to her from the stairs. She looked up from her rant at Helmut to see Aleksei striding toward her.

"*Bellissima*, I can see you have a few things to tend to. The sun is already nearly fully risen and I must leave you for a short time. Get some rest and I will see you this evening. Good day to you too, Helmut." Aleksei kissed her softly, then headed down to the lower levels of the castle to clean up, then to the family crypts to rest for the day.

Missing an opportunity to have an overdue snuggle with Aleksei irritated her more than it normally would. Intellectually she knew she was tired and pregnant and just needed some quiet time. Preferably it would have been quiet groping time with her tall hunk. Instead she was discussing dangerous, armed, headless men in the hallway of her home with her boss.

"I hate my job."

"Now, Gillian, you are a wonderful therapist and an exemplary soldier." Helmut patted her on the shoulder in a fatherly fashion.

She jerked away from his soothing gesture. "You figure out something for Leopold in there that we all can live with or I quit."

"You won't quit. Now, come on; things will look better after some tea and breakfast. Let me get Leopold settled in with Cass for his intake, then I will personally make you something in the kitchen."

"You'd better be suggesting steak and eggs and not that crappy sausage you made the other day."

Helmut laughed. "I know you love my cooking."

"Of course I do. It's right up there on my list of 'Things I Love to Avoid,' between hangovers and spiders."

He hustled her toward the kitchen. She was still grumbling when he headed back to their newest client. On the way, he called for Cassiopeia, knowing that she would hear him wherever she was in the castle. The library was secure enough from the sun to let her do Leopold's initial paperwork before she went to rest.

Gillian wasn't serious about quitting. He just knew it. She couldn't quit. This job was in her blood and her soul. There was a waiting list of Beings who needed her help and who needed it at the Rachlav Institute. Her little makeshift family needed her too. Helmut expected Aleksei and the rest of their group would make that point very clear to her that evening when they could be reunited. Right now, everyone was home safely, which meant today was going to be a good day.

"A unique idea in the paranormal genre."
—Laurell K. Hamilton

Meet Gillian Key. She's a Paramortal psychologist who can treat the mental distress of non-Humans. And she's a Marine Special Forces operative who can get physical with them when the situation calls for it...

Key to Conflict

By TALIA GRYPHON

"I dare you to put this book down."
—Rosemary Laurey, author of *Midnight Lover*

"A fast-paced adventure tale set in a fascinating... alternate reality."
—Robin D. Owens, author of *Heart Dance*

M177T1107

Don't miss…

Key to Conspiracy

by

TALIA GRYPHON

Recalled by her commanding officer, Gillian finds herself in Northern Russia after a devastating earthquake. Away from Count Aleksei Rachlav, the irresistible Vampire she left behind, Gillian is vulnerable to the Dark Prince himself—Dracula—who would like nothing more than to use her as a pawn in his escalating war with Rachlav. And when Gillian is sidetracked in London by yet another mission, one that goes horribly wrong, she finds herself at the mercy of one of Dracula's minions, a creature who rattles her like no other: Jack the Ripper—reborn…

"A unique idea in the paranormal genre."

—Laurell K. Hamilton,
#1 *New York Times* bestselling author

penguin.com

**Explore the outer reaches
of imagination—don't miss these authors
of dark fantasy and urban noir that take you
to the edge and beyond.**

Patricia Briggs	Karen Chance	Anne Bishop
Simon R. Green	Caitlin R. Kiernan	Janine Cross
Jim Butcher	Rachel Caine	Sarah Monette
Kat Richardson	Glen Cook	Douglas Clegg

penguin.com

M15G0907